psychoraag

suhayl saadi
psychoraag

Black & White Publishing

First published 2004
by Black & White Publishing Ltd
99 Giles Street, Edinburgh
Scotland, EH6 6BZ

ISBN 1 84502 010 3

A CIP catalogue record for this book
is available from the British Library.

The publisher acknowledges subsidy
from the Scottish Arts Council towards
the publication of this volume.

Scottish
Arts Council

Cover design: www.hen.uk.com

Printed and bound by Creative Print & Design

It is only the reflection of a story
The sweetness of a belief of innocence
Images other than truth

> from 'Sun Fire Majestic',
> The Colour of Memory

ACKNOWLEDGEMENTS

The author would like to thank the following:
Alina Ayub Mirza, Nadia Afza Shireen Hawwa Mirza-Saadi,
Salim Uddin Ahmed, Shahzadi Shahgul Afza Sultana
Tabassum Ahmed, Shahzada Shehryar Ghulam Ahmed,
Shakeel Imam Ahmed, Sharif Sultan Ahmed, Shahzada Dawar
Masaud, Amjad Ayub Mirza, Mohammad Ayub Mirza,
Sarmed Ayub Mirza, Shahzadi Shireen Mirza, Zohrabai
Ambalawali, Gaan Saraswati Kishori Amonkar, Faegheh
'Googoosh' Atashin, Shazia Azhar, Kanan Bala, Aziz Balouch,
Rabia al-Basri, Baiju Bawara, Khurshida Begum, Mehboob
Begum, Shamshad Begum, Doctor Bhar, Alison Bowden, Sam
Boyce, Campbell Brown, Jenny Brown, Pastora Pavón Cruz,
Victoria Eugenia Reina Gil, Hakim Mirabilis, Christopher M.
Dolan, Caroline Mary Donaldson, Shihab al-Din ibn Baha'l-
Din Fadlullah of Astaribad, Ruqa Farrell, Joe Fisher, Andy
Gailey, Patricia Grant, Haji Hafiz Imam, Aamer Hussein,
Robert Alan Jamieson, Noor Jehan, Alasdair Joss, Hemant
Kumar, Raj Kumari, Gerry Loose, Martin MacIntyre, Kevin
MacNeil, Pankaj Mallick, Michael Marshall, Patricia
Marshall, Ibn Maymun, Mehrunisa, Raj Melby, Samia
Mikhail, El Mirlo, Lyn Morgan, Ashraf os-Sadat Morteza'i,
Ibn Nafis, Edith Rahim, Eric Rahim, Lalitha Rajan, Bino
Realuyo, Reshma, Mark Rickards, Rogerius Rex II, John
Rotherfield, Geeta Roy, Kamal Sangha, Rameen Shakur,
Saame Sita, Adam Arnald Slotsky, Stílogo, The Reverend Sir
Edward Ingle Synnot CB, Rachel Taylor, Ranjana Thapalyal,
Hamish Whyte and all at Black & White Publishing.

The author acknowledges the help of the Scottish Arts Council Writers' Bursary Scheme.

This book is dedicated to Alina Ayub Mirza
with gratitude for her activism, engagement and love.

MIDNIGHT

Salaam alaikum, sat sri akaal, namaste ji, good evenin
oan this hoat, hoat summer's night! Fae the peaks ae
Kirkintilloch tae the dips ae Cambuslang, fae the invisible
mines ae Easterhoose tae the mudflats ae Clydebank,
welcome, ivirywan, welcome, Glasgae, welcome,
Scoatland, tae *The Junnune Show.* Sax oors, that's right,
sax ooors, ae great music, rock an *filmi* an weird, weye-
oot-there happenins an ma rollin voice. Whit a
combination, eh? It's wan ye cannae resist. Wance ye
tune in, the dial sticks. Aye, Ah'm in control ae yer radio
sets – aw the music plays through me. Ye're oan ma
wavelenth an that's a pretty weird place tae be! Radio
Chaandni broadcastin oan ninety-nine-point-nine meters
FM. Moonlight, moonlight, moonlight! *Arey,* Mister
Moonlight, stay oot ae ma windae – this is ma show!
Right?

So. It's deep summer, right, it's hoat as a used tandoor
and, thenight, it's ma last night, it's the buildin's last
night, it's the radio station's very last night. It's twelve
o'clock a.m. or p.m. or both or neether. Is it rainin? Who
knows? Not the weatherman. Ah am the weatherman. It's
midnight – the moon's nearly full. Ma name is Zaf –
that's zed ay eff – and this is *The Show of Madness.*
Junnune. Hoat 'n' rollin. Eighty-four degrees. Come along
fur the ride. And how are ye? Where are ye? Who are
ye? Are ye drivin or workin or jist sittin at hame in yer
livin *khanas,* ye sad people? Naw, naw, only jokin. Ah'm
the saddest ae the loat. You're happy people – we're aw
happy noo. Right? Ecstatic. Look it up in a dictionary.

We're *junnune*! No the band, no the filum but the radio show. *Haa ji*! Ah'll put my ear up tae the mike. Don't all answer at wance. But, naw, it's different thenight. Thur'll be nae phone-ins thenight. Bad jokes, mibbee. Tae aw ma auld, auld friends. *Theen maheenay*, wow! Huv we been goin that loang? How mony oors is that? How's yer arithmetic, then, eh? *Mujhe bathao*. Ninety nights, sax oors a night. That's five hundred and forty oors or thirty-two thoosand, four hundred meenuts or wan million, nine hundred and forty-four thoosand seconds or . . . stoap me now, please! Argh! Actually, Ah did that oan the spot, aff the tap ae ma heid! See? Ah'm a genius. Bet nane ae you tap-ae-the-class smooth-haired swotties even goat past the oors. Ha-ha! Ye'll fail, ye'll sink. Be scared, be very . . . Nivir mind. If ye believe that, ye'll believe onyhin. Ye win some, ye lose some, gals 'n' *bundhay*. Relax. OK, so, afore ye aw start phonin in tellin me that ye hud the answer before Ah gave it tae ye or that ye've wurked oot three months in micro-nano-giga-seconds, doon tae the thirteenth point, or before aw you parents ae swotties – macro-swotties – start phonin in tae tell me how much ae a bad influence Ah am oan the pristine Asian youth ae today, yesterday an themorra, let me tell ye thur'll be nae phone-ins thenight. Ma decision. Ah know, Ah know, ye wur just waitin wi yer fingers poised ower the plastic, see-through buttons ae yer mobile, jist waitin tae phone Uncle Zaf. But this night is special. Mibbee you'll nivir hear ma voice ivir again. Who knows? Life is too sensible, *hai ke nahii*? That's why we huv radio an TV an cinemas an bingo halls an music an books an weddins. Aye, right. Ye can think aboot that. But nae phone calls this time. Ye can aw jist relax yer minds – you can aw jist float doonstream. This night, ye're goannae gie yer fingers an yer voices a wee rest. Tonight's fur listenin. Dreamin. Madness. *Junnune*. I love ye all! *Sumjhe?*

'Naxalite'!

Zaf pressed the button and slid down the switch. Deck A: Asian Dub Foundation – great way to start a gig or a radio show. High energy. Amphetamine dancers. There were two decks for CDs in the console – Deck A and Deck B – and Zaf's idea, throughout the three months, wis to alternate them so that there would be a fairly seamless transition between tracks. This would involve considerable shooglin about of CDs, cases, bits of paper . . . Zaf wis never really certain of what he would be playin three tracks ahead but he liked it that way – each night would kind of evolve from nuthin. Normally, he would pile up CDs by the wall so that he'd just pull one down off the stack. And, usually, throughout the night, there would be phoned-in requests. It wis one way of keepin people interested, of holdin them on the waveband. Tonight, in the absence of a phone-in, he had left everythin to chance or whim or need. Tonight, he wis in the dark just as much as his listeners. He wasn't prissy about the songs though – there were no hard-and-fast rules and, sometimes, he would interject before the end of a track or just as another wis beginnin. It wis the mark of a DJ to do that – to overarch the artists, to butt in, to play God.

He leaned back against the swung chair and folded his arms behind the back of his neck. Closed his eyes, then opened them again. Let the tube light flood in. Let his brain ride with the bass. Deep London Underground chords, janglin, monsoon guitars, cocaine drums, shouted vocals, the nineties' tale of early seventies' revolution in West Bengal, land of the darlin *daryaon*, the god rivers, an angry-man song in purple

Jamaican Cockney. Bang-jang-jang! Asian Dub Foundation. Darkness, beards, sweat, number-one haircuts. Clued-up, burnin eyes. A reckonin of sorts.

N-A-X-A-L-I-T-E: P-O-L-I-T-I-C-A-L S-E-X.

The cubicle was twenty-by-twenty in feet. Two of the walls were almost completely covered in grey sound-damping cones but, to Zaf's right, was a partition wall with a shared glass window stretching from the ceiling to about three feet above the floor. Above him, attached to a fake ceiling, was a cold strip light that created its own architecture of shadows. Directly behind him was a door and straight ahead, some ten feet beyond the arc of the console, beyond the various cables, boxes, amps, half-empty plastic bottles and other miscellaneous objects, was a large sash window with huge panes of glass. And, beyond that, the night. Originally, his cubicle and its twin next door would have been part of the same room or they might have formed part of an elevated gallery or cloister. Zaf imagined monks or priests or Proddy pastors – he couldn't be sure which – leafin through voluminous bibles an mibbee sinkin down on to their knees in the moonlight and prayin to their dark broodin god to surgically excise the seed of terrible temptation from their bodies. The physicality of muscle on stone. But all that wis long gone – if it had ever existed – an, now, all that remained wis Zaf an his imaginins, the crazy dance of his loves, the pressure of foam and polyvinyl-somethin-or-other against the seat of his jeans, the flicker of neon siphonin through the cradle of his skull, the atonal choir of his life up to this point.

By day, the ground floor functioned as a community centre. Before that, it had been a church. Radio Chaandni was tucked up on the upper floor, in what once must have been one of the long galleries. Because they'd got a licence for three months in a row, they'd been permitted to cover the walls of each of the two cubicles with small foam cones. It was not quite soundproof but it was better than having just bare walls and a mica table, which was what they'd had the first time around. It always felt flat and dry like the inside of, well, like the inside of a radio station. Not that this was a real radio station.

Deep in the night, there would be little to do between tracks, some of which, he would make sure, would stretch to five or more minutes – especially the old songs. Eating carry-outs and sipping various carbonated drinks had their limits in terms of stimulating mental activity. During the long periods of boredom, Zaf had tried, for nigh on three months, to find evidence of the building's dank past. He had walked up and down the long corridors and had run his palms along the yellow wallpaper as he had searched for what might have been fissures or unseen hollows. Like Sherlock Holmes, he had rapped his knuckles on the horsehair plaster until they had begun to throb but still he had found nothing. The building held no secrets, no priest holes, no buried hearts. There was no trace whatsoever of the old stone or of chanting choirs or of formaldehyde. It was as though the entire past of the building had been erased. And, yet, more and more, as the weeks had progressed, Zaf had found himself playing the old songs and so what the listeners had been getting had grown into a mixture of music which spanned some one hundred years. The whole of recording history. Before radio, some of it. Certainly before the community centre.

Everythin wis ready – he always made sure of that. Three months wis a long time in radio-land and, durin that time, Zaf had honed his trade. There would be none of the amateurism he'd seen in a lot of the people who were attemptin to run this station. No. The mike wis positioned just so and he'd pushed his chair right beneath the rim of the console so he could feel the metal press down against the muscle of his thigh. There wis a small buzz of static from the mike. Zaf killed it with a tap from his index finger. Tap. His seat went up and down with rotation and sometimes, deep in the night, he would spin, round and round, ending up either lower or higher than when he'd started. It was time for a spin. He pushed off, lifted his legs to avoid knockin his knees on the bottom of the console. He rotated three hundred and sixty degrees, twice over. Seven hundred and twenty. He'd never been that good at arithmetic but three months in this place could have made anyone a numbers maestro. It wis like bein in a cell and chalkin up figures on the wall. Figures were easy. Facts were a different matter. And people, most definitely, were facts.

Zaf stopped turning. He was facing the partition window. The shadows ran past him slowly and then went into reverse for a little. In the cubicle next to his, a man's shape moved across the wall and then crumpled. Above him, the more curvaceous shadow of a woman began to move – slowly at first but then faster – and her shadow bent and arched over his, both shapes seeming to merge into one and then to lose shape altogether. Zaf tore his gaze away and focused down on the controls of his console. It wasn't the done thing to have sex on the air. The Radio Authority – or Ofcom or whatever it was they were calling themselves these days – would definitely not have approved. But then, he thought, they'll probably be tucked up in their beds and, even if they're listenin to the radio, they sure as hell won't be listenin to me. He wasn't sure whether the couple knew they were being watched and, if they did, whether they cared. Perhaps, like actors, they enjoyed bein spied on and the whole thing had been just a performance and, night after night, for three months, he had watched the spectacle and been unaware. Mibbee, all along, it wis he who had been the spectacle. Suddenly uncomfortable, he painfully fought down his own arousal. Ripenin figs. The trick – negative thinkin. Dwell on the bad things. But it wis dangerous. They could get you when you were off guard, the bad things. Wis that what had happened to those guys who'd ended up as flotsam driftin around the streets of Pollokshields and Kinnin Park? The ones with hooded eyes and baseball caps. Sometimes, they would drift into gangs and into blood and guts and expensive white cars. Cheap white women. Aye, miniskirts and breezy flesh – legs taperin just enough like the shape of music in moonlight. The earthy joy of degradation. He'd known it and, for a while, it had been like teeterin on the edge of a cliff – soles flattened on stone, spreadin arms and legs, breathin in and then . . .

He wondered whether, one day, the gangs would reach a new level of maturity and divide up the city like bits of halva. He'd heard somewhere that the gangs already ran everythin. Drugs, protection, porn, dogs . . . radio stations. But then someone else had told him that this wis just a myth, spread by the gangs themselves. Mibbee the truth lay somewhere in between – in the place where you couldn't grasp it.

He hadn't sequenced any CDs tonight. It wis a bit of a risk really – a bit irresponsible – but he had planned it that way. He'd drawn up a kind of playlist but now, as the show started, everythin wis up in the air. He had a pen and a piece of paper kickin around somewhere on the console. He would just pick up the music as it came – let chance take its hand. Mibbee it wouldn't work – mibbee this wis the night when he would come a cropper. The laughin stock of the city for ever and ever, *ameyn*. But he knew what he liked and he knew what he wanted and this last show of all wis goin to be different. 'Naxalite'. It wis the only way to fly.

Zaf went over to the window and gazed out at the darkened street. It had just stopped raining and the walls glistened. The nights always seemed darker after it had rained. He could hear the water drip from the roof gutters. Three floors. It was a long fall. A messy death. Up there, in his cubicle, he felt safe from gangs and girlfriends, past and future, safe from sticks and stones and from those he had loved. Now, there was only the ever-present hum of the static and the music and the sound of his own voice falling deep into the night. The studio's electric lighting meant he could make out only the brightest of the stars and then only when he glanced obliquely at them. Seeing but not seeing. Sending his voice out, over the airwaves, spiralling into the darkness of space.

God, it wis so bloody hot. It wis still threatenin rain. But, then, it wis Glasgow and it wis always threatenin rain. Or snow or hail. Even in summer. He'd known it snow in June, for God's sake. That wis the thing about this city – the time wis always out of joint. Asian Community Radio wis a bit like that – anythin could happen at any time. Like the electrics packin in without warnin. Or like Ruby 'n' Fizz screwin in the room next door. Ruby 'n' Fizz went together like rock 'n' roll.

At last! He'd found his blue biro and the page that had been torn untidily from one of those ring-bound reporter's notebooks. He wondered whether reporters actually used those pads or whether the term had become somewhat archaic – like police boxes or milk boys.

Ruby 'n' Fizz, they seemed joined at the hip, those two, and they giggled constantly and they only got away with it because their audience knew less than they did and because, in Bollywood Heaven, everythin would be forgiven. *Bollywood*

Heaven – the programme they ran. Kind of 'Guess the Tune', 'Guess the Actress', 'Guess the Hero' and so on. They'd finished actually broadcastin over five minutes earlier and now Zaf's show wis on the air but Ruby 'n' Fizz hadn't switched off their machine and had merely pulled the controls down to silence. It wis a kind of turn-on. For them mibbee. Zaf had the terrifyin thought that, at any moment, they might break into his music with a cacophony of climaxes and then it would be Pollokshields Hell, not Bollywood Heaven, for all of them.

The humidity must be a million per cent, Zaf thought. His evenin shower had already worn off and wis bein replaced by a transparent skin of sweat. In spite of the soundproofin, he wis still able to hear vague noises – shufflin sounds, a creak here and there – yet he figured that, in the next room, the controls would be set at zero volume. He wondered at what point they would reach climax and whether they would reach it together. Without glancin at them, he tried to fill their shadows with bitterness but that didn't work so then he tried to wipe them from his mind as he might the memory of a bum programme or a bad affair. It wis just like pullin the volume control down to silence. It wis that easy – if you knew how.

Time to warm up. Lean back and stretch. It wis a workout an he wis a finely tuned athlete. He could sense every centimetre of his body – as though each hair, each tiny diamond segment of skin, had turned into a magnetic receiver. This wis how it felt on the good nights. Better than sex, really. It wis just one long up. He let out a deep breath slowly and felt the air within the booth vibrate, just a little, and then become still again. He glanced up at the clock. Three minutes past twelve. Almost time to go. He wis meant to have put on the pre-recorded News 'n' Weather at midnight but, at the last minute, he'd decided to slip in Asian Dub Foundation as the openin track. The News could wait. It would be the same bulletin anyway, all night, every hour, on the hour. And . . . THE WEATHER. The only reliable thing about the Weather wis that it wis totally unreliable. So, by six a.m., the whole climate might have changed, the season performed a volte-face, and yet the pre-recorded forecast for the night and the day ahead would remain unflinchinly reassurin. It wasn't his voice, of course. Well, it wis but not the same voice. Not live. And don't forget the Adverts. No, do forget the Adverts – the only thing that mattered wis the music. Concentrate on that and the night would be his. About the only thing he had now. He wis like a junkie – he had sold and stolen everythin for this show. In three months of broadcasting, he'd probably spent more time in the twenty-by-twenty cubicle than he had at home in bed with Babs. He would get back to the flat at seven a.m. which wis just about the time Babs would be getting up for work. She drove a big power bike, a second-hand nineteen-ninety-nine Kawasaki Vulcan 1500 Classic, painted metallic blue, the colour of the sea in deepest summer. It wis strange, that, for a woman, a nurse, to be powerin off in the saddle of a bike usually steered like a buffalo by leathered, hairy male bikers. A dainty pink scooter would've been more appropriate, Zaf thought, with one of those smooth, shiny, close-fittin helmets to match. Babs's machine wis a bit too macho. But, no, when he thought about it, basically, there were two types of serious country motorbikes and, therefore, two kinds of rural motorcyclist. The first were mostly to be found in England, where it wis drier and where old metal didn't rust quite as fast, and these were the veteran models, the old machines that invariably had been 'Made in England'. The men (it wis generally men) handled each component of their machines with the care they might have lavished on a lover. It wis a kind of clingin to the past but, more than that, it wis a buryin of oneself in the metal bosom of the Golden Age of mother-machines. The other type of country biker wis different. They drove the most up-to-date models possible – the computerised, silicon-seamed androids. Theirs were the sorts of bikes you could jump on to and be in Nice or Santander or Interlaken in a few hours. Well, bein a nurse, Babs couldn't really have afforded one of those but she'd got as close as she could sensibly manage. And, after all, she had never been a shy, retirin type of person. She'd always been into outdoor pursuits. She'd been brought up in the deep south, in Galloway, where she had been surrounded by the land and the sea. She carried them with her wherever she went. The hills and the ocean breathed in her head. At times, he could see it in the blue of her eyes, a shade that shifted with the quality of the light.

Like the time he had been ridin pillion and they had been rompin along a bumpy, unmetalled, one-track road – up in the north country which some Viking, with a sense of humour, had named Sutherland. They'd been steamin along and the wheels had been kickin up dust all around them so that they could hardly see the sweepin ancient mountains, the gleamin silver rivers, the clear blue sky. His arms were looped around her pelvis, his fingers were interlaced with one another and his elbows pressed down tightly on those bits above her bum that some call love handles. Her belly was soft yet taut an she wis speedin up, goin down the gears, revvin crazily along the stones an earth of the track. He tried shoutin at her to slow doon. What wis she doin? But his voice wis sucked up in the slipstream and his breath wis swamped with the billowin white dust. Then, at the moment of perfect acceleration and total invisibility, she had twisted around and kissed him on the lips, long, deep an hard, a metal-and-bone motorcycle snog, exquisitely timed and utterly terrifyin.

She would be off to work on her bike, early in the mornin, while he crept home on foot. She didn't wear leathers, though, and somehow this made the thing even more incongruous. Like seein Florence Nightingale and her glowin lamp arrivin on the back of a tiger. Growlin at the crossroads. Dinnae mess wi me. It wis a wakey-wakey sound an she wis a wakey-wakey kind of a person. The lady of the dawn. The sharp, clean outline of her motorcycle against the sky or its reflection in the unbroken surface of a freshwater loch. 'We're like passin ships in the mornin,' she'd quipped and he had smiled. She wis like that – spontaneous and funny. She never had to think before she felt, before she spoke. The words just came out like a river – clear and rushin and confident. He envied that. Yet a motorbike seemed a transient thing. It made it seem as though she had jist dropped into his life for a sojourn, a temporary phase which, at any moment, might end with her leapin into the saddle and powerin off into the mornin, carryin only the clothes on her back. Her long, sleek, gleamin back. Sometimes, when she felt really randy, she would wear no underwear. Just jeans on leather. He desired her then, as he got things ready for the broadcast. The compact discs, the tapes, the console, with its hundred switches, which somehow had become more familiar to him than the way she smiled or the counterpoint of her body against his. She would be fallin asleep – the near-transparent skin of her lids would be closin over the blue. Her breathin would be slow, regular. Complete.

Sometimes, the mike wouldn't swing properly and would sit at an awkward angle so that he would have to prop himself up against the back of his chair and lean forward, like John Lennon had done in 'Imagine', and then he would almost spit into the metal. Come to think of it, he quite liked that. Some nights, his voice felt like a muscle.

Zaf inhaled. He wis still able to smell the plastic primary-school grey of the cubicle but he knew that, as the night wore on, he would lose the scent – not because it would have vanished or dissipated but because somehow, breath by breath, it would have slipped into him. By the end of every six-hour session, Zaf would have become the room. And, as the weeks had gone on, he had found it more and more difficult to define an existence outside of Radio Chaandni and his life on the air. Christ Almighty. Not that there wis any air in that small space. He felt suffocated. Trapped. *Ya Ali*! He had the sudden urge to get up and walk out. To leave the console, the cubicle, the clock, Ruby, Fizz, the memories . . . fuck. He slid the switch. Held his breath. Exhaled. Breathed in again. Slowed things down. Tried to focus on things outside of himself.

He looked up. All he could see of the next room wis a single dreich wall and, hovering across it, the combined shadow of a man and a woman making love on a chair but, really, it was not like that at all. The dark shape hung over the wall, its movements slight, hardly noticeable, so that it reminded Zaf of a slowly beating heart. 'Naxalite' swept in juddering waves across the stagnant air. Zaf had rolled up the volume, to try to blank out the sounds coming from next door but the grunts and groans still managed to slip through the cones and straight into his head.

He wondered how he had managed to survive the last few weeks without goin completely insane and then he laughed – he must've been bloody mad to have done this thing in the first place. Glasgow Asian Community Radio equalled chaos and *cairry-oots* and great fuckin ego trips. Guys would strut about with one side of their heads stuck to black plastic mobiles like some kind of alien wis about to suck out their brain. Again and again, presenters would turn up late or not turn up at all or else turn up halfway through a programme – it would become evident that the person hostin it wis very subtly stoned. That wis the only subtle thing about the station. Generally speakin, Radio Chaandni, 'broadcastin on ninety-nine-point-nine meters FM', hovered somewhere around the far edge of grossness – the aim bein to cultivate the lowest common denominator in all things. It wis culture on the run – here come the *jhankarian*! That could've been the station motto, like that TV weather thing – 'Bringing you the weather, whatever the weather'. An, in Glasgow, the whole thing wis mixed in with wind and rain and the sleek sound of water flowin down fractures in the pipes. After three months of this, it wis no wonder Ruby 'n' Fizz had resorted to screwin on air – it wis either sex, drink or the mobile. Zaf knew which he would've preferred on that hot, damp August night, on the floor above some used-up, run-down community centre towards the west end of the city. But you had to have the gall. And he, Zafar, did not have it.

> Our heads may be different
> Our bodies of many colours
>
> But look closer in the darkness
> Our souls are One

He spun round in his chair, turning the grey walls to blur, and slammed his shin against the leg of the console. Fuck, shit, fuck! He rubbed at the bone and swore again but even his expletives didn't stretch far enough. Not like Ruby 'n' Fizz next door. They were meant to have been presentin a quiz programme on Mumbai Cinema – eleven till twelve. It wis no great sweat. They didn't have to know much about anythin since all the answers were printed on neat little green cards. Yet, sometimes, they still managed to get it completely wrong. They got their decades mixed up – like the sixties became the seventies and the eighties and nineties just merged into one another in the way that time can (but not on the radio, Zaf thought, not in public on the air when your voice, that which wis you, wis in full earshot of complete strangers) but, since their audience wis probably gettin it wrong in the same way they were, in the greater scheme of things, it had never really seemed to matter. Whereas, if I make a mistake or even a semi-mistake, he thought, feelin the gall rise in his throat, we get hundreds of phone calls (well, not hundreds – tens mibbee), even if it's three in the bloody mornin. Who the hell listens at three in the mornin, for God's sake?

Cats in the jungle
Lopin round the towns
Feline fightas
Comin up from below
Burnin fire in the night
Eyes, stars, teeth

Awright!!

The Ganges guitar sounds of the song about the doomed *Bangali* revolutionaries announced the end of the track and Zafar realised he'd forgotten to sequence the next one. He'd been that desperate to shut out the sounds from next door. He thought about playin two or three more tracks before startin to talk but decided against it. He'd scribbled down a couple of songs but he wasn't sure he would go with those. He wasn't sure of anythin. This wasn't workin. Fuck. Oh,

God, don't forget the Adverts! They were not all his voices
– people sometimes did their own commercials. Cash 'n'
carry and restaurant owners posin as actors, dancin Mumbai
before a row of grain sacks or bouncin beneath a plate of
steamin, hyper-chillified food. An all of it in sound! Blind to
the world. 'Eat this and die a thousand contorted, Kama
Sutric deaths in solo!' The same roll of ads would be repeated,
hour upon hour, the sponsors gettin their piece of brain.
Maghas. Sometimes it wis hard to keep a straight face. But,
then, who the fuck wis he to judge people? What had he
done with his life that had been so wonderful that he could
sit in judgement like some kind of surrogate big white man?
Zaf wis as riddled with holes as the next person. But at least,
he thought, at least I admit it. I'm not perfect, OK? Sittin
there, in his wee crystal radio set, singin and makin pronounce-
ments. Mibbee, in a dark, wet corner of the city, some drunk
hooker wis bendin down over a gleamin puddle to worship
him. As the sound died, he took a deep breath and slid the
switch upwards. It wis like makin love. First time would
always be the same.

Dunno boot yous oot there but Ah know Ah've always
been a Dubber. Awright, tonight? That wis the first an
there's lots mair tae come! Dum-dee-dee-dum-dee-dee-
dum. Hey! It's sivin meenuts past midnight, Saturday
night. This is *The Junnune Show* and Ah'm Zaf – that's
zed ay eff. Can ye spell? *Salaam alaikum, sat sri akaal,
namashkar*. Welcome, again. And, as always, a special
hello to Babs. This is what they call 'the graveyard shift'.
Funny that. Ah've never seen a grave bein dug at this
time ae night. Onyweye, Ah hope ye're all ready fur a
grand finale cause this is the final night ae the show and
it's also the last night ae Radio Chaandni – it's the last

time we'll be high-wirin on the ninety-nine-point-nine FM waveband. And we'll miss yous, so we will. Hope you'll miss us, too. Don't answer that!

That wis ADF, of course, and Ah hear they're aboot tae tour again so Ah'll be the first one queuin fur tickets – dunno boot you. Onyweye, Ah'm sure we wish the lads aw the best ae Scottish luck. Ah wis always a Naxalite. Whoops, might lose ma job fur that! Mibbee Ah'll get away before sax after all. Only jokin. Otherwise, Ah'll be wi yous, whurivir ye are, right through the night. So lighten up and don't fall asleep at the wheel. Or, if ye're sittin at home in yer armchair, then start tappin yer feet cause there's a lot mair guid music tae come! There'll be nae requests tonight. Tonight, we're goannae play the stuff we like – that Ah think will be similar to the stuff yous like – so, hopefully, we'll all be *khush*. We'll be hearin more fae ADF later oan in the programme and there'll be the usual oorly news bulletins but, otherwise, it's sax oors ae *pukka* solid sound. Oh, an, if ye hear sumhin in the backgroon, don't retune yer sets – it's no interference, it'll be a *daavat*!

He moved closer to the mike and spoke more quietly and with a deeper voice, the sort of voice he would normally acquire after drinking a small brandy.

This bein our last night, we're goannae be hovin a *daavat* so the folks in the radio station will be dancin tae the same sunes as yous. It'll be a party – inside an oot.

He leaned back again. Ruby 'n' Fizz were reaching orgasm. Shit, he thought, they'll come together, right in the middle of my patter. He bent forwards, his lips almost touching the mike.

Let's cut the talk an huv another track. But first the News 'n' Weather. Ah know – mair talk. Whit can Ah say?

He switched over to the pre-recorded CD. The same news, the same weather. It changed from day to day but, really, Zaf found it hard to remember even one single item of what the Prime Minister had said or of what the First Minister had not said or of whom some glitzy, anorexic movie star, baskin in a cat-suit, in the shallows of Bombay or Mumbai or whatever the hell they called it nowadays, had slept with or danced with or cuckolded or shot – and what difference wis there anyway? They got these things from the big commercial English Asian station, Radio Sunset, which wis based in Birmingham, in return for a modicum of cash – of course, nuthin came for free in the minority ethnic business communities any more than it did anywhere else.

After a while, Zaf would find his mind runnin along two separate tracks so that he would be readin the news or, at least, his past self would be readin the news, his voice, sensible to the point of insensibility. That's what a full honours university education did for you. It enabled you to sort out the bullshit from the bullshit and to do it with an intense and profound seriousness, born of the pursuit of excellence – otherwise known as gettin the grades – and, all the while, his other cerebral railway line would be emanatin an alternative news broadcast across the city of Glasgow and its satellite estates. And this other version of the truth went somethin like this: 'Fellow citizens, don't believe whit Ah'm tellin ye – it's maistly lies – but, maist of all, don't believe whit ye believe.' Mibbee, one day, he would actually come out and say it but, whenever the crazy thought had entered his mind

– and over the three long months, it had occurred to him more than once – Zaf had been unsure whether he could actually put what he was thinkin an feelin into words. No, it would probably come out either as a long bloody scream or else as music. After all, it wasn't so much about what you said, it wis more about who wis listenin. It wasn't just Zaf who wis on multiple wavelengths, the whole bloody population of Glasgow wis tunin in on totally different levels – each person was listenin to a different Zaf, a separate show which bedded down inside each person's skull, their very own receiver. Sometimes Zaf would try to picture his audience – he would suck up the soundwaves and play them into light behind his eyes. Someone listens, right enough. Tired ex-gangstas, dyin eyes, hangin around in musty rooms; hot blades, sleekin back their sable hair, dreamin of a fast club lay; young women on the brink who no longer desired to sing with the voices of girls; minicab drivers who, in another *zameen*, had been government ministers; doctors and nurses dancin on the long caffeine shift; lovers with thin walls, slidin up the volume to hide both the sounds of pleasure and their own guilt; members of wacky religious sects, mud-wrestlin with their souls; *madrasah* junkies, avoidin mirrors; off-duty, multiculturally-inclined strippers; on-duty, curry-lovin polis; hookers of all descriptions; junkies on all kinds of prescriptions; mothers whose babies wouldn't go down; city *biviis*, with *kisaan*-heid hubbies, up in the night to move down an out; *mitai*-makers – 'Purveyors Since Nineteen Seventy-Two' of sweet, sweet happiness; multi-*balti*-millionaires with twenty-four carat worries; tramps clutchin bags of rancid eggs; migrants from north, south, east an west; those who'd never fitted in; clerks with scores to settle; parkin wardens wearin false moustaches; aficionados of cross-over, the Kings of the Night; kebab-shop runners; and internet-crazed insomniacs.

Motorbike girls whose limbs stretch deliciously in leather as they run up your close stairs to deliver your *haraam* pizza . . .

His *maa* never listened – he knew that. His papa . . .? It wis possible. Deep in the night, anythin wis possible. And what about Babs? Did she listen? She had said that she didn't, that she wis too busy sleepin, recoverin for the early shift. Real work. But, sometimes, when Zaf had got home, he had noticed, in her eyes, a certain look, a weariness, yeah, but somethin more, somethin deeper. Wanderin music. The lust of migratin Celts. He swept his arm around and gathered up a particular CD from the long rack over to his left. The name of the band was The Colour of Memory and the song he wis thinkin of wis called 'Changed Days' from their album *The Old Man and the Sea*. He opened up the CD case, glanced at the liner notes. Black-and-white photographs of the band, young faces, lookin mysterious, their eyes glistenin with hidden knowledge. One of the women reminded him of Babs. He removed the CD and put the case down again, carefully though. Changed days. Aye.

Outside, the rain was fallin again, steadily like slivers of glass through the darkness. Zaf slipped the disc in and pressed the button to start up Deck B. Then he got up and went over to the large sash window. He ran his thumb down the wood, felt the cracked white gloss. Beneath the white, there wis purple and beneath that . . .

He stared into the blackness. His own face glared back at him, black, transparent, the worried eyes, the chin a little too large, the mouth crumpled at the corners as though from the pressure of keepin too many words unsaid. He ran his fingers through his hair, which he felt had overgrown, and he scratched at the roots, at the skin of his scalp. He let his eyes close and let the music flow into him. Celtic rock. Holy stones. Good music – ancient and modern, sad and happy. Songs from the lighthouse, from beyond the rocks of this land. The warm, pulsin rhythms of the electric bass, the woman's voice, like the soarin flight of an eagle. 'Changed Days'.

> As the sun sinks to rest,
> My thoughts are with you, my love,
> While sleeping . . .

There had been times when there had been no one, except him, in the entire building. He'd kept busy at those times, had not allowed his mind to seek out old fears in new places. Sometimes, Zaf had wondered whether the place wis haunted, perhaps by some unfortunate fallen nun, who had cast herself from the parapet, or mibbee by a walled-up Counter-Reformatory priest. The Covenanters, the Young Pretender and all that. Headless Mary. Saint Thenew, mother of Kentigern, martyred upside down and then forgotten by those whom she had blest. The Poor Weans' Dinner Table. The Tobacco Barons. East End, West End, South Side. 'The Parish of Govan' emblazoned in stone across half the buildings in the city. Rabbie Burns, the drunken taxman who, alone among taxmen and goin by all the plaques, busts and dedications, seemed to have slept in every woman's bed in Scotland. The battles between the Night Men and the immigrants from Donegal. The rattlin of the trams. The sound of marchin boots. The seventy wars of the British Empire which had been fought with Scottish soldiery in the van. Long, dark coffins, grievin widows, children barefoot in the tenement closes. The Great Exhibitions, the Diamond Jubilees. Zaf hadn't thought too much about that sort of thing. Hadn't let it get to him. Everythin had a past and you couldn't go about shoulderin it all. He opened his eyes. The face in the glass looked ridiculous – a Stan Laurel figure, up there on a rainy summer's night in Glasgae. He let his arm drop and gazed at the buildings opposite where the windows were long and always darkened. Better ridiculous than scared. He turned away. Found himself glancin over towards the next room, to where the shadows of the lovers had been. They were still there. In spite of the heat, his face wis covered in a cold sweat and he wis tremblin.

He had gazed through the windows countless times durin the past three months. Ninety days – it sounded like a prison sentence. Only, at first, it had seemed excitin – exotic, even. 'Midnight tae sax, man, midnight tae sax – do the requests and, in between, play whitivir you like, man,' Harry had said. 'Well, whitivir you like within reason.' But, as in any relationship, the exoticism had faded with the drudgery. The song wis endin. Celtic twilight. Zaf drew up the almost clean sheet and wrote, slowly:

ADF – BLACK WHITE

Well, after all, it is an Asian station, he thought. All the bits, past an future, that daily jostled and sang the state of Asian-ness into being, that reconstructed somethin that wasn't real from somethin that wis. A dancer's shadow hoverin over the hot red soil of South Asia. Old India wis shaped like a crucified Jesus. An, like some white-walled cavern chapel, Radio Chaandni bellowed out its hymns into the unlistenin darkness of Glasgow. Wee drops of Punjab and Oudh and UP and Baluchistan and Sindh and Madhya Pradesh and Sri Lanka and Tamil Nadu and Bihar and Bangladesh and Orissa and West Bengal and Karnataka and Kerala and NWFP and Himachal Pradesh and Andra Pradesh and Assam and Goa and Gujarat and Meghalaya and Tripura and Travancore and Pondicherry and Mizoram and the Dominions of the Nizam and Jharkhand and poor bloody Kashmir and Chandigarh and the old islands of Andaman and Nicobar – the prison islands or were they the spice islands?

Every one of these places had many different languages, most of which were mutually unintelligible. So what? Even people who talked the same bloody language couldn't agree on the slightest thing – they went to war with one another as often as anyone else. Zaf wis not goin to favour one stupid tribal group over another, the way some of these organisations did. Protectin their own. Keepin the others out. Imprisonin themselves, without fully realisin what they were doin, holin themselves up in cellular jails, surrounded on all sides by *kaala pani*. Black water prisons. Of course, it wis all rubbish, this stuff, this ascribin of characteristics to a whole group of people based on their tribe or their religion or the *mulk* from which they had journeyed. Aye, it wis impossible to get it out of your system – any more than an Orangeman could banish the echo of the whistle or a Catholic the pungent taste of dark Roman wine. Nonetheless, Zaf would try. If you gave up, if, at every point of dialectic, you simply threw up your hands into whatever shape happened to signify your deity's quantum line, if you cast off the mantle of responsibility for your own actions by takin the easy option of tearin the individual sinews off other people, then you were really numbin the instrument of your soul, you were makin ready for genocide. Ultimately, that wis what it led to. No joke. The great pyramid, the route from reification to deification – first you change the present, then you deny the past. Then you are the future. Which is tantamount to sayin there is no future. No way. Fuck all that – that wis what wis wrong back 'home' in the subcontinent. That wis why it wis so fuckin in-continent – it wis why people emigrated the first chance they got. But it wis takin over here, too. In subtle ways, British ways. Or, sometimes, in less than subtle Amrikan ways. All that flag-wavin and bible-bashin. What all those folk were interested in, if only they knew it, wis not God, the Tetragrammaton or *Hazrats* Isa, Israel or Ali, nor wis it Vishnu, Shiva, Rama or Rub and it certainly wis not about love or submission to a supra-human power. What it wis about, deep down, wis cotton and paper. Money, money, money. Like Mister Raj, the *pesay*-man – the *High Heid Yin* of the radio station. The guy who juggled all the coins 'n' cotton. Every time he saw the *pesay*-man, Zaf had the terrible urge to call him Taj instead of Raj. Like his big round head and his broad-shouldered suits gave him a strange resemblance to the Taj Mahal. There wis somethin very cheap, gleamin and touristy about Mr Raj/Taj but there wis also somethin deeply tragic as well – just as big city provosts tend to assume the swaggerin shape of the High Courts in Edinburgh and small-town major-domos take on the expansive fakery of the local municipal hall. They said folk took after their pets. The truth wis, they took after the stones. No, even if Zaf's mind wasn't totally balanced, his music sure would be. It wasn't so much an agenda – it wis more a feelin, a desire. The mike smelt of *methi*. Jesus! Who'd been usin this room before him?

Changed days, these. Why d'ye think Ah dae this? Tae change the day! Or the night. Aye, Ah huv ma reasons. Thur's method in ma madness! That wis the name ae the soang. 'Changed Days'. No bad, eh? *Chalo*, let's sing it thegether:

As the sun sinks to rest,
I am with you.

Enough ae that! Out-ae-tune? Och, weel, at least Ah try.
An, onyweye, it's too early tae be singin. It's always too
early for me tae be singin. Ye might aw switch aff yer
sets if Ah really get started! Ah'm not Lata. Ah cannae
do the soprano bits. Jist thought Ah'd make that clear.
Nae mair ramblin. Next tune!

A gentle pressure was all that was required. Deck A.

Zaf tapped his foot in time with the bass line of the music
(it wis another ragga-rap thing – drum 'n' bass wis all there
wis) and he sniffed the air. 'Black White'. ADF again. A song
of shrinkin universes and mixin genes. Switchin skies. A
supremacist's miscegenate nightmare.

Babs made love with a meticulousness that wis frightenin
and she expected the same from him. She would taste different
parts of his body as though he were a meal. She said his
nipples tasted sweet – she had a sweet tooth. Once, at the
height of their love-makin, she had cried out, 'My brown god,
give me your seed!' and, with her calves, she had pulled him
deeper into herself. He had felt he wis dissolvin, like rough
brown sugar, into her and yet, in the same moment, he had
felt the separateness between them widen and the two feelins
made him sense that he wis about to be torn apart and he had
almost stopped there and then. It was like she had poured cold
water over the fire of his body. Then he had managed to lose
himself for a few seconds but, afterwards, he had lain awake
for hours, the back of his hand lyin flat across his forehead,
thinkin. Before, he had always tried to see their relationship
as colour-blind but, that night, he had realised that it could
not be. Only in madness might such a thing be possible. She

needed his brown-ness – just as he needed her white. They were both conquerin territories. Three hundred years. Zilla's shadow. Nuthin wis equal between them.

He spun his chair round. On the door behind him was a poster of the station logo:

The top right-hand corner had peeled off, exposing the tape against the grey plastic. The smiling moon face was a bit like that smiling sun face that used to be everywhere, just a few years ago – that round, yellow one, nicked from New York, that the City Council would have had everyone believe was the real face of Glasgow. But the light of the radio station wis reflected light. Zaf wasn't sure what that meant but he wis sure it must mean somethin. On one side of the poster were several postcard-sized versions of the same thing and then a calendar advertising a local grocery shop. Lots of wee moons, scattered among the dates. On the wall to the left of the poster, he had Sellotaped up a photo of Babs so that, when he was seated, she would be more or less at eye level. Although lots of other people used the cubicle, Zaf had spent more time than anyone else in the twenty-by-twenty box which, rather grandly, had come to be termed a studio. He had become familiar with every crack and it had got so that he would know beforehand in exactly which direction the shadows would fall and at what time. But he had never experienced the room in full daylight. He would leave at six a.m. sharp, as soon as his broadcast had ended. He peered at the picture of his girlfriend. The photo had been taken two years ago, just before they had met – he knew it had been just before because of her hairstyle. She wis a straw-blonde and her skin wis slightly waxy and gave off a light golden hue. Her nose wis just a little too broad and the nostrils flared almost as though she wis constantly tryin to sniff out somethin. Her lips were plush, like the fur of a cat, and she had a habit of poutin them when she felt happy. She spent her spare time knittin or else watchin TV. She'd watch anythin, from highbrow art movies to glitzy game shows where grinnin people would be paraded about like animals on plastic studio floors. The flickerin images seemed to hold her attention, to hypnotise her. Zaf couldn't stand half the things she watched but he loved the fact that she watched them. She wasn't thick though. Babs possessed an instinctive perception of things as they were, of the world unveiled. Everythin she did she did deliberately – everythin from the way she sat and painted each toenail a subtle, dark shade of blue, to her possession of a powerful motorbike, to the sudden manner in which she'd moved in with him. She let her body make the decisions. But, then, thought Zaf, it's easy for her. There's no fracture between her body and her mind.

The music pulsed on, ADF beamin out their message of hope and unity, of rainbow community, but Zaf wondered whether it wis all just a big hoodwink? A superficial take on an impossibly deep structure, seven-eighths of which wis unpalatable? Too much of all that lovey-dovey stuff depended on there bein some kind of level playin field to start with. It depended on a delusion. But, then, what wis the alternative? Mibbee the dream wis the precursor to the reality. And, anyway, he wis one to talk.

He drew himself back to the photo. She'd always claimed that it had been taken by one of her girlfriends. But the image wis slightly blurred – as though the hand that had held the camera had trembled a little, just at the critical moment. He went right up close to the shiny paper so that he could almost smell its silver. Only a lover, he thought, or an ex-lover could have taken a picture like that. And Zaf had noticed the twitch around her lips, the lips which so often he had rapturously kissed, and he had pretended a kind of studied nonchalance and had allowed her not to elaborate. We all need lies to keep us sane, he'd figured. She wis smilin but not broadly (he had touched the extremes of her happiness and it had been different) and sunlight came from her left so that the long strands of her blonde hair seemed almost luminous. Almost. It wis just a photo, he kept remindin himself. In the background – though there wasn't really much background, it wis more or less a straightforward portrait – he could make out the slurred shapes of summer so he figured it must've been taken in a park of some sort or mibbee by the banks of one of the big lochs up north. The bonnie, bonnie banks ae Loch Lomond . . . The paper had become creased towards one of the upper corners and the white line of this fold extended downwards and diagonally across her face, amputatin her right ear. It wasn't a perfect photograph by any standards but it did somethin for Zaf. He'd carried it around in his wallet for ages before, finally, he'd assigned it to the wall of his cell. Sometimes, he wondered why he'd not picked an image of his love which he had set up and created for himself or which, at the very least, he had caught on film, the way most people did, so that, again and again, the picture would trigger memory until the memories themselves would become the image. Perhaps it wis because, in possessin that part of her life which he had never really known, he had felt that somehow he might be able to possess the whole of her. Zaf ran his tongue tip along the line where the flesh of his upper lip met the skin. The stubble felt like sandpaper. A midnight shadow. He tasted salty. Babs wis hardly ever salty – sometimes she might taste of elegant mild cigars or else of coffee or, deep in the night when they were close to bein one, she would make him feel he wis swimmin down a tunnel of warm, fast-flowin blood. It wis like he was inside the arteries that ran through her body and, in the total darkness, there wis no longer any separation, no longer any colour, no thought – just their being, the fugue of their breathin, the rise and fall of her firm, small breasts as they formed silhouettes against the emptiness beyond the window.

Zaf jumped as, in the distance, a motorbike blasted off into the night. It got so you could tell the make an model by the timbre of the noise it made. Every bike had a different voice. You became like one of those naturalists, trackin down the different species. He knew that this was not Babs's machine. Her bike wis clean – she polished it down once a week, more in the winter. Waxed it with love. And, throwin on her dun-coloured dungarees, she dismantled it too. She would handle each component with the greatest care, as though it were a precious organ or a gleamin, steel baby. She knew exactly how it worked – its precision components, its filters, its cylinders. Its map wis drawn inside her head in a way he could never be. At times, Zaf had found himself jealous of the bike, of its perfectly designed blue body, its chrome neck, the unvaryin trajectory of its wheels, her hands runnin all over its structure, the engine oil smeared on to her face. Love paint. Stupit bugger!

Sometimes, especially durin these past three months, Zaf had wondered exactly what role he filled in the life of this active woman. Two years must mean somethin. But Babs wis bone fide Scottish, blue and white down to the marrow, and so she hadn't talked. Well, she did talk – they had conversations and, when they were intimate, they shared whispers that were like songs or prayers – but she didn't really talk about anythin to do with Zaf 'n' her.

Zaf sighed. Women were like music – deep and unfathomable.

The electric black-white unity of Asian Dub Foundation was discharging its last sparks and Zaf swept himself back to the console. Lips, mike, breath, switch, go.

Namaste ji, salaam alaikum, sat sri akaal, welcome tae *The Junnune Show*. Ah'm Zaf – zed ay eff – an ye're listenin tae Radio Chaandni oan wavelength ninety-nine-point-nine meters frequency modulation. It's hauf past midnight an we're gettin intae the groove! Whativir groove ye're in, Ah'm in there wi ye. Whit a thought, eh? So switch aff yer mobiles, prick up yer ears – don't misquote me now – an get ready tae swoon an sigh. If ye've been listenin fur the past hauf oor, ye'll huv noticed that the music's swung aroon fae hard Asian dub – city music, ye might say – tae airy-fairy Scoa'ish stuff. Weel, Ah don't know aboot you but that's whit maist ae us are livin, folks. We're no breathin Bollywood here an we're no stampin oot bhangra in the *zard* fields neether. Right? This is today music – it knows nae boundaries an we know nae boundaries. We are the sky, we are the sea. Hey, did Ah ivir tell yous that Ah wis a *shair*?

Zaf paused for effect. An image of Babs, naked in the night rain, flashed up on to the celluloid of his brain.

No? Weel, now yous know it aw.

He pressed the button. *Jao, jao, nunga* soangs! Naked Celtic rhythms again. The Colour of Memory. The female vocalist breathed the lyrics of 'Always With Me' as though her body itself had become an instrument. Those swirlin, transformin knot patterns. Green glens. Echoes.

> And we fell
> We fell
> Into the day of the dead

He got up and switched on the kettle. Crap instant coffee, panned, like fool's gold, on the scratched mica of a wobbly side table – that wis what Radio Chaandni stretched to. Zaf would've preferred it filtered, at least, but that wis what you got on a cheapie wavelength. The music might be magic but the drink wis shite on wheels. Or, to be more accurate, shite an powdered milk on stilts, stirred slowly with a bent, verdigrised spoon. Still, it kept him awake through the long, long hours of the show. He alternated it with builder's tea, stewed for ages with two teabags, that wis thick as tar. The kind of stuff that made you shiver as you sipped. The kind of beverage that burned the memsahib right out of you. He measured his cups though – he'd found that, after a while, too much caffeine would begin to have a reverse effect. It would end up sendin him to sleep or mibbee into wakin dreams which wis worse. Copper ends to ivory canes.

The song swung between two poles – the words of the singer, strong, breathy, light, a voice of clarsach spaces and bodhrán mountains, unchangin in their unimaginable antiquity, and another silent voice, a sound that wis like an anti-song, a negation, an inhalation that never ended but swelled in his chest until it wis as big as the world and as long as time.

Anyway, even instant coffee wis considerably better than two-litre plastic bottles of ginger. Zaf had this theory – which he had tested at several recent weddings, *Eid Melas* and other assorted socio-familial events – that the Glasgow South Asian metabolism no longer required *pani*. If anyone asked for 'just water', there would be a slight hesitation which masked a tacit response of 'Ah! So you're a poor person, then.' Peasants drank water – the wealthy imbibed E-numbers. Their souls had become fully carbonated. This wis how they would float up in the social scale. Back in fourteenth-century Firenze, if Dante Alighieri, in his exile, had had Irn-Bru, he wouldn't have needed Beatrice. He wouldn't have needed poetry. But, then, Dante wasn't Asian or Scottish. In fact, Zaf had been forced to the conclusion that loch water wis positively detrimental to the health and well-being of the New Subcontinental physique. He'd heard it on the radio – soft water, *pani*, denuded miraculously of its mineral content, wis a slow serial killer. But somethin he'd never heard on any programme, somethin he'd never read in any pamphlet, leaflet or tome, wis the theory that the warm milky tea, that folk called '*hamaray chai*', wis also a burnin, silent, gurglin murderer. If Zaf had been a judge, he would've sentenced *hamaray chai* to the gallows or mibbee to be stoned alive, in some basement dive no one, except habitual *pani*-drinkers, had ever heard of, to be rocked and rolled till the blood flowed and the brains drained. A waverin, theremin death. He sipped his coffee. It wis OK – it wis palatable only when it wis so hot it threatened to burn the linin off your mouth. A DJ with a dragon lung.

'Ye'll always be with me, won't ye, Zaf?' she had said, deep in the hay of the lochside night. 'Ye'll nivir leave me.

You're ma first love, ma first real love.' Corny lines among the dead stalks of corn. His seed lyin silver in the gold of her body. Her limbs outstretched, a rood of muscle and bone and need. Time compressin and extendin them both into ciphers, into light, into nuthin. 'Ah'm with you – Ah'm here,' he had whispered to her curled, foetal form, the red mush tyres of his lips turnin against the rubbery cartilage of her left ear. Strands of her hair halfway up his nose. Her gold trackin up to his brain. He tossed the spoon down on to the mica. An effective and elegant assassination. Aureate locks sharpened with a long bicentenary of practice, angled straight towards the frontal lobes. Destroy your self-awareness, erode your faculties of judgement. This wis where the playin field began to get uneven – inside your head.

The sides of the mug were still hot so he swapped hands, right to left, and scratched the crown of his head. The light comin in from the street had altered in some subtle aspect which Zaf could not quite place – some shift in the simmerin rhythm of the night had occurred while the northern song had begun sendin its clear glass waves out through the darkness. Some coffee spilled over the lip of the porcelain as Zaf got up and tried, for a moment, to forget his audience. His *baratherie* of burned coffee drinkers, the loose agglomeration of hounded, black-eyed escapees from the swirlin, tawny tyranny of *hamaray chai* and bright-orange ginger litres. '*Pani, pani*, ivirywhur . . .'

The Colour of Memory. The substance of things which no longer existed. But what about the things that were in-between – where did they fit in? It wis all very well to say that whatever he and Babs had had wis ebbin away, faster than sunlight off a tenement roof, yet the women he'd loved would always be there, in his head, gathered around his body, definin him. They marched alongside him, a shadow *fauj*, they matched every step, each one elicitin in him a bottomless sense of loss. It wis a bloody epic. Not that there had been that many of them – women. Zaf wasn't some kind of Don Juan who went around fellin every piece of skirt he came across. Even the image seemed anachronistic. In one part of his head, he sincerely believed in the equality of women and men in all respects, on every level. The problem wis it had remained an intellectual concept, somethin he had learned, a received wisdom that had been handed down from somewhere – one which, on good days, he imagined he had internalised to the extent of bein almost unaware of its existence. But it wasn't the good days that mattered. A person wasn't defined by what they did, thought or said when the sun wis shinin, the music singin up the major keys. It wis what you did on the nights when there were no shadows, when the rain came down like shinin spears, down through the hot, suffocatin nights of the auld taverns, the sweatin, lathered horses with their nostrils flarin at the moon. It wis what you did to people, when they didn't match up to your dreams, that counted. How you treated those you loved and who loved you when everythin wis goin down. That wis how you would be judged.

Some ill-defined movement, down in the street, caused the shadows on the cubicle walls to shift and dance. The lush Celtic techno-folk was sinking deep into the dark notes, the minor scales, the forgotten sequences. It wis those and not the others, he thought, that cut the shape of your soul. And, risin from the deep loch, wis somethin from the past-that-wis-ever-present. Zaf felt a creepin sensation spread over his body, beginnin from his chest and movin outwards. This wis not Babs or any of the normal, fallible, physical women he'd either had or imagined havin. This came from somewhere unfathomable – it derived from a much older template. The pulsin, electronic folk music, very Scottish, he'd thought would evoke Babs and their cosy romantic beginnins but, instead, this other, this heaviness, wis risin through the notes, envelopin his body, crushin him, takin over, just as it had done before. As she had before. Movin backwards, jig 'n' reel in reverse. She – the one before Babs. Manic, red-faced ceilidh dancers, high-steppin through the substance of his brain, punchin out holes, great, dark, bottomless lochs in his soul. Her shape.

He could feel her weight, physically, over his body. Even though it had been four years ago, she had left her imprint – the timbre of her breath, the windin notes of her voice – though, unlike Babs, she had never sung. With her burnin, screamin bones, she had branded him. Zilla, his first love. A love without innocence, without light. A shadow music. Zilla, Babs. Zilla. Babs. Zilla-Babs. Fuck.

Zaf gripped the sides of his head.

Fuck, fuck, fuck!

But even his words were mere punctuations in the beat and pulse of the music which was no longer bein played by musicians. And he wis the stupit, bastart, tragic figure at the centre of it all.

Still holdin his head, he got up and began to pace around the room. He felt totally unable to stop the music. Deck A. Deck B. It wis runnin out of control – this night, his life. Fuck sake, she could push her way through anythin and be here, now, with him. As he breathed song into the warm night, he would be breathin Zilla. The soul inside.

'Always With Me' wis fadin away. There was nuthin better to galvanise Zaf into action than the prospect of silence. He had to keep the music playin. Six hours of non-stop *junnune*. It wis his only hope of stayin sane. The tracks might be unpredictable but what lay behind them wis far, far worse. He let go of his head and became instantly the cool professional. By the end of the three-month life of Radio Chaandni, perhaps Zaf would emerge a better liar than before. That wis somethin. A preacher with a long tongue, a Wee Free:

Lie down with the beast!
And be damned to the hellfires of
Eternity!

Hope ye enjoyed that. The music's real. Dig it. *Sumjhe?* That wis The Colour of Memory an 'Always With Me'. An, afore that, ADF's 'Black White'. Celtic rock an Asian dub. Hey, we've goat ivirythin oan this show. It's crazy, it's whisperin an it's wonderful! It's *junnune*! Ah aim da greatest! Have ye heard the wan aboot the boaxer an the shoapkeeper? No? Weel, mibbee Ah'll tell ye it wan day. Or mibbee not! Ah don't jist do jokes oan this show. Ah do jokes that make ye laugh till ye burst. Or cry till ye drown. Ah'm a bundle ae laughs. A right likeable character, eh? But thenight, Ah've run oot ae funny lines, folks, so ye'll need tae think up some ae yer ane. Tonight, it's jist me, ma voice an the music. And whit music! Whit ye've heard so far hus been jist a taster ae whit's tae come. An who knows whit's tae come, *samaaen?* Who knows whit lies ahead? It's hard enough tryin tae figure oot whit lies behind! Mibbee that's jist as weel, eh? Now, Ah'm askin the questions an you're feelin jist a wee bit insecure – am Ah right? It's no the role ae the DJ tae be posin deep an profound *savaalat* tae his listeners who, after aw, are probably relaxin aifter a hard day's work or a hard night's play. Ah'm meant tae be the loast voice inside the centre ae yer heids, the voice that tells ye the answers an mibbee even THE ANSWER. *Javaabaat aur savaalaat.* But whit if the joakie husnae goat ony *javaabaat*? Whit if the whole, lang river ae Qs an As is jist a skin, like these here radio-wave voices ye hear when ye press the tunin button, or, if ye've goat wan ae those haunted valve sets, when ye twiddle the *kaala* knob? Now, don't get me wrong, Ah'm no suggestin that ye go aff an leave Radio Chaandni, broadcastin oan ninety-nine-point-nine meters FM. Ah'm no telling ye tae defect fae Radio Chaandni, fae *HAMARAY LOAG* an dive intae some other musical river, a caulder wan mibbee or wan wi an iced heid. Mibbee then ye would walk away in the mornin wi a different set ae voices dancin aboot inside yer brain. Cause iviry piece ae music ye listen tae, iviry person who comes intae yer life, iviry breath ae soang fae the dark river ae the *raat* that runs under the skin, changes ye, forms ye jist as much as yer mither 'n' faither or as much as yer lover. So, because Ah don't know whit's comin next, whit track Ah'm goannae play next, thur's nae control oan this last episode ae *The Junnune Show*. Or, if thur is, then it's beyond me. Madness, music, life. It's a river that emerges fae total *tamas* an flows through oor lives fur a while an then flows aff again intae darkness.

Zaf swung back and sipped from his coffee mug, spilling a bit on the left side of his shirt.

Heavy stuff, eh? Don't worry, ye're no alane. Ah'm oan this ship, too, even though thur's nae rudder, nae sail an the tiller has wandered aff fur a kip. So, wu're sailin oan a sleepin ship, a boat ae dreams. Your dreams, ma dreams an the soangs an tales ae those we thought we knew but who huv nivir really been known tae us because they've always been a part ae us.

Zaf removed a compact disc with a black-and-white cover from the rack. Deck A. Smooth, deep Rafi. The closest sound to Heaven, this side of the Gates.

Enough ae the hype. Now it's gettin late and we're movin cool intae the night. And Ah know it's rainin oot there, oot ma windae, but nae worries, you'll be indoors, mobile phonies, at home or in the shoap or in yer car or whurivir an Radio Chaandni will stay with ye right through the night. And tonight – oor last night – Ah'll be playin aw ma favourites an, since ma taste is *kaafi* broad, as they say, then Ah'm sure thur'll be sumhin here for ivirywan. Now fur somehin mellow.

Baw'wabaat.

A scent was rising from the fabric of the building or perhaps from the night beyond – a scent that was powerful but which, like most smells, was difficult to define. Yet it grew even stronger now as Zaf closed his eyes and massaged the lids. Already, he felt so tired. It was not a fatigue that could be remedied by any amount of coffee – it was a weariness that went back centuries. Perhaps he had been wrong before. Perhaps the essences of the church's previous occupants still hovered, somehow, within the stone. It was a dry, tight, musty smell – a stench of bones and empty stomachs, of human beings reduced. Or perhaps it was that of skin, of palms touching in whispered supplication, in a mystical conjunction of blood and wafers. But, if the church had been filled with congregations – not of transubstantiating Roman Catholics but of iconoclastic Calvinists – then the echoes would emanate from the rising howl of metrical psalms. A Last Word, over and over. The War of the Farishtas, here on the upper floor where stone griffins, blinded for centuries, once had alighted. Perhaps all of these voices, singing into a swaying, darkening sky, had hewn the wood and fashioned the stone and forged the gold. And now, again, Zaf was raising the music up into an architecture – a mosque of many domes. Countless notes – one music.

He slid down the voice-control as the warm, God-like tones of Rafi began to pour through the night. Slow cellos rolling like waves on the Karachi sea. Hanging in the nets, the scent of bhang.

> You broke my heart
> As though it were a toy
> You left me one companion –
> Sorrow

A voice from behind him.

Thu're at it again, those two!

Zaf almost jumped out of his chair. He spun round. 'Christ, Harry! You tryin tae give me a heart attack or whit?'

Harry did not apologise but came in through the door. He was small, light and handsome in a gay kind of a way. His mother was Scottish and Harry had always straddled several worlds, each of which was equally mysterious to all of the others. Harry was a democratic secret, a miscegenate time bomb which Zaf thought might explode at any moment and change everythin. His cheeks had reddened – Zaf wasn't sure whether this wis because of the rain or through embarrassment at the copulatin couple. 'Khilona'. In a world of wind-up toys, though, Harry wis a humanoid. Zaf could see why the guy might've broken some big men's hearts. Paths of sorrow.

'Ah'm fed up wi this fuckin crap . . .'

'Are ye comin to the party?' Zaf interjected, in an attempt to stop him from goin on about it.

Harry shrugged. 'Yeah, Ah'll be there. Who's organisin it, anyway?'

'I thought you were, man.'

He shook his head. 'No this time. Ah've had it wi organisin. Someone else can do the work fur a cheynge.' He jerked his thumb sideways. 'Like them mibbee – wance they've left aff ae each other.'

'Or Raj?'

'Hah, that's a joke. He'll do aw the money thing, the book bit, but, when it comes tae gettin yer honds dirty, ye'll no see him fur dust.'

Harry slumped down on the only other chair in the room and crossed his short legs just above the ankles. His jeans looked old and in need of a wash. There were dirty marks on the insides of the legs. He closed his eyes and rubbed them and then he sighed. Zaf felt the song flow through Harry's being. 'Khilona'. A mumbled half-lyric:

> My heart got busted.
> *Dil toRay jathay ho.*

Harry had spent his life swimming against tides and it showed. He was looking haggard, his skin lacked something vital and his eyes flitted this way and that as though he were perpetually searching for some task or challenge into the resolution of which he might pour his energies. Zaf wondered whether he wis on speed or cocaine. Rhino dust. Zaf pictured him, on the first night of the run, leanin there against the jamb of the door with his earring drippin towards the floor – the guy wis trendy, right, but he wis known locally (within the buildin, anyway) as 'The Station Master'. Zaf supposed someone had to be. Harry wore his hair up, almost spiky. It wis dyed brown but, around the edges, you could still make out where it wis goin grey. He wis shorter than most Western women and always dressed in denims. Faded blue, like the eyes of the men he preferred. He had a moustache like Freddie Mercury's. And he might've been mistaken for a Parsee, except that he wis a Sikh. Aye, The Station Master wis the trendy one and, when he wis around, no one else wis allowed to be. Still, he got away with it because he ran a tight station. Well, it wis a damn sight tighter than that other lot had been – the ones over the water. Radio Pardesi. The rivals. Stupid name. Radio Foreigner. Talk about shootin yourself in the foot! The two stations never ran at the same time – one would follow the other, like American prison sentences. Two hundred and fifty-one years on community radio for bein rude to your granny. But Zaf had a lot of respect for Harry. The guy had been around in the seventies and had trained as an actor when the only roles for an Asian had been either as a gigglin guru or else, once a year, as one of the three wise men. The thespian equivalent of cleanin toilets. Harry'd said to Zaf that, in those days, when it came down to it, Asian pussy had been hot but Asian cock had been a threat – simple as that. Harry wis a man torn and mibbee that wis why he wore his hair spiked as if he'd just had a large dose of coke. It wis what had driven him on, through one doomed project after another, until, finally, he'd ended up on the air – or, to be more accurate, behind the air. 'There's not enough professionalism,' Harry would keep sayin as though professionalism wis some kind of elusive quality amenable only to adepts of the Harry Singh School of Radio Broadcasting and not just a job status. Like if mibbee we got paid, Zaf thought, then we just might be a little more professional. No hope of that though. It wis like the bad old days which the auld-timers liked to go on – and on and on and on – about. And who could blame them? Long, dark days when most Asians, here in Scotland, had worked as pedlars, wee men in boats, hawkin their trinkets and pieces of cloth through the *pishaap* rain from door to boggin door. They'd tramped their way from Dunnet Head, in Caithness, to Portpatrick, in Galloway, from Aird Uig, on the extreme west coast of the Outer Hebridean Isle of Lewis, to Boddam, just south of Peterhead – aye and they'd had some good, warm, metal mugs of tea along the way and some wonderful welcomin smiles and sales. Yeah, OK, they'd had some utter shite, too. And the women, once they'd followed their husbands, upside down across the great main of the skies, were swept into a life where, apart from doin all the housework and raisin the kids, they'd also had to reel light years of thread across the vastness of the city and to lose *sairon* of heart's blood in the interiors of merciless sweatshops, often run by other Asians – places that made those of Hispanic LA seem like ecologically tolerant cooperatives. No wonder those guys and gals were hobblin around on sticks by the time they reached sixty. Their hearts had been worn down – not broken by the thick aromas of romance but desiccated slowly by the unremittin need to transmute themselves, day after day, from somethin they once had been to what the 'new life' demanded of them. No wonder they had clung on to weird attitudes. It wasn't their fault, Zaf thought – for most of their lives, they'd been under fire. They all thought that their words, their actions had been for the best. Most of the time and for most of the people, they probably had been. And that wis the scary thing. They'd been travellin salesmen without a motel, gypsies without a caravan. To leap from peasant-farmer to this – it wis a strange story and it had been the story of the world, over the past couple of hundred years. Ranks of men and women pulled from the burnin furrows of southern poverty and slung into the towns and cities of the north where, in winter, the icicles tinkled merrily from the sides of their *barras* and where the blood that whirled from the spools of their sewin machines congealed and froze. A decade on, some of them had set up corner shops which, in those days, had been called tobacconists or confectioners or news-agents. In a place that stopped the flow, it wis hard enough to swim with the tide and, like Harry, Zaf too had dedicated his life – so far – to swimmin against it. Time for a folk song.

> Oh, Punjab, *tuu meri dil toR*.
> Oh, Scotland, you, too, are breaking my heart.
> Oh, Life, I am but a toy!

The dark crescent moons that hovered habitually below Harry's eyes had become even darker than usual. Just beneath the skin, lines fissured through the elastic, cartographing the course of the bones. The creases at the corners of his eyes, the protruding cheekbones, the slump of his face, all gave him the appearance of a man haunted. Soon, Zaf thought, the skeleton will force its way out through the muscle and skin and will bare itself to the cold wind. Zaf hadn't really thought all that much about ageing – about his own ageing at any rate – but he could tell from Harry's face that he feared it and ran from it. Mibbee that wis why he was so bloody energetic, always thinkin up schemes and schemes-within-schemes and schemes-within-schemes-within . . . What the fuck. We were all runnin from somethin.

At one point, several years ago, Harry had decided that he was, in fact, gay. This was after he'd shacked up with at least four women (though not simultaneously – it wasn't bloody California, for God's sake) and now he had a regular partner, a lover who was very blond and almost vegan. Harry, on the other hand, was vehemently carnivorous – he sometimes joked that it really wouldn't have done for a gay lion, a Glad-to-be *Kooni* Singh, to have been veggie. Anyway, back in the seventies, there had been very few gay men in the west of Scotland and certainly no Asian gay men so Harry figured that he'd been, in some way, ahead of his time – though, of course, at that time, he hadn't known he wis gay. Anyhow, the thing was so convoluted, Zaf felt he had really lost the plot somewhere or mibbee there wis no plot. As he glanced sidelong at Harry, the mess of all those extinct relationships seemed burned into his face – a scar for the loss of each lover. You don't ever get anythin for nuthin, he thought.

'You look knackered, man,' Harry said as though in riposte.

Zaf sighed. 'I am knackered. Three months is a long time.'

'But you chose this slot yersel. Said you were a night owl.'

'Yeah, but you can get too much ae a good thing.'

After a while, you begin to hate that which once you loved. It occurred to Zaf that perhaps he looked worse than Harry. Mibbee this show of long nights wis agein him rapidly. An image of Zilla pushed up into his mind. Skin a dark coffee-brown and hair sleek and soft and blowin in the night breeze. He pushed it away.

'But you'll be back.'

He shook his head. 'No way. I'm not doin this again – not even if we get a permanent licence.'

Harry glared at him. His electric hair with its fringe of grey around the edges. Grey electric greaser. 'You think we'll get a permanent licence? Ah don't think so. Not when the community itself cannae agree on which toilet tae use. Ye've goat wan MSP fightin another an wan mosque fightin the next mosque. An that's jist wan religion, fur fuck sake! Unless ye get yer ane act together, no one's goannae look twice at ye. The Sikhs are the same. There's nae unity.'

Zaf had noticed that, when Harry got angry, his accent would become more and more Scottish until he would be really flowin and dashin over killin stones like some lost mountain tributary of the Clyde. And, yet, somewhere deep in the mix, it wis always possible to detect the dust syllables of East Punjab. Gurmukhi. From the mouth of the guru. Harry's family had drizzled into Glasgow from a small village that lay to the east of Amritsar, some thirty-odd years earlier, when he had been around five years old, and so he wis, technically, first generation but, psychologically, he belonged to the ones beyond. Anyway, Zaf hated those kinds of boundaries – hated bein defined by his status of bein other – felt trapped by that whole thing. Mibbee that wis why he'd dumped Zilla – because he'd not wanted to be cast in his own skin. He remembered that, once, Babs had dyed her hair a rust red and had put on intensely pale make-up. It had changed her appearance altogether but he'd liked it. The Celtic look. And Zaf wanted to be like a lizard and to be able to slip from one skin to another, whenever it suited him – to go from pub to club to mosque to whore and not even to sweat in between. To be like a white man. Well, that wis the fantasy, anyhow. No, he reminded himself, I did not dump Zilla, after a four-year relationship, because she wis a Paki – nor because my mother thought Zilla wis dirt because of her background and because she'd been disowned by that background. No, I left her because she wis a fuckin junkie an because she wis goin down. Zilla wis medium brown and she'd never forgiven herself for it. And neither had anyone else. He shivered as he recalled the sight of the inside of her left thigh – the dun colour of the skin puckered with darker brown puncture marks and a tattoo in the shape of a crescent moon. Blue. Five years apart wis a long time. Five years and all the chances in the world.

'Listen, Ah'm headin off. You want anythin?' Harry's earring glinted as it caught the light from the fluorescent tubing. Blue gold.

Zaf shook his head slowly. He was still tryin to disengage from Zilla's thigh, from Rafi's song. He didn't want to eat or to talk unless it was on the radio. He wis known as the silent man and for good reason. People talked too bloody much. So much hot air. But, through the mike, in the silence of night, Zaf could wax and flow like heroin. Harry rose and put his hand on Zaf's shoulder.

'See ya later. You'll be comin tae the party.' It was not a question.

Even though, on one level, he hated him, really Zaf was in awe of Harry. Two hundred years ago, all the toys had been forged from metal and stuffed with movin cogs. Those things still worked – but their hearts had long been broken.

Zaf looked up at The Station Master. 'What about this place?'

'You can put on the Sunset Radio stuff for a while. It disnae matter. It's the last night.'

Harry, Harry, Harry. His name wis like a prayer. Zaf could well see why certain men might be attracted to The Station Master. Like Zilla, he had that same swirlin cocaine magnetism that drew the unwary into their orbits. Mibbee he wis one of those who wis as easy lyin with a woman as with

46

another man. Mibbee Harry wis really bisexual. Who wis to know? Mibbee Harry didn't even know himself. Sometimes Zaf had tried to elide himself into the mind and body of a woman – to view men the way he felt a woman might. And sometimes it had worked. He had actually got himself quite worked up on occasion. Jesus! All in the mind, as they say. But the woman he became wis always Zilla. She wis like a fuckin alter ego. Well, then, for years, he had been screwin an alter ego. How twisted wis that? That wis the effect Harry had on people – made them bent and screwy like him. He wis a fuckin lysergic bhangra – a snake of many colours. A slippery slope.

Zaf looked down at the board. 'Mibbee,' he said. 'Mibbee I'll come down for a while.'

But, then, he thought, mibbee it wis jist the Harry and Zilla inside of himself that he wis thinkin of. That made him feel better and worse at the same time.

Harry made sure he closed the door quietly as he left the booth. Always the professional, Zaf thought. He'd left behind the smell of cigarettes. Harry smoked because he was an artist. That wis all. Zaf had never been able to master that kind of act but, then, he thought, why should I? – I'm not an actor. He forced himself to be mechanical, forced himself to become merely a cog of the console with its reassuring angularity, its uncompromising solidity, and he even managed to inscribe the title of the next song on to the makeshift playlist. And that, at the height of Mohammad Rafi's virtuosity.

The violins coursed up and down and, in spite of the fact that he had been playin this music, night after night, for almost three months, Zaf still felt his insides go soft every time he heard that bit where Rafi's voice flowed like the Ravi River – before the pollution had come – slow, slow and majestic. And he felt that, if he had leapt into it, he would have known instantly that Sikander, Emperor of the Greeks, had been there, in that same place, before him. And mibbee Mohammad Rafi had been there too and mibbee he had been there before even Sikander since surely the voice must've been the first of all musics. Tonight, Zaf had brought in his favourite songs. He wasn't goin to play the LCD stuff. Lowest Common Denominator. Not tonight. Fuck everyone else. Fuck Raj/Taj, especially – Mr 'You-Can't-Play-That-The-Sponsors-Won't-Like-It'. Well, screw the sponsors. What did they know about music, the human voice, birdsong . . .? As far as Zaf wis concerned, Mohammad Rafi, not Elvis, wis King and The Beatles were his *Shahzaday*, his Royal Princes. And, after them, came Kula Shaker, ADF, Junoon, Sheila Chandra, Mukesh, Talat, Kishore and the two Kaleidoscopes and, then, a hundred others – all of them swimmin, like Alexander, across the Jhelum, the Ravi, the Chenab, the Sutlej . . . and he had only stopped at the last, the Beas, because, one night, some fuckin subaltern hadn't been able to go on any further.

> I am only a guest for a few nights.
> Why are you turning your face from me?

The song wis like dark red wine – it poured from the singer's throat and into Zaf's brain as though such a thing wis completely natural. Tragedy – it wis natural. He had been listenin to this stuff since he wis – since before he could remember. It wis part of his spirit. He could no more separate himself from its sinew than he could tear the skin from his skeleton. The big break. How many of those had he had? In the end, you always came back to what you knew – you returned to the place where you had begun. 'Khilona'. But fuck that! Tonight, there wis no stoppin him. This wis the night and Zaf was goin to cross the last bloody river. He would sink into the burnin heat of Hindustan and would pour, like melted gold, into the future. He looked up. The shadows in the next room had disappeared. Ruby 'n' Fizz had ceased to copulate. Funny, Zaf thought, I didn't notice them leave – but, then, that wis the power of Rafi. Man, his voice could even rip you away from a shadow puppet porno flick. *Khuda-ke-liye*! He laughed, cynically. Cynicism wis the eighties, he thought. My kindergarten. He'd been weaned at Thatcher's breast and, boy, had the milk been sour! Music had been his one salvation. A degree in ethnology – one of those they used to call 'useless'. It had been the kind of thing a girl might've done prior to nuptial arrangements being made – so his father had said. Sociology before fuckin. The cynicism again. But Thatcher's reptilian era wis long gone. It wis further away than Shakespeare. And what had come of it? Zilla. Fuck Zilla. Fun is the song that money can't buy. Well, they'd proved that one wrong. The only thing that money couldn't buy wis good fortune. The cubicle had fallen silent and not even the twitch of the electrics broke through the darkness. Panickin, Zaf segued on to the next track and tried to whisper like that guy, the late-night disc jockey – but he found his voice movin a little too quickly over the notes. What he needed wis an anti-coffee, a downer, an elegant slowin of things.

Fae mellow, tae mellower. Here's Sheila Chandra. Not many ae ye will know her. Remember 'Monsoon'? 'Loneliness'? OK. Showin ma age!

Showin a lot more than that. God's sake, get a grip!

No? Well, fur those ae ye who cannae remember or who're mibbee too young tae remember or even fur yous who nivir knew in the first place, Sheila-*jee* wis a singer who kept the flame alight in a time ae *tamas*.

He half-turned towards the window.

It's *kaafi* dark thenight and it's rainin. But it's no as dark as it wis then. That wis the time before radio stations or at least before Asian radio stations, ye know? The era of Mister Big White Boots, the yuppie-duppie grey suit brigade, *pesay, pesay, pesay* . . . oh, never mind aw that – it's loang since deid. Thank Goad. (Now Ah'll definitely get fired – only jokin, *samaaen*, only kiddin, Mr Taj – Ah-Mean-Raj.) Ah, words, words . . . Ye ivir felt like ye wur stuck between a rock an a hard, hard place? Iviry day, eh? Ah thought ye'd say that. Weel, oan this show, we escape. In the black night ae summer, we rise up an *ouRo*! Sounds good, eh? Ah wish. But dinnae listen tae me, rattlin oan. Ah'm Zaf-The-Naff – zed ay eff. Listen tae her. This is a track cawd 'Mecca' an it's fae the *Roots and Wings* CD – or wis it oan the *Quiet* album? Ah've goat them baith hereaboots. Ye know whit? Ah cannae remember! Sheila C's music seems tae slip like silence fae wan silver disc tae another. *Khamoshi, khamoshi, khamoshi.* Ah've nivir been thur but Ah wish Ah hud. The grass is always greener.

The song wis like a Hindu *bhajan*, a rhythmic repeating mantra but with only one word, Allah, at its centre. A whole song, five minutes and twelve seconds, consistin of a single, cosmic word. A name, stretched, extended, explored through voice, tranced toward eternity. Alif – he wrote it but it

should really have been with a fountain pen or a quill.
Runnin or flyin.

$$I \cup$$

Long, slow, loopin. 'Laaaaam'. 'Raaaaam'. Peace.

While the music slipped over the airwaves, Zaf picked up
the freebie paper, glanced at the date – three days old. He
began to pore over the small print. When Zaf wis in the
station, he wouldn't read the big stories about corrupt
councillors or sex-romp moderators but, insanely, would
find his attention drawn to the small ads section or else the
classifieds or mibbee the stories about some local fund-raisin
event where the text, big, rude and hearty, would always be
fleshed out with the overweight figures of smilin, white
schoolgirls. No one looked good in the newspapers. Zaf
found himself fascinated by all this stuff. Real stories about
real people in the dead of night. Hyperreal. Dot-matrix farce.
Mibbee that wis what an arts degree and a dead-end job did
for you. Enabled you to sort out the rubbish, from the rubbish. Or mibbee that had been his father.

◎◎◎◎◎

The windows of the drawing room of the *haveli* house seemed
almost like pools of water in the light of the setting sun. The
glass was filigreed by arabesques of wrought iron and, beyond,
in the garden, Jamil Ayaan could just make out the closed
white flowers of the jasmine plant. Lahore in the early spring.
Over in the corner, in the window recess, the Bakelite volume
control on a wooden radio had been turned down just after
he had arrived. But, though it had not been switched off, it
seemed to have lost its tuning because he was sure that,

underneath everything, he could make out the low, dissonant sound of static. Carefully, he put down his teacup and stared at his knees in an attempt to fight down the blush which had colonised the skin of his cheeks ever since she had entered. It was his third visit to the house of his *maalik* but it was only the first time he had met his superior's wife. Thick tea poured elegantly from a slim, Farangi-style, bone-china pot. Perhaps it was the strangeness of the new or the overwhelming effect of her perfume which hung heavily around the dark Chinese furniture in the closed air of the drawing room. Or perhaps it was her face cut clear as a silhouette against his brain. The swish of her cream-coloured silk sari. They had been married for two years, his boss had been telling him, but Jamil had burned his mouth and throat with the milky tea so that his replies had emerged hoarse like those of a rickshaw driver or a *paan-wallah*. And there was no doubt that he felt like a servant, an underling, in her presence. He remembered her from the first time – just two weeks ago or thirteen days to be exact. She had become imprinted on his being like an image from a flashgun. He had dreamed of her but that was too light a term – too superficial. Every man dreamed of an ideal woman but this woman was a real physical presence here, in this room which smelt of *Ruh-Afza* – in this pink and apricot house with its four floors, two of which were occupied by the extended family, the third rented to some tenants and the rooms on the roof being said to be the dwelling place of a very ancient *djinn*. They'd shown him up there on the first night, his superior and his superior's wife. Rashida. That was her name. Spoken slowly, it was like a poem. Rashida. It was like the sound of swaying grass or the sweep of waves across the sea.

Visiting the top floor was a courtesy, part of the ritual of hospitality, for all visitors. Up they had gone – the Boss,

Rashida and him, Jamil Ayaan, son of a clerk made good. She had been right in front of him as they had climbed the winding staircase – her being had been less than two feet from his hands. How small her feet were. How elegantly painted the toenails. The timbre of her voice which he could compare only to a bird's flight through a clear blue sky. The manner in which she held herself, even as she stumbled on a crumbling step, the same step, Jamil thought, as he quickly proffered a hand, that had been trodden by lovers, long-dead couples who had sat on the roof, far from the elders downstairs with their smoking, burnt water hookahs and their ground glass monocles and their eternal complaints about the state of the State. And the lovers – those long-dead *ashik-e-mashuk* – had extended the tips of their fingers until they had just touched and they had gazed at the stars, which were brighter in those days, and at the moon, which was always crescentic and silver, and they had listened to the plaintive, single-stringed melodies of Ghalib and Zauq drifting across the rooftops from the area down by the river, where the whirling civilised courtesans plied their trade. The smells of the city had entered them, had possessed them, so that they no longer had been individuals, treading their separate paths, but had become part of the old, white-washed stone, the glazed tiles of the magical *mohalla* mosques, that no one could ever seem to find twice, the smells of burning wood and sweet incense that wafted westwards that night, towards the darkness of the sunken river. And a look had passed between them in that moment, with her husband, his *maalik*, carrying the torch up beyond the next bend in the stairwell, and they, in the darkness below, holding on to each other and giggling soundlessly because they both were afraid, terrified of the *djinn* which had danced between their bodies, their souls. Her skin a shade of burnished gold, her eyes deep wells of amber and jet. Oh, how he longed to drown in those eyes! The poets were right. Those old songs. A man might give anything . . .

And, now, here he was again and once again at the invitation of his *maalik*. Tea and *mitai* and a discussion about the long decade that had passed since the British had got out. At times, Jamil found it difficult to remember why they were talking about this until he recalled that it was Pakistan Day – that auspicious date in March when the nation commemorated the poetic dream of Allama Iqbal come to fruition through the political organ of the Muslim League. The day, a quarter of a century ago, when the die had been cast and the goal of this country's creation had been announced. And now it was flags and streamers in the streets and a public holiday. A day of annunciation. Jibril and Maryam. A time of fluttering golden wings, of kites swooping down upon one another, and the inaudible sound of strings being cut. The shattering of powdered glass. A day of change. And he felt a longing – a feeling that sucked him dry and left him powerless. His body was barely functional, his mind a haze of days. It was like the desire for wealth but, whereas that desire left him empty, desperate and filled with hate, this other desire made him feel as though, at any moment, he might simply take off and fly. He had spent the past few weeks soaring high above the ancient and venerable city of Lahore, over the tops of the *chenar* trees, the winding streets, the flat roofs, far away from the growl and rumble of the sculpted black cars and the men who howled beautifully from the points of minarets. He was terrified his wife might suspect. Women knew about these things. But, then, nothing actually had happened. It was like being in a film – one of those flickering nineteenth-century ones. Maurice Sestier, a Grand Lumière in Bombay. Colorello and Cornaglia and their tented film shows. Real and yet not real. But definitely already out of control. What was one look, a touch, a shared sensation? Infidelity? What was that? A term invented by the gaolers of this life, the monocled regiment who drew all night on their serpentine rose-watered pipes and who had lost, or perhaps had never experienced, the taste of real wine. And Jamil hadn't tasted it either – not till these past few weeks. Once sipped, never forgotten. His marriage had been arranged by his parents and, over the four years they had been in wedlock, he had grown to appreciate that certain fondness which arises through habit – that sense of self which permeates through the walled gardens of familiarity. And he had a son. But what Jamil was experiencing now was like a mountain or a waterfall. It was of a different order, it belonged to the wild cosmic scheme, it was right – he could feel it – it was correct even though it was immoral. But there must be a plane where the moralities are not bound by the conventions and requirements of this world – a place to which, usually, we remain blind except at moments of intense revelation. Jamil felt like a prophet who has just rolled a stone away from the mouth of a dark cave. In reality, whatever rocks had moved, he no longer cared whether or not his wife found out. He was beyond that. And, somehow, he knew that Rashida was with him, at least in her mind. He had seen the sweat break out along the line of her top lip – those lips of hers, so thin and yet so rich with blood, he could almost sense their touch and pulse, so like music. Rafi, perhaps, or Talat. Suraiya, definitely. Songs of loss, of guilt, of hope in the monsoon rains. Harvest-time. A season for loving. A fragile *chirya* that's what she was – a tender, fluttering bird in a cage, around whose form he needed nothing more than to wrap his arms. Up there, in the chamber of the *djinn*, there had been nothing. No furniture, no curtains, no electric light. Just an oval mirror, fixed to the wall.

His father, the refuse scientist. Perhaps he wis listenin to *The Junnune Show*. Zaf glanced up from the paper. Sheila Chandra wis still intonin her weird version of the *zhikr* and the drone made it sound more like a Sufi *kalaam* than the sort of thing which might be played on a hip, hot radio show. Fuck that. Tonight wis his night. He would play whatever the hell he bloody well liked.

A couple of lights on the console flickered – red, red and white. Red. Red. White. Morse code for the deaf. An alphabet of three words. It wis definitely a low-tech operation like in those silly sci-fi series from back in the seventies. Men in polyester Peter Pan outfits and grinnin Mormon haircuts. And the women with Bambi eyes and hair that fell in lazy waves around their faces. Pastels. His father had never actually worn a polyester tracksuit but it must've been decades since Jamil Ayaan had clothed himself in natural fibres. His papa wis one of the last of the vest brigade. That wis somethin that had always got Zaf whenever he'd visited Pakistan. The way in which, even in a hundred and ten degrees, a man would retain his vest as a virgin might her hymen. Vests were a British thing which the British, en masse, had long ago abandoned. He had always thought of his father as middle-aged with an elegant greyin beard and a voice like a conductor's baton. Not abrasive, not crude, like those of some men, but guidin, helpin and, at times, disciplinin. He struggled to construct an image in his mind of his papa as a young person – it seemed somehow obscene. He closed his eyes and folded his arms behind his head, swung back.

Once, perhaps.

Zaf is sitting on soft sand. His father's face is framed in sunshine and is smiling and his smile fills the world. There

56

is clear water just beyond Zaf's reach. He can hear and smell it. From the other side of the loch, a range of dark green mountains casts shadows across the water. A pair of arms lifts him under the shoulders and suddenly Zaf is high above himself and is filled with light.

He opened his eyes. Fuck that, it's all gone, he thought, and quickly he returned to the chubby schoolgirls. But it kept botherin him. Every time he tried to grasp the image of his father by the loch, it would slip away like sand in water and all that he would be left with wis his own, stupid face. Sheila Chandra's voice swooped and dived like the flight of a white-winged lark while the music pulsated all around, growin almost imperceptibly faster.

When Zaf had gone to Pakistan, things had seemed unutterably vague as though the pollution and the clouds of dust and the bastard heat had jumbled all the reference points. Whenever he had been there, Zaf had felt himself fill with guilt. He'd always had the feelin that he had done somethin not quite right but what that somethin might have been he had never been able to grasp. Pakistan wis a bad dream. A mess of crazy traffic, blisterin, suffocatin heat and rows of stern countenances – and, everywhere, the scent of decay. He knew there wis more to it than that. He knew about the arcane and eclectic bookshops and the mind-blowin Symbolist-Expressionist galleries dreamed intae being by people whose art would never ever gain recognition in the West. And he had heard of the small projects – the groundwork that folk were doin against all the odds in stinkin, foetid villages no one knew the names of beneath the infinite heat of a lunatic sun. They were drawin up the good from the old, old land. And he had experienced the unadulterated warmth of family gatherins – that deeply civilised, seven thousand years of hospitality of which folk in the proud, fragile West simply could not conceive. They had never gone to visit the grand-parents – the disgrace had been too great and they had communicated only by letter. He remembered seein one of his grandfather's letters and had marvelled at the delicate *Nastaliq* words which had been penned in thin blue ink. Zaf felt that he had understood nuthin. Much later, he had learned that, occasionally, they had sent a little money, mainly for his upbringing, but, by the time he had found this out, they were long dead. In spite of the urgings of his wife, Jamil had not asked for loans from the local big businessmen. He had prided himself on the fact that he wis an educated man and, besides, unlike most of the Pakistanis in Glasgow, he had not come from the poverty-stricken villages around Faisalabad, or from those which clustered about the slopes and rivers of Indian-occupied Mirpur, but from the great and magical city of Lahore. The myths of his forefathers stretched back more than three millennia.

He went over to the window. Hauled it open just a fraction. Then a bit more. The rain wis fallin vertically and he stuck out his hand and let the water hit against his palm. It felt cold and sharp, like tiny spears, and it made his skin tingle. He looked through his reflection and thought, I'm like Gulliver – a giant of the airwaves but not quite real. Not yet. Mibbee I should get into religion in some way. Not like those idiots who think that the way you wash your hands is more important than how you treat your wife. That would be ludicrous. Those guys were merely mergin the worst elements of Wahabi Calvinism and Scottish Catholicism and comin up with a form of faith that no one, bar themselves, could ever really learn to love. They were just wearin other masks and he'd had enough of masks. They were conformin to a partic-ular stereotype because, essentially, it wis always easier to do that. The thing wis his *maa* had constantly put down his father and, in so doin, had lowered herself to the level of stereotype in the eyes of her son. At least, that wis the way Zaf figured it. That wis what a university education did for you – you learned, slowly, how to despise your parents and then you spent the rest of your life tryin desperately not to feel guilty about it. A vicious cycle. At every stage in his life, his papa had tried to buck the trend, had gone against the flow. He had mocked those who had done what everyone else did and, yet, Zaf thought, whenever he had tried to follow his father's example, in some small way, Jamil Ayaan had put him down. Like only he could be the adventurer. His papa had attempted to do what should have taken two or mibbee even three generations to achieve. He hadn't wanted to compromise, not even once. And look where it had got him.

Across the street wis a deserted building which once must have been straw coloured but which had been lamp black for as long as Zaf could remember. It was four storeys high and, like half of the buildings in Glasgow that had gone up around the turn of the nineteenth century, its walls had been cut from pale Giffnock sandstone – the other half had been hewn from the red-coloured rock that had come from further south, in Ayrshire and Dumfries-shire. It wis the third floor that drew his attention. The three sets of windows were longer than any others in the street or any that he had ever seen. They seemed obscenely long as though, at some time, the glass had been pulled and stretched and rendered into a kind of Gothic nightmare. Like in *Frankenstein*. High Gothic. Giants again. Heroes and jokers. There were no curtains and Zaf had often wondered what went on behind the dark glass. In the three months he'd been there, not once had he spotted any livin being on that floor or on the floors above and below. So it had to be the dead. Nuthin odd about that. It had happened always. Havin made history, the dead then became it. His hand had gone numb. He pulled back in.

Sheila wis fadin fast and a jarrin noise wis comin from the floor below. There had been the break from home and then there had been Zilla. The clangin grew louder. Zaf glanced at his watch. One a.m. He broke in, cuttin off Chandra and her ethereal voice. 'Alif-Lam-and- . . .'

The time is wan o'cloack. Ah'm Zaf-Zaf-Zaf and Ah'm yer ghost. Host, Ah mean, host. Aye, whitivir. Ye're listenin, this mornin, tae *The Junnune Show* oan Radio Chaandni broadcastin oan ninety-nine-point-nine meters FM. That, of course, wis oor very own dear Auntie Sheila the Chandra an the track 'Mecca' fae wan ae her aulder albums. OK, stay tuned hereaboots, don't move an inch – oh, weel, ye're allowed tae go tae the bog but don't be readin the paper in Urdu, Punjabi, Bangali, Angraise, Gujarati, Francisi, Farsi, Icelandic, Gaelic, Kashmiri, Swahili, Pashto or any other lingo. Right? So, ye can skip aff tae the lamp post, right, but don't move a radio-dial inch, ye know whit Ah mean? Cause there's loads mair superb music tae come. Five oors ae it! Before ye ring in tae moan aboot language, Ah said oors. OK? Not whoors. Oors. Tick-toack, tick-toack. Geddit? OK. An, when ye come back tae ma mooth, there'll be a *ziafat* fur insomniacs like me. Or vampires. Urgh! Givin masel the *shithers*!

Zaf leaned into the mike. Whispered. Now he wis rollin at the right speed. Now he wis Mister Saaaaans.

Ahhh, thur's nuhin better, in the deeps ae the nicht, than a wee bit ae clean terror. Lang teeth. Gleamin eyes. *Bhookee annkh.*

Annkh. Saamnp. Memphis on the Nile. Sleepy asps. Broken circularity. *Baat-chit, raat-*shit. *Saans. Saaz.* Snake charmer.

Z

Don't do this at hame. Thur is nae such thing as a vampire, kids. Believe it. Onyweye, we've goat so much mair lined up fur yous, Ah cannae even remember how much.

Zaf glanced down at the scrap of paper on which he had scribbled the playlist but he had made so many scribbles he found that he could barely read his own writin.

Yeah, Ah mean, Ah don't have them lined up jist yet, folks.

Fuck sake. What wis he sayin? He needed a zip over his mouth. A permanent bloody zip.

As Ah said at the start, Ah know as much as you people aboot whit track's goannae come next. It's excitin, isn't it? Or sumhin. So ye'll huv tae stay wi us tae find oot whit's happenin! See ye soon. Be sure an be there. Ye don't want tae be left behind fur deid. Fur the vampires! News 'n' Weather comin up!

He flipped on the News and got up.

ONE A.M.

It wis a thing he had made a habit of – gettin up, while the News 'n' Weather were pacin out their sensible and very borin algebra, and walkin quickly around the cubicle, almost along the line where the walls met the floor. It wis partly to keep the blood flowin through his legs, partly to enable him to take some very deep breaths but, most importantly of all, it wis so he could make contact with somethin physical, somethin real. Six hours of bein on the air could freak you out big time. Assumin the cloak of invisibility came with a hefty price tag. So Zaf moved round and round the cubicle, slowly, like a bad tai-chi performer, and, as he walked, he trailed the ends of his fingers along the grey cones so that, by the end of the whirls, his skin would be electric and, by contrast, the world around him would have become static, solid, tenable. Two-thirds of the way through the News, he would turn and go anti-clockwise. He knew exactly when the point came – he wis a timepiece, a swayin grandfather clock, his body wis all cogs. Because he had done this for nearly three months, a hazy brown line had formed, at waist level, along the tips of the cones. It wis like a border, dividin the room into two separate halves.

It wis not just his hands that acquired electricity by this circular movement – the soles of his trainers, already plasticked up beyond chemical possibility, now seemed to Zaf like tactile receivers, synthetic skins through which he felt he wis able to perceive of everythin that wis goin on below. The first cog.

He heard bangin and scrapin from downstairs. He banged his foot down a couple of times – not as a warnin but just to test the boards. These floors were not original. They had been inserted at some point, Zaf thought, most likely whenever the old church had been converted. Deconsecrated. Given over to the ruttin material world of the devil. Unlike the congregation who would have been hard skulled – incontrovertibly unconvertible. Stones were easy – flesh wis more difficult. More jagged, arrhythmic noise from the room below. The same sequence of news items, over and over, hour upon hour – his own voice comin back at him in a mockin parody. Sometimes it would seem as though the News wis rollin backwards like the spokes of a cartwheel – that events, both trivial and important, were occurin in reverse. If it went on long enough, by the time *The Junnune Show* ended, Zaf, Radio Chaandni and the whole of Glasgow would have arrived back at Genesis. Day Zero. Darkness movin over the waters. A world from nuthin. Altaqween. He closed his eyes but the room wis still spinnin. The sounds were solid – it wis almost like he could see them.

Downstairs, Harry and Fizz would be luggin amps and other bits of equipment around and managin, as always, to seem incredibly busy. But, now, there were footsteps comin up the stairs. Zaf's eyes sprang open. Magic lanterns! He began to pace. Then he realised he had never stopped. Ruby 'n' Fizz were standin in the doorway, closin off the darkness. They glanced at each other – he saw that – and then they joined him in the cubicle as he moved around the walls. In the background, the News wis treadin on as it always did. Fizz came over an sat on Zaf's chair an began to do wee G-force turns with his feet jist off the ground. Ruby wis leanin against the far wall, with one of her long legs crossed over the other, and wis surveyin the whole thing with a somewhat dopey gaze. Well, it wis one in the mornin. Normal time for nuts like him. And not everybody wis a nut but Ruby went to clubs so she should have been used to it.

'Are ye no goannae gie us a hond, man?' Fizz gestured at him.

Zaf kept movin. Round an round. 'Ah cannae leave the cubicle,' he grunted.

'Why not?' asked Fizz.

Zaf looked at the controls, the plastic levers and buttons and the dials with their little flashes of white lettering marking their functions: noise level; frequency; Deck A control; Deck B control; microphone volume; phone-in connection; head-phone switches; faders; the very limited panoply of basic broadcastin.

'Because the stuff might go out ae control,' he said. 'The machines, the music.'

Another shared glance. The fuckers. 'Ye mean like in that filum wi Big-Hal-The-Big-Computer?' Instant American Pacific guttural. 'Are you alright, Zaf? Zaf . . . ? Please stop that, Zaf.'

Fizz wis such a funny man. Stand-up bloody comedian. 'Is the party gonna be down there?' Zaf asked.

Fizz nodded. 'It's a bigger room.'

And, Zaf thought, nobody's been screwin in it recently. It would be filled wi the scent of neutrality. Like Babs. Jesus! Every time the News 'n' Weather came on, he thought of her. It wis like some kind of Pavlovian thing. Rain – salivate. War – ejaculate.

Round and round.

NEWS – INHALE SERIOUSNESS – BABS
WEATHER – EXHALE SCOTTISHNESS – BABS

A rancid taste in his mouth. He swallowed hard three times. Hardwood throat. Zaf and Babs liked to sip strong, black coffee seamed through with sugar. But there were limits. He remembered the time in a restaurant when they had drunk Turkish *kahve* – she'd gulped down the thick treacle like it was bad medicine while he had savoured it more slowly, the way you're meant to, and had let it massage his palate. Her face had been a picture. They'd been in stitches over it. He wondered what would happen to all that afterwards and whether it had meant anythin. Memories. Old photos. Green-and-white. An arc of grass. Wood, linseed oil, quietude. The sound of a hardened ball, strikin seasoned white willow – a sound without echo, a thing complete in itself. A world, a crooked staff. Babs, Zaf and Jamil – three-way cricket.

Jamil had on a floppy white hat that made him look a little like an umpire. He sprang up and began to chase about the fringes of the garden. Babs too was puzzled at first but then she got up and joined him and soon they had the basics for a cricket match. Usin sticks, branches and a dog's lost ball, Babs an Zaf began to play a kind of *gully* cricket. Babs wasn't much good. She'd always said that cricket wis a game played by the English for the English. To which he had replied that, no, cricket wis a game played by Pakistanis for the Pakistan which they had lost or which mibbee they had never had and that the game fulfilled a role which, for Scots, had long been assumed by football. But, today, it didn't matter since, with every run they made, Jamil would throw back his head and laugh and clap and call out, 'Qaisarr, zndabad!' Someone brought out a radio and the sound of Cornershop's 'It's Good to Be on the Road Back Home' rang over the wall and down the street.

Zaf stopped his rotation just long enough to be able to scribble down 'Good to Be . . .' on the piece of paper that he had decided would function as a playlist. With his blue biro, he would try to predict which song wis comin next. In a smooth continuation of the same movement, he inserted a disc into Deck A. That wis the way he felt with Babs – everythin ran smoothly, like the internal mechanisms of a well-oiled motorbike.

!!Broom-broom!!

Swingin, easy rock cowboy woman rides again. Bums on black saddles. The air in their faces. Youth, beer drinkin, sunshine songs. Road music. Cornershop-on-wheels.

Hand. Mike. Switch. Sound. Behind him, Ruby, urgin him on – the way the presence of a woman always did.

Hi there, *samaaen. Sat sri akaal, namaste ji, salaam alaikum. Bonjour, Buongiorno, Subax wanaagsan, Neehaa, Günaydin, Buenos días, Dobro jutro, Làbas rytas, Bom dia, Mirëmëngjes, Guten morgen, Maidin mhaith dhuit, Molo, Boker tov, Shubh subah, Kalai vanakkam, Go Eun A Chim.* Hiya in fifty thoosand tongues! Zero wan five or five meenuts past wan. Bet ye thought Ah wis skimmin doon a phrase book. But, naw, you'd be wrong. Ah've goat loads ae tongues in ma heid – thu're aw there, wagglin away, almost singin. A babble. Hope ye're still there. Here. Hope ye're still listenin. Hope ye're ready tae spin. Whoosh!! In ye go, Tijinder Singh. It's deep night, the city is sleepin, ivirywan is layin doon tae rest. But we're different, are we not, *Junnunies*? We're jist stretchin an risin like the moon – we're gettin ready tae sing. We're leapin on tae the silver machine. We're oan the road again!

Deck B.

This is when it starts getting seriously freaky. No one can stop us noo, you 'n' me. If thur's a power cut, we'll go oan. If an asteroid hits the Dear Green Hollow, Radio Chaandni will be shinin bright. If this night is the Eve ae Kiamath, if this is the *Shaam* ae Truth, then we'll rise up, singin back trumpets tae *Hazrat* Israfil. An whit'll we be singin? Ah, noo, that's a mystery. Ye'll huv tae tune in, right the way through till sax in the mornin, tae hear the Magic Number. They're aw *jadui hindsay* – Signposts on the Path. An here's wan fur the road.

Reconstruct a cricket match. Raise it from the ground, *Hazrat* Israfil. *Il muladaad.* Set us on the road home, via swingin guitars and a tall, interlopin blonde.

Durin the fourth game, he began to feel dizzy in the mid-afternoon sun and he let himself be bowled out for a duck. I'm a mad dog, he thought, as he collapsed on to the grass. He lay on his back and gazed up at the sky, which wis spinnin round and round, and he closed his eyes and let the sun flood over his body. Opened them. Closed them. Opened them. A row of birds climbed higher and higher into the blue until they were just specks. He fixed his gaze on the specks, watched them waver and dance until they disappeared. Babs came up and stood over him and her silhouette turned the sky black. She held her hands out, palms facing downward, and offered to help him up but he rolled over and began to play with the tiny blades of grass. Down near the soil, a small red insect busied about for a while and then vanished. He felt the sun burn the skin of his neck, just below the hairline.

A game of cricket, in the summer sunshine. An old, imperial pastime risin up here, in Glasgow, in the twenty-first century.

Him, his papa and Babs in a walled garden. A fleetin paradise. She wis game for anythin. Flexible, like, she would've said in that Galloway lilt of hers – the intonation slidin up a little at the end a bit like that of a New Yorker or like the vocalist in Cornershop. A long-forgotten insecurity. She wis a good fielder, her broad white feet were planted firmly on the well-cropped grass as though she had been seeded in that earth – she knew where she wis at. Her limbs, her complexion were proportioned to suit the Scottish vista – the etiolated, northern light. Like with a lot of white people, sunglasses made her look hard, cruel. Bonnie and Clyde. Ridin on the running-board. It wis somethin to do with the narrow line of her lips, the fall of her cheekbones. They'd joked that the shades had made her resemble a secret policeman skulkin in some doorway east of the old iron curtain, along some narrow, cobbled street, west of the big silver Volga. Zaf'd kept sayin 'vodka' instead of 'Volga' and that'd doubled them up even more. It wis her drink – Vodka-wi-anythin. Doubles, triples . . . It made her think clearly, she always said. Lucid brain. Of course, you couldn't voice those thoughts about the shades to anyone else – they would've been seen as objectionable, deeply racist or just plain sick but that knowledge didn't stop you from havin them. They were intrinsic to the rhythm of their relationship, the beat of her soles on the soft, green earth as she fielded the balls he put out. They were part of the reason he had been drawn to her. 'It's Good to Be on the Road Back Home'. Aye.

He heard her voice, almost as if she wis there, in the cubicle. He looked up, thinkin that mibbee she had decided to pay him a visit after all. To power down the hot, dark streets of Glasgow on her fat, blue motorbike and to roar up the stairwell and to burst into the loop of his world. The world he had always kept to himself.

'You didnae get ma note?' she asked him.

He felt somethin surge through his body like a shot of caffeine. There wis a woman standin before him but it wasn't Babs. Different build, other presences. Music from another string. A red soul string. Ruby.

Zaf wondered just how they got that – the right balance. A sense, in their music, of hipness, of roamin chords and jangled thrum. A kind of Country music – or mibbee Western. Zaf had never really understood the difference though he supposed it might be somethin to do with the accents or the paralysin self-pity which defined the former, as against the buffalo vistas of the latter – but, in any case, the guys 'n' gals of Cornershop were ridin the great, gleamin, collective motor-bike of road songs, the wheelie-machine that had been movin an rollin since Ibn Battuta, Geoffrey Chaucer and Iacobbe d'Ancona. Silk routes, sapphire mountains, earth voices. Songs of the folk. Crazy dreamers, treadin the Path. Heel, arch, toe, heel, arch, toe. Walkin the line. Finger-trailin along the walls.

Zaf kept his eyes on his trainers as he rotated. He could just picture the scene in the room below – plastic bottles, disposable cups, orange lights, the usual accoutrements of late-night social gatherins – and, as he did so, he began to feel uneasy about the whole thing. He really didn't want to go to a party tonight. He preferred the intimacy of mouth and mike, of whispers in the room inside his head, to the noise and bawl of twenty people bathing together amid flashes of electricity. Mibbee I'm goin nuts, he thought. He circled slowly round and round the room and, as he did so, he tried steadfastly to gaze downwards and yet, again and again, he found himself drawn back to Ruby and her jeans. Her white trainers. Everythin about her wis long. Her face with its large chin, her eyes which drooped downward from the bridge of her nose, her body, her thin legs. He could see that, beneath her skimpy T-shirt, her breasts would be small like those of a white woman. Zaf wondered if that was why he felt attracted to her – because she reminded him of Zilla who reminded him of some mystical Northern goddess . . . but, then, he thought, I've already got Babs, I've got the real thing – I no longer need to dream. But what if the real thing didn't match up to the dream? What if it never could? What then? But it's the small things we dwell on. We mythologise the unimportant. Like the way Zilla would buy eggs, say, or the manner in which Babs would peel and eat an orange. Nothings, really, but they hooked us. We became life's junkies. The smell of cigarettes began to seep up his nostrils and he realised that she had lit up. Hadn't asked anyone if they minded. He could hear her drawin in the whitened tobacco. She wis in the cubicle with him, her breath sucked away the air, drawin in . . .

She spoke and he almost leapt out of his skin.

'How's the show gan, Zaf?'

He straightened up, rocked back on his heels and only just managed to regain his balance and keep movin. She wis everywhere. He shrugged to try an offset her effect on him.

'It's OK. Ah'm playing what Ah want tae. It's the last night, after aw.' Why did he do that? He felt like kickin himself in the shins. Every time he spoke to Ruby, he found himself slippin intae a broad Glaswegian of the sort which he hadn't really spoken since he'd been with Zilla – except on the show.

'Listen.' She waved her cigarette about. She was still leanin against the wall, legs crossed at the ankles. 'Ye wanna buy a mobile phone? Ah can get ye twinty, wi a third aff the price.'

'Ruby . . .'

'The best. Man, ye know, the wans wi those kind ae *Star-Trekkie* flaps oan the ootside?'

'Ruby, Ah don't want twenty mobile phones.'

'Aye, ye do. Ivirybody needs a mobile phone. Ah can get ye a really guid monthly rental, tae. Ye don't like the K.U.S. 420? Well then, what about a Red Mango 666? Interactive, holographic, organic, brain-an-hip-friendly. It's the size ae a postage stamp. Comes wi a fake platinum ring. Ye can wear it oan your pinkie. A new generation.'

She twisted her hand up intae the air as though she wis performin a delicate medical procedure or the top end of a balletic whirl. The ring she wis wearin wis solid gold, though, an there wis nae screen. It wis jist a ring. Not a weddin ring, not even an engagement one, jist an ordinary, twenty-two carat Pollokshields Pakistani *guRee.*

'It'll tell you whit the weather is in Hawaii. It's really useful that weye.'

'The weather in Hawaii's always the same . . .' Zaf began but she wis unstoppable.

'Different colours. Ony shade ye want. Ah can get ye whativir colour ye need, man.'

'Ah don't need any colour . . .'

'Aye, ye do. Ivirybody needs colours, man.' She wis amazin. She could switch fae ciggie-totin vamp tae aggressive, petty-capitalist saleswoman in the space of a second. Her cousin sold mobiles. So she wis sellin mobiles. She could sell you anythin. Well, except the things that weren't fur sale.

'Yeah, hey, listen, Zaf, man, listen, phone me – Ah'll gie ye the quotes. Then ye can decide. Think aboot it. Take yer time – relax. Ye're too serious about iviryhin.'

He sat down and placed his palms flat on the surface of the console. Solidity. Silence. Time to break it.

Bye-bye, then! The bhoys ae Cornershop sing 'Baa-baa, y'all!' as they roar off intae the night. Hey! That wis 'It's

Good tae Be on the Road Back Home'. That title is a journey in itself! But Ah'm sure glad they know where hame is. But, then, again, do they? It's the journey, say the sages, no the destination. Mibbee the road ends right here, thenight. Mibbee the last note is lyin in wait, silent, dark, an mibbee it's searchin fur iviry wan ae us an noat the other way roon. A knotty problem, ye might say. But it's ma problem, *samaaen* – it's Zaf's dilemma. Which soangs will Ah play an in whit order? Ah, whit a difficult life it is! Knots, filigrees, *Nastaliqs*. Syrian steel. We're goin back, folks. Back an back . . .

Those rhythms ae the Sea Peoples bangin oot the strides ae the great river-crossins, dancing wet wi the arc ae the sun's path. An this wis the end, this city, aifter here, there wur nae mair crossins, nae mair lang loops across the waruld. So they settled here, in the green hollow, an, in time, they grew tae love it an tae call it 'dear'. The doors tae knowledge, the paths tae hell. Here it is, the journey electrified. Alternative Current. Sparky knots, silver bangles. Hear them, ringin. *Chaandi-ki-chuRia. Chunn-chunn-chunn.* Well, whitivir. Let's continue oor journey noo an we're goin deep Celtic here wi The Colour of Memory an 'Rigmarole'. Ha! That's this show. Lots ae roads, aw ae them leadin nowhur. That's where we want tae be, right?

Deck A. Runnin, jiggin from the Isle of Mull. The swoopin vocals of the modern Celtic rock band filled the air, the woman's voice seemin to bounce off Ruby's lithe body, the rocky brow of her brain, as though suddenly, in her mobile madness, she had become the centre of the universe.

He looked at her and shrugged. How old wis she? Twenty-two, twenty-three mibbee. And what difference did a few years make anyway? Zaf irritated himself when he thought in this manner. It was like he was bein the spectator again. Watchin people. He would watch women, just for the hell of it, to make them feel as though they were being watched. And they always knew. Always. And whether they'd like it or not would depend, of course, upon who wis doin the lookin. And that kind of depended on what or who wis fashionable at a particular moment in time. It wis strange the way fashions change. The two basic rules in all this were: you are what you wear and you are as others see you. It wis a circle really. A loop. There wis no way out. Until recently, Latino had been hip and Paki hadn't. East Euro used to be but hadn't been since the hookers and beggars and rouble brides had arrived like wanderin, amnesiac Celts from across the Oder or the Don or whatever the big final frontier wis called these days. Indian had always been hip but only if you were a guru, a communist or a sitar player. All that had changed in the last few years and now it wis cool – that was the word – cool to be connected, in some way, to the land which lay somewhere to the east of the Middle East. For some odd reason, however, Pakistan wis seen completely differently. In fact, most of the time, it wasn't seen at all. He wis convinced that, when the vast majority of people in these slim-waisted islands heard the word 'P-A-K-I-S-T-A-N', they thought of three things. Firstly, the land of his mothers wis perceived as bein a repository of the dirty, the oppressed, the smelly, the cunning and the inscrutable. An mibbee it wis but it wis hardly alone in that. Secondly, the place of purity rang the fear bells of perpetual immigration, of a movement of population that had no beginnin, no startin point, no real homeland. People were always seen as immigrants and never as emigrants or expatriates. They were pictured as nameless, liquid hordes that would pour in – even though, at no time in the half-century or more Pakistan had been in existence, had they ever poured in. And lastly, in this great, pyramidal misapprehension of a whole people, Pakistanis had remained completely inaudible. They had no music, no voice, no breath. In many ways, they were seen as incorporatin everythin that wis bad, dysfunctional and regressive about South Asia. Whereas that good old fat, post-imperial clever clogs, *Mata Bharat*, née India, née née the Jewel-in-the- . . ., mysteriously (and, quite possibly, cosmically) had acquired all that wis admirable, even enviable, about oriental culture. Sexy – in a kind of golden shower, pure, ashramic kind of way. And, as such, it remained perpetually cool. Zaf hadn't figured out yet just what the essential element wis in this new-found popularity and, in some respects, he didn't see it as that important to know – just as long as it went in his favour. Folk thought of young, hip guys 'n' gals as Indian. Whereas the crabby auld-timers with the specs, the sticks, the jumpers and the assertive teeth were assumed to be inherently Pakistani (or else Bangladeshi but that wis another story). The whole thing wis fairly superficial anyway. Like a weak joint or an expired E. Still, it wis better than bein spat at or killed.

He'd given Zilla her first joint. She'd coughed for ten minutes and had nearly puked her guts out and then she'd gone over and put on a tape. Mukesh's 'Bhooli Hui Yaadon'. 'Forgotten Memories'. More songs of torn hearts or borders that closed and never reopened, of final partins and last glances. Of black metal trains, burnin noisily away on the line to the *qabaristan*. Zaf had read somewhere that a person's disembowelled intestines, when stretched, would cover a pair of doubles tennis courts. But the human heart wis infinite. Forty, love. You are what you eat? Nah, you are what you love. And their love had been shared over the acrid, risin smoke and black *maajoun*, 'a taste of Tangier'. That mustachioed guitarist, with fingers that seemed to dance across the strings as though they were speeded up and slowed down at the same time. Such things were possible in the world of the white flower. Swayin, *maqam* nights with Zilla. Such things went back as long as breath. And then she'd asked for more. And he'd given her more. Much more. Like the two babies she'd killed. Aborted before she'd got hooked. Before her will had weakened. But that wis the way of it. You couldn't control everythin that happened to everyone who wis within ten miles of your life. Things just happened and sometimes – most of the time – no one wis to blame. Like time, guilt wis just a concept dreamed up by those who needed to imagine that there wis some kind of an order to the world. Cause and effect. Newton, the Apple and the Lie. But the world wis like Radio Chaandni. Life pulsed with random malevolence. There wis no order.

Ruby exhaled, sendin an elegant smoke ring across the room. Zaf wis just aware, from across to his right, that Fizz wis watchin them. Fizz, the wee man. The action man with the Anil Kapoor quiff. He wis the sort of wee guy who would drive a super-turbo-charged hatchback (either black or scarlet) and who would play techno music loudly with all the windows wide open. Every time you saw one of those things, there would be at least four guys, all dressed identically, hangin out the doors. They would be shoutin like fuckin sirens, roarin into the night. They were all voice, those guys, and their voices would bounce off of the sandstone and glass like fuckin boomerangs. The whole thing wis one big hi-fi system. It wis sad. No, it wasn't. They got the birds. Good-lookin birds like Rubina – tall elegant women of the type that strutted about the city centre on sunny afternoons in May. All legs and blossoms. Flighty, too. Zaf had never quite worked out just what Ruby saw in Fizz beyond the wheels.

But, then, he had never really worked out what had drawn him to Zilla. Babs had been different. She wis white. Reality is nine-tenths of myth. He and Babs had met at a party – a mutual friend had introduced them. It hadn't been love at first sight but had been more of a kind of a gradual thing – an intense pattern of curiosity and desire that had led, by degrees, to a mutual infatuation and, thence, to the lunacy of love. He remembered the song that had been playin the night they'd met. 'Rigmarole' – the track he wis playin now. Words. Whispers howled across the darkness.

> Bending off the ecstasy of someone else's dreams,
> We fall into
> The fire of lies . . .

Babs wis one of the Galloway Irish, as they were called. The accents were so hard to tell apart that people used to think she hailed from somewhere across the Irish Sea – somewhere like Bangor perhaps – and they would ask her about 'The Troubles' and about 'sectarian violence' of which she knew next to nuthin. She worked as a nurse in one of the big Glasgow hospitals. It wis a regular job and he knew she wis bloody good at it. Zaf had always thought that she wis the sort of person who, when confronted by a stranger at the door, might just say, 'Come in, then . . .' Well, kind of. And she had more or less said the same to him and he had obliged and now they were long-term lovers. They might have got married except that there would've been complications – the whole bloody family thing for a start. He'd only met Babs's family once and it had been enough. Her father wasn't a farmer but he might've been. He owned a catering company that fed the workers on the rigs up north and he had hands like big white slabs of fish. Talk about stone faces.

Christ. You'd think he wis the fuckin Archangel of Satan. Gallows Way.

Selfish love . . . fuel for ashes

The singer seemed almost breathless. Her words, enunciated between the thrummin keyboard phrases, were insistent as though she sensed that, already, time wis runnin out. And Zaf had felt like escapin with his new white girlfriend, runnin away from the eternally judgemental, hung-up families of East Pollokshields and Kinnin Park – far away to some vast, empty place where they would be able to lose themselves, where they would be able to become just two tiny figures, specks of dust in a classical European vista. But they'd had to go through the rituals of the Sunday dinner table. The dreadful rattlin of forks. Jesus Christ! Some Sabbath! And the thing wis they had been tryin so ridiculously hard to be polite all round. Of course, it wasn't worth it – better that they had acted insouciantly and have people try to please them, to have the buggers grateful for a smile or a concurrence. But he'd never been any good at those mind games, the broad panoply of bourgeois fakery. He wis a liar but he wis a bad liar – and that wis his savin grace. God, what a rigmarole! Later, a red-faced Babs had explained that they didn't get many . . . uh, cosmopolitan types down thereabouts. He had felt embarrassed for her. He had pictured them spendin most of their time up mountains or under water. Or drivin along dirt tracks, trekkin along bridle paths. And he had only taken Babs to visit his mother on a handful of occasions. It just didn't feel comfortable. His papa had liked her but he didn't really count. It wis strange how they got on – Babs and his papa. Mibbee it wis her nursin experience, he thought. And, so, apart from a few friends, they had ended up keepin very much their own company. Which had been fine for a while.

When they'd first known each other, he and Babs had ridden on an impulse, one mornin, up north. They'd gone on the big bike and Zaf remembered the elation he'd felt at havin her, all around him. She was drivin, of course, and, after a while, as the humpbacked mountains began to open up the sky, he realised that he wis breathin very deeply, almost as though he wis on the point of fallin asleep, but he wasn't drowsy. The sun wis streamin off the metal and reflectin in the wing mirrors and he could see Babs everywhere, not just the body of flesh and bone on to which he wis clutchin for dear life but out of the corner of his eye as a figure somewhere up on the flanks of the bens and the figure wis movin ever so slightly and it wis at that moment, which seemed to stretch into a kind of infinity, that he decided that she would be the love of his life. They'd moved in together soon after that trip. It had been a short romance – spannin weeks rather than months. He sighed there in the radio studio and suddenly felt intensely awkward, as though he'd left one of the buttons on his jeans unfastened, and so he bustled about and pretended to be busy. So much of our lives is pretence, he thought. So many lies, evasions, self-deceptions . . . and all for what? In fifty years' time, we'll all be dead. All the people comin to this party tonight, most of whom had had somethin to do with Radio Chaandni would, by the end of the twenty-first century, be pushin up weeds or else simply would have become an imperceptible part of the carbon cycle. And it won't matter what they had done in their time or whom they'd slept with or whether or not they'd drunk a glass of wine on *Eid* Day. Only their voices, spirallin out towards the far end of the solar system, would still be real. He thought of the first radio broadcasts, of the fragile, cracklin sounds which seemed to have come from another epoch altogether. On the airwaves, as in death, finally, everyone would be equal. All the ambiguities, deceptions, elaborate fictions would be wiped clean and only the pure sound of the empty places would remain. His papa's dreams would have become meaningless and so the pain, which had come from their lack of fulfilment, from the slow, degenerative death which, day by day, had infiltrated his soul and his body, would no longer have meanin and would have no power over him. He'd heard from a friend that, in the Lahore film industry, actors would screw one another indiscriminately, all over the houses of the sets on which they were workin. He had visualised men and women, clad in the solemn costumes of soap opera, fuckin hard, fast and cold in the kitchens, corridors and foyers of Lollywood. The desperation of the damned. Once you'd let one tiny part go, the whole ship would begin to sink. But what, for God's sake, wis the alternative? A kind of masochistic, anorexic version of religion? All stick and no carrot. No fuckin thanks. He'd take Lollywood anytime even though it was a pathetic imitation of Bollywood. But he would never have the opportunity. In Glasgow, it wis all clandestine, *anjaana*, the daggers would be unsheathed and sheathed again before you'd even had time to swill back a glass of vodka.

'Rigmarole' wis sinkin into some kind of Celtic twilight. Time for the Ads. Sales – the opposite end of the world. Ruby had finished her smoke and had gone over to the window, which was slightly open, and, with a smooth crescentic motion, she flicked the cigarette into the darkness. Zaf followed her over but she had already begun to move back to the wall as if there was some kind of hook there to which she might attach herself. It was too late to stop, though, and so he walked straight up to the edge of the sash that reached to the level of his upper thighs. He felt the cool air blow on to his T-shirt, just below the waist, and it lifted the edge of the thin white cotton so that the material moved like a soft hand over his skin. He leaned on the casement of the window and pressed his cheek against the cold darkness, glanced sideways, tried to avoid seein himself. He looked down, across the street, at the tops of the trees whose leaves were being buffeted by the rain and wind. They rustled and swayed and, in the near-darkness, the street smelled of marijuana. It wis the aroma of narrow lanes at night, as the junk of the day slipped and merged and danced. Down to the right and further along the street, he noticed a man balancin on the edge of the pavement. At first, Zaf thought that the man wis a drunk but then he saw that the figure wis standin on one leg and that he wasn't at all unsteady. As his eyes grew accustomed to the dim street lights, he began to make out more and more of the figure. He saw that his other leg was not missin but trailed out behind him like a dead branch and that he had propped himself up by means of a long crutch. He must've been tall, since he seemed tall even from the upstairs window, and his silvery hair wis bound back in a ponytail. He stood with his back to Zaf so that he was unable to see his face. He hadn't noticed this guy before yet he seemed somehow familiar. Some of the man's hair had come loose from the band so that it fluttered about in the wind and rain and the whole thing seemed to Zaf a little ludicrous. What the fuck wis he doin out at this time? Didn't he have anywhere else to go? And them – the ones in here – what were they doin? Where were they goin?

His cheek wis numb. He pulled away from the glass and breathed in sharply. He spun round and was dazzled for a moment by the light. He blinked hard, twice. The room wis different. Zaf realised that Fizz must've left the room –

must've gone to the bathroom or somethin – cause now he wis back. 'De-deh!' announced Fizz, his arms outstretched. He wis smilin.

The place seemed far bigger than before in spite of the defunct sound system that had been dumped over in the far corner. Ruby wis kneelin on the floor, facin the largest amp of the system. She ran her palm down over the nettin at the front, examined her hand and then blew the dust off the skin. Her jeans were pulled tight over the upper part of her legs and her top had come loose so that the small of her back wis visible. Brown, wiry. 'It's not been used for ages,' she said, turnin to Fizz.

'It belongs tae Raj.'

'Whit made him bring it in?'

Fizz shrugged.

Zaf felt as though he wis no longer in the room. They would go on endlessly addressin each other and totally ignorin him. They'd done it before and would do it again. It would be no good speakin to them about it and, anyway, doin so would only seem petty, childish. They were lovers with all the selfishness and rudeness which that entailed. They worshipped each other and everyone else could go to hell. He had become just a faint brown line smeared on to the cones, a dead whorl in a bad year. But he understood. He'd been in love. Mibbee he still wis. He turned back to the window but, this time, he did not press his face up against it. The buildins on either side of the street seemed to have moved slightly further away from him than before. He remembered hearin somewhere that the whole world, and even the space outside the world, wis expandin so fast that you couldn't feel it. That wis the way most things happened. Most important things, anyway. Like growin old or fallin in love. He wondered whether he might be expandin along with the stars but he couldn't see them because of the rain. He waited till his eyes had, once again, grown accustomed to the dark and then he looked down and to the right. The figure had vanished.

A hand on his shoulder made him jump. He turned around. It wis Harry. He wis speakin. When had he come in? His words didn't seem to make sense. 'Is that the Ads over?'

'What?'

'The Ads – they'll be finished now. An the Jingles. Ye'd better go back on.'

Zaf felt Harry touch his elbow. The pressure wis warm but insistent. The same in his eyes. Bastard blue. Harry wisnae a bad guy but Zaf felt the bile begin tae rise in his throat. He looked at his feet, tried tae anchor himsel tae the flaer and he realised that his fists wur clenched. He hudnae finished his fuckin round yet. His circlin ae the cubicle – the movement he performed durin the breaks in the music: News, Weather or Ads. Damn them all – they hud stopped him from performin the ritual that kept him sane in this place. He hudnae realised that 'Rigmarole' hud overlapped wi the commercials. Deck A, Deck B. He must've pushed the right buttons but he hudn't realised he wis doin it. And now he wis losin it fast. Harry wouldnae let go of his airm. Thur wis a tinglin comin fae his elbow an it spread doon the bone so that he wis unable tae feel the pain that the nails made as they dug intae his palms. He hud tae get control. Come oan! he said tae himsel. Come oan, Zaf. Slowly, deliberately, Zaf let his fingers uncurl. He turned and glared at the control panel. Without lookin up, he disentangled himself and pushed past The Station Master and stumbled towards his chair, which Fizz had hastily vacated, past the big black boxes of the sound system, past Ruby, who was sittin cross-legged on the fake wooden planks, and he sank down on to the chair and rested his hands on the smooth grey metal as though he wis some kind of ancient Mesopotamian magician about to summon up demons from the deep. He felt their presence at his back, their merged, sexed breath on his neck. Cross-legged Ruby, the instant hippie, and bumblin, buzzin Fizz, who, so recently, had been with her, in her, and Harry-the-Actor, Hari, Hari, Hari. He didn't hear them leave but, all at once, from behind him on the exposed skin of his lower back, through the opened door, Zaf felt the wind billow up from the fire escape and the wind carried the voices of the dead and the smell of places long demolished.

He was just in time. The Ads were about to end. Happy chappies, some with yellow turbans wound tightly around their skulls, intonin about just how totally unique their ornamental golden plastic hankie-box holders were. Who invented those bloody things? Zaf wondered. They were everywhere. Surely, a sociological survey would reveal, one day, that there wis not a single household east of Ibrox football stadium or west of Gorbals Cross that did not possess at least one of these glitterin cuboidal bastards, nestlin comfortingly on a window sill. In ten thousand years' time, when archeologists would come to excavate the area around the city that once had been known as 'Glasgow', they would find not gold or medallions but yellow plastic hankie-box holders, perfectly preserved, utterly unbiodegradable and resistant even to ballistic nuclear conflagration. They would name the civilisation that had existed in the deep green hollow 'Polypropylene Artefact Culture' – and its finds would be instantly recognisable by the presence of lovely little roses and twirlin stems with no thorns on, moulded in cheap, yet holy, plastic and painted the colour of angels. These, the ones in banana-skin turbans, should be put on trial at The Hague for diminishin the quality of life for so many visitors, for trashin their sensibilities, for causin them to weep with laughter and dismay until they would need the entire box of two-ply hankies simply to wipe away the tears. Ach! There were worse things.

He glanced around. The others had left but they'd forgotten to close the door. Wankers.

Zaf would still sometimes forget to sequence tapes and discs properly and would then have to rush to avoid the worst disaster possible for a radio station – SILENCE. Quickly, he jammed on a CD. It was not the one he had planned to play and he'd barely glanced at the cover as he'd slipped it out. Breathless from runnin round the enclosed space and from the excitement of a near miss, he ran the voice-control up to maximum. Whoops! Too high. Didn't want to wake the dead. Scribbled somethin, without really lookin, on the paper that wis meant to be his playlist.

OK, folks. Hello again. That's that.

That's what? he thought. What the fuck am I sayin now? Deep breath. Just one.

Ah'm Zaf and ye're listenin tae *The Junnune Show* and Ah'm yer host thenight – this mornin, Ah mean – it's ten meenuts past wan oan this hot summer's night. Glad ye steyed wi me. Hope ye're happy too. Nae mair hankie-box holders, please. Ye know the wans. Forget the flower! After pebble-dashin, the gaulden plastic hankie-box holder is the Emerald Tablet ae Sooth Asian Scotland. Sooth-sayin. Alchemical, ye might say. Theophrastus Bombastus. Melt the gauld! We're goannae be playin music that sets the night oan fire, as the man said.

Here's somethin completely different.

Why am I soundin like some fuckin Bible-Belt DJ? Christ!

The music began slowly. It was hardly anythin at first and Zaf wondered whether he might not have made yet another mistake on the air. The familiar and somewhat comfortin sense of imminent panic flooded through his body. Like someone walkin over my grave, he thought, and then he smiled. After fear, came release. But why did fear always have to come first? He waved away his philosophisin as the song burst into apocalyptic funk rock. Kula Shaker. Upperclass English. 'Great Hosannah'! Sock it to me!

> If we stand here together
> We can laugh at what we've done
> All our time has been wasted
> And there's nowhere left to run.
> There may be trouble up ahead
> Will we be sleeping in our beds
> Or will we arise to a new world . . .

We'll lie in our beds, thought Zaf. Definitely.

A pricklin sensation crept up his back and he shifted awkwardly in the chair but the feelin wouldn't go away. He leaned forward so that his lips almost touched the metal of the mike. He felt the edges of the skin begin to tingle – not from electricity but from expectation. He could taste his own breath as it returned, cold and metallic, from the black mesh. It was like the first kiss of a new lover, only better. Once the breath had left his lips, it wis no longer his alone but belonged to the whole world. On the radio, he wis immortal. Invisible, formless, perfect. A god. No wonder dictators hit the radio station first, he thought, and he leaned back again.

> Will we arise in our time
> At the dawn of another meaning
> Will we awake at the break
> Of a Great Hosannah

He couldn't concentrate on what he was doin, he had no idea when the track would end and his body seemed to tremble all over – though he knew the window wis now shut. Or was it? From time to time, durin the past three months, Zaf had had the creepy feelin of bein watched, usually from behind where the door wis or ahead from the big sash window or mibbee it wis from the darkness of the other studio. Whenever this had happened, he had gone over to the window and looked out. The preposterousness of the idea that anyone would be able to shin up the drainpipes, leg it over the sill and stand and stare at him would usually be enough to dispel any irrational fears. But, this time, he wis reluctant to get up and walk towards the glass or even to look round. And, yet, he knew the longer he put off doin this, the greater his panic would become. He ran his index finger up and down over the surface of the console. He had come to know this machine almost as well as he had known the skins of the women he'd been with. Better, perhaps. Slow, slow, the sound of tablas massed in long lines that stretched towards infinity. Middle frequency, ganja tones.

> Well, if there's nothing left to do
> Just hold your breath and hope it's true
> That we'll arise

He tried to focus on Babs and on what she might be doin. She would be asleep – she'd never had much difficulty sleepin alone and certainly not after three months of havin had no choice. Perhaps it wis a kind of adaptive thing – her basic sanity meant that she would never come to depend on any man. On anyone. They had argued, almost every day at first, about his doin the night shift at the station. 'It's just a fuckin ego trip for you,' she had said and the truth in her words had stabbed him like tiny skean-dhus so that he had shouted and raged at her and had stomped around the flat, knockin over unbreakables. But his rage wis bellicose, empty. These last few weeks, she had grown quiet. Her silence frightened him. He would rather she smashed things, broke plates, ripped up photographs, whatever. She had never done any of those things but it would've been better than this awful mute resistance. They hadn't made love for weeks – a mutually inflicted punishment of chastity – but now he ached for her. His finger slipped across the matt metal of the control desk, liftin off the patina of dust, and he could feel her shoulder, exposed, crescentic, as it emerged from beneath the sheet. He imagined a moon shinin through her window (she seldom closed the curtains except when he wis around – until Zaf, she had always woken with the dawn) and, in the soft, cold light, her body shifted slightly, alterin the contours of the cotton – her hair a mess on the pillow. He tried but wis unable to get behind the closed lids of her eyes. Strange, he thought, I can never see her face unless I look at her picture. It wis like tryin to remember the face of a dead person.

That wis the Kula Shaker and 'Great Hosannah'. The Man Wi The White Hair. Swayin, swingin psychedelia. Karmic love, among the rocks. *Arey*, Shaykhar! *Yeh kya hai?* Such things are unspeakable. Not unsingable, though, or unwritable. Nae weye! There've been whole books written about it. 'It'? Whit's 'it'? Ah hear ye ask. Cause Ah know ye're aw totally innocent *bundhay* oot there in the cosmic, karmic darkness ae space 'n' time 'n' Glasgae. They say the moontains create bizarre magnetic effects. Believe it, *loag*. And, as ye aw must know, this city lies sprawled between two ranges ae bens – weel, hills, onyweye. Mibbee those effects play oan the brain – mibbee they stew the *aql* till it's heavin an burstin an bleedin wi power. Spin the city roon an roon, fae the caul black hill tae the warum white sea, an it's a transmitter. Hey! *Sumjhe*? Have ye thought of whit that means, *meray doston*? Ah gie ye five seconds.

Zaf let the airwaves fill with quiet. He said nuthin for so long that he could feel N-U-T-H-I-N blow back from the bulbous mouth of the mike, he could feel its heavy flanks crush like poison gas into his face. The weight of the darkness, a Hindu darkness without end, twenty thousand million generations ranged, one upon the next – a series of lives runnin through time like tungsten through bronze. ON, OFF, ON, OFF, ON, OFF, a suffocatin, barely imaginable night.

It means Ah can read yer thoughts. Creepy, eh? This is the freaky show an ye're tuned in. An Ah'm sittin here listenin tae yous. Ye're breathin ma breath. Ah know yer iviry thought, yer iviry desire.

Stop, stop, stop. Jesus.

OK. Only jokin. Wild, but, eh? Man, here's another wan fae the Kula Shaker. 'Mystical' – ye know what Ah mean – 'Machine' – beep, beep, these wee red 'n' white lights – 'Gun' – *Happiness Is a Gurrum Gun*, that's the title ae a Bollywood movie. Makes it alright, doesn't it? Onyhin is OK in Mumbai among the gloss an steel ae satin shirts.

Nuff talk.

Track Two. ON.

GO. BANG, BANG! YE'RE MYSTICALLY DEID!

The urge to turn around grew inside him until he felt as though his chest would explode.

> You're a wizard in a blizzard
> A mystical machine gun

The music wis swingin in big, powerful telecaster arcs. Big wheels – like in The Who. But this wis a new royalty. Kula Sekhara. Thousand-year-old Mods of God, changin forms, turnin guitars to sitars to *kitharae*. Middle notes, the words between the lines. The songs before the songs. Darkness. He gripped the armrests and spun round. Blinked.

The rain wis still fallin. The window wis closed. There wis nuthin else.

But, just before he had blinked, Zaf thought he had made out a shape against the glass. A face. Shit. Zilla. The woman wis an acid flashback. A bad trip. Some kind ae fucked-up orgasm. Beyond the glass, the wind had got up and wis sendin the branches of the trees on the opposite side of the road into all kinds of bizarre dances. He let his hands relax. Massaged the palms. Fuck. For a moment or less than that, Zaf had really thought she wis there, in the room, standin behind him, dressed, as always, in black leather. Chic. A magazine junkie. Between the dots, flyin mystical bullets. Scratch the gloss and it wis a sewer. Mostly, the crap-fuckers would be more like incontinent retards caught up in somethin which they would never have been able to control. But Zilla had been different. That wis what had drawn him – like a vein to a needle, he thought, bitterly. Well, he wasn't all to blame. He hadn't realised that she had become a junkie – not at first. It wis just the occasional joint, mibbee an E or two and that wis all. No more than wis normal. Her eyes had given nuthin away. They'd just got blacker. Let's just say she'd hid it well. Or mibbee, at that point, she had only been sniffin. You couldn't tell if someone wis just a sniffer. They could walk around like the average person and not raise any eyebrows. And Zilla had never ever been just average.

He'd first noticed her when he'd gone to college. Or, at least, that must've been the first time. There wis no possibility of them having met prior to that and, yet, right from the start, Zaf'd had the odd feelin that he had known her always. It wis a feelin that had grown stronger the more he had seen of her. Mystical crap, obviously, but, still, he hadn't been able to shake it off. It wis unusual to see an Asian girl goin out with an Asian guy. It seemed somehow that the two entities were mutually repellent – as though there wis a danger that they might catch somethin from each other. Blackness mibbee. Or shame. Zaf had never gone out with an Asian woman till he'd met Zilla. Before that, it had always been white girls who had usually been at least two social classes beneath him. He remembered that one of them had called him a snob. Or had that been Zilla? He recalled her face without difficulty. The tiny blemishes around the cheeks as she'd turned towards him one day and said, 'You're a snob, Zaf.' But then it wasn't her face at all and the words belonged to some indistinct white girl. Before Zilla, they had all seemed indistinct. She wis tall and wis like a tree charred black by lightnin. Long, wavy hair, dark eyes, lips like the blades of a scimitar. Yeah, Zilla could've been an *Asian Babe* if she'd wanted but she'd had other demons to ride.

At first, he'd befriended her out of pity. No, that wis a lie. He had convinced himself that he would somehow be able to save her from whatever it wis that pursued her. Her eyes had a hungry look and she seemed constantly to be on the verge of goin under but then, somehow, she would run like a wolf on ice and manage to escape through to another day. But, eventually, he thought, the great city of Glasgow had trapped her in its vein. Silver bullets. The music wis still rockin through the night. Kula Shaker. Lads from the south, turnin through the cartwheel gods of Hindustan. Crispian, the man with the old soul, man of miracles! Silence, then fast tablas, then power guitar, then tablas, then more power guitar, then more tablas, then silence.

And, for a while, Zaf had tried to run with her through the cold night. She'd made up a story – or mibbee it wasn't a story – about how her parents had tried to force her into a marriage with some *hunda* from beyond the back of beyond. She'd run away from home and had gone to live with some tall white guy or other before findin her own place. She hadn't really got into college, though lots of people seemed to think she had, but somehow – perhaps through one or other of the white guys she hung around with – she had managed to insinuate herself into the circles in which the college kids tended to move. Well, they were not exactly circles – they were more like ellipses. Anythin to do with Zilla would always come to be bent – twisted in some way or other. That bitch wis so coiled inside herself that it wis surprisin she ever managed to stand up straight at all. And Zaf saw her there in his dark night cubicle – he saw her thin arms, her bony shoulders, that no moon had ever softened, an she wis all needle and black and, at that moment, she wis leanin against the glass of the window as if she were about to fall right through the transparent darkness into the rain beyond.

Fuck!

He turned back to the console. He rubbed the sweat off the back of his neck and cursed himself. Even now, five years on, she could still get to him. Durin their arguments, Babs had always said that he wis still in love with Zilla. To her, the radio station, with its intense exclusive Asian-ness, its revellin in a kind of aural subcontinental architecture, had come, somehow, to stand for Zilla. It had occurred to him that mibbee Babs thought that he might be havin clandestine meetins with his ex. If that was the case, then Babs really didn't know him as well as he'd thought. She'd never come out and said it though – she'd never closed that last arc of the ellipse. And he'd never confronted her with it either. Sometimes, lies were the only truth there wis. Mibbee that wis what this night wis about, the stuff he wis playin, it wis a first for a South Asian radio station – mibbee he wis tryin, single-handedly, to build a bridge of cantilever guitars, of sound, between himself and Babs. In the past, they had not needed bridges – in the past, they had been selkies and music had been their sea. The end of flirtation wis slavery, he thought. And between the two wis madness. *The Junnune Show*. The song wis endin. Tablas, tablas . . . fadin away to silence. He cut in.

That wis the Kula Shaker and 'Great Hosannah' and 'Mystical Machine Gun'. Told you it wis a bit different. *Haa ji*, we've goat iviryhin oan this show. We've goat Rafi and ADF, we've goat Sheila C an Kishore Kumar. But we ain't got nae bhangra. Not tonight. This is a bhangra-free show. Now, Ah've nuhin against bhangra. It's great music! It's a nivir-endin dance in yer heid. It's harvest, it's hot rain, it's life! Aye. But there's mair tae life than bhangra, right? Mair tae life than rhythm-an-beat and *Arey! Sanu, sanu!*

'Futtuk-in-the-buttak-haiy!-futtuk-in-the-buttak, futtuck-in-the-buttak *arey*!-futtuck-in-the-buttak'. Ye know whit Ah mean? Ah know the lyrics say more than that, OK. But ye know whit Ah mean. We're no jist spinnin, grinnin dancers – we're no jist clowns in glitterin dresses. We're mair than that. Deeper. We've been here, there an ivirywhur, fur thoosands ae years, an we can draw oan onyhin we like. Dig it! OK, it's *baara* meenuts past *aik* o'clock and here's a thing fae Junoon. Remember this?

Christ, no. Why did he have to add those last words? Remembah, remembah, remembah! He wis beginnin to sound like the host of some crap nostalgia show. 'Roll up! Roll up! Leddies and gentlemen, let me introduce to you the one and only, the most beauteous beauty in the waruld, the Goddess of Five Decades, the Queen of the Night, the greatest of all Glasgow singers.'

Fuck that.

Zaf let the track begin and he scribbled down the titles of five or six others to come after. From the floor below, he could just about make out the beginnins of music and the sounds of feet clatterin on the boards. He set the console on autopilot and went over to the window. The street was deserted. The place where the one-legged man – who wasn't – had stood was awash with the dark water from an over-flowing drain and, of Zilla, not even the shadows remained.

The wall of the building on the opposite side of the street seemed to quiver and change shape and, for a moment, he thought he had slipped into reverie. It sometimes happened in the middle of the night. He reckoned that, for a good proportion of the time he spent broadcastin to the sleepin city, he wis actually, technically, electrically, asleep himself. Eyes open, mouth movin but what wis pourin out wis all dream. He blinked and then realised that the heavin effect was bein created by the lights projected from the room beneath his cubicle, from the party which had just begun. He could feel the thump of the beat ram up through the soles of his feet. It flowed through his body and almost knocked him over. He made out shadows movin across the pale stone. The ones with *hijaabs* and beards would come but would not dance and would leave early to pray not for a better world but for their own personal salvation. They were spiritual touts. Gamblers on the empyrean. He could almost see the sharp corners of the scorecards pokin out from of the back pockets of their jeans.

He had turned the switch down almost to zero and it wis only after the song wis well in that he realised that it wis his own radio broadcast they were playin over the speakers downstairs and that the song wis simply the next part of 'Saeein' by Junoon. 'The Mystic'. The music sounded entirely different through all that old stone and wood. A bit like the distant, swayin noise of a football match through the night rain. The light and shadows came from the flickerin lamps of the sound system. Reflected in the windows of the buildin across the street and in the darkness of the stone, he could vaguely make out the shapes of people, just their top halves, as they stood about in groups of three or four and he could tell that they were clutchin drinks and fidgetin, the way folk do at the start of a party. He could picture it too, the room below, even though his feet were on their ceilin – yet, like a *farishta*, he could feel everythin through the skins of his soles. Midnight to six. He was like a worm crawlin through the night. He could feel and see the world.

You are in my body
You are in my mind
You are in my soul

That song should always be played loud and breathless, he thought, but then he wasn't certain whether he might actually have whispered the words under his breath like in one of those B-movies they always talked about but which he could never remember havin seen. Folk seemed to be passing from room to room – milling about as they do at parties. Zaf should've been able to recognise most of the people in the cubicle yet, gathered together in clusters of shades, they seemed anonymous – their heads all the same shape like in the bas-reliefs from ancient ruined cities. Without meanin to, he found himself takin a step back.

'Eh, Zaf!' shouted a guy from one of the groups. 'Zaf!'

He turned towards the voice. A 3-D face – Fizz. He had come back up to the studio. What the fuck wis he doin here? But he made sure that he didn't actually speak the words.

Fizz wis holdin a plastic cup filled with a red fluid which, Zaf guessed, wis red wine and not *Ruh-Afza* but the cup wis still almost full and the surface of the wine jigged up and down with Fizz's every movement so that Zaf began to fear that it might spill over the edge. Two other men looked on.

'Best fuckin radio station this side ae NYC.' Fizz's reference points were always North American. He dealt exclusively in superlatives. If somethin wasn't Number One or if it couldn't be expressed in those terms, then it wasn't worth talkin about. Thinkin didn't come into it.

Zaf nodded, slowly.

'Three months is the longest any Asian station's been allowed,' Fizz continued. 'It's about time they gave us a full licence, the bastards.' He sipped from the cup, slurpin a little.

Zaf thought of Fizz 'n' Ruby's *Bollywood Heaven* show and suppressed a shiver when he thought of it goin on forever. But, then, there were worse things. By now, more people had filed into the cubicle. Jesus! The place wis like Glasgow Central on Cup Final mornin. The hard, red iron of conversation through a rusted brain. Still, it proved you were alive. Old Firm.

'It's only a matter ae time. Mr Raj hus goat aw the right connections. He'll make it happen.' This came from a guy Zaf didn't know – an angular, almost ungainly man in his mid twenties, with a thickset jaw and a three-piece suit. Six feet tall, at least. He wis wearin specs of the fashionable narrow type and his black suit wis obviously expensive and woollen and must have been cut from the finest cloth. Italian, most likely. Must be one of Fizz's friends, he thought.

'Where's Taj?' Zaf asked without knowin why.

Fizz shrugged. 'Should be comin alang, later. Ye know whit he's like – always addin up figures, tottin up the *pesay*.'

'That's what it's all about,' retorted the three-piecer.

'All what's about?' Zaf asked but no one seemed to have heard. The music had just been turned up. Junoon's lead singer Ali Azmat's voice wis like that of an elemental, powerin up from deep in the bowels of the burnin Scottish earth.

> Your love is like a deep sea
> Your love is always there
> But mine is just an illusion . .

He looked at Fizz. 'Where'd ye get the drink?'

Fizz didn't answer. It wis probably just as well. He would've made a fool of himself whatever he'd said. Funny how some folk seemed to possess a knack for doin that, Zaf thought. It wis like an anti-talent. Fizz wis one kind of guy. He had on a bomber jacket and wis about half the size of his friend but that wis the way he wis. He liked to be the wee man. The fast talker with the gelled hair. Snappy, snoopy. Like that. Like Starsky from that ancient American cop show. Or Shah Rukh Khan. Yeah, that wis it. Chinos and arched eyebrows and a body posture that made it seem as though he wis about to leap on to someone's back. Well, in a way, Zaf thought, he wis. Zaf felt better. He'd been tryin, for weeks, to put him in his place, to turn him into cartoon. Once you had defined someone, made fun of them, held them in, they'd have no chance. But fuck. Mibbee that wis what Ruby saw in him. Mibbee she liked that kind of an image. Mibbee it turned her on. Christ. The other type of guy wis the kind who drove open-topped sports cars – usually white but sometimes red – and who wis the conduit for a large number of vices mainly revolvin around drugs. *Munnashiath*. Son's Ruin. And, more and more, Zaf thought, daughter's ruin too. But he shoved that one aside before it had time to do damage.

Arey, Junnunies! Good tae see ye again. Or not. OK, jist wait a meenut, put yer ear tae the groon and jist listen. Fur wance, don't talk through the air, real or virtual, silence your microwave voices, jist haud yer braith an listen.

Zaf paused. The power of the pregnant pause. Somethin lawyers might get taught, he supposed. A Gregory Peck pause. Deep voices in the courtroom, knowin looks from beneath heavily arched eyebrows, the dark weight of justice pourin down to drown you in its infinite silence.

Go oan! Live a little! Get doon on the flaer or the grass or the road – do this at home, folks! – and put yer left lug tae the earth. *Kaan* do! It's goat tae be that wan. The Shaitan ear. Ye hear a different music wi that side. Know whit Ah mean? Wait . . .

Zaf got off his chair, pulled the mobile mike off the console, placed its flat, round metal stand on the floor and twisted the neck down so that its chain-mail mouth was almost touching the boards. There were three or four people in the cubicle now and Zaf wis aware that they were watchin him. His trainers were almost vibratin with the pulse and beat of the music as it drew to ecstatic closure – a beautiful mess of guitars. Brian O'Connell's sinuous bass and Salman Ahmad's virtuosic lead – that guy sometimes played in bare feet and now Zaf understood why. As the music died (such songs never die – they just fade away), he pulled the mike back up and, still holdin its stem, he began to pace around the room. He whispered into its metal.

Whit aboot that, eh? 'Saeein'. Dodgin between the boadies ae this waruld – it takes ye tae anither place.

A universe governed by strange, paradoxical laws. The mesh wis hot but Zaf's lips were hotter. Shaitan mouth. Then he realised that his skin wis burnin and he had to pull away from the mike.

Someone very brainy had brought up a bottle of red wine and some plastic cups. They'd placed the lot on a wee round table over in the corner by the door. Zaf went over and poured himself some. He glanced around to make sure that Harry wasn't there. He'll go fuckin spare if he sees me drinkin on air. He'll go *paagal*. Quickly, Zaf swallowed half of it and grimaced. It tasted cheap and plasticky. Bulgarian, probably. The sharp sensation of alcohol hittin the roof of his mouth carried with it a frisson, the attraction of the forbidden. Every mouthful, every swirl, every poppin cork carried with it a barrel load of guilt. He wis Muslim, he wasn't supposed to be drinkin, it wis against the Law. By engagin in such activities, Zaf wis drawin one inch closer to the infinite black sea. He would've thought that, as a Sikh, Harry would have had mair taste when it came to *sharaab* but then it occurred tae him that it had probably been Raj/Taj who had set the budget for this party. Imagine settin a budget for a party. Stingy bastard! He glanced around searchin for a conversation to leap into. Zaf didnae particularly like parties but, once he found himself in the situation, he would tend to relax and flow with the music. As long as there wis music, he'd be OK. He scrambled around the console, leanin over a couple of bodies – God's sake! Had they not had enough ae consoles an mikes an glitterin lights that they had tae hog his? They were like death's heads circlin a burnin flame. He glanced down at his cup. This wine wis stronger than it looked. The odour of sweat wis beginnin tae fill the room. If these people didnae leave soon, the walls would swell like the sides of a balloon. *The Junnune Show* would either burst or fly. He tossed the biro on tae the console and slammed in another disc. He tried tae guess which one it wis and then he laughed. Strange, he thought, how Ah've forgotten which CDs Ah meant tae put on even though Ah stacked them up myself just five minutes ago. Mibbee Ah'm goin senile. Presenile. He swigged another mouthful ae the wine which now didnae taste so bad. There wis a certain exquisite lucidity which only came the mornin after a night of drinkin – it wis a feelin that enveloped the whole world, that anthropomorphised the sky and the trees and which also made him feel as though the essence of everythin lay just beneath his own skin. He looked forward to such a feelin. It would last for around three hours, after which, it would crumple, like some night-time moth, in his head and desiccate slowly on the sun-drenched pavements. But that feelin of lightness, of elation, would be hours away. Right now, the *laal* liquid lay heavily in his stomach – a not unpleasant feelin – and radiated a warmth throughout his body as though it were some kind of alien being.

Fizz's tall three-piecer wis gazin at him through his trendy oval specs. He disliked that – it always made him feel like he wis bein inspected, a speared specimen under glass. In the past, before the *Madness Show*, it had always been the other way around. Another mouthful. Beyond the rim ae the cup, fae out ae the shadaes, he saw Raj approach. Christ! The man wis a silent *singh*. A big sleek-backed cat. Oh, no, that wis Harry. He wis mixin up his authority figures. This *maalik-sahib* wis a cobra. That wis it. A leather skin swirl that ye nivir turned yer back oan. He had the urge tae put the cup down. He fought it, wantin, at all costs, tae blend in, tae stay firm, tae fight them oan the beaches. His lips were missin a cigar, but.

'Hi, Raj.' He had almost said, 'Hi Taj.'

Raj/Taj nodded.

Zaf pulled himself together. He realised that The King of the Airwaves wis about the same height as himself. He hadn't noticed that before. Mibbee proportions were different up here in the rarefied breath of *The Junnune Show*. Length, breadth, people. Different. Raj wore his hair across his head in a gel sweep and his immaculate pinstripes were unaffected by the fact that it wis almost two o'clock in the mornin. It was his face, though, that betrayed his exhaustion. Usually, Raj's skin would be smooth and his features formed in such a way as to render to his face the spherical appearance of a *golu* but, tonight, Raj looked ten years older. His lower lip, normally bulbous, now seemed swollen to the point of repulsion. The folds around his eyes slumped downward and the line of his jaw seemed to waver slightly so that, for the first time in all the years Zaf had known him, he seemed as though he was on the verge of tears. He's older and younger in the same moment, thought Zaf, tremblin slightly. The skin of his throat jigged up and down against the white plastic. Somethin wasn't right. His tie had been loosened. His words, his thoughts, everythin.

'You look like you've had a long day,' Raj said.

He wis one to talk, Zaf thought, with his face like that. 'It's the last, thank God.'

'Yeah.'

Zaf sipped.

'You want some wine?'

Raj shrugged. 'Why not?' His voice was ragged.

Zaf removed the cork and poured the blood-coloured liquid into a plastic cup.

> Oh, heart,
> Drink and roam the streets

The sound of Kishore Kumar's voice belted around in the darkness which, Zaf had tae admit to himsel, wasn't quite as dark as it had at first appeared. You could get used to anythin. 'Ye Kya Hua Kaise Hua?' Somehow, in every song, that singer wis really always askin the same question: Why? Of course, he must've known, back then, in nineteen seventy-one, that there would never be any answers, that his sentimental song would go on forever like one of those tape loops The Beatles used to play around with. Tears flowin backwards like salmon, back up the ducts, back into the brain. Kishore, songs of the sea, tales of drownin sailors, of lungs, white with the salt of this life. Aye, the air up here wis different.

Raj sipped the stuff and swallowed hard. Put the cup down. 'It's been a fuckin awful day. Fuckin shite, man.'

Zaf almost dropped his cup. Raj/Taj had never sworn in his whole life. Zaf had known him since they had been at school – Raj had been a couple of years above him but, even then, the guy had been a complete bloody swot and a mama's boy, right down to the ironed seams of his undies. Zaf had never once heard him swear. 'Why? What happened?'

And now, as the wine, like blood, began to leaven his brain, he noticed that there were stains across the pinstripes of Raj's jacket. Diagonal, just below the collar on the left side, where the useless wee angled bits were, and the stain cut across the slit which wis meant for a flower. 'What happened?' he repeated.

Raj looked him, straight in the eye. 'It's not the first time I've run this fuckin radio station but it'll probably be the last.' Comin from Raj's mouth, the expletives sounded doubly obscene. It wis like hearin a nun swear – or his father. He went on but he had lowered his voice so that Zaf could only just make out what he was sayin and had to crane forward like an idiot. 'Have you heard of the Kinning Park Boys?'

'The Kinnin Park Boys?' Zaf repeated but Raj signalled to him to be quiet. Raj glanced around at the other people in the room. He's scared, thought Zaf. The fuckin arsehole's petrified. The Kinnin Park Boys were a gang of about thirty or so lads who came mainly from one family and who lived in the Kinning Park area of the city or, as it wis sometimes known, 'Wee Faisalabad'. Zaf had wondered why they had not been named 'The Wee Faisalabad Boys' or even 'The Little Boys Fae Faisalabad' but that would've been too ridiculous. After all, they were tryin to be a genuine gang just like the horror boys of Bedford-Stuyvesant or the tribes in the Bronx or Harlem or whatever. Until the eighties, Kinnin Park had been controlled by Orange Gangs, fuckers of the extreme Proddy persuasion who had been brought up on porridge spiked with nail bombs and bread wrapped in auld blood-spattered flags from the Battle of the Boyne, sixteen hundred and ninety, and who terrorised not only Catholics but anyone who wis in any way different. In Glasgow, that meant Pakistanis. Aye, in those days, you wouldn't have heard 'Ye Kya Hua Kaise Hua?' anywhere along the length of Paisley Road West. In those days, it wis the sort of place where crooks would open pet shops as money-launderin outlets. Pretty, pretty Polly. Zaf had never lived in Kinnin Park. His stompin ground had always been the Shiels – in some senses a much more cosmo place, especially out towards Govanhill, though not in the heavily veggie kind of way of somewhere like Woodlands. But he had heard the stories of firebombs and of Nazi morons, in black bastard bomber jackets, racin up and down the streets that rotted with rain. In those days, Zaf remembered, the tenements had all been different shades of black. Reddish-black or greyish-black. Glasgow had been a place to run away from and, generally, the only people who actually came here were those who, like his parents, had somethin to hide. Anyhow, the *baratherie*, from which the Kinnin Park Boys had sprung, had all migrated from one particular village outside of Faisalabad, alias Lyall-pur. And, eventually, when they had got sick of bein gobbed on by guys in Rangers scarves and, after one particular incident where one of their women had been GBH'd by an arse-face from Ibrox, they had got together and had taken over the crime scene in the entire area. Zaf had never been sure exactly how this had been done – a *Khooni Raat*, a Night of the Long Knives, perhaps – no one ever seemed

really to know but there it wis. A fait accompli. Kind of Al
Pacino in a *shalvar kamise*. 'Ye Kya Hua Kaise Hua?' The
Kinnin Park Boys were simply the younger elements of this
mini Cosa Nostra.

'What about them?' Zaf asked insistently.

'They wanted exclusive advertising on the station.'

'What?'

'They want . . .'

'I heard you. But what's it to do with them? They're just
a bunch of arseholes. How could they think . . .?'

'Because, Zaf, they own the fuckin station.'

Zaf felt the room begin to reel. Over tae his left, he made
out Ruby talkin to wan ae her friends. Her arms were bare
and, in her right hand, exactly level with her right breast, she
held a glass – not a plastic cup but a proper glass – stylishly,
like Madhuri Dixit. He felt like he wis breathin through the
skin ae his feet.

'But Ah thought it wis different sponsors. Businesses. And
a grant fae the Cooncil.'

Raj waved him away. 'It is. But the Kinnin Park Boys –
or their fathers – own the biggest part. It's their way in and
up. How do you think we managed tae get the three-month
licence?'

Over tae his left, Ruby wis still teasinly sippin her drink.

'They made all the businesses in Wee Faisalabad pay up
or else. They're already intae heroin and now they're movin
intae broadcastin as well. They've got links aw the way up.
Wherever there's money, there's also fear. The two go thegether. And that's whit the gangs are all aboot. Money an
fear.'

Get yersel thegether! Get yourself together, straighten out
your words, down among the lush chords. This wis the
opposite of music or at least of that music which, like comic

Italian operas, constantly, painfully, sought resolution – songs such as 'Ye Kya Hua Kaise Hua?' But South Asian arcs were that much more extreme – they heaved and tugged unashamedly at your emotions and Zaf generally disliked those songs with big bellies that brought you back safely to a sonic asylum. It wis too easy – its sophistry rankled. That wis the difference between romantic and sentimental. And, like the young Rishi Kapoor, Raj wis usually the incarnation of resolution, of comfortable elegance. That off-centre parting in his hair, a diagonal Indian streak of respectability – all the blue deities must've visited the same barber. You would buy a used car from this man, wouldn't you? No freebie plastic hankie-box holders in the back window, catchin the light, blindin you. Some songs you had to play even if you hated them. The flipsides. Silver disc jingles gleamin into the back of your brain. Front brain connected to the midbrain, midbrain connected to the hindbrain. Merc wheelies runnin smooth and silent over black roads. But, tonight, he wis fucked. Raj's middle-class accent seemed to have dropped away like the lank strands of his hair which fell now across his face and which he had to keep flippin back like Michael Sarazin or Beau Bridges used to do in those nineteen-sixties' films. Nineteen sixties in American films – nineteen seventies in Indian ones. Rajesh Khanna, Amitabh Bachchan, Rishi Kapoor – oh, Goad, there he wis again, Rishi, Rishi, Rishi. *Arey*, VOMIT, *bhai*. Those Indian film stars never lost control.

Kishore's song had ended and the Ads were back on. Zaf suddenly had a crazy image from *Sholay*, the curry western from the mid seventies. It was the bit where the big baddy, Gabbar Singh, is standin on top of the dusty hill, just before nightfall. He's laughin a kind of exaggerated, psychopathic laugh which echoes around the entire valley where the population are cowerin in fear.

'So, what happened today, then?'

'They wanted it to go on – if we were to get a permanent licence. Ah told them Ah couldnae guarantee anythin like that. A radio station isnae a bloody corner shop. It has tae be broad based and cannae be in hock tae wan family. Besides, if it got found out . . .'

'So . . .?'

'So they beat me up.'

'What?' Zaf almost gagged on his drink.

But Raj finished his wine and poured himself some more. His hand wis tremblin.

Zaf looked closely at Raj. So that wis why he had seemed odd. Now that he wis really lookin, Zaf wis able to make out the beginnins of bruises around his left eye – and his lower lip really wis more swollen than usual. He'd been done over. Zaf remembered one particular Kinnin Park lad who wis known as Zafar. Not Zaf but Zafar. An, in those two wee letters, there lay a chasm of difference. He remembered his namesake from school, where Zafar had been one year above him. He wis fair, almost white, and he had blue eyes – the sort a woman might die for. Lookin into Zafar's eyes wis like puttin a seashell to your ear. They reminded you of far-off, sunny places filled with whitewashed buildins and lost echoes. Except that, after it, at the end of the symphony, you would go deaf. *Neeli annkhey*. He didn't have many advantages but that went a long way. The gangsta-tae-be had always been *gey* good at electrical and mechanical things. Good with his hands. He wis a part of the extended family that ruled Kinnin Park but, since his father lived in Pollok-shields, Zafar had grown up alongside Zaf. Well, 'alongside' wis puttin it a bit strongly – in the same century might have been more accurate. The same century but another world. He remembered the fear in which he had been held even by boys two or three years his senior. From very early on, he'd been known as 'The Psycho' and with good reason. On his second day at school, aged only eleven, Zafar had broken another boy's nose. Actually smashed the bone so that later, agonisinly, he'd had to have it rebuilt like Michael Jackson. Legend had it, Zafar had been jumped from behind by the older boy but had managed to turn and pin him down on the ground where he'd proceeded to bash the back of his head off the asphalt of the playground. And then, when it wis obvious that he had won, Zafar had looked around at the circle of boys (and girls), who were chantin at the tops of their voices 'Kill him! Fuckin kill him!', and, with an elegant swingin motion, he had brought a double fist down on the face of his victim. No one had dared to even breathe on him after that. He wis like a walkin Alex Harvey song. 'Give My Compliments to the Chef'. He'd gone through school with a record longer than a butcher's knife and, officially, had left the moment he'd turned sixteen. Unofficially, he'd hardly been seen in the playground for two years prior to that and, instead, had frequented the edges of the school, sellin dope and filth to any of the kids that wanted it. And plenty did.

Raj saw himself as a big businessman – mobile-and-all – with paper money hangin out of every orifice but he didnae realise that there wis always a price to be paid for that kind of advancement and, if it wasn't monetary, then it would be somethin else. Payment in kind. Nuthin in this world wis for free. Zafar, the gangster, had always understood this and so had Jamil Ayaan but the knowledge had led them down totally different paths. Zaf hated himself for soundin like his father. A defeatist. If anyone had stuck their neck out and tried somethin, he had always been the one to put them down. It wis a Glasgae thing or mibbee it wis a Jamil Ayaan thing. Fuck that. Zaf took Raj/Taj by the arm. Auld wumman. 'You should go and bathe your face – otherwise it'll just get worse.'

Raj nodded and left without drinkin the rest of his wine. The side vents of his jacket had got creased in all the wrong places. Zaf glanced around but no one seemed to have heard a word they'd said. I should've gone with him, he thought, and he drank some more wine. Then he put down the plastic cup, sat on the chair and swivelled his body till it wis right against the mike. Snake-sex. Saaaaaaaaaaaaaaaaaaaaaaaamnp!

Here we go! We're ridin high, up in the sky! We're a mythological machine monster. Ma brain, your brains, thoosands ae yous, aw trailin along in the warum darkness. The city is like a big brain pan, a burnin, sizzlin *haandi*. Sweet dreams, eh? Sweat dreams, mair like. Wu're comin up tae two o'cloack, ante meridiem, an Ah've jist discovered Ah've loast sumhin. Whit huv Ah loast? Three guesses. Mibbee we should huv a competition:

GUESS WHIT YER DISC JOAKIE HUS LOAST IN THE DEEP, DEEP DARKNESS AE THE NIGHT!!

Apart fae his brain, that is! Is that no right? Don't answer that!

The paper with his playlist wis a mess. Song titles had been written in capitals at first but, as he'd moved down the sheet, the writin had become more disordered until the last few lines of blue ink were barely legible. They seemed to have been written by a spider. Hastily, Zaf scrawled the words:

Over the three months of his radio life, he had developed the technique of writin with his right hand while, with his left, he would flip open CD cases, slide out the discs and slot them, sometimes singly, sometimes in pairs, into Decks A and/or B. Not that he'd ever been as extreme as tonight with regard to the randomness of the track listin but, nonetheless, over the ninety nights, he'd refined his skills like a keyboard player or a dancer. Different sides of the brain. Day and night. Deck A: Deck B. It sounded like an ocean liner, one of those massive white metal ships that shifted populations across unimaginable seas, across five hundred years of Renaissance blue. Columbus, Columba, Conquistador. Carryin Arabic triple rhythms from Aragón to Argentina. *La jota*. Damascus silver. Quaich dreams. *Jaams*. Jams. 'Brimful of Asha'. Cupful of hope.

Go Asha! Go!

Pop music, easy summer songs, strummed Saturday chords. Love, in tight white jeans. Fresh-faced girls wanderin down Buchanan Street, past that specialist kilt and tartan shop. Away in, son, and pick yer family! The Fairy Clan. Sons of the ugly men. Mind you, he'd heard that now they had designed a 'Commonwealth Tartan' that anyone could wear, a pretty blue-and-white woollen skin to wrap around yourself at football matches. Not rugby ones, though. Somehow, it wis easier to meld in with the football crowd, except perhaps the Rangers brigade. A class thing mibbee, Zaf thought. Or, sometimes, as with Celtic and Hibs, an immigrant, underdog thing.

Zaf wis alone again and it felt like a relief. He wis surrounded by the twangy sound of Cornershop singin 'Brimful of Asha' in Gurmukhi. Asha. Hope. Dancin. Dreams.

Jhangley-jhangley-jhangley! Gee, folks, these are the chugga-chugg-chugg boys. Next door, iviry brother hus wan. A seller ae dreams. Cups ae iviryhin. Golden hankie-boax holders. Cornershop! 'Brimful of Asha'.

He could sense that, twenty feet below, nobody wis dancin. It wasn't that type of party. Not yet, anyway. Raj should listen to more of this stuff, Zaf thought. He should freak out more. Let his hair down. Dig the madness. Too much sanity wis bad for you. Yep, Mister Raj/Taj wis out of the loop! But then, Zaf thought, it wasn't him that got me on this radio station. It wis Harry and it wis me. And, mibbee, in a funny kind of way, it wis Babs, too. Because Babs had known Harry from back in the days when he had been workin as an auxiliary nurse on a hospital ward where she had been a staff nurse – actin work had completely dried up and Harry'd had to do anythin to earn a crust or two and things had begun from there. He didn't know what things. Harry wis gay but, then, there were some who saw themselves as bisexual so anythin wis possible. And, somewhere in Harry's past, there lurked some women. Sometimes, Zaf would feel intensely, burninly jealous of Babs, especially when things weren't goin too well. He would picture Harry Singh, ridin pillion on the Kawasaki, his hands wrapped around her waist, his long, brown fingers taperin down to the hollow of her navel. He could feel the actor's touch on her skin. He remembered hearin a story about one guy who'd married a *goree* – a big blondie, long legs, blue eyes, a real good-looker – but one day, seemingly without warnin, he'd taken her off to the Highlands, stuck a hosepipe in the car exhaust and shut the windows. End of story. A double suicide. Romeo and Juliet with a multicultural angle. Beginnin of myth. His loves were like tigers. Untameable. Lusts, really. Because, if you loved someone, really loved them on an equal level, then it was impossible to feel jealous of them. Jealousy came from a sense of inadequacy. Yeah, right. Fuck that, Zaf thought. Ivory towers. Cod psychology. Just so much crap. His father and mother had never been equal in any sense yet they loved each other in a way that Zaf found inconceivable. The love of a man for a woman. Then there wis the love for a people. A *baratherie*, a tribe, a nation. But real love hardly came into that. Zaf had a long line of people he knew he had to kowtow to and Raj wasn't one of them. Not any more. If the Kinnin Park Boys had duffed him up, he wouldn't be runnin any more radio stations this side of the border and Zaf didn't want to associate with a loser. It wis tough but that wis life. His father had been a loser. He'd got the woman he wanted but then he'd lost everythin else. Lucky in love, loser in life. The cheap wine wis beginnin to make the bones around his ears ache and that made him despise Raj even more. Penny-pinchin – and for whom? For what? For the Kinnin Park Boys? For their fat-cat fathers, the pride of Wee Faisalabad? Fuck him. Ah! The bosoms of sanctity! The male vocalist sounded hip-easy, bumpin along his funny song, light rock, pop violins and all – he wis too easy, like he wis bein hyper-ironic or somethin. Very London. Straight faces, stiff lips. Mind the Gap! Ooh sooo coooooooool. Everybody wis so fuckin suave and icy, like they knew where it wis at and weren't tellin. Like they were not weak, brittle human beings, like they were uncrackable. Oh, yeah, sure they were! Everyone wis just a dog, a lizard, a fish, crawlin around in their own shit. Like it said on those perverted websites, the only truth in the world wis besti-fuckin-ality. Still, it wis a good song. Upliftin. That wis why he wis playin it. Right now, he needed uplifted.

III

He sipped the wine and then felt like spittin it out again. Why am I drinkin this, he thought. Why do we fill ourselves full of crap all the time? Mibbee we lack imagination – but perhaps it's more than that. Perhaps we like doin it. Mibbee it's a masochistic thing. He wondered whether Babs really had had somethin with Harry back when sex had been desperate and deadly and you could've so easily killed yourself with just one fuck. Or, at least, that's what they had told you back then. In the semi-darkness of the room, with the shadows of the people bumpin into one another, Zaf thought he spotted Babs, there among the throng, but then he saw that it wis just another shadow on the wall. Nah, he thought, Ah would've seen her by now if she wis here. Either that or else she's a bloody good actress. He began to feel the acid bitterness of jealousy well up in his gullet. That wis the thing with white girlfriends – you never knew what they might be doin behind yer back. They could lie almost perfectly through the blue of their eyes. Mind you, it wis gettin that way with Asian girls too. Take that Ruby for instance. Now she had begun life as a Mashriki, an Easterner, full of chastity and bitterness. He remembered her from when they were kids. Her father had been no stricter than average (and, in the Shields, average wis pretty bloody strict – especially for girls). She'd been plain Rubina then and had always worn *shalvar kamises* and had raised her scarf and dropped her eyes at the sight of boys. But then she'd gone to uni and, within months, the whole fuckin thing had fallen apart. He remembered the first time he'd seen the new Ruby – he hadn't recognised her and had walked right past her until she'd called out to him, 'Eh! *Behen-chaud*!' Now, Zaf had thought, I may be many things but I'm not a fuckin sister-fucker and he'd turned around, all ready for a fight, but then he'd seen who it wis and all the fight had gone out of him like *sharaab* out of a bottle. *Behen-chaud* was Ruby's term of endearment. If that's what she calls her friends, he thought . . .

But, then, it wis permitted. The real world wis virtual and the mobile-phone world wis truth. *Filmi*-scenes. *Hijaab*-shouters. Girls, with pink cells clamped to their ears or, rather, to the sides of their headscarves, decibellin one another across the street, makin cars almost crash into lamp posts. A *geet* life. *Arey*, Asha, ye've goat a lot tae answer fur! A brimful. A *geet* revolution. Six hours of turntable madness, of laser lunacy, of autohypnosis on the wheel rims of rattly cassettes. The Gramophone Company of India. This wis Zaf's *Junnune Show*. But, against the backdrop of the August night, it wis the show that played him. Zafre Zaf and Red Ruby. Two different kinds of reality.

And there she wis – chatterin away as usual. He could almost hear her. Amidst the syncopations of the music, he could almost make out the unstoppable gear of her voice. Sellin mobiles, mibbee. Pushin words, invisible connections. A text massaaage:

CANNY RUBY CAN

A mobile romance. Snogs-on-the-hoof. Lips, ears, brains. Gimme those microwaves – aaaaahhh!!! Safe sex. Well, it would fry your brain but your honour would be intact – and we're not talkin high-court judges.

The other people at the party were totally oblivious of the fact that, only a couple of hours earlier, Ruby had been busy attainin some kind of a climax with that wee nerd, Fizz. What kind of a climax Zaf wasn't certain – he really couldn't see what she saw in him. Sometimes he felt that there just weren't any reasons for anythin. Take virginity, for example. There would've been a roarin trade for surgeons in repairin torn hymens (usin, no doubt, the famed Neapolitan Technique) but for one thing – advertisin it would have been impossible. In Italy, the whole concept wis a bit of a charade so that you wondered why they bothered any more but, among the Asians in Glasgow, it wis for real. Both virginity and its loss. But, as in all things, reality wis hidden, totemised, and so the power of the intact hymen lay in secrecy, in myth. A veil over a veil. Ruby wis from the Shiels and Fizz wis too and so wis Zaf but Zaf had moved out and up, as they said, and now he wasn't really a part of the Shiels any more. If he hadn't left when he did, he would, most probably, have joined some kind of a gang for a while and then eventually ended up working in the family *dhookan*. The gangs in the Shiels were loose agglomerations, unsworn orders of shiftin alliances whose internal logic changed from day to day along with the wholesale prices of produce and, especially, of drugs. All over Pollokshields, Queens Park and Govanhill and reachin as far south as Hampden Park Football Ground and Cathcart Road, where the rag trade had grown up, there were lines which you wouldn't find on any map. Boundaries drawn in blood. Well, in bhang an spittle anyway. The lines were burned into his back and, even though Zaf had upped and run years ago, the cuts would be there forever. It wis like a tattoo. It would be there when he died. The thing with the Shiels gangs wis that they differed from the Kinnin Park Boys in one major respect – while you could become part of a gang in the Shiels and, as a general rule, the boundaries would not be of a religious or racial nature, in Wee Faisalabad, not only did the gang members all belong to one religion, they were also part of one *baratherie*. One big, happy family. The gangs were a mixture of tragedy and farce. Mostly, they were just pretendin. The big action, the hard criminality, would usually be happenin around the next corner, which might

mean some warehouse or other or else the dog-shite streets
that ran through auld Govan and Possilpark or it might
mean a meetin between the dead and the dead, out along the
unmappable terraces of the great, unwashed East End. But,
sometimes, Zaf thought, pretence could be more dangerous
than reality. It could get out of proportion and could lead
you into things that you were not ready for. On the fringes
of the gangs, there wis a certain amount of toin and froin
with organised crime. The guys in white sports cars. Skid
marks on the tarmac. Machetes. The Hockey-Stick Murders.
Hoverin behind it all, the grey figures of the Russkis. A town
enclosed within a town. At the centre of Glasgow, there had
always been a Gorky – the city not the writer. Some folk even
maintained that, somewhere along the line, there were links
with a certain Mister E, so-called on account he was the
biggest contractor of Ecstasy in Scotland and wis deemed
untouchable because of his thoroughly legitimate business
and council links in the city. Tannin salons and second-hand
car dealerships. And there were others. The thing wis, no one
really knew where the truth of it all lay and so everythin –
the techno, the howls, the hookers, the drugs, the roarin
pretence, all of it – tended to boomerang back into the local
community and, in the Shiels, there wis a constant sense of
imminent, barely suppressed violence. Like everythin in Glasgow, like everythin everywhere, this whole business wis
historical. Zaf had learned all about this type of thing at uni.
He had studied the migration patterns of his own people –
quite dispassionately, as though they had been geese. By
degrees, he had learned to dissociate. *Cognito ergo sum*.
That wis the best migration pattern of all. The one that you
couldn't stop even if you'd wanted to – the one that never
ended. The one in your head. What wis that, he thought –
the unseen switchblade that slices through your life along

some dark invisible line so that, without realisin it, you become separated from the whole of your past and everyone in it. One day, you turn around and there's nuthin behind you. And that wis scary. Like Zilla. Zilla wis scary – always had been. That's what had attracted him to her. That and a whole load of other things. She hadn't been born in the Shiels or in Kinnin Park either. Zilla was from another part of the city altogether. Somewhere out in the East End where there were almost no Asians and where the Celtic flag flew over every second building. Well, Zaf thought, not really but, after a heavy night on the town, if you listened carefully enough, you just might hear the sound of a flag, flutterin somewhere up there in the darkness (though no one in their right mind would venture east of the Trongate after nightfall).

Her parents had moved to the Cathcart end of Battlefield Road when she wis fourteen. Old enough to lose her virginity and not blink an eyelid. But her real haunts had always lain in the East End. And Zilla had taken him back to the waste grounds of her childhood and had shown him to her pals, all of whom had been white and Catholic. Zilla had always maintained that Catholics got on with Asians better than Protestants did but Zaf had said that he really hadn't noticed the difference. She had said that that was just because he wis basically stupit. Like so many of the Asian youth, he wis educated but ignorant. They'd gone to college and got their bits of paper that said they were members of the Glasgow bourgeoisie and then they had slipped into jobs and cars and wives but, all the while, they were still fuckin *kisaan*, as John Lennon had said all those years ago. Yeah, Zilla had been a bit political back when it had definitely not been cool to be. Back in the time of Madonna's 'Material Girl' and all that crap. On the edges of aerodromes and beneath the earth's venerable crust, a storm through the desert of the mind – that was the late nineteen eighties. The Summer of *Ishq*, Mark II. The early clubs and the pulsin techno and the Manchester baggies. Love in aircraft hangars, swingin among the ghosts of dead air aces. And back and back and back – 'Happenings Ten Years Time Ago', sunk deep into the clock of his mind. Telecaster genius, it wis Arabic pop art played by guys with minds opened to the sky. Explosive, azure music. Duellin guitars. Zilla wis a duel. Twenty paces, back-to-back, seein nuthin of the other – not even a shadow. And he had enjoyed the blindness. They had lived like bats in a world of sound and night. That had been before she had totally fucked up on the point of a needle. Then, it had been fun. Kind of hedonistic bein 'Eight Miles High', like in the videos. Not the Hindi videos. The rock videos. The AIDS adverts. All that stuff. Choruses, in the twelve-string jet-stream, swoopin down to the street – a perfect psychedelia. That thing he does with a plectrum – there wis a direct line from Ziryab to Roger McGuinn. Birds both. But that wis before. Coloured lights before the darkness. Zaf felt his wrist tremble and, quickly, he put down the cup but he spilled some wine over the edge of the plastic. It dribbled like heroin down the side of the cup. Or like the tea which his mother made perpetually, as though the act itself was a transubstanti-ation of a previous life.

◎◎◎◎◎

Their affair was conducted almost in silence. The difference between open relationships and those which are clandestine lies, in essence, in the amounts of noise generated. Even the most brazen adulterers, even those who strut in heels amid billowing, invisible clouds of eau de cologne, tend to creep through the *mohallay* of their infidelity, remaining somehow awkward, even at the height of their elegance, avoiding eye contact with anyone outside the binary axis of their deception. Perhaps, for them, this sleight of existence is their final adventure. They move about their changed world as though they were starring in some tremulous B-movie (betrayal is always black and white), except, of course, there are no cameras, no action, only the disturbing sense of incipient detection, of imminent revelation, of shaming damnation and worse. Perhaps their silent music did not arise simply from the need for discretion but lay in something deeper, something inherent in the relationship itself. Words were dangerous but they could also be clumsy things and the love which had sprung up between Jamil and Rashida was anything but clumsy. It was fortunate that Jamil's boss was often out of town in connection with his work. Because they could not be seen together by anyone who might know them, they did not frequent the usual locations for socialising in the city but, rather, they would meet in the *mohallay* where seedy establishments, huddled on the corners of streets, would sell them *nihari* and steaming hot tea ladled from blackened iron pots into cracked, flowery white cups. And they would sit on rickety cane chairs and watch the street children play makeshift cricket in the ditches and against the walls. There was no chance of Jamil burning his mouth in those places.

They booked into the cheapest hotels in town – the ones where nobody else seemed to go and where no one asked any questions. The men at reception bore the irritating insouciance of those inured to servility, they seemed perpetually on the verge of laughter and there, amidst the low buzz of radios resonating through the wall, in a first-floor room that stank of mothballs and dust and diesel, and drowned out by the sound of lorries revving in the yard below, he peeled off her thirty-foot long sari and he watched as, one-by-one, the slatted shadows of the window blind revealed themselves against the golden-brown of her skin.

And, as in the films, there was always a go-between, a servant, an actor, who grinned and lied and grew a little richer with every falsehood cleanly enunciated in a good, a heavenly, a *paridaezical*, cause. Nothing was ever written down. No telephone calls were ever made. Jamil and his lover hoped that their infidelity would be lost among the winding *mohallay* of the old town, that their trail through history would become as elusive as the flying metropolis of top-floor *djinns*.

And they succeeded – no one discovered their secret liaison, there was no showdown in the *haveli*, no blood-and-fire screaming resolution. There was only the quiet *ragam* music of the natural, the black note tablature of the inevitable taking its course. But, after a while, they found that, in their very success, they had arrived at a dead end. Where does an affair go if it remains undiscovered, its dialectic perpetually unresolved? Either it loses purpose and peters out, destroying itself, or else it takes over and changes the course of history.

Night was the best time for escape. In Pakistan, the darkness had always been more intense partly because of the lack of street lamps and partly because of the contrasting brightness of the day. Her husband was away again, up north somewhere, dealing with pale-faced tribesmen and mountain-top wooden forts. Rashida had her bag all ready, except for her face mirror which she had been unable to find that day. In a crazy moment, she had stolen one object from her *majaaz-i-kunda*'s house and that was the radio. It was hardly a sensible thing to carry across five thousand miles – especially not in the trunk of a small car – and Rashida never knew just why she had decided, on impulse, to lift the thing. But she was carried on the heady swell of a greater madness – it was as though every little action or thought held meaning, even if that meaning remained elusive. Her decision to leave with Jamil had been made months earlier, one burning midsummer's night, and it was she who had proposed the idea to her lover. They had been standing naked before the slatted blinds as the hot air sifted between the blades of wood. They could make out every conversation from down in the alleyway – they could hear the rub of every match on stone, each tiny explosion into the air, the fibrous contact with rolled *tambaku*, the inhalation through the seams of cracked teeth, the curling white smoke rising towards the stars. She had felt the night air burn the sides of her thighs, her back, her ribs. It had blown the loosened strands of her hair across her face and he had lifted them off, gently, with fingers that trembled with the intensity of the illicit. She had lost him in the valleys of her eyes, the tawny light from her body had swirled around him, enveloped him in its fecund scent. And Jamil Ayaan had swooned and turned away from her, as though to leave, to gather up his clothes and run down the broken staircase, out into the teeming *mohallay*, into the swirling smoke of cigarettes, the unending press of the poor and the darting, dodging forms of urchins. He had closed his eyes and imagined, for a moment, that this was just a dream – that these nights, rolled up into old carpets, had been as faded gates to heaven. Wool and silken sinew, the tiny joyous pressures of physical contact. On the outside, everything had looked the same these past few months – or had it already been a year? An age? Time, in such places, ran along different threads. But the dissembling, to his wife, his son, his *maalik*, had steadily become more dif icult to maintain – its fibre had grown thinner with each passing day in the hotel. Jamil Ayaan had not looked into anyone else's eyes since he had first gazed into hers that evening in the house of the *djinn*. He had not been capable of feeling anything except for her. She had been his mirror. Perhaps his wife had noticed – he had become like a blind man or a dead man. At first, the mendacity had been easy – it had come naturally as it might to any man, lying inside his wife, dreaming of other women. But, when the dream had turned to flesh, the fiction had become little more than a shimmering veil. And perhaps Rashida had sensed his dilemma – there had been something in his lovemaking, some subtle withholding that had told her that she had to ask him that night or else not at all. So she did not allow him to turn away. She held him and pulled him around so that he was facing her again. And there, as the wind rose and the slatted blind began to sway like a dancer between the lovers and the world, Rashida had asked him to come away with her, to leave his family, his country, his skin and to go with her across the dust wastes of the west to a land faraway and known only through the flickering monochrome of newsreels and the taut cadences of Tommies and memes across white marble floors, the still lingering echoes of Empire. And, since the pull of dreams is stronger than the anchor ropes of reality, Jamil Ayaan had agreed and had buried himself in her embrace, an embrace that was to last for forty years or more.

Rashida had abandoned her mirror with its golden back and stem. Perhaps one of the servants had stolen it or perhaps it had been borrowed by one of the *djinnies* who lived upstairs. Perhaps, one day, it would be found on the staircase, two steps up from the ground, the gleam of its metal, turned to lead. She thought only once about the mirror as she gazed out into the darkness that was total there among the fields and rising hills of western Punjab. The road to Taxila. Her sleepless lover at her elbow as he changed gears, his hand brushing against hers in a rhythm that was almost musical.

They had rolled the windows right down but it made little difference. The heat lay heavy on the roof of the car, a very basic Ford Popular, and, as it swept through the darkness, its black metal hide made only the slightest indentation in the sea of night. Through the metal, she could feel the ground shift beneath her feet. The earth of Pakistan was like flesh. To leave would be to relinquish a limb. But there was no other way. It must have been written in big *Naskhi* letters across those five rivers, the lines in her skin. Soon, they would lose the trail. Soon, she would lose the scent. One by one, the stars slipped into invisibility, as the velvet curtain of the monsoon moved westwards across the sky, until, as the runaway lovers crossed the border between the Land of the Five Rivers and the North-West Frontier Province, there were no longer any lights in the firmament and every breath was molten lead.

They had planned it like *daakoos* – like spies, they had a complex multilayered scheme of deception, of sleight of hand. *Al-taqiyya*. The British authorities had asked very few questions – Mother England needed labour like an old *sharaabi* needs liquor – and Jamil had bought the car, his first, with most of his life savings. They had brought only three buckram-skinned trunk cases – their dream was light as silk in the breeze – and as much money as they could amass. They left no notes, no record of their passage. They would slip from this land and from their previous lives like fresh snakes from old skins. The people they had left behind – his wife and son, her husband, everybody's families – would find out soon enough. Rumour travelled even faster than the night monsoon. But, by that time, they were out of reach, they would be living in another world, their car would have turned from black to gold and they would be able to lie in each other's embrace for the rest of their lives. Theirs would be a different archaeology. They would move as far north as it was possible to move – up the slim English island to a place that was even beyond the frontiers of England, a northern place whose latitudes were virtually unknown. The bigger the crime, the farther one has to run. Rashida quivered with the delight of the prohibited. Yes, she was scared, she was terrified, yet it was her fear which gave her strength. If she could do this in the deep dark heart of the tropical monsoon, then, in the land of the open sky, anything would be possible. Theirs was a sin but a joyous one. A sin born from love could not remain forever sinful. No more seedy hotels. No more frantic afternoons. They would live in the full glare of the sun and the wind and the rain. Truth would be their *rajarasa*.

And now the water came down, as though from the furthest circle of heaven, banging like silver ingots on the car roof, on the barely-metalled military road, on her arm as she rested her elbow in the place where the glass had been. She let the rain sweep down on her, soaking her to the bone, purifying her body for a new life, a different path. The monsoon was like music, the pull of its rhythm sweeping her westward and north to the land of holy water and dreaming stones and circle crosses. And dead wolves howling amongst the stars.

⊙⊙⊙⊙⊙

Zaf carried the square piece of plastic from the stack to the console as though it was a three-thousand-year-old precious artefact, a key, a piece of music, from the old metropolis of the Greeks. Taxila – sandstone ruins, dancing weeds, stupas and platonic love. Burning light from metal mirrors. His mother would often sing as she cooked – just as long as she thought nobody wis around. He remembered her tremblin voice mixed in with the sounds of dishes bein clanked together in the sink. The mornin pourin in through the glass. It all seemed so far away. 'Chho Lene Do', Mohammad Rafi, all that.

> Let me touch . . . your lips
> They are not lips, they are wine cups

Or she might sing somethin from *Pakeezah* – that film with the doomed actress, Mina Kumari, in the lead role. It had taken twenty years to make, from the nineteen fifties to the nineteen seventies, and wis part monochrome, part Technicolor. Or wis that *Mughal-e-Azam*, he wondered. Those old films merged into one another like long-dead ancestors. *Aba-o-ajdad*. Anyway, as the last shots were bein framed, the director had made a mask for her to wear in the final scenes. The scene where she is bein rowed in a boat, down the deep, dark river, the reflection of her face ripplin slightly on the gentle waves. 'Chalte Chalte'. She wis a drunken poet dyin of cancer. Flickerin candles castin a net of tenuous luminescence. Beneath the death mask, the hideously deformed, beautiful woman's face. The silent wings of bats. At the river's end, the truth.

Then there had been that song 'Mohe Bhool Gaye Saava-riya' – 'My Lover Has Forgotten Me'. Cryin, singin, lies. Lovers always forget, rememberin everythin only at the moment of their death.

And somethin wis wrong, five years later, here, in the party. Somethin just wasn't right. Oh, fuck. No music. He had let things run on for too long and the console had run out of tunes. His autopilot had just crashed. Silence. At that moment and possibly for several seconds before (he had lost count of time), Radio Chaandni, broadcastin on ninety-nine-point-nine meters FM, had been broadcastin precisely nuthin. In one movement, Zaf put down his cup, blinked and forced himself back to focus on the console. It had finally happened. He really had fallen asleep at the wheel. He shouldn't have blinked. From the corner of his eye, he saw the cup teeter and then fall off the edge of the table. Red liquid spread across the floor. Bloody cosmic wheel. It wis more like a stairwell with no 'up' direction. In the few seconds before this had happened, Zaf had dreamed that he had been downstairs and wis late for the broadcast. He had dashed past a group of people, almost knockin them over, and he had run out the door and up the stairs, takin three at a time. Folk had glared at him while the plastic cup had trembled, as though it had acquired a sense of chemical being, before both Zaf and his *jaam* had fallen off the edge of the world. Zaf found that he had real difficulty, now, knowin which version wis the real one. You went through life, he thought, collidin with yourself.

Speak, speak, speak. Now!

Salaam, friends. It's the weepy time – we're in the waruld ae sadness, ae tragedy, ae melancholia. Ae loast opportunities and loast people. Ahhhh! Enough ae that. Life's enough ae a downer as it is. So let's switch the groove. Deck A, Deck B – load em up wi happiness. Or at least, wi madness. Chaba Fadela's 'N'Sel Fik'. Maghrebi madness. Dance an spin oan the island here, dance the night aweye oan *al-Jaza'iriyah*, in the liftin darkness ae Radio Chaandni, ninety-nine-point-nine meters FM. Wu've goat Mediterranean *mohabbat*. Behr-e-Rum. 'You Are Mine'. Dig it. *BaRa gana*!

He scribbled down the title and artist but, because he wis tryin to manipulate the disc into the machine, his writin resembled a hermeneutic form of shorthand, a kind of hidden Hebrew or mibbee a revealed Arabic. The syncopated quarter-tones of Chaba Fadela's voice cut in Kufic across the mornin, words transfigured from stone to music to air. It wis a duet with Cheb Sahraoui – a call-and-response thing – and, after a few bars, it became hard to distinguish between words and instrumentation so that the whole was like a flat-woven kilim or a rough woollen prayer rug. The sort of rectangular piece of architecture on which Zaf might rest his forehead and palms – the pads of his toes, the front of his skull just touchin the twirled sheep hairs, the tip of his being in contact with the dreamin earth. Such a rug would leave an imprint that would last for hours afterwards. Mibbee all night. Midnight to six. Hands turned south and east. Radio prayers.

A heaviness had come to rest on the city. There wis a difference from before – Zaf could feel it in the air, in the light and in some other indefinably altered quality. Somethin left over, perhaps from the days of the church, of the massed arches of prayin hands, fingers pointed, as one, towards the dark vaults of heaven. Ach, this place could get to you if you didn't watch out. If you let your mind run out of control – if ever you began to believe the turns and loops, the deep-cut dives of the music. When you began to see, in the margins of the poolin shadows, in the uncertain pre-dawn light, the massed, glissadin forms of angels, then you were well on the way to a glistenin, terrifyin lunacy. Six hours of solitude replicated, night after night, with effectively nuthin but the mike and the songs for company – now that wis a recipe for madness. Time to get up and pace about. To mark out reality – even if it wis a lie. And, somehow, this song, this risin, lyrical piece of rai, whose words Zaf had no hope of under-standin, seemed to penetrate his brain, the muscles of his limbs, the lengthenin rubric of his bones, so that he felt, liftin inside him, the urge to dance or, at least, to move about, to do somethin purely physical. To abrogate his mind, his voice, and simply to lose himself in the Rif Berber fractals of the Maghrebian night. A long coastline of dark rock and billowin sand. Khairuddin Barbarossa.

He got up and went over to the window. Gazed into the middle darkness of the street, looking at nothing in particular.

He stopped and it hit him in the head.

For a moment, he thought he wis in the wrong room. He had the urge to run, to exit backwards in a speeded-up movement like in the old comedy shorts. *Keystone Chaandni.* But he didn't and, instead, he stood quite still by the partition window to his right – the glass a few feet from his temple. Shimmerin light. Gold into lead. A fuckin bullet.

It was Ruby's face that did it. The eyes were starin, insane, and the mouth wis in a state of rictus, the lips stretched taut across the front teeth like skin across the frame of a drum. For a crazy second, Zaf thought she wis dead. Then a sound came from outside of him and grew louder and louder – a scream like the feedback sometimes emitted from bits of audio equipment if they'd been moved too close together. Metal on metal. He felt that, if he didn't move, he might not be noticed. It wis like he wis in one of those nightmares he'd had as a kid. The type where you feel that anythin you do might influence the dream. As though dreams were susceptible to magic. But there wis no metal in nightmares. No metal and no magic. The scream wis comin from Ruby as she mounted to climax. Zaf moved very slowly backwards so that his feet made no sound on the wooden floor. Pad, pad, pad. His expression was as fixed as hers. Her eyes had closed. That was the only difference. He knew that he had to move before she opened them. Till then, he would be invisible, like when he wis on air or mibbee like when he went down south and mingled among the crowds in the centres of cities. There were so many Asians down there, no one noticed him. That was quite nice in a way. But scary too. Like bein in an airport terminal, along with ten thousand other anonymous travellers – waitin for the plane. He moved backwards and a shiver went up his spine as he thought he saw Ruby open her eyes. Wasn't certain. Wasn't goin to stretch forwards to check. No way. He felt the sweat slide over the skin of his face but didn't dare wipe it off. It's OK now, he told himself. I'm out. I can move again. His limbs began to move stiffly as though he had just woken up. An old man's legs. Usin his sleeve, he wiped the sweat off his forehead and crashed into the chair. Ran up the switch. But 'N'Sel Fik' had not yet ended an Zaf wis in no mood to mess with either Chaba Fadela or the listeners. Or Ruby. So, more slowly, he slid the switch down again, right down to the zero line and then some. He wis movin into negative sound. Mibbee his words, his breath, his being, would go out to the silent ones. Upside down. Right to left. Subliminally *Nastaliq*.

'N'Sel Fik' drifted away over the dunes, the red and white sandstone ruins, *argento saans* goin south.

Midnight tae sax. Hold yer breath! Two a.m. News 'n' Weather.

Dream signature.

TWO A.M.

After the Walkies, come the Talkies!! *Salaam-alaikum, sat sri akaal, namashkar.* Guid mornin, ye're listenin tae *The Junnune Show* oan Radio Chaandni an this is oor very last mornin broadcast comin tae ye oan ninety-nine-point-nine meters FM. Ma name's Zaf – zed ay eff – it's two o'cloack in the mornin, we're deep an swingin an Ah'll be yer host fur the next . . .

He glanced at his watch.

fur the next four oors an there's plenty ae good music still tae come so stay tuned in. That wis the News 'n' Weather an noo here's some commercials tae keep yous aw deid happy. Ivirybody's jolly happy! An Ah'm dancin in the rain.

Once again, into the breach. In ten years' time, he would still be dreamin of giant sacks of plain *ata* and his brain would be a chewed-up mess of sound bites culled from the speeches of council leaders. This wis the stuff of life. This wis what mattered – not all the music he wis playin. That wis his problem, really. He had lived his life dreamin of the perfect chord. It never came. Far better, surely, to keep your head down and let your belly expand over the hard plastic arc of a saloon wheel. To burn your books and take the silver. And, anyway, what wis an *avara gurd* like him doin pretendin to be some kind of moral mountain. He hadn't climbed a single grassy verge – let alone Ben Bloody Nevis. No transfigurin epic voyages were possible nowadays. For the rich, it wis caught in the gloss of exotic brochures while, for the poor, it wis whorin kidneys or jumpin barbed wire. Reuel Tolkien and Staples Lewis ruled, OK – with the rood of Charlemagne chauvinism, the linear predictabilities of Farangi fantasy. Or the *zabardast* hippy trail in reverse – tserevE.

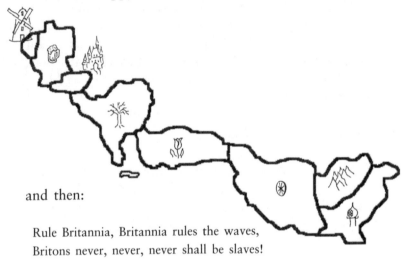

and then:

Rule Britannia, Britannia rules the waves,
Britons never, never, never shall be slaves!

Halleluia to that, brother! The end of the News. Into the Weather.

Rain!

Freakin out in a big glass house. Love and sunglasses among the fronds. Zaf, the Fab One. Zero Graffiti – *Bardo Thodol* rules, OK.

Rain!

He scribbled a title across the dog-eared piece of paper that wis lookin more and more like an ancient parchment map with a set of bizarre blue symbols for coordinates, sweepin curves for mountain ranges and no shore in sight. 'Rule

Britannia' versus the most amazin B-side of all time. Catch the gleam of plastic and, beneath that, the glint of silver. Magical music. The voice of Yahya slidin down the edge of a blade. A Head, right enough. Two thousand years ago, *Hazrat* Salome *Anha* had danced to its rhythm. Seven veils, hey! Even Sikander, if he'd heard it, would've rocked. Changez Khan would've swirled. And Jalaluddin Rumi had written the lyrics – Zaf wis sure. Whenever he listened to that song, Zaf found himself inside the brains of millions of silkworms, spinnin threads across five thousand monsoon miles, shieldin him from the . . .

Rain!

Yet that intro was like the entrance to heaven. Old Uncle George's fingers, the keys to nirvana. *Bajayen*, Jorge!

Zaf spoke.

Fab, zero. Dig it. The end ae the Weather that wis no really the Weather. Fooled yous, eh? Ah feel fine. How aboot you? Put oan yer shades an fly!

Deck A. ON. GO. Into their heads, every one of them. Silkworms.

As the chords and vocals ran backwards to the end of the song, Zaf wondered whether the tape loops in any of his listeners' heads would be doin the same. Mushroom choirs. The altar and the grave. Below him, in this church, bodies once had been carried, feet first and unseein, out the door. Tears and blood. Glasgow rain. It wis difficult to break through the wall of every thing but, mibbee at this time of night, as folk approached the lowest ebb – which would be around four a.m., he thought – their minds might just become a little more fluid. He felt like a river – his words, the waves that sharpened rocks. White water rapids. Speed up.

Ye're listenin tae *The Junnune Show* an thenight – Ah'm soarry, this mornin – we're playin a real mix ae auld an new, of Eastern an Western an aw points in between. An beyond. Or, tae be mair accurate, the soangs that let us hear the truth ae the fact that the waruld is aw wan. That thur's nae 'East' and nae 'West' – that's jist a great big lie cooked up by those who, even if they wantit tae, could nivir hear the real music. Mibbee some ae ye huv nivir even thought that such a thing wis possible – mibbee ye've nivir heard a loat ae these soangs afore. But this is the music that Ah've been listenin tae fur years. It's the *mausaki* ae ma life. It's made me whit Ah am. And whit's tha?, I hear ye ask. A disc joakie? Whit's sae special aboot that? It's no exactly a useful joab, noo, is it? Ah don't own a fleet ae cars. Ah don't even huv wan motor – thur are nae Merc wheels runnin beneath the skin ae ma honds.

He glanced at his palms, at the lines runnin into one another, at the fingers angled together in the shape of a dome so that, as he sat there, it wis as though he wis prayin – the Muslim way. He let his hands come apart and then he leaned into the mike.

Ah'm jist a human being. Behind this voice is me.

He pulled back.

Very cosmic, eh?

He had almost said the last words in a fake Indian accent but somethin had held him back.

Now fur somethin really old. Well, old in rock music terms, onyweye. See if ye can guess who it is. Nae phone-ins, remember – the phone's well and truly aff the hook an thur's a *daavat* goin oan doon here. Just listen and guess . . .

Deck B. Go!

Zaf leaned back and sighed as the first sitar runs of The Beatles' 'Within You Without You' began to *kathak* through the night air. He almost glanced towards the wall of the next room but then stopped himself and, instead, he got up and went across the landing to the bathroom. Doused his head. Wet his hair. Let the cold water run like tiny snakes down the back of his neck. He looked at himself in the mirror. His face wis brown. Well, light brown. To have described it as olive would've been stretchin it a little too far north and west. Latte might've been about right. Yeah. He liked that. The slightly sweet coffee they made high up in the northern mountains of Pakistan – the milky liquid which frothed from the spouts of gleamin steel machines mounted by the sides of the roads. Warm glasses cradled in your palms. *Murree* coffee. Aye, that wis it. The whites of his eyes were streaked with red and his growth of beard was already two days' worth. He ran his hand over the skin. Fine sandpaper. Number Five. Just a guess. He'd never been into that DIY nonsense. He'd never been into the physical things. Bodybuildin and all that. Carryin the weights in the hope that you might lift yourself up in the world. He'd heard of some guy, hyper-fit, tuned like a fuckin grand piano and only twenty-nine years old, who'd collapsed and died one spring afternoon, right in the middle of Argyle Street. Anabolic steroids, they'd said. They, whoever the fuck they were. The folks in the valley.

The suburbers, descendants of the *soobedars*. The kind of people his parents had always wanted to be. What an aspiration. Love among the bead-counters. The superglue of society. The rampant DIY fanatics. Always makin things, stickin things together, buildin dreams. Paintin over cracks. Zaf pulled his lower eyelids down. The flesh around his eyes was like that of an alien. Mibbee I am an alien, he thought, and then he laughed but his laughter wis hollow. If I stare at myself for long enough, chances are I'll turn into somethin else. Mirrors were dangerous things. Vampire killers. He remembered a time when he had hated himself so much, he had deliberately avoided mirrors. And yet, sooner or later, he would always find himself lured by one of the glass sirens and would then spend ages gazin stupidly into his own face like that big Dutch cow in the old master. Gazin into the mirror and not knowin what you were lookin at. The thing wis, if you were white, then you were that bit closer to a state of bliss and, if you were very black, then it didn't matter to you – there was nuthin to be gained from tryin to pretend that you were a little less black. But, if you were in between, now that was the real locus of purgatory. You would do almost anythin to seem a degree or two lighter than you were. Purgatory wasn't a place up there in the sky. It was right down inside of your skin and it turned and twisted until you were turned and twisted and you couldn't think straight any more. Until you were so fuckin crazy, you couldn't follow their rules. Yeah, right. Zaf had been the original chip-on-the-shoulder case. He would be arrogant to his own people but would find himself unbearably obsequious with any white person. Charmin to the point of idiocy – as though he had wanted to obliterate himself, to merge his being in their white-ness. He had wanted, so badly, to be accepted and loved that he would've been willin to have scraped the blackness from his skin, cell by fuckin cell, until all that would've been left would've been the bones. And they were white. *Burzakh*. For a long time, he had wished that he wis white. The aspiration of all good Asians, finally, wis to be as pale as possible. To marry white, to generate white and to strive incessantly for depigmentation. It wasn't that he had wanted to become a true Scot or a real Englishman – whatever the hell those things were – but, rather, that he had aimed at some elusive quality of white-ness which probably had never really existed but which was all the more prized because of that. His image had chased him repeatedly through the days and the years until, finally, inevitably, it had always caught up with him and, every time it did, his eyes would be transfixed by the alien face in the mirror and he would die again. Glass deaths. There wis a kind of masochistic joy in that. It's the chase that's important, he thought, but then he found he had forgotten the rest of the sayin. Chase the dragon. Mibbee that wis what had driven Zilla into drug addiction. She had never been able to face herself. But that wis bullshit. The kind of thing dreamed up by social workers and psychologists. Zilla hadn't got into drugs because she'd wanted to run away from herself – she had got into drugs because she had wanted to get right down deep inside of herself, to spiral down into the darkness that lurked some-where at the bottom of the well. But the mistake she had made was not to realise that the well had no bottom, that human night went on forever. It wis not puragtory, it wis *jahannam*. That wis God's revenge. There wis no escape. There wis illusion and there wis sex and that wis it. Fuck. He pulled away from the face. Spat into the sink. Swirled away the spit. The water had dried on his skin. He felt cooler now and yet, somehow, more fragile. His hands were rapidly growin cold and he ran the hot tap at full blast but still the water took ages to get hot and then he burned his hands in the scaldin water. Dried them. Went back to the studio. On his way, he noticed that Ruby 'n' Fizz had left again. Probably gone back down to the party, he thought. God. Zaf felt that, if he could get through this night, then he might be able to get through anythin. Suddenly, he needed Babs. Not in the flat but here, right by him – her eyes gazin into his, her hand on his hand, the soft lilt of her voice meldin with the dyin sympathetic strings of the sitar. The blades of her shoulders, the sharp twin protuberances at the bottom of her neck where the collarbones almost kissed, that hillock which he loved to feel move beneath the rugosity of his lips. Her long, thin fingers, the nails transparent pink. Within her without her, he thought, my life goes on. Sometimes, he felt that he would have given her anythin. His money (not that he had any), his mind, his soul. Everythin. But his own obsequiousness disgusted him. And disgust hardened him. It always had. Right now, he thought, I need her but in ten years' time or mibbee even five, who knows? That wis the way of the modern world. Disposable love. Recyclable. Reincarnatable. We were all one. One what? He closed his eyes and let the music seep through his skin.

As he turned the key, Zaf blinked slowly just to make sure he wis alive and awake. The flat wis completely tidy – everythin wis arranged just as it should be. The *Marie Celeste*, he thought, with its unused table napkins and just one upturned chair or else the *Cutty Sark* drownin in two centuries of firewater. That wis Babs for you. He almost smiled. Felt on the edge of somethin. Freedom mibbee. Whatever that wis. He went into the bedroom, tryin to avoid lookin at her neatly arranged clothes. He did not glance at the bed but allowed his gaze to be drawn to the big bay window. The light of the mornin wis streaming through the glass so that all the imperfections – the dust stains, the trails of dried rain, the tiny sand bubbles which denoted the fact that the panes were not of the best quality – became enhanced, larger than life. Through the window, the white newness of the mornin light grew filtered, fake, unreal – he remembered the way the muscles at the sides of her lower ribs had moved when she'd bestridden him, the skin ripplin over the fretted bones. Beneath his fingers, she had been electric.

In the far corner, just next to an ethnic occasional table, was a pair of white sandals. The straps lay loose and the leather had worn away around two of the punctures. Summer by the sea. Ayr, the long beach. Rows of dormer windows, seagulls, ships. The way the pinky-white skin of her feet grew a darker red at the toe ends, the Venus Blue paint she had applied to the nails as they had sat on the edge of the quilt in an airless hotel room. The touch of her soles on his back as they had made love deep in the western night. He could hear the sound of her soles on leather as she walked, leisurely lopin in shorts, the way she did when she was off duty. He'd deliberately hung behind her and had gazed at her figure as he might've watched himself in the glass of a window. Beyond her, around her, the rhythm of the pallid Irish Sea had swirled and dipped and fanfared and the seaweed smell had filled his head until Zaf had felt himself grow quite dizzy and had suggested that they sit for a while on one of those benches dedicated to the dead. She had laughed at him for being so unfit. And he had laughed too even though he'd had no breath left. He had hung his head and followed the Florentine blue veins of her feet up through the structures of her corpse, right to the opening and closing of her lips. Yunus and the Whale. Love among the peasants.

He felt a great emptiness in his belly. He inhaled and drew

the back of his hand across his lips.

On the kitchen table wis a bright-yellow mug half-filled with cold coffee. The mug bore the inscription, in big, red letters:

SMILE! IT COULD BE WORSE!

and, beside the smilin mug, Zaf noticed a scribbled note. He shivered and glanced up at the window which was not open. He picked up the note. The edge of the paper wis jagged. It had been roughly ripped from her pad of good water-marked writing paper. It was unsigned. Everythin wis real. Each sensation, every thought, each fear held equal weight. It wis like he could take a cosmic pen and draw a plan of the night and it would be a thing in eleven dimensions and it would be played back in sound. A voice, close to orgasm, barely human, gratin monosyllabic in the darkness:

'BABS! BABS! BABS!'

Another mornin. The park, the crest of a hill, close to a sleek white flagpole without a flag. Forty feet high. A possible scenario or a mixture of scenarios.

'Ye got ma note?' she said.

'Whit note?' he said.

'Ye wandered about in the park, after ye'd been up all night,' she said.

'Aye. It wis a sunny mornin and Ah'd been up all night,' he said. 'Ah didnae want tae wake ye up.'

'Yeah, but ye do it iviry night. Mornin, Ah mean. It's a bit crazy.'

He shrugged then regretted it. But he couldn't take back a shrug. Words mibbee. Actions never. She started high and her pitch rose along with her volume. Her face also got redder. Like a ripe tomato. Wanker-bitch.

'Ye dinnae see it that way. Ye nivir look at whit ye're doin, Zaf. Ye drive ivirybody else fuckin mad. And fur whit?'

That's it, Zaf thought. That says it all. She can't see why anyone would want to do that. It wis a long time since they'd been to that loch up north, where she'd swum through the night like a dolphin. What happens to folk, he thought, when they settle into habit? They end up in prison – that's what. But mibbee I'm just immature. Zilla's prison wis heroin. And his wis Zilla. And Babs's wis him. Mibbee.

'Sorry,' she said.

She slipped her arm through his. He allowed her to do this – he didn't pull away but didn't reply, either. They were awkward, deliberate. Like bad diplomats. The sound of the traffic grew louder. A couple of kids were playing hopscotch in the road. 'One, two, three, four . . .' He'd heard that, in Punjab, the game was different. The numbers, the shape of the dance. Different. They said nothing until they reached the end of the street. Then he pulled away from her. Not violently. Coldly.

'Why don't you come back tae the flat, Zaf?' She wis pleadin. Her accent wis gettin stronger, wis swellin intae Galloway Irish. She, too, wis goin back.

'There's a note . . .' he began. His voice wis distant, like the sound of muffled church bells from across the hills. Holy, holy, holy.

'Whit? Ah know there's a note. Ah left it there. Whit're ye goin oan about? Ah thought ye hudnae been back tae the flat. How d'ye know there's a note? Why are you fuckin wi me, Zaf?' She paused. He felt her body tremble, just a little, whether with excitement or from fear, he wasn't certain. Her voice was crackin. 'Fuck the note. It disnae mean onythin.

139

It wis jist anger. Rage. Forget it. Ah'll destroy it. Burn it.'

'Ah need tae think,' he said.

'No, ye dinnae. Ye've done enough thinkin fur wan person. It's bad for ye. Too much thinkin.'

They had reached the edge of the park where it rambled into the back-ends of some shambled, yet expensive, tenemental streets. The sort of place where a musician might reside for a while. Sleek, black buckram cases rushin through the summer rain. Guess the instrument. Imagine the music. Zaf felt somethin expand inside him, in his belly, his chest, his throat. He couldn't breathe. He wis drownin in the cold arms of the Kelvin River. There it wis – a hundred feet below. Then the river swelled and burst its banks.

'Shut up! Jis shut the fuck up! Ye've trapped me fur too long!' His voice fell.

'Trapped . . .'

Her face had collapsed. He felt guilty. Shite. He looked into her eyes. Dream blue. He'd died so many times for those eyes. Not any more.

'Ah nivir trapped ye, Zaf – ye trapped yersel. Dinnae think ye can jis gie me a tossed awa thank ye and that'll make ivirythin awright.' She wis silent. He could feel the chasm that was openin up inside of her. He felt sorry for her. It wasn't fair. She'd been right all along. When she'd harangued him about the radio station, when she'd refused to listen to his broadcasts and then had listened anyway. Her fear about him 'n' Zilla. He hated it – he hated himself – but you couldn't do anythin to change the way things were. Life wis a dark tunnel . . . existence, flickerin images on a kitchen wall. But, in the end, it wis all there wis.

He moved away. He wis aware of a distance between them that had always been there but which now, in the hard light of noon, had become almost palpable.

'Where're ye goin?' She'd sensed somethin and her voice wis unsteady, already unfamiliar. But her face wis red and she'd pushed her chest out so that her wee breasts seemed suddenly much bigger. She wis drawin in air, breathin fast, ready to fight. 'Ye cannae jis walk away fae me. Dinnae you jis fuckin walk away. Ah've put a lot intae this relationship. Too much.'

She glanced back up the street and then back round at Zaf. Her face wis anger but her eyes were wellin. She spoke slowly and her words came out like lead. Slow silver. 'Days, nights, Ah've worked like a fuckin dog . . .'

She took a step towards him and, for a moment, he thought she would reach out and grab his arm, hold him to her. Force him back. Crush him, beneath the combined weight of their pasts. 'Ye dinnae jis walk away fae me – no aifter two bloody years. Ye fuckin ungrateful black bastard! Go back tae yer fuckin whoor, go an screw yersel intae her filthy cunt. Ah hope ye're both very happy thegether. It's all ye deserve. Arsehole. Bastard. Wanker.'

She'd not known rejection. Uncertainty. The crack in the soul. Well, now she wis learnin, Zaf thought, now their skins were bein stripped away and the filth wis pourin out. The air between them seethed with her rage. But it wis jist hot air. He wondered why she wis so upset. After all, she'd been the one who'd written that note. She'd admitted it. Mibbee, he thought, mibbee it's because she's been rumbled. She's been tripped up. It had always been there, runnin beneath their relationship, the implicit threat of her takin her white-ness and goin elsewhere. She'd been the one who'd really always been in control. Well, that wis changing now. He knew he wis bein a bastard but there wis no other way. It wis for the best. Or mibbee it wasn't. He wis beyond knowin. His head reeled. He felt light. The sound of sitars.

'Ah'm jist goin doon tae the coast.' It wis a lie but, once he'd said it, the prospect began to assume solidity. 'Tae stay wi friends fur a wee while. Ah need tae get away . . . Ah need tae get ma heid sorted oot. Ah'll pick up some hings . . . later . . .' His voice trailed off. He knew his lies were unconvincin. He'd never been a good liar. To be a good liar, you needed to know where your own truth lay.

'Ah'll phone ye,' he ventured. Then, with relief, he remembered where his mobile wis. Then he wasn't sure.

'Dinnae fuckin bother. It's ma flat. Ah'm cheyngin the phone. Ah'm cheyngin the locks. Fuck you. Arsehole!' She wis cryin. Her body wis startin to shudder. She glared at the tiny, well-pruned bushes to her right. In the bright sunlight, it seemed, for a moment, as though they might ignite and burn with her fury. 'And dinnae come back fur nuhin!'

He turned around and began to walk. She stood still and her arms went loose at her sides so that she was like a doll with the stuffin knocked out. He could feel her muscles tremble and he could smell the cold sweat of her rage. Her belly wis almost doubling her over and she wis havin a real struggle to stay upright. Her anger wis the rod up her spine. He felt her glare scorch his back as she watched him leave – just as he had watched her that night as she had swum away from him into the clarity of a full moon so, now, she gazed, unblinkin, as his figure dissolved into the burnin sunlight. He felt the wells of her eyes flood over the paper-thin lids and she wis sobbin, her stomach wis almost retchin, castin up its contents, and he could hear her but he accelerated away so that he wouldn't be able to hear her any more.

On both sides of him, the trees were massive and the leaves sighed as a breeze caught the edges of the afternoon. There wis a man mowin the lawn. The man had on jeans and a checked shirt. His hair wis short and fair, like that of a cornflakes father. Zaf closed his eyes against the sunlight, the impenetrable blueness of the sky. Ye couldnae cry wi yer eyes closed. Just before he turned the corner, she called out to him. He couldn't decipher the words. Couldn't even tell whether or not they had been spoken in anger.

He reached the crest of a hill and paused to get his breath. The sun was poised over the western horizon. It wis later than he'd thought – either that or the nights were beginnin to draw in. He'd needed to get out of breath, to run without runnin away, to push his lungs to explodin point. It wis either that or crack up. And he'd cracked up enough for one day. He could see the city laid out all around him. There were several ways he could go. He might go left and follow the river upstream through the centre of town. Perhaps he would cross the softly flowin water again and pass by the mosque as, for so long, it had passed him by and then he would walk between the white and black tower blocks of the Gorbals and over the soft, wet grass of the Glasgow Green towards Bridgeton where everythin wis either disused or misused or tassled and sashed with purple and orange. Once, Bridgeton had been a roarin crossroads. He remembered the old photos of when the street had been piled with mounds of horse shite and thronged by muscular, aproned women, their sleeves rolled up above intact veins . . .

But, then, all his life, the pasts of other people had blown at him, had buffeted him so that he had barely been able to stand on his own. The pasts of seamstresses, soldiers, children, ancestors. Of the dead, the near-dead. Of the church and the abandoned tunnels that disembowelled the city with their stink of old engine oil. Dead mandolins. A rubric of the insane.

The sun had reached that second apogee which occurs in the early evenin and the sky wis burnin blue. Zaf felt the heat embrace him, he felt it run through his body like lust or like a drug. He breathed deeply. Closed his eyes against the glare.

The thing wis, it wouldn't have made any difference. No matter where you went in Glasgow, sooner or later, you would end up in the midst of squalor and heartbreak and, in your nostrils, there would linger a sense of your own transience. If not today, then tomorrow or the next day. Escape wis just a dream.

He felt the asphalt beneath his feet begin to seethe and melt and it occurred to him that, if he stood there for long enough, he might never be able to move from the spot. He might become like one of those imperial statues that skirted George Square. He might melt into granite. No land wis pure.

No wonder Zilla had wanted to be high all the time. Mibbee he would get out altogether. Take the sea bus to Ayr or Saltcoats. Or the boat to Rothesay. Somewhere gentle and decaying, somewhere filled with the forms of those who needed time and space and the smell of seaweed and deep fries. Wind. Solitude. He needed a bath. Perhaps, he'd stay there, by the seafront, for a few days. Get his head sorted. Then, mibbee, he would move in with a friend for a while. Sooner or later, he'd have to get a job. Somethin concrete, somethin real. Like, mibbee, he could become the voice on the end of a helpline. He almost laughed at the image of himself as some kind of disembodied good Samaritan. At some point, he'd have to go back to the flat to get his things. But, right now, he couldn't face another confrontation with her or with anyone. He could get by with the stuff he had on and the few clothes he'd tossed into his bag. He could always buy some new clothes in Ayr. If the blood didn't wash out, then he would burn the old ones. Burn them to hell. He opened his eyes.

He put the note back down carefully, as though to have damaged it in any way might have endangered the fragility of the mornin in the house which, for nearly the past two years, they had called home. She had called home. It was Babs's place really. A country girl, she had made this city her life. It had not sucked her down into its sewers. Not yet. Mibbee that wis why she rode a motorbike. For a quick getaway. Just in case. The light made dancin patterns of the leaves on the walls. Everythin around him was movin and yet, there, in the kitchen where they had eaten together so many times, where they'd filled their stomachs with the food which they had cooked with their own hands and where their hands had touched momentarily, sometimes lovinly, sometimes irritably, sometimes wishin the other wis dead, there, Zaf sensed no movement. Nuthin. They'd been lovers, consecratin their flesh in each other. Around this table, they had refashioned their bodies. He ran his index finger around the rim of the mug, felt the stick of her lips in the place where she'd drunk. The surfaces remain the same, he thought. They lie to us – we force the lies out of them – and yet they never alter. She called his father 'Papa' which must've seemed strange to her since, in Scotland, the word was usually used to refer to someone's grandfather. And Jamil had always smiled back at her – that warm, full, middle-Indian smile of his. Teeth ranged like tablas. Strange, Zaf thought, he never really asks who she is. It seems he's quite happy to accept the fact that a *goree* is in his house, real close up, at the table, in his bathroom, in the bedroom, even. Mostly, he'd felt good about the bond which had grown up between Babs and his papa but, now, it wis a knife twistin in his chest. Whatever had linked Babs to Zaf wis erodin like a folk tale, wis sinkin like silver heads into the sea, and she wis makin it very difficult for him. Everythin he did could only be provisional, relative. The flat wis a museum. She wis the curator – he an escaped artefact. Everythin wis defined by its relation to her. It is the small, the inconsequential, the transient, Zaf thought, which ultimately kills us. Through white sandals and stained porcelain, her innocence had grown monstrous, Edenic. Yunanis an Yehudis. Fuckin guilt. He hated the flat, the note, her loving, carin, motherin, nursin archetypal bosom, belly, buttocks. He felt like a fuckin statue, teeterin in the kitchen of his past, weakly dreamin of her lips. The bones of her fingers that, now, would not rest with his. No Crusader lions for them.

As he left the kitchen, his foot scuffed against somethin. He looked down. It wis a scrunched-up ball of paper. He knelt and picked it up. It came apart like an ancient manuscript and, yet, it had been written on the very same paper as the one that he'd found on the table. But the writin wis far clearer, not scrawled at all but planned and written out slowly, carefully, in the modern equivalent of copperplate. He gazed at the note, his eyes followin each curve and swirl of the pen, the tiny blue streams of biro ink . . . he wis familiar with the tectonics of every line. Every title. Music, into words, into stone. Brick by bloody brick, we build our own prisons around ourselves. He screwed it up in his palm and tossed it on to the floor. Then he reached across and grabbed the other note off the kitchen table and he tore it to shreds. The slivers stuck to his jeans. He really should've changed his *kapRae* but he didn't want to linger.

He swung the small holdall that he had stuffed with clothes, toothbrush and a copy of the previous week's *Glaswegian* up on to his shoulders and quickly left the flat. She hadn't even finished her coffee. As though it had been a medical emergency. An image of his papa's body rolled naked on to the morgue block, cold in the Central Mosque. White sark, skin dead.

Waitin for the last, the tidal wash. As he closed the door, the smell of Babs, her perfume, the sweat of her flesh, the wasted blood, which she had shed for him, blasted into his face so that he felt as though he would suffocate, there, on the piss-shite of the landin, trapped between floors. Between lives.

He woke up. The song wis endin. It wis the incipience of silence that had woken him. Fuck sake! He couldn't remember fallin asleep at the mike. He was seized with terror at the thought that he might have said somethin on air. So he said somethin on air.

The Beatles' 'Within You Without You' – fae the album *Sgt Pepper's Lonely Hearts Club Band*. Ye thought that wis auld? Get a handle oan this. Talat Mahmood, Aulya of the Ghazal. 'Chal Diya Caravan'. We're aw leavin sometime. Optimistic, eh? That's why ye tune in tae *The Junnune Show* oan Radio Chaandni, ninety-nine-point-nine meters FM – cause, hereabouts, ye don't get ony lies. Here, ivirythin ye hear is the truth. Goad's ane.

Even the words of the songs? He thought. We'll see. Deck A.

> The caravan is leaving,
> And I am here, bereft.
> On the hem of my shirt,
> My tears have written
> Our tale . . .

Talat wis like a drug. His voice wis the arc and plunge of a falcon. It could pull you in, take you over . . .

The song was about the moon and death and lost loves and it drew him back to a time before the tenements, to before he was born, when the world had belonged to his parents.

◎◎◎◎◎

It had all begun on that journey, back in the dusty ol' fifties. Jamil Ayaan and his new bride-to-be jogged at fifteen miles an hour along the old military road that ran from Lahore to Rawalpindi while, all around them, over the burning airwaves, Talat sang his songs of parting.

Like Alexander, they were running from Punjab but, unlike the old Yunani, they carried with them neither treasure nor triumph but only the fragile, bleeding seeds of the possible. A whole night and day it took to get to the Afghani border where the sun burned relentlessly against the desolate mountain slopes. The light was brutal. Iron. The monsoon had never reached this far and had exhausted itself, along with the pursuing police, just before they had entered the Tribal Zone. *Gee haa*, her *majaaz-i-khuda*, her metaphorical god, and his *maalik* had summoned the forces of law-and-order to stop these seeds of chaos from escaping. Past Taxila, Attock and on through the Khyber Pass road where the ghosts of dead Tommies rose up in dust swirls and saluted and grinned at the old car and its dazed occupants. A massive bribe, first thing in the morning, got them past the flags and over the frontier. 'Chal Diya Caravan'.

On their first night out of the country, in some wild hollow of the ancient province of eastern Khurasan, they drew the car to a halt and tried to fall asleep. Their aim, such as it was, had been to find a town where they might seek out some place to stay but they had forgotten that the land of the Afghans was defined by an almost biblical emptiness. *Kha urasan*. They seemed to have lost the moon and Rashida was terrified of bandits, of wild beasts, of the unremitting blackness of the night. All around them rose the hulking shapes of bare mountains and the only sound came from their own frantic, heated breathing against the wind-screen. With the sudden descent of day into night, the temperature dropped thirty degrees or more and the lovers huddled up against each other and wondered just why they were doing what they were doing. Surely there were easier ways, less dangerous paths they might have followed? What was so wrong with gleaming white boats? But they couldn't have lied about their names – these were the days, long before illegal passports became easier to come by than a flute of French champagne, when things had to be done the British way, by the book. And there would've been no captain's table for them, no perfectly ironed tablecloths and sterling silver services filled with Angraise *chai*, no portly cigars after dinner, no breaking off the dead tobacco heads against the rail of the upper decks . . . Now, in the bitterly cold night that was made even colder by the sudden and unheralded arrival of a brutal moon, the Peninsular and Oriental Steamship Company liner, with the Yunani-sounding name, *Symyrna* or *Cypriana* or something similar (Greek via Oxford via the back streets of Eastern Thrace) and the sleek, billowing shape, with its prow pointed always ahead, now this silent leviathan that was slipping invisibly, impossibly silently, through the dark waters of the magical Arabian Sea, Solomon's Sea, seemed, to Jamil and Rashida, a hugely desirable yet totally impossible dream. 'Chal Diya Caravan'.

They had wrapped as many blankets, towels, jumpers and jackets around their bodies as was physically possible in the confined space, within the cabin of their car, yet sleep remained formless, elusive. Just as he sensed Rashida's breathing begin to subside into a regularity, a depth, that signalled the shallowest ebbs of *neendth*, Jamil heard a sound. It was not unlike an owl's hoot and, at first, he thought that it was coming from his right but then it came again – this time from the left and behind. A series of three perfectly pitched cries, midway between the whine of a big cat and the song of an *ulloo*. Rashida had not woken up. Her breathing had grown deeper and her body was settling comfortably into an attitude of repose – of serenity, almost, he thought, as he gazed down at the side of her cheek, suddenly illumined in the pale moonlight. As she breathed, the tiny, fine hairs of her cheek rose and fell in tiny waves. This was something he had never noticed before. It seemed odd to him that there might be anything about this woman, who had filled his world with light, of which he might yet remain unaware. On the back seat of the car, hemmed in among bundles of dirty clothes, sat the wooden radio Rashida had brought with her. Before they had left Lahore, he had been on the point of arguing with her about it but, then, something, which he still did not understand, had stopped him. He wondered how long it would take for them to learn everything there was to know about each other – how many years – and, then, once they had reached that point beyond which there was nothing new, where the music held no possibility of subtle improvisation, where all the *maqams* lay flat and dead beneath the fingers of the lutenist, whether they might begin to retreat within the confines of their own imaginings, to a place of dust and unreality, to a life of essential solitude. But, then, of course, he thought, since we do not even know ourselves, how can we ever really fully know another person? Ah, Jamil thought, the *falsafa*-mongers, the prophets and seers had wrestled with such things for centuries and no one yet had found a solution. It wasn't something a grown man, a mature indi- vidual, need worry about, especially not if they were stuck in the middle of nowhere with their adulterous lover, in the middle of the Kafiristani night.

The cries now had intensified – as though whatever creature was making them had crept closer to the Ford Popular. And, although Jamil was aware of the possibility of danger in these wild places, there were no rules – yet even that thought gave him an odd feeling of circularity, a sense of appropriateness.

After all, it was they who had broken all the rules, who had burst the bonds of marriage, of respectability – it was they who had crossed from the newly planned cities of the Land of the Pure to the old, deserted marches of Khurasan, land of dead Sufis and wandering drunken kings. They had flown from a state, where love – the various different kinds of love, as fixed, immutable entities – had been directed, by text, social convention and animal instinct, to a place where love was no longer possible or, if it was, then it circled in the darkness, high above the ground, like a plague of vultures, and where it had to be hauled violently from its dream sphere, its moon time. Jamil felt his whole body shudder. Such a terrible love could lead only to madness or worse.

The howling had become constant, a long high-pitched sound with no gaps, no rests, as though whatever inhuman thing was making the sound had no need of breath. Surely, she must awaken. Now, surely, the spell of wildness would break. Jamil forced himself to stop shivering, partly because he thought the movement of his knees and abdomen might accidentally wake up Rashida and partly because any movement there, in the cramped confines of the Ford Popular, was inherently uncomfortable and led to a drop in body temperature that just made things worse.

He had heard the legends about this land, tales spun from the cavernous looms of servants, all of whom, of course, believed absolutely every superstition they had ever heard in their lives. He had imagined that this might have been because of their lack of education or else a certain deficiency in rationality or perhaps because the intense, unbroken darkness, that essential quality of the *gaon* from which they had arisen, the lack of electricity, of sewage disposal, of both the symbols and reality of modernity, had led to strange reversions. But now, as the moonlight billowed and rippled around the bodies of the escaped lovers and as the noise rose to a scream and his heartbeat raced as though he were climbing one of the massive mountains that surrounded them, Jamil realised that it was because the old servants – the poor people of the villages and the fields, who, in desperation, had moved to the *shehron* – had always existed so close to the earth's surface that they knew that the true nature of the interface consisted not of soil and air but of intermittent shades of light and shadow. In this sense, the *gharibon* lived in a place that held no coordinates and where the moonlight shone perpetually and the music played at frequencies beyond human hearing. 'Chal Diya Caravan'.

It took them three weeks to get from the Durand Line to the white cliffs. The journey across the massive plateaux of Iran and then Anatolia, in particular, seemed to take forever. Light years, dark nights. As they travelled westward, the names of the towns became steadily less familiar until, eventually, even the script of the language changed. Both Jamil and Rashida wondered many times whether this epic journey of theirs would be worth it. When the tiredness became overwhelming, when they felt as though they were the only people in the whole universe, when even love had withered in the burning salt flats of the Dasht-e Kavir and the sky and earth had become enemies so that even the slightest touch from another living being would have felt unbearable, at those times, they clung only to the knowledge that there was absolutely no possibility of going back.

The car aged rapidly – new cracks opening up with every hundred miles. It broke down five times and, once, it even half-sank into quicksand. All these forced halts necessitated long sojourns in dust-bowl villages that once had been poetic oases. They were places where philosophers and *shairs* had tripped on light and figs and metaphorical wine and now they rocked and turned with the hollowed-out skulls of wild dogs and the jawbones of mules. In such places, it was difficult to find even a mechanic to repair the car.

They had heard that Persian and Turkish food represented some of the best cuisine in the world yet all they got was stale kebabs in various shapes and sizes. The taste was always the same. It was road food, rough meat, the dog-ends of old goats. There was no joy in such a meal. And there was not much more beneath the stars.

They had sex six times on the journey and each time it was a rapid, animalistic act, quite bereft of the tenderness which had imbued their love-making in the back-street hotel in Lahore. It had become a dry release, a desperate clawing for hope, for connection and, even more than that, for redemption. Deep into the swarming night, they clutched each other's exhausted body along with the papers they had carried, the official documents that would guarantee work for Jamil Ayaan once they reached England. But now, as the howling reached a climax and seemed to subside, only to build again, the wine seemed bitter indeed.

◎◎◎◎◎

In those days, it had been far less difficult to travel all the way from the Indian frontier to the English Channel. Now, a few decades later, Zaf thought, the physical movement wis easy – the mountains and deserts and seas had been conquered. It wis the politics that stopped you – the people. Once again, he thought, Papa wis ahead of me. 'Chal Diya Caravan'.

He got up and paced about as the Talat Mahmood song drifted away into the past. Then he sat down again. But still no sense of ease came to the cubicle. The urge to weep bloated his belly, forced his innards up through his windpipe. Zaf had to cough hard, almost to retch, to get his throat open again. At first, the STOP button didn't respond. Fuckin machines! Minds of their own. Or mibbee they were just tired. He had to try three times.

Welcome back, all ye *Junnunies*. Thought that wis tough? We're no finished yet. Ye'll not able tae switch aff while this soang's playin. Ah'd be willin tae lay a bet oan it. It's an addiction – Junkie Radio. OK, then. Let's get auld again. Not literally, mind you. Auld songs, Ah mean. *Dilon*, ragged, ancient with disuse. How's this fur heartstrings? 'Chalte Chalte'.

Deck B.

> While I was walking . . .
> I came across someone.
> Suddenly I stopped.
>
> The waiting night,
> It will end, sometime.
> These candles
> Are dying down
> As I am burning,
> Fading away . . .

The young Lata's voice, plaintive yet intense, a *trobairitz* voice, singing of a love tragic in its formality, a love that spanned the centuries of darkness and blood, the deep canals of misery.

◎◎◎◎◎

When the couple arrived in Britain, there was little problem finding work – the trade ministers had long been calling for labour from the ex-colonies to help out great *Mata* Inglistan in her time of need – but the work was shit. Literally. Jamil Ayaan, or Mr Khan as henceforth he was to be known, went to the Sewage Works hoping to obtain a post if not the equal of that which he'd had in Pakistan then at least one which might have held the prospect of promotion. But he found himself at the end of a very long queue. This did not put him off, since England was famed for her good queuing sense. Far above the line of men – none of whom were white – a series of jet trails scored across the sky. As he waited in line, 'Chalte Chalte', Zaf's papa marvelled at the manner in which even the clouds in Britain were orderly and straight.

Of course, the reason he had clambered up the arc of the world, all the way to the land of rain and whisky, was because, up there, there were almost no Asians. He had figured that it was better that way. But, by the time he managed to reach the front of the queue, all that was left were jobs in detritus. Not in the theory of waste, not even in the planning of waste management, but in the actual cleaning of the channels through which the sewage of Scotland poured. Jamil felt dismayed for a while but, deep in the night, he had whispered to his new Scottish-registered wife, once a semblance of tenderness had returned to their love-making, that it would be only a matter of time before they would recognise his talents and his education and lift him out of the dirty water through which he was being forced to wade, leptospirosis-and-all, 'Chalte Chalte', day after day after day. The sewage would be diverted through other passageways, in order to allow for the cleaning of valves, ports and so on, but the tunnels were never completely empty and the smell . . . Jamil had often wondered why the British had a reputation for being constipated and now he was finding out just why.

◉◉◉◉◉

Whenever Zaf thought of his papa, the stink of sewage came to his mind. In spite of all the chemicals they used, in spite of the numerous *balti* baths in which his father had showered himself, nothing could ever completely remove the smell of waste from his body. He always said that his best years had been spent wadin around in the detritus of the British Bastards. 'That's what they did to the colonies,' he'd told his new son (something which he had never said to his firstborn), 'they enticed us with sweetmeats and whisky and then they swallowed us whole (without chewing) and, when all the goodness had been digested, they excreted what was left. We are the shit of Empire.'

Zaf thumped his fist down on the console, thumped it hard so that it hurt. Goodbye, 'Chalte Chalte'. Goodbye to youth, Lata. Goodbye to Papa. Goodbye, Deck B.

Ah, sad songs. Remember the auld filums? They used tae be shown at cinemas in Glasgae but those places are long gone noo. Cinemas wi elegant, filigreed balconies an men smokin, thur breath risin like blue angels intae the air. Before ma time, though! They nivir show those auld

classics in the cinemas noo an the new movies . . . ?
Well, thur's nae comparison, right? But it's no sae guid
oan video. Nah! It's like a footba match – it's jis no the
same. Or like love. Ha! Hey, listeners, wu're gettin deep
here, deep in the night. The risky time. Whun things join
up or die. Know whit Ah mean? Whit time is it,
onyweye? Let's see . . . two thirty-four and twelve
seconds. 'At the first stroke . . . beep, beep, beep. Do not
adjust yer sets.' That's ma hobby – checkin the speakin
cloack. Sad, isn't it? Each to their ane, Ah say. Each to
their ane. And whit gets you through the night? Mukesh
mibbee. 'O Jane Wale Ho Sake To LauT ke Anna'.

Deck A. ON button. Self-punishment. Flagellation. Black
monks.

> You, who are leaving, please return.
> A person, who crosses to the other side,
> Never returns

Every time he heard that song, Zaf felt like cryin. The black-
and-white songs always made him remember the old smells
of a seventies' childhood. The sweet scent of rain as it hit the
tarmac – a scent which, as a child, he had hated – now
became transfigured somehow into a feelin of imminent death.
Very strange. Sentimental tosh – jis brain connections, nuhin
more, the west ae Scotland part of him would always retort,
but, during the song, that part of him would remain on hold,
its volume control pushed down, near to zero. It wis not the
stuff that got broadcast that wis important – it wis stuff that
did not. Mukesh and those other great singers had come
along just after the Partition, that great division through the
flesh of the people which, once again, had completely trans-

formed the Indian subcontinent. It had been a painful birth, an agonisin one, with a psychopathic midwife and, at the end of it all, Mother India had rendered unto the world two infant Lands of the Pure. One, to the east, was washed clean in the waters of the Ganga Jumna while the purity of the land that lay to the north-west of the great Golden Temple resided solely in the purity of its people, in their collective virginity. Once, as a child, when he had gazed at a map, Zaf had thought that Pakistan looked like a woman on her knees. It wis the sort of thing which, once noticed, could never be dispelled and so now, whenever he came across a map of the region, no matter how hard he tried to focus on the physical contours of the Hindu Kush or on the innocent pale brown that wis the Thar Desert, the political boundaries would slowly emerge and take over and, after a while, all he could see would be this burqa-clad mendicant woman. Pakistan prayed as his mother had prayed the night she had heard of the death of her own long-estranged mother or, more recently, after his father . . .

> You who are leaving,
> Please return,
> Someday,
> Any day . . .

After the laughter had come prayers. Zaf knew that she had prayed for forgiveness or redemption or peace. Or because she had had no alternative. He sank into the song, one of those from which he had never really escaped.

Earlier that day, when he had arrived at his maa's flat a good few hours before the *Junnune Show* wis due to start, she had been watering her plants. In the absence of her man, Rashida's daily activities revolved around the various hanging baskets, cacti and other plants which she'd scattered around the place in a defined order of which only she was fully aware. Gardenia, aloe vera and things with bizarre, almost Esperanto names like *kalanchoe mirabella* or *spathiphyllum cupido* or *anthurium fiesta*. Zaf had become used to such obscure, Latinate names from the small pieces of card which she kept stuck in the pots, as though to remind the plants themselves of their own genera. All of these could exist only in subtropical temperatures and, day and night, winter and summer, she kept the thermostat turned full up so that, as Zaf entered, he wis hit by an entirely predictable wave of stiflin heat. If he'd been wearin his jacket, he'd have removed it but, since he wasn't, he found himself wipin his brow and beginnin to breathe, like an overheated dog, in a shallower fashion than usual. It wasn't her age that wis drivin her hypothermic – she wasn't really that old – it wis her increasinly fragile association with a land with which she'd had, at best, only a skin-deep relationship. And this wis her attempt to reconstruct the heat of Pakistan. It was her theme park, her micro-Disney. Yet, in Pakistan, as in the southern states of the USA, Zaf thought, the people did everything they could to escape from the fire outside, to spend as much of their lives as possible dwellin in the air-conditioned murk of their drawin rooms. This thing with his mother, the plants and the windows, this wis another strange transmutation.

The noise from the TV had been audible from out on the landin. South Asian satellite channels, all providin a mix of songs, films and news, films, news and songs, news, songs and films. And, in between, as a kind of leavenin substrate, BELLOWIN ADVERTS. LOUD 'N' LOUDER. The box kept her company. She wis as he remembered – her *shalvar kamise*'d, slightly rotund form bent over the green fronds by the window. The door had been unlocked. Zaf's mother had avoided the almost ubiquitous paranoia which most people over a certain age seemed to harbour. A fear of everythin. No, his mother wasn't like that. She had never hidden in tunnels. This retreat into the burnin heat of Pollokshields had been a conscious decision on her part. Perhaps, Zaf thought, as he stood there, watchin her pour water carefully from the spout of her can around the roots of a purple orchid, perhaps this hydroponic hothouse wis her orchestral accompaniment, the green stems her dotted minims, the broad speckled leaves her double-released semiquavers. The symphony issuin, carefully, carefully, as her love wis dispensed in measured volumes. She'd paced herself, had Zaf's *maa*. She wis a costumed, jokin marathon-runner and perhaps now this place had become her green electric orgasm.

She wis wearin a cream-coloured and fairly roomy *shalvar kamise* and flat, embroidered shoes to match. Now, at last, Rashida wis once again able to don clothes which were more than merely functional. And she had always had good matchin sense – it wis one of those family myths that cling to a person throughout their life, sometimes with good reason, sometimes not. The outline of her face in the window light rendered a mood of tragedy to her form. Her long nose wis just a little flared at the ends of the nostrils, as though she was constantly findin her way by smell and, when she closed her mouth, her upper lip just overhung the lower. Her hair, now filigreed with silver and smoothed back against her scalp, he remembered as once bein long, black, silken. In those days, she would wear it bound up in a kind of bun but, when she washed it, she would let it swing before her face and over her breasts and Zaf would pretend to be scared and through the pretence would come the reality of fear and he would shriek and beseech her to reveal her face, to show him that, beneath the curtain of sable hair, it wis, after all, only her. He found himself smilin at the memory. It was as though the person in the magnolia *shalvar kamise*, at whom he was gazin, wis quite different from the one that he held in his mind. Zaf wondered which wis real. Perhaps, on this night, at this time, only the voice of Mukesh really existed.

He wis transfixed by his mother's form as she moved through the bright air. When she had her back to him, she seemed intensely vulnerable and he felt a great wave of melancholy sweep over him. It wis so powerful, this pathos, that he had physically to swallow it down. If he let it take over, like the Devil's touch, it would double him up, wrestle him to the ground *kabbadi*-style and turn him to a breathless, quivering remnant.

That wis what he always felt about people, about gettin close to them, really knowin them. The truth. Aye. You just ended up bein hurt, feelin a little closer to death. Because raw human truth is too hard to deal with, we turn those closest to us into caricature. This allows us to disregard everyone except number one. But what of her desires and fears and dreams? He felt ashamed that, over the years, he had scarcely considered that she might possess these. Oh, yes, it had crossed his mind on an intellectual level but not really, not deep down where it mattered. All that studyin, all those songs, those loves, the physical contact with the different women in his life, the forms of whom seemed harder, cleaner, more defined than that of his mother, what had all of this made him? How had it changed him? And it had changed him, there wis no doubt about that. You couldn't live among words, music and . . . and what? Love, sex, what? He'd been rovin around, lookin for somethin and he didn't even know what it wis! Zilla had been right, he thought. He really wis just a gadfly. There wis nuthin deep about him. Or, if there wis, then he had let it burn away long ago. He had never even glanced into his mother's depths – he had never pierced the pearl. His father had perhaps on that night of jasmine when he had first seduced her, or she him, or perhaps on that long car journey across the tracks of old empires or during the long, dreich nights of return from the sewers but now . . . If she'd been born into a different generation, another life, then . . . who knows?

She spun round, a little surprised to see him. She squinted into the sunshine. The ghost of Mukesh hovered in the background. 'Zaf,' she said, 'is that you?' Her voice had a certain familiarity, the recognition of which can only come after a period of separation. He was silent for a moment. He had been torn from his reverie. She straightened up. Walked over and kissed him on the right cheek. The smell of her perfume recently had become mixed in with somethin else – not sweat exactly, more a slightly sweet smell like that of rottin fruit. It disturbed him. 'What brings you here?' she asked.

He shrugged, then went over and turned the TV off. The soap opera. Narratives of crisis. He'd had enough of those for a lifetime. For a while, anyway. He sat down heavily on the sofa. His parents had nearly always spoken to him in English except when they were angry or upset or when they had forgotten.

'I just thought I'd come and say hello. I'm goin away for a while. Mibbee to the coast. Stay with a friend.'

She came over and sat opposite him, on the hard chair that she'd got for her back, and she put the thin green watering can down. A drop of water dripped on to the tile-topped table. The house was clean as porcelain. 'You're still in that . . . flat? With your friend?' She leaned across and stroked his chin. 'You're growing a beard. Like a *maulvi*.

Maybe tomorrow you'll be marching around with those itchy Jamiat *loag*, quoting Hadiths all day long and claiming your parents did it all wrong. *Jazakallah sharran!*'

Zaf felt anger rise like bile in his chest. It wis wan ae her jokes. Double-edged. Ha-fuckin-ha. 'No, I just haven't shaved. *Maa*, her name's Barbara. Ye know that.' She looked askance. He knew that he would be better to keep his cool, to remain calm.

'You never come to see me any more.'

'I'm here now, aren't I?'

She looked him in the eye and smiled. It was hard to separate those two emotions – calmness and coolness. The latter wis just another betrayal, a lie, a mannerism acquired from this rough, superficial, northern civilisation which meant absolutely nuthin the moment he walked through the door of this house. It wis the antithesis of the music of the great Bengali singer. He smiled back. Her eyes were a tired brown, the skin wrinkled as though she'd been up too many nights or as though she had laughed too much. But, once, they had been full and rich and beautiful and she had sat by the mirror and outlined the edges of her eyelids with a thin black pencil. The monochrome photographs had imparted, or perhaps elicited, a greater richness, a mythic-ness, and Zaf's picture of his mother arose partly from those few old pictures and partly from his own snapshot memories of her standin by the old porcelain sink, singin *filmi* songs as she cooked and washed and cleaned in the sunshine of their mornins together while his papa wis at work beneath the earth's surface.

Sometimes, he longed for those days before walls and adult pride and silly jokes, when the only silences were the rests between notes. Before Zilla and Babs and the others. When music had been spun in air for the beauty of its calligraphy. Courtly love. The watering can dripped on to the tile. Outside, the children's ShielDi yells did not quite break through the foliage.

'I'm making some tea. You want some?' He nodded. She grabbed the can. Got out of her seat, a little too quickly. Groaned.

'Is your back botherin you again?'

She limped towards the kitchen. 'I don't take the pills – they make me sick. I do the exercises every morning but, some days, it's bad. Aie! Getting old. Don't do it, son.' Zaf hissed with laughter to hide the pull of sadness.

As she boiled the kettle, the sound of the radio came from the kitchenette. He went into the hall. Picked up the phone. There wis no tone. He banged it down and tried again. 'The phone's not workin.'

She continued to make the tea, stirring a large pot on the gas. Hot, milky tea. A bellyful. 'It's been off for a few days. I'll need to get it fixed.'

'You've not been cut off?'

'No, no, it's just some fault. I'll ask someone to fix it.'

He put the receiver back on its saddle. Mixed in with the familiar scents of *methi* and 'Spring Fields' air-freshener, the place smelt of old age. That wis it. The rancid smell, that certain kind of sweat. Though she wasn't so old, really. It reminded him of funerals, of the scent which came off dead bodies. Then he realised it wis him that wis stinkin. '*Maa*, I'm goin to have a shower.'

'*Jaldi karo* – the tea'll get cold.'

Zaf turned the water to almost scalding and he burned the night from his skin. Because the bathroom wis just a thin wall away from the kitchenette, he could hear the sound of Radio Sunset, the Middle-England-based Asian station that controlled most of the airwave franchise and which had been founded by some guy with janglin gold bracelets and a big blue swimmin pool in a hot place. 'O Jane Wale Ho Sake To'. Drowned in clarity. Comin up for air.

The stickiness of the night wis beginnin to reek through the pores of the walls and the floor – he could taste it when he licked his lips and when he trailed his tongue over the stubble above and below. Pungent, acrid flats. The cubicle wis divided horizontally into two halves by the brown line of his sweat. Because both floor and ceiling were the same shade of grey, if he bent over and gazed, upside down, at the cubicle, the whole thing became a swirl of steel and, as the blood sank with gravity into the channels of his head, Zaf found it easy, hip-easy, to see the floor as the ceilin and vice versa. It started as a joke, a bored quasi-experiment. But, then, he attempted simultaneously to slot the next compact disc into Deck B and to scribble down the title of the song while half-suspended, balanced the wrong way up, on the swingin, turnin chair. On this night, in the wee box that wis Radio Chaandni and especially in the even weer box that wis *The Junnune Show*, the distinction between night and day, earth and space, sound and structure, had shimmered like a set of anachronistic alchemical algorithms in the face of a brand new number and, now, as Zaf, his *Madness Show* and the music drew toward a place of crossin, a marcher time, the differences seemed to disappear altogether and everythin became fluid. Or, at least, molten.

He pulled the microphone down, bent its back almost to breaking point and spoke from his belly.

OK! Fae oldies tae goldies! This comes fae wan ae Amitabh's better filums. At least, it's better till aroon two-thirds ae the way through, when it starts tae turn silly like aw the rest. The moment when he jumps intae his movie jeep, ivirythin turns upside doon. That wis always the end fur me. The poetry (an aw filums are poetry) gets loast sumwhur aifter that. It faws intae a safe rut. Aye, Hindi cinema hud an opportunity at that point an it blew it. It played safe, folks. Hollywood also plays safe, *samaaen*, although in a quite different manner. But Ah'll nivir forget it. A glimpse of whit might huv been. Ah think ae it often, in the manner ae a *shair*. *Hazrat* Percival. *Kabhi Kabhi*. Ah'll mibbee be able tae make sense ae it aw. 'Kabhi Kabhi Mere Dil Mein'. Or mibbee it's not tae be made sense ae. Mibbee some hings – maist hings – exist in two warulds.

He swung back up again.

Am Ah makin non-sense?

But he'd forgotten to grab the stem of the mike and so he wis speakin into thin air. Thick darkness. Rainwater pourin down the windows, streamin like clear rivers, *daryaon* you could never cross for fear of seein, reflected in their crystal skins, your own *surat*. The heavy *jild* of your past, washin back at you. 'Kabhi Kabhi'. No wonder Amitabh had leapt into that jeep. Even his long legs couldn't have straddled the steep bank of the river, the deep waters of silence into which the poem wis drawin him. Rashida and Jamil had never stopped singin the poem and, by degrees, it had pulled them into madness.

Quickly, Zaf jerked up the mike. Its thin chrome neck wis slippery with sweat from his hands.

OK. Here we go. Kabhi, Kabhi, Kabhi, Kabhi, Kabhi, Kabhi, Kabhi, Kabhi, Kabhi.

Same river, different moon. It had torn them apart.

Deck B. Button-*jee*. On!!

Love-music. Goldies.

'Kabhi Kabhi'. The tale of a tragic, poetic love, a flickerin flame in a niche.

> From time to time,
> The thought of you
> Comes into my heart

Goin down. Suddenly, Zaf longed for the Ayrshire coast, with its retired colonists, the pieds noirs of Alba and its dank jardinières and its exceedingly rich, by-appointment-only complementary medicine specialists. *Doctor No*. Mysterious sports cars, driven by tweeded, elderly grouse shooters, who all seemed to speak as though they'd had cotton wool stuffed into their mouths at birth, but really there wis nuthin ridiculous about them – they were really retired special agents. Trained killers. As a child, he'd been taken there on a fairly regular basis. So regular that, for a long time, he'd grown sick of the thought of the place and had avoided its open coastline, its clean, white ice-cream parlours. He had preferred the inland lochs up north towards the old Mounth line. The sea held too many questions. It wis a swirlin mirror in which you would never be able to hold an image long enough to grasp it. But, then, one of his friends had moved to the balmy seafront and he'd gone to visit and, after the long gap of adolescence, Zaf had marvelled again at the dark bulk of Arran and the Kabbalistic triangle of Ailsa Craig, the island which did not really exist, unless you were a bird.

AMITABH WIS NOT A BIRD

He had stood naked on a summer's mornin in his mother's plastic bath-cum-shower, with burnin water trailin down his body, and suddenly it had all been back, right there, the whole fuckin night. Three long months of it. He had segued 'Kabhi Kabhi' and then the song that wis on now. Deck A. 'Sutrix'. Talvin Singh's swirlin, subconscious tablas. The water dripped off his body and his body wis a drum skin beatin in the foetid, poundin rhythm, black as fishes' bowels, that emerged from lakes deep within the *jungle ki kokh* of Madya Pradesh. The womb of India. The water wis swirlin up around his ankles and wis pourin out over the bathroom carpet. The *Madness Show* wis out of control. It had run beyond him and wis spiralin into space and into the brains of amphibians. Straddled minds. The plug wis stiff and, when he yanked it out, the chain snapped off. Wordless screams.

'What happened to you?' she asked as they sipped the tea.

Doodh puthee. The tea wis thick, bulky, sweet and re-minded him of childhood illness and winter days. Howlin winds outside the glass. Inhuman, Siberian forces. But the wind wis in his head. 'Sutrix'.

Zaf bit off some biscuit. Spoke with his mouth full. Sat back against the sofa. He made a conscious effort to relax. Not easy with Vladivostok cyclonin in his skull.

'You smelled like you'd been down the sewers.'

'Very funny, *Maa*. It's the radio station – my show.'

'You're still doing that?'

'It had a three-month run.'

'Does it pay?'

'It's finishes tonight. Tonight will be the very last night.'

'You haven't shaved, it looks like, for three months.'

'Oh, for God's sake.'

He got up. Swallowed the tea hard and it burned in his chest, his stomach. Ripped the linin. Fuck. It always ended like this. Did she not know that life wis too fuckin short? She should know. Everybody spent their lives, crawlin around in dark tunnels, occasionally comin up for air or else to die. Or did they all have the desire to live unrequited, forever blind, trapped inside their own egos, windin down into their cist sheets.

He banged his cup down. Stomped across the room. Turned around. 'Ah'm leavin.'

'But you've only just arrived.'

'Yeah. That's how long Ah can stay here. Mibbee that's why Ah nivir come.'

Her face fell. He looked away. Focused on the *spathiphyllum cupido*. He knew that she would have aged a whole decade. Next to the *spathiphyllum cupido* wis a stupid pink porcelain decoration comprisin a figure which seemed to emerge from a cornucopia of crenellated leaves. Some half-nude nymph with a kind of throw or toga draped around her lower trunk. Or mibbee a sari. *Goree*, of course. It wis OK like that, up on the shelf, burned into stone. It wis OK to worship or despise but the rule wis you never screwed your gods or your devils – it brought out the demon in you. And that wis what all this wis about – all this porcelain shite, the glass, the quadrangles, the culs-de-sac, the constant, overarchin darkness of *izzat* or, more particularly, the incipience of its loss.

He wondered why in hell he'd returned on this mornin. Perhaps his judgement wasn't what it should have been. Any sense of lightness he had felt on his way across the river had been completely banished and, in its place, Zaf felt an immense weight, the squat pillar of a *mandir* stuck right through his gut. This house disembowelled him every time. The armour he had acquired the hard way, over the years, melted after about ten minutes of porcelain teapot *doodh puthee*. He wis like some demon in a myth who could never return to the land from whence he had come but who wis doomed forever to try. 'Sutrix'. He would never again fit into his old, perfect shoes. He didn't ask why she hadn't listened to any of his shows. 'Does it pay?' That was typical. His nurse wis keepin him. His woman. He wis spongin off his *goree*. He had slipped into *joothay* the *goree* had fashioned with her magical, albino fingers. Everyone had to be a shoemaker. That wis what she meant. A sponger, a user, a waster. What wis so wrong about that? They'd sponged off our people for long enough. Bled us dry. It wis time for a little mutual recompense. His *maa* would've understood that, the revenge aspect, but not in the way it applied to her own son. The life he led wis too openly lazy, too brazenly Farangoid, to have been granted her approval. He knew that, to his *maa*, Babs and he lived like rats in a sewer, humpin each other at every opportunity. Spunk and hog grease everywhere. *Ganda, ganda, ganda.* He heard the clink of cup on saucer. He turned around. Her back wis hunched over the table. A powerful wave of pity almost took him off his feet. He went and sat back down. Smiled weakly at her. Poured her some more tea.

'Stay for lunch,' she said. Her voice was steady, unemotional. She had learned to pace herself. They didn't talk.

He wanted to open a window. Chuck out the plants, soft green suckker-fuckkers. Listen to the fired earthenware smash on the pavement. 'Sutrix'.

Her lips were a question mark. Why had they grown so alien? Why had he left her kitchenette to roam like a dog around the dung heaps of the big, white city? Why did he wear jeans all the time? Why wis he rude, crude, uncivilised, like these Westerners? Farangi – Franks, as though it was still the fuckin Crusades. Why wis he growin older by the minute, by the beat? *Queu, queu, queu?*

He shrugged. Ran his fingers over the stubble on his chin. There were no words between them. No answers. Hadn't been for a long time. Not really, not since the music had sewn its notes across both their lives. 'Sutrix'. 'When she's gone, then you'll know . . .' Somewhere, deep inside him, there wis a vague plexus of undifferentiated love and, whenever he sensed its presence, the yearnin would almost tear apart his fabric. Ear to ear. 'Kabhi, kabhi, I remember the love which once was pure but which, long since, has been washed away in the puddles and tunnels of Glasgow's dark land.' But that wis just immature, infantilist male, garishly tableau'd. Too many Bolly flicks. Too much gigglin Govinda and trendy Shah Rukh, of the *theen* expressions, and that heavily-arched, broodin guy whose name Zaf couldn't recall but who resembled the young werewolf Oliver Reed. His mother had a name, which he hardly dared intone, and she had a past beyond, behind, the photographs. She'd had an education and could've become somethin more than simply a mother but, in those days, such adventurousness had been rare, difficult. Frowned upon by the frownin ones. The leap across hemispheres had been the end of her own life and Zaf's birth had been the last nail in the coffin. From the moment she had stepped on to the shores of this island, she had become less than real. Her life had become transposed on to his and on to that of his father. She had turned to celluloid, she had no face. And they had done this, Zaf and his papa. And all the other papas, right back to wheaten Aadam. And even he had had his Lilith. His dark, silent fuck. But *Hazrat* Layla *Anha* wis stronger than all of them. All the bearded prophets had quailed at her strength. She wis bigger than the sky. Bigger than God. 'Sutrix'.

Now Zaf needed to seek out another love, a different kind of love where he would no longer sit at the climax of the song. 'Kabhi Kabhi' – the alternative version. The real version. No jeeps. No runnin away. 'Sutrix' mibbee. It might be a beginnin of sorts. You could never really tell where the beginnin would be until the end.

He had got up to kiss her. At the last minute, she had averted her lips. Her cheek had tasted dry, rough, unmade-up. Her arms had remained at her sides. She had smelled of a perfume that had been the thing a hundred years ago. Nuthin wis the same. His hand had touched her flank and she had seemed about to crack, like porcelain. Broken leaves. The thought of her terrible fragility cut him up and it wis all he could do to gulp back the tears. In silence, she had turned away her lips, her mouth, because they would have tasted of the grave. Sentimental bugger, he thought. Too many soaps. Too much music. For a moment, he felt he understood those stern iconoclasts who had smashed musical instruments and torn up score sheets. Ripped skin. Burned leather. 'Sutrix'.

For a moment, he felt the insane desire to boost the signal. He went over to the big red switch by the wall and moved his fingers up to within a centimetre of the plastic. It wis somewhere he had never been before. No reason to. It felt hot – as though, like some cheap whore's cunt, it wis drawin him in, encin him. He pulled away at the last second. He mopped the sweat out of his eyes with the back of his hand but the bones felt hot against the jelly-and-skull of his orbits. Boostin the signal would be like droppin a pebble from the Devil's Bridge. It wis spreadin madness.

Those heavy sad songs were fadin at last an Zaf needed tae change the mood.

OK, *Junnunies*, that wis the end ae the tragic stuff. Ah wouldnae want ony ae ye tae go aff an jump intae a jeep now, would Ah? Stay wi me, people, an Ah'll take ye tae places ye've nivir dreamed ae. *Darone khawb*. Cause Ah figure that onywan listenin tae me noo, tae this crazy, this *junnune*, show, must be haufweye *paagal* themseles. *N'est-ce pas?* Whit's wi the French? Ye see, good listeners, the night, Ah'm the man ae a thoosand tongues. 'Don't be disgustin, Zaf!', Ah hear ye say. Or even if ye cannae say it, ye think it. Ye see, that's part ae the problem. If ye cannae say whit ye think, then ye're already haufweye doon the *saRak* tae perdition. *Azab jahannum*. Enough lecturin. Next track.

Zaf fingered his playlist. It wis just the length of a *kisaan*'s hand and, even with writin vertically as well as horizontally, he had run out of space. So he flipped it over and started to scribble down song titles on the other side. His writin had changed since midnight – from bein not bad to now bein like some kind of hieroglyphics. Different times, other scripts. Priests high on asp juice. A thousand years from now, no one will know. Our dreams, our nightmares, our everythin, will be as dead as the breath we exhale. Och, fuck that. Fuck that stuff about bein in the gutter. He needed to get out of this city. It wis killin him.

A long, long fall. Whoosh!!! Slam!!!
  The 13th Floor Elevators: Holy Acid – in the desert. Silver Towers. The Lone Star State. 'Slip Inside This House'. One star is all you need. Mushroom Love.

Deck B.

The quiverin, ever so slightly insane sound of the theremin made the walls of the cubicle shudder. It wis as though the old church wis rememberin some clandestine meetin of the Glasgow Theosophical Society – the high frequency voice of the invited speaker, that old mystical Russian con man perhaps. Nineteen Eighteen. The singer's tremulous voice, hauled back from the nineteen sixties, Anno Domini. Mad Roky. Perhaps the two, the Kaukaf Georgian and the mad-eyed Texan, had been the same, all along. Austin, Texas and Glasgow, Scotland, by way of the Old Man of the Mountains. On ghost frequencies, distance didn't figure. Ninety-nine-point-nine meters FM. Everythin wis *junnuned* into existence. It wasn't quite as crazy as the total schizophrenic madness of Red Crayola's *Parable of Arable Land* but it wis still howlin Caucasian avant-garde. Wondrous noise. Zaf let his eyes close and he began to spin.

Whenever the family had deigned to return, it had seemed a clandestine, shamefaced journey. Their sin had grown with the longitudes until, by the time they had touched down at Lahore airport, both his parents' faces had looked as though they were about to face a High Court trial. Which, in later times, they might have had to do but, durin the seventies, the laws in Pakistan had not yet descended into those of Old Israel and so, as long as they had managed to keep out of *sharif* society, they had managed to remain safe. Zaf had always thought that, apart from the desert areas, Pakistani meta-geography consisted essentially of icebergs and moun-tains. They were everywhere if you looked. The average, middle-class family (though, in a land of extremes, the concept of average wis hard to come by) might well have secreted, say, a couple of rogue abortions, a loaded *pistole*, at least one large financial scandal and, possibly, a minor drug problem. And that wasn't countin the teacup whisky parties and the *dubeez* prostitution that went on in every second *mehman khana* – the closer to the gleamin white buildings of the National Parliament the guesthouse lay, the more likely it wis to be an eggs-on-toast brothel. Zaf figured that, apart from mibbee cotton an heroin, whorin, of one sort or another, must be one of the country's largest sources of income – except that, of course, it wouldn't be declared. It wis the same in ScotPak society. And it wis different. Here, it wis all icebergs. The sort that sank ships. Nuthin wis fixed and the community wis so small that, if you had a problem, there wis nowhere to run except into yourself. And the bergs kept poppin up, just when you least expected them. Zilla wis an iceberg and so wis his *maa*. Secrets held power and they had it. His *maa* had lived her life below the waterline while Zilla, dear, dark, totally fucked-up Zilla, had exploded out of the sea very early on. But, essentially, they were both the same. They sweated tragedy. Zilla had been overwhelmin – it had been like ridin a rocket. Babs wis more subtle. Her power over him came from her maturity, her balance, her rootedness. And she wis white. When he wis with Babs, he felt complete.

The sound of the theremin and Roky's tremblin voice seemed to build the sense of unreality, the feelin that the cubicle walls did not really exist – that stone wis water and music stone.

Sometimes, Rashida would sit in the bathroom and weep and sing simultaneously and he had known why. He had sensed it. But, then, he hadn't deserted his family for a man and his crimes had not yet been burned deeply enough into his soul to destroy it. While she'd sung, Rashida must've thought that she had been on her own but Zaf had often listened, both as a young child and later sometimes as well. When she'd thought he had gone out with his *avara-gurd* pals, he would kneel beyond the jamb of the door and listen to the words of sorrow and loss – of perpetual parting at frontiers which, once crossed, could never be recrossed; of children lost by chance in trains which had left the station just a moment too soon; of the ghosts of long-dead mistresses who nightly cast themselves from the ramparts of Mughal castles; and of the general sense of tragedy that had hovered over her life right from the first day she had met Jamil Ayaan. It would have been impossible to have slipped into that kind of feelin in Scotland – as impossible as love in the rain. Here, thought Zaf, it would be a deep kiss and then a quick drunken screw – that way, there would be no danger of tragedy ever catchin up with you. Mibbee that was why life here had become so fast – mibbee it wis because everybody wis so bloody keen to escape the fate which, sooner or later, would be theirs in any case.

That could've been Zilla's motto – run away and keep runnin. She'd escaped from somewhere in Battlefield and had gone as far as she could go. Back to the East End where she'd always felt at home. And she'd holed up in some stinkin bedsit on a street where big-bellied guys wi pink skin would hang out of windows and pee into half-full cans of cheap lager. Wee guys with earrings and number-wan haircuts – they were the salt and scum of the earth. Celtic supporters. He remembered walkin the gauntlet through these guys, the first time he'd been to the flat. It had been rainin, as it always wis, and they'd run all the way from the bus stop to the street on which she lived. Garngad Street. The auld East End that had gone from dirt-poor bothies to dirt-poor tenements and where, once, the city fathers had turned a country house into a loony bin – Garngad Asylum. The asylum wis long gone but it seemed as though the inmates had hung around. Zaf had been used to dunderheids, neds and the like but this wis totally different. It wis as though he wis in another country. As though, somewhere along the bus route, they had been taken backward in time and now were half-runnin, not through the Glasgow, City of Architecture, City of Culture, City of Kak, but alang the roads of somethin from Dickens's time but without the corny consciousness. It wis not so much faces at windows (no danger, here, of net curtains and aspidistras) as faces through windows. When he glanced at the people, they seemed flat – as though their features had somehow become rubbed over like charcoal on paper. He couldn't tell one from another. A couple of guys haunted each close entrance as though they might've been on the verge of somethin and it wouldn't be enlightenment. All along, Zaf felt there wis somethin wrong – not the dog shite runnin down the walls, not the imminent violence, not even the silence broken only by the sound of the rain hittin the tarmac – there wis some other terrifyin thing which he couldn't quite put his finger on . . .

Her flat – which she shared with three others – wis a rundown council shithole. Three floors up, dampness streamin, like spunk, down the walls and the swayin stink of piss an shit everywhere. Like so many of these places, Zaf remembered, it would've been constructed durin the nineteen seventies – the 'Shoddy Decade' when everythin had been fallin apart and when the architecture had been eloquently designed to reflect this. It wis no wonder that almost no buildings from that time were still standin. It occurred to him that, in a hundred years, when they would come to look for examples of the architecture of the period, they would find none. There would be a great white blank where the mid-twentieth century had been. But it wis while he wis sittin in the kitchen – the only part of the entire tip where the smell of fries outweighed the stink of excreta – that he realised, with a kind of a cosmic bump, just what it wis that wis missin from the whole place. There wis no rhythm to the street.

A dusty frontier post. He could see it. The red wine mibbee. Metaphorical or not, those dervishes had had a point. Nineteen-fifties' magazines. The Geographical Society, spiritual descendants of the Theosophists, exotic hunters with elongated portable lenses. Hip, hip, here we go again! Metempsychosis. Guards in green uniforms, Brylcreemed hair. British but not British. The skins still looked as though they had been sloughed off by the Angraise, twelve years earlier, and then donned assiduously (there must surely have been some slim, humble *derzi* plyin his transfigurin trade of skin alchemy on some burnin-gun corner in Peshawar), by Punjabis, Sindhis, Bengalis, Pathans, Baluchis, Baltis, Kalash, Chitralis and all the rest, but, underneath, everythin had changed. The uniform wis just a camouflage, a veneer. Strip off the cotton and buckram and wool, the golden pips and strips and braids and what you got wis desolation, howlin wolves, a cold moon.

It wis a world away from Zilla and the rain and the street with no music and yet Zaf felt that, somehow, the two were linked. Not in any direct way, not like the way in which he breathed from his lungs out into space. The seams of human tragedy ran far deeper than that. His fall into Zilla had been a gradual one, like the sinkin of notes into a symphony. But, when you sink into a person, Zaf thought, you are really tumblin down a black hole into their world. Their muscles mould you and you are burned by their sun. Their horizon becomes your horizon.

The street with no music, the barren slopes of Afghanistan. His mother should have turned back there and then. But it had been too late. Already, she had crossed the mountains and had reached Glasgow. Her voyage had ended the moment her heart had decided, between flutters, that she would follow Jamil Ayaan even unto the gates of *jahannam*. She had taken the big break and it had broken her. Right there, on the crisp, late winter's mornin when they had first met, that had been the moment. Everythin had been triggered by a look, a phrase, a sleight of hand and, at some level, she had chosen it all.

Zaf thought that he had never known when to decide that the act of taking a particular path might or might not be important. But Ah wis always an amateur, he thought. Ah never possessed the art of livin. Only the artifice. He had drifted into Zilla and then, when he had touched the edge of her abyss, he had panicked and run. And who could have blamed him? What had been an exploration had grown into a demon king. Maharaja *Khashkhash*. He had watched it creep, like a shadow, over Zilla's body. Another, a far better, lover – King Heroin. They used to say, on the street with no music, that, at the end, a junkie would lose their shadow. They had seen it, in the urine-soaked, pus-drenched madness of the night – with their needle-bitten bodies, they had seen it. And he had seen it, too.

It wis night-time summer in the East End. A rare, almost heretical, occurrence. The heat rolled in thick waves up the dashed pebbles of the walls, over the jungle of satellite dishes, and sank down again into potholes in the tarmac. Nobody had fans – the shops had sold out on the first day – and people just sweltered and drank. He woke up, stiff from lyin on the floor on a buggered mattress, and found himself bathed in light. He wis closest to the window and he realised that the moonlight wis streamin, like goats' milk, in through the glass. He wis naked and must have felt hot durin the night because, at some point, he had thrust off the sheet. His body glowed in the pale light, the bony protuberances accentuated like in a Beardsley print. The sweat lay in tiny droplets on his skin.

She lay with her back to him. He could hear her slow breathin. One day, he thought, she won't be breathin and she will have she have OD'd and then I'll have to go and ID her body. A mortuary slab, silver and white with taps like cake decorations. He pushed the thought away. Gently, he lifted the sheet off her. His hand touched the small of her back but she did not awaken. Narcotic sleep wis a deep one. Her skin wis smooth, burnin. As Zaf peeled off the cotton, he watched the moonlight creep over her limbs, her back, her breasts. Her body wis sleek like that of a porpoise.

On the wall opposite, he watched the shadows. Then he dropped the sheet on to the floor. He arched over her back, gazed at her face. She had assumed that strange, expressionless state which he remembered. The state of fugue that she would attain after a hit. He fell back slowly and let his eyes drift into the distance. Glanced up at the wall. The peelin wallpaper, the stains of seepin damp, the holes like gunshot wounds. Halfway up, a cheap print lay askew and its frame cast a long shadow in the shape of a finger across the wall. The picture wis of a small girl with long dark hair and in her hair wis a flower. A white flower. The girl wis smilin. He felt himself dissolve into her smile. It wis then he realised that she had no shadow. God. He looked back down at Zilla's body, caught the fall of her breast as she exhaled in the moonlight, the sweep of her shoulder and then he glanced up at the wall, at the child grinnin, off-angle. He froze. The sweat solidified into goose pimples.

His hand felt like lead. It wouldn't rise. Then it did and he waved it slowly about in the moonlight. Watched its shadow move. Brought it down so that the tip of his index finger just touched the hillock of her pelvis. He wis shiverin. His hand trembled. The contact wis electric. She snaked like a wire through his body. He forced himself to look at the wall. He saw his hand poised there and below it . . . nuthin. Just the girl, her unchangin face. He wondered who she had been. Imagined her, old now and incontinent in some flea-bitten nursin home where no one knew that she wis still hangin on the wall. Ten green bottles, ring-a-ring-a-roses . . . He pulled his hand away.

He wis tremblin all over. Wis aware of the moon and of her slow breathin. He knew her pupils would be tiny, black zeros. He did not turn to check. Let it go to hell. He pulled the sheet back up from the floor and slipped it over his head and he stayed that way until the first slivers of day slipped in through the glass when, eventually, he fell asleep again. Later, when at last he got up, Zaf wis no longer certain which part of the night had been dream and which waking reality. His head felt light, as though he had been awake the whole time, and his skin itched. The music had changed again. Somethin loud and discordant.

'Ah want out,' he said as they stood between the mantelpiece and the coffee table. The tattered residues, incongruous now, of a flat which once had been designed for families to live in. She wis facin the peeled-off wall.

'Oot? Oot ae whit?'

'Yeah. Out ae this.'

She turned. He looked at the carpet. It wis threadbare, greasy, the legacy of too many trainers an late-night cairry-oots and, every so often, the pattern wis punctuated by the odd cigarette burn.

'Ye mean me – ye want oot ae me?'

He looked sideways, out the window. There wis no curtain

here, either. Just one sheet of glass between him and the silence. 'Yeah.' His voice sounded small and seemed to come as though he wis speakin from the end of a long tunnel. He turned towards her.

'Yeah. Ah'm leavin.'

She did not reply but knelt over the table and picked up her fag packet. Searched about for the lighter. Then gave up. 'Gotta light?'

He shook his head, slowly. Then he exploded. 'Ah'm sick ae yer fags an yer dope. Light yer ane fuckin fag.'

She flung the cigarette down and deftly stepped on it, crushed it intae the carpet. Diamonds. The carpet pattern. Seventies. Slade, shite housin, yabba-dabba-fuckin-doo. Before his time. Just. He wis aware that she wis starin at him, gangsta-style. He could feel the heat on his forehead in the place, right between the eyes, where she wis tryin to burn a hole in his face. Zilla had always been a gangsta. He refused to look back. He felt himself becomin aroused. Fuck. He shrugged and turned away. Outside, everythin wis silence. People here didn't get up till after twelve, sometimes even later. Sometimes, they never got up at all. She had moved closer to him and he could feel her breath hot on his neck.

'Ye just cannae handle it,' she sneered. 'Ye're a fuckin coward. You'll end up like yer faither, livin in the sewers.'

He swung round. 'Oh, aye! That's rich, comin fae you, ye fuckin whore! Ah don't want tae end up like you, wi yer punters an yer dope. Fuckin great life, that. Oan the game. Only it isnae a fuckin game.'

'Don't tell me it's no a game. Ah'm the one livin it, no you. You were nivir livin onyhin. You're jist an amateur. A coward.'

'Amateurs stay alive.'

'Good line. You're full ae good lines. No much else. Onyweye . . .' She became suddenly coquettish. 'Onyweye,

Ah can earn five times what you do in the space ae an oor. Wan oor.' She measured the words as though she were layin out time on a table top. Outside, the sound of bottles smashin on tarmac broke through the mornin air. It wis a different sound from that of windows bein broken. Sometimes he would think it wis the singin of Garngad birds – much in the same way that a cat's cry in the night might be confused with that of a baby. He looked her full in the face. 'At least Ah've still got a shadae.'

He regretted this as soon as it had left his lips. She laughed an it wis the kind ae croakin, cynical sune which he hud sometimes heard, late at night, echoin doon the waws ae the street-wi-nae-music. He hud imagined it would be oan accoont ae some failed deal or other – a deal wi life mibbee. She moved towards him. Her eyes wur empty. Wolf's eyes. He tried tae slip backwards, away fae her, but thur wis only the waw at his spine. He glanced up at the ceilin an she hud him by the neck. He felt her body press against his. He tried tae wriggle away but, even then, even oan that mornin of his departure, his attempts fell away like the skins ae losers an he could smell the stink ae opium seethe through her pores intae his muscles, an, sumwhur in the backgroond, above him, below him, he thought he heard the sound ae sumhin comin doon fast.

Discords. Luvin, dancin.

'Will ye, won't ye? Ah'm goannae make ye. Wan day, Ah'll come back, an Ah'll fuckin make ye. Don't turn yer back oan the night, Zaf, cause Ah'll be there, in the shadaes. Ye're fucked.' An auld word. An aulder profession.

Helter, helter, helter skelter

And then she hud traced the blades ae her nails too gently

along the saft skin ae his cheeks. And she hud rammed his heid against the peelin, seventies' wallpaper an she had fingered the buttons ae his jeans an pushed hersel up aginst him, aw the while whisperin, almost singin, 'Wan day, Zaf, when ye're no lookin, Ah'll creep up behind ye. Ye cannae escape me, Zaf – Ah'm yer shadae. Ah'm yer soul.'

An aw the while, he had been tryin tae chase doon the music which couldnae huv been comin fae the street – cause Garngad Street hudnae run wi ony music since the asylum had vanished – but he could feel the dark stane bloacks ae the madhoose tear shreds fae his back as he spiralled doon in some deid lunatic's dream an he had known then, as he'd swum aroon in the thick, boilin opium waves, that sumhin inside ae him wis slowly bein broken as she almost fucked him against the wa between the windae an the door. Haufweye doon the slide, a skull hud cracked and would nivir be whole again. Two soangs, playin simultaneously.

Yes

Yes

Yes

Yes

Yes

Yes

Yes

Yes

Yes

Yes

Yes

Yes

The last echoes ae the soang ebbed wi the blood that wis poundin through his heid an his airms an, jist tae try an cool himsel doon, he went an washed himsel in the sink an then he left. But it didnae work cause the heat hud slipped oot an spread acroass the whole city. 'You're Gonna Miss Me'. Mad, screamin, chemical Roky. Acid theremin voice. The ghosts ae Garngad singin bass in solo harmony. We are legion.

As he almost ran doon the street, Zaf thought he heard her laugh again but then the sune wis swallowed by the noise ae birds leavin.

He opened his eyes. His heart wis beatin like the leg of a beatbox and he had forgotten which songs he'd been playin or, at least, he had forgotten puttin the discs in. Somewhere, in there, had been The Beatles' 'Helter Skelter', like in the middle or mibbee through the spaces between the notes. The swayin slow time. The discs were slippin an slidin over one another, silver on silver. He gazed down at his palm. The lines were like waves, changin all the time. An effect of the light or else of the darkness. Yet the movements of his own body were becomin alien to him. He wis outside of himself or inside of himself or somethin. The last of The 13th Floor Elevators slipped away, out of the old house, and Zaf could feel its seepage more definitely than he wis able to feel his own legs. He needed to speak, to bring himself back. To return from the suffocation of the cist. OK. Go. They don't know jackshit. But he did.

Hi there, ma people, ma buddies, *meray doston*, ma fellow loons. *Salaam alaikum, sat sri akaal, namaste ji, halo ma-tha. Ji, ji, ji, Octoober kaboother*, that wis 'Slip Inside This House' and 'You're Gonna Miss Me' by a band that naebdy will huv heard ae cawd The 13th Floor Elevators an, in between sumwhur, sumhow, The Beatles' 'Helter Skelter'. Dunno how that happened but it did.

This place hus a mind ae its ane. Onyweye, *halo ma-tha*! That wis Gaelic fur 'Hello!' Now ye know. Ah'm full ae facts. Ye get only the truth at wan meenut tae three oan this boilin, broilin, seepin, slidin summer's night. Soon, Ah'll be hovin ye dancin in circles, roon an roon an roon, like in those Heilan reels, ye know the wans, the *raqs* ye didnae want tae do at school but which, unless ye sported a pyramidal beard or a *hijaab* (or baith!), ye hud tae dance or be damned furivir like the banshees an vampires ae Alba. Hoat *siller*.

He wis flippin, fur fuck's sake. Mibbee they'd all fallen asleep. Mibbee he'd fallen asleep. Again.

OK, three a.m. Welcome tae the News 'n' Weather an tae the music ae the sensible universe. Welcome, the nutters ae the waruld.

THREE A.M.

He felt light-headed and the sweat lay cold beneath his T-shirt. He forced himself to breathe more slowly as he walked around the edges of the cubicle like it wis a cage and he wis a big cat. A paper tiger. A deep, rhythmical pumpin wis comin up through the floorboards. He could feel rather than hear it. Techno, he thought. It might transmit and be broadcast over the airwaves. A pulse beneath a pulse. What the hell. It wis the last night. He felt the sudden desire to get out. To simply walk away as he had done that mornin, five years ago, when he'd left Zilla. He'd needed to escape then, to save his life or his sanity or his soul. He had felt himself fallin deeper and deeper into Zilla's existence and he knew that, if he hadn't left after that last time, then he might never have been able to. No matter how degraded he'd felt when he'd been with her, he'd been powerless to resist the hunger which he'd had for her. Zilla wis his devil dust. You couldn't dabble with Zilla. Not like you could with a white girl. Two dead babies. It wis enough. He had never gone back to the East End after that – except once or twice on the train to Edinburgh when he had kept his eyes buried in a book or else had turned his Walkman up to full volume so that the passengers on either side of him had begun to shift about in their seats and give him dirty looks but he hadn't cared and had only turned it down again once the train wis out of Glasgow. Time for talk.

Boom, boom, boom, Ah'm running oot ae words. Ivir get like that? Ivir hit the *raat ka dil*, the point ae nuhin, when thur's jist braith an silence?

He put his lips right up to the mesh of the mike so that he could almost taste the iron. He inhaled and exhaled a few times, slow and loud.

Don't turn aff yer sets – it's no the *mohalla* perv. It's me, Zaf – that's zed ay eff – an Ah'm blowin oot ma *ruh* at yous aw oan ninety-nine-point-nine FM an, as ye may huv guessed by noo, if ye're crazy enough tae still be awake oot there in the real waruld which is no really the waruld, this is the *Junnuuuune Show* oan ninety-nine-point-nine meters FM an we're broadcastin oan that wondrous an excitin an pioneerin multicultural, multi-ethnic, polyglottal stop ae a radio station, Radio Chaandni. Aye!

He drew back, placed his right hand on his heart and sang into the mike in a fake crooner voice.

> Mister Moonlight, come to me, be mine,
> In a deep, deep vat of wine!

Sorry, *samaaen*, *maaf kijiye*, Ah'm jist a wee bit oot ae practice. Ye'll miss me when Ah'm goan, so ye will. An if ye don't, then why not? Shushshsh! Be khushshshsh! Smooth music. Saft oan the ears, hard oan the hairt. Earlier, we played a tribute to Talat *Sahib*, the King of the *Ghazal*, 'Chal Diya Caravan' – 'The Caravan is Leaving'.
    Yeah, we're goin even mellower noo wi Mister Mukesh. This'll take ye back. And then, aifter that, some other stuff . . .

Fuck. He wis losin it. Words.

Don't worry aboot themorra – jist live, breathe – that's
whit Ah think. *Shayad* that's kind ae what aw these
soangs are aboot, isn't it? Whether it's LA California,
Austin Texas, Mumbai India or Karachi Pakistan. Or
even Glasgae Scoatland. Scoatland, in Urdu, is a wee man
in a coracle, croassin the ocean. Ahoy there! Aye. But
that's a dangerous philosophy. Mibbee that's whit we
need – a wee bit ae danger. But how can ye huv jist a
wee bit ae danger? Ony real risks huv tae be big or
they're no risks at aw. Ye know whit Ah'm talkin aboot.
Some ae ye came fae the *gao* an made it here in Glasgae.
And thur's nuhin wrong wi that. All power tae you! But
some ae you didnae make it an that's life and it's hard
and ye're bleedin an thur's nuhin you or anyone else can
do aboot it . . .

Fuck. Fuck. Fuck.
    He rammed the switch down. Needed air. Went over to the
window. Pushed. It wis stuck. He looked around, desperate.
He felt his nose wis blocked, his throat wis shuttin off . . .

Come, beloved, you have to go.

Behind a tape machine, he found a metal rod which he
jammed through the handles of the window and usin the
heels of his hands, he rammed the rod upwards. It seemed
obscene, somehow, to be doin this in the middle of a lush
Mukesh song – it seemed to betray a lack of respect. But he
wis losin it. The sash weights clunked inside the wood as
though they hadn't been moved for decades and, millimetre
by millimetre, the window groaned open. Zaf stuck his head
out and tried to slow his breathin. The rain had eased up but
the air wis still cool and damp and his face felt like a flame.

He closed his eyes and let the fire subside.

He wis in a car, an old Austin Princess saloon, the model that wis shaped like an early school calculator circa nineteen seventy-seven, but without the buttons, and it wis dark green, the colour of crocodile-skin – as in Louisiana swamp not Monte Carlo – shoes. But, like everythin in Scotland, it wis second-hand or mibbee third-hand and mibbee the paint had been sprayed on by some previous owner. A cheap lot. His papa had bought the hulk because, at that time, everyone wis buyin cars. White folk were also flyin off on Spanish holidays but, of course, Asians didn't need either holidays or sex. They could make do with a journey from Glasgow to the far north, to the Nordic pole, to the end of the land – Balloch, Luss, Tarbert, Crianlarich, Tyndrum – and then into the big country – Glencoe, Fort William, Fort Augustus, Inverness, the Black Isle, Wick, John o'Groats, Dunnet Head. Aye, they should rest and be thankful. In Zaf's memory, the time of day on this journey seemed fixed at sunset. All three hundred miles. Lookin back on it, the rickety old Princess would've taken a long day to cover the roads that wound around the banks of the vast, luminous lochs but now, in the cubicle, in the glassed valve of Zaf's head, the entire voyage had occurred beneath the halaal'd sky of a single summer's evenin. That wis what a Psychedelic Castlemilk did for you. That wis what happened when you turned guitars into sitars and violins into *penas*. You changed the nature of the sky. Aye, the Cosmic Rough Riders had a lot to answer for. More than they knew. Their gun wis definitely loaded. Blue ink. The playlist.

Anyway, back in nineteen seventy-seven, the car trundled up the rugged face of Alba and, though Zaf could not remember ever reachin the north coast, he supposed that they must have. Perhaps he had fallen asleep in the back seat as the big darkenin mountains swept past. But that wis the thing. You didn't remember destinations – it wis the journey . . . argh!

Self-help rubbish. What nonsense all that stuff wis! If there wis one thing you couldn't do, it wis help yourself. You were what you were. Aye, OK, there wis some level of responsibility which you bore for your immediate actions but, really, he wis here in this cubicle tonight because, a couple of decades ago, his folks had decided to take a trip to the Midnight Sun. Perhaps it had reminded them of their original, their epic, voyage. When you've driven all the way from Lahore to London, the jaunt from Glasgow to Dunnet Head wis a fart on the wind.

But, in this case, Zaf did remember the journey's end. He must've woken up when they got there because he remembered gettin out of the car and seein the sky suffused with blood, right across the sea, right to the limit of his vision on the purple line of the northern horizon. Lookin inland, oval-shaped lochs lay embedded in flat scrubland and the surface of their waters wis opalescent and barely movin. The air too wis oddly still. His mother and father were clad in their functional clothes – his papa in a rumpled suit, though for once without a tie, and his *maa* in a thin *shalvar kamise* – and they went and stood a few paces in front of him. The place wis totally deserted. It wis where the road ended. From where he wis, it seemed as though there wis nuthin between the sky and the darkenin land except for those two silhouettes. As he caught the strong whiff of salt that lifted from the sea loch, it seemed to Zaf as though his parents were holdin apart the edges of the world, that only they stood between him and Armageddon. And yet, at the same time, he had become brutally aware of how small they were.

OK. So he wis in the old hulk of the deconsecrated kirk, in the metaphorical entity that wis Radio Chaandni, because of somethin that ran between himself, Babs and his papa. Glasgow, Lahore and . . . No, not that.

Music! Yeah, that wis it – he wis spinnin through the darkness of this hot, humid night on account of *saaz*. And so were the Cosmic Rough Riders and The Beatles and Mohammed Rafi and Kula Shaker and Janki Bai Allahabadi and all the rest. They – the sounds they made – had come together over Zaf. And where this night would lead would depend on the songs, on the music. It wis not just that the music had suddenly assumed a mind of its own – the artists had always been conduits merely – but rather that, in the place where the radio transmissions faded to nuthin, up by the big mountains of the north, even the *saans* he breathed as it reddened turned miraculously into music. That wis why it had always remained with him – a blood fall, hangin through half the sky, a red dome, set over the supine body of Scotland.

Somethin had altered – some quality of the light. He could feel it through the skin of his lids. As he opened them, he thought he caught a fleetin glimpse of what might have been a figure movin away at the far end of the street. He blinked and there wis nuthin – just the sound of water runnin down the pipes, the long shadows of the street lamps . . .

He could hear the music from below and suddenly it wis out in the night, in the street. Downstairs, a window must've been closed and then opened. He had the sudden fear that the window here, in the cubicle, might slip down on his neck and crack his spine. He thought of his head rollin in the gutter. A squashed voice box. 'Nae mair transmissions the-night, folks. Wu're aw *bas khutum* hereaboots.' The caravan had left. One by one, its burnin lamps had been extinguished.

Bye-bye, Talat, *Khuda hafez*, Mukesh. He began to laugh. The sound echoed back from the buildins opposite. He stopped. He felt there wis someone behind him. Pulled back into the room. Fuck! Bumped his head on the bottom of the window.

There wis no one. He massaged the back of his head. There'll be a bump, he thought. Deck B. The Cosmic Rough Riders' 'The Gun Isn't Loaded'. Karachi to Glasgow in twenty easy strings. Sitar'd. Chilled out, the way a DJ wis meant to be. He would beat the techno yet! Zaf liked to close his eyes whenever he listened to that song. Its sweepin Makrani chords led him down a path into some woods, the night moon shinin overhead. A balmy, summer's night, just like this one, except there wis no rain, no strange girlfriends, no real memories. Just the hootin sound of an owl and a rustlin of leaves. And, from the depths of the forest, from a place where he knew the silence and the darkness would be total, Zaf thought he made out the faintest glimmer of a light.

The music wis mellifluous and swung heavily – the way Sindhi strings did. It wis the music of the desert and the forest – these were sounds from the furthest places. Circles of notes that would swallow you up if you weren't ready for them, if your life wasn't attuned to their wildness. A rough cosmic ride. The band. The Castlemilk escarpment, Glasgae, goin south. These peripheral estates consisted of great borin blocks of fast-food housin where nuthin ever happened. The inevitable video shops, the corporate pubs, the off-licences filled with cheap toxic wine. Yet, from these post-war after-thoughts with their ration-sized rooms, there had arisen this amazin band of Riviera joy, of Californian harmonies and Rajasthani rock. A curlin, swirlin night among the dunes, with a tassled, gyspy dancer hoverin on the brain. Smokin, tokin guns. Unloaded. Cosmic Rough Riders. Fuckin, fuckin brilliant! Such music carries you back, Zaf thought. No, that wis wrong – in its magnitude, such music wis timeless. The *doodh* down there in Castlemilk must be somethin special.

Again, he opened his eyes.

The cubicle wis incongruously shadowed, as though this place, this old kirk, wis refusin to be taken in by the *saadhus* of Castlemilk. He could feel it all around him, its walls closin in on his tiny space, its stone, unmoved by sympathetic sitar strings. The marches, the peripheries, might shift and shine in the face of an Indian moon but, always, the centre would hold. It wis an unspoken precondition of bein Scottish. There would be no alteration in the span of notes – it would remain mathematical in its obdurateness. He tried to reconstruct the forest, the moon, the night breeze waftin against the flat bodies of the leaves. The sharp aroma of pine or birch or rowan. But, once you had to build that stuff yourself, it wis too late. You were back on the escarpment, back in cold, rainy Castlemilk, and you couldn't see the sky. You couldn't stretch a leaf.

The room wis beginnin to feel creepy. This place wis fuckin old – a hundred years mibbee. Barefoot children long-dead. A dog-tired seamstress. Those old photos where no one smiled. Wis it because they'd had to stand for ages in one position or might it be because they had sensed that their images would be stared at a hundred years later by their uncomprehendin descendants, who would have emerged from a completely different world, and also by those who were not their descendants – by interlopers. The air in the room began to smell of early mornin – the kind of dank, empty smell which had sucked away the hope from so many generations.

Come, beloved, you have to go.

The songs were meldin into one another – they were losin their borders. For Zaf, if not for Scotland, the outside and the inside were mergin and that wis scary. It made him shiver as though a ghost had slipped from the stone into his body. This wis what happened in the middle of the night. Things lost their bearins. Stuff slipped out and down, thoughts got misplaced, people went wanderin. Talkin to yourself drove you mad. And Zaf had been talkin to himself every night for three months or mibbee for his whole life. The sound of his own voice wis the only music he knew but it had become like a fuckin anaconda – it writhed away from him every time he tried to pull it in. Three months compressed into a single, impossibly dense night. No dreams would survive this night. They would either be forgotten or else, like the uncannily sharp images in the old, heavy photographic paper, they would remain merely as totems – devoid of real substance. Myths for sons and daughters.

When his parents had come to Glasgow, the ghosts of the past had still been very much alive – the old women, their backs bent almost double, who walked like jackknives along the streets; the outside toilets where it wis too cold to be able ever to dream; the thin-lipped men with long, hard faces and hair greased to the point of madness; the Orange Marches where blood-spattered banners would be hauled from houses of God and made to flutter in the rain; grizzled men, dressed in old sewer-green suits, slumped in doorways with broken eggs dribblin from the ends of a paper bag; a deadpan voice on a black screen intonin the football results, as though they were obituary notices, for what seemed like hours; and, later, when the green-jacketed Indians and Pakistanis had begun to drive the big Irish Tricolour buses through the city streets, the casual hate that had been directed at them. The last bus aggro. That wis the bit Zaf remembered. The tail end of the seventies, the fag end of Enoch Powell and all that crap. The Rough Riders had stabled their horses, the sitar cases were bein unloaded by sepia Far Western men in shiny waistcoats and Mukesh wis back and wis singin again of love and loss, of partin forever. Deck A. Let's go, let's go, let's go. 'Come, Beloved, Let us Go' – 'Chal Ri Sajni Ab Kya Soche?'.

The Friendly City. Aye. Friendly as long as you were a tourist. His parents had brought no photos with them from Pakistan and had only acquired a few when Jamil's father, Zaf's *dada*, had died. Jamil had gone back for the *chehilum* and had brought back a rickety cardboard box, labelled 'Wazir Khan', filled with photographs. Who the hell Wazir Khan wis Zaf had never been able to find out. Mibbee it had been a street or an area or a *chowk* – a crossroads buried somewhere in the middle of the old town, in a part of Lahore which had grown up in small squares, bordered by *haveli*, and now with the ghosts of *djinns*. And mango stones. Don't forget the mangoes! No scene from the Lahori nights would be complete without at least *theen aam*. Three because it wis a magic number and because, even in monochrome, it suggested possibilities of the illicit. Zaf remembered siftin through the old photos and bein shown who the strange black-and-white people in them were. The names had meant little to him and, anyway, they had been known only as parts of names or even by polite nicknames. Bits of people like 'Laal' or 'Meel'. What the hell kinds of names were those? Meal, deal, orange peel? Red oranges. Jesus! Fruits again. Yeah, the South Asian subcontinent wis a *gey* fruity place and every juicy, aromatic, Expressionist piece of flesh wis heavily symbolic but only in those slightly silly books with titles like *A Summer of Kathak on Chillies and Parrots* or *Dreams of the Mauve, Saffron and Unusually and Vibrantly Different Lives of the Verdant-Eyed Mughals*. In such books, the past had been frozen hard between exotic covers, the story glued to the spine. Not like the loose photographs that were the only legacy of his parents' old country. Some of those in the pictures looked as though they had already been dead, even as the flashgun had gone off. Zaf had been frightened by the images but also drawn to them. There were some photos of his papa at college but none of his *maa* and none with both of them together. There were also a few which his parents didn't like to talk about – as though to have talked about them might, in some way, have brought bad luck to the family. The photos from Pakistan evoked quite different smells from any photographs of old Glasgow that he had seen. Smells of cow shit and *methi* and of the sort of melancholy resignation that can exist only in the *gao*. He had always been fascinated most by one of a child standin alone and barefoot. On his head was a turban and behind him stood the ramshackle wall of a mud hut. He must've been around seven or eight. Zaf had never been able to find out who this was and his parents hadn't seemed to know either. Probably some servant's child from the *gao*, they had said. He wis wearin a loose *shalvar kamise* so that only his face, hands and feet were visible. The boy's eyes were big, round and black and his face almost shone in what must have been the camera flash. Zaf could almost smell the burnin glass. The photograph, probably taken usin a Box Brownie, was a very good one because it had not gone sepia but wis clear – white and black – so that Zaf was able to make out every feature, every curve of the boy's face and he felt as though, at any moment, the child might leap out of the paper and come to life. He had even given him a name. He had named the boy Zafar. Zaf wis Zaf and Zafar was Zafar and he had been able to talk to Zafar any time he'd wanted and to share secrets with him. He became like the brother he'd never had.

As he grew up, Zafar had faded more and more into the background until, eventually, the box of photographs was relegated to the cupboard under the stairs, right at the back behind all the polish and the brushes and the useless plastic buckets. Zaf had almost forgotten about his namesake until this moment. It must be the music, he thought. Mukesh's voice swirled all around him, minglin with the smells of the night and addin to them – the scent of *raat-ki-raani* – and, in the jasmine wind, Zaf had an image of Zafar – of his eyes like bright, clear marbles, of his glowin skin which he knew would be smooth as honey and of his solemn mouth, of a face, old before its time, which wis now long past. He felt he would be able to reach out and hold him and to run the boy's warm flesh beneath his fingers.

The air blew cold on the back of his neck. The next song. 'Bhooli Hui Yaadon'. 'Forgotten Memories'. Cracked dreams. Deck A again. Deck B wis empty. Unlike every other track Zaf had played durin the night, Mukesh's words did not lead to some kind of ark. The song wis on its own. There were no segues from this one – it segued into everythin. He wis reluctant to break the spell – it would almost be like turnin the photograph of someone you loved face down. He looked at Babs's picture and thought how utterly different it wis from that of Zafar. The two people he had confided in most were held in his mind as images, stills. It didn't matter that one wis at the bottom of a box in a dark cupboard nor that it had remained unseen for over a decade – somehow, that made it seem even more sacred. He wondered just how much of his love for Babs wis merely love for her as icon. Mother Mary, *aajao*. Speak words of wisdom.

In reality, he knew nuthin about the boy in the *gao* in Pakistan-before-it-wis-Pakistan – before the land had become suddenly pure, before it had been purged of somethin impure.

He knew nuthin of the Scotland before. It wis a complete mystery to him and would remain so always. He knew the Glasgae of the white-trash housin estates. He wis familiar with the clubs and the pubs and the dives and the toxic cafés that they frequented – far more so than he wis with the street plan of Lahore. He had felt the heat of the pot as it melted, slowly – someday, everyone would leap out, coffee-skinned and highly cool, like in the song but that wis fifty, mibbee a hundred, years away or mibbee it would never happen at all but, right now, every rivet, every smile stretched back two centuries to the slave ships and the freebooters and, yes, he could smell the stench of human sweat and detritus and blood mixed in with the oak and elm and starched collar bibles of the great sailin ships which had been built by the bonnie banks of the Clyde and there wis no escape from the fact that, every time he had screwed a white-trash girl, it had somehow made him feel better.

Zaf had wandered through this city his whole life. He had given his spirit to the buildins, the parks, the broken neon signs and the people. The soul of Glasgow had penetrated the core of his being. He had allowed it to enter him and, like some dissolute whore, he had welcomed it, had allowed it to fester within him and he had held back nuthin. And so, now, when he needed some of that spirit back, just for a while, just for tonight, the city wis not forthcomin. It turned its hard Presbyterian face away from its own children, it averted its thin lips. So why on earth should it bother to acknowledge a changeling like Zaf? He no longer recognised himself in this place. The city had changed. Or mibbee he had changed. That wis precisely what those people who lived in halaal universes were tryin to avoid – the leakin away of spirit, the consumption of their being. They, and others like them, were negotiatin new paths, they were redrawin the courses of rivers, pullin the land this way and that. It wis kind of like when he wis on air. On the radio, everythin he did felt real. It wis the only place where he felt human – when he wis alone with just his voice. Every night, he wis goin back to the beginnin. To Altaqween.

He had never confided in Zilla. When he had been with Zilla, it had been a masochistic trip, a spiralin into the hell that wis himself. He had felt his body enveloped by the fluids of the sewers and had felt the ticklin ends of rats' tails as they'd swished past. Glasgae rats were miles better . . . Zilla had metamorphosed into a junkie whore and he had contributed to her degradation – he had fiddled while she'd danced for the White Man and then he had dumped her in her own shit and now he didn't know whether she wis dead or alive. He really didn't and he loved her and might've made it with her if only he had been able to lift her out of whatever filth she had sunk into, if only he had been able to make her feel better. If only he had been white. But that wis a load ae crap. Just another aspect of his addiction.

The music swelled and pulsed. Mukesh's voice could make a fuckin stone weep and, beneath it, from downstairs, there rippled the ambient Asian techno of the meltin pot an Zaf felt his boady begin to tremble in the breeze that wis pourin in from the night an he felt his spine straighten an the tears rolled, they fuckin rolled, doon his cheeks as he glanced back at Babs an saw that she wis really a guid person, a really guid person, an that he wis exploitin her at some level an he knew that he would probably peye fur it oan some level an someone hud said tae someone, an he hud heard ae it, that he wis jis feedin aff ae her, that she wis jis white meat an he wis jis feedin aff her – yet, withoot her, he hud been jist a big black hole – weel, no literally but figuratively. Aye she had a guid figure, taut breists, thin as she wis. Thur wis nae doubtin that

– but, then, so hud Zilla.

A voice, light and tremulous in the mornin that wis yet to come. 'Ah know. Ah know what Ah said. Ah didnae think. Ah wis wrong. But it's over now. Mibbee ye hud tae do the radio thing an noo it's oot ae yer system.' That wis typical Babs. People had to get things out of their systems. Before Salvation, lay Purgatory. Hallelujah! She'd been a nurse for too long. She knew, too well, how to change the subject, how to retreat from confrontation. Her small breasts moved up and down beneath the lemon-yellow cotton of her blouse. It wis like he could see right through to her skeleton. Her slim bones were built for runnin, for flight. Outside, her motorcycle gleamed and perspired like a medieval stallion – its blue spine moist with the sweat of her body. He could make out the points of her nipples. But things were different now. Two years. Make-or-break time. And, on the lance of her thin form, he had broken.

But thur wis thin and then thur wis junkie thin and Babs wisnae a junkie – that wis the difference. It wis nuhin tae do wi colour or religion – fuck sake, whit hud Zilla's religion been onyweye? An he wis damned lucky tae huv her an he should thank his lucky white stars – Babs that wis – an Mukesh wis cryin-singin tragedy upoan tragedy an he, Zaf-Zafar, he couldnae fuckin bear it ony mair an he would huv tae get oot ae here or he would go fuckin insane – like he almost hud that last night in Zilla's moon-flat.

He could feel the moon burn the skin on the back of his neck white. The clouds must be clearin, he thought in a moment of clarity, a moment of illumination. The pulse from downstairs wis growin stronger while Mukesh wis fadin. Like their songs, these guys just turn to spirit, he thought – unlike young soldiers who simply die. He had heard that a million people had attended Mukesh's funeral. A burnin pyre, a smashed skull, the end of the end. The boy wis dead, he knew that. Zafar, his brother, wis dead. It wis not possible to be encapsulated in the darkness of a Box Brownie and survive. There wis a sadness in his eyes and Zaf knew that, even then, even as the photographer had raised the camera and pressed the button, Zafar had seen the instant of his own death and that, after that moment, there had never been any hope. Not in the Land of the Pure, not in the Friendly City, not in hell itself had there been any hope of redemption. Zaf moved forwards and pushed the voice switch up to maximum. The music would play on but the silence of the room and of the night outside would sweep over the music and would move through it and then mibbee the Asian community in Glasgow, the Glasgae community in Little Faisalabad, the gangstas, the seamstresses, the barefoot children would hear the sound of themselves, would gaze into the dark mirror as they had glared at Babs 'n' Zaf (may Almighty God fuck them since, at those moments, Zaf had felt like he had been trapped like a fly in the lens of a camera, that he had been actin a role and he had felt the cracks that lay between them begin to open up and he knew that, without Babs, his knees would turn to clear jelly an he had felt himsel begin to sway) and, mibbee in the mirror, they would learn somethin or feel somethin or mibbee some white-trash arsehole might just tune in and smell the scent of the night jasmine, the queen of the night, and finally understand that Combat 18, the NF, the BNP and all the rest of that crap were just more ways to screw yourself and that the real strength lay in the seam-stresses with their bobbed hairstyles and in the *barfit* weans whose ghosts still scarpered through the back closes of auld Glasgae and that blood never fed souls but love does.

Here's sumhin wild. It's the middle ae this night an we're huvin a party! You an me, jis the two ae us, eh? Or the five million, mair like, or the saxty million, or the . . . Delusions ae grandeur, eh? It's whit happens tae ye when aw ye've seen or heard fur three months is the sound ae yer ane voice. An that's no a very pretty sune! Ye heard it earlier, right? Croonin's no fur me. So, in that vein or artery, let's huv this.

Scribbles on wood. His pen had half snapped, the transparent plastic cylinder had turned opaque with the crack. Too much pressure. Soon, the ink would run thick and blue like sticky blood. The frantic quarter-tones of 'Roller Coaster' spun through the night air and Zaf could feel them permeate every *pathaR*, every brick, every block of blond-on-red sandstone in the city. The Thirteenth Floor, where his parents had got off. All their lives, they had been watched by that enormous eye, the one that lived and breathed on the spike of a pyramid. *Boori Annkh*. Their lives had been truncated, their beings gathered in by its convex gaze. As the Rough Riders once had trotted up through 'Chal Ri Sajni Ab Kya Soche?', so now the Elevators were ascendin through auld Mukesh's 'Forgotten Memories'. This wis more than a trip. The eye had directed them all to its logical conclusion – the zero-point.

◎◎◎◎◎

Jamil Ayaan had hailed from the new middle classes in northern India which had themselves been caused to emerge during the early part of the century to help run the Raj from the top down, as it were. As was the raison d'être of such classes, he had worked unimaginably hard (there is no parallel

in sunny Scotland for the manner in which Jamil laboured)
and, eventually (after only one fail), he had graduated from
a college in Punjab in engineering sciences and had been set
for great things – or so the family legend went – possibly
even for nuclear weapons or dams or something of that sort.
Haa ji, it had been all kites and crescent moons and pleasant
monsoon rainstorms, kind of like in the *filmi* films – a
wavering branch, a tragic heroine and a very dead poet. But,
somehow, through some wink of a *djinn*-infested *haveli*,
amidst the inchoate static of burning glass, Jamil Ayaan had
fallen in love and, more than that, he had fallen in love with
this married woman whose face resembled a stanza from
some Mughal miniature. Even back in the fifties, love marriages were not completely unknown but to have descended,
in such a manner, into an adulterous relationship was definitely not the sort of indecorous act in which a citizen of a
young republic should have engaged.

Zaf sometimes despised himself for the way in which he
saw his father. Ah can only mock him, he thought, because
Ah could never do what he did, could never follow in his
footsteps. And, when the two lovers had eloped in an ancient
Ford Popular one broilin July night with the monsoon weepin
and laughin all around them, they had left behind Jamil's
son. That wis the first, the original, betrayal. The monsoon
in Punjab is hard, fast and short, like the sex between
adulterers, and, as they had moved westwards, away from
Lahore, the rain had grown more desperate. Or, at least, that
wis how Zaf saw it in his mind. This, he thought as he lit
up a long cigar and blew imperfect circles towards the ceiling,
this wis the time of Raj Kumar Mukesh and he had always
been able to picture Mukesh, the great, sad singer, as he sang
through the night rain that wis utterly different from Glasgow
rain, of love, death and the poetry of exile.

Dover, the gleaming, white cliffs of Albion. 'Clover, plover, roll me over!' And thence to London, the city of clocks and bridges and very polite bowler hats. It had been hot and sunny. An uncharacteristically boiling spring for the south of England. Or perhaps they had brought it with them, the lovers, with their *gurrum-masalaa* lust. Or so it appeared to the fusty landlady who agreed to put them up and who, in return, had put up with the dark, discordant *taal* of their love-making, on condition they consume the flesh of a pig with fried tomatoes and mushrooms every morning. And, beneath the pasteurised morning moon, they ate from gleaming white bone-china plates. Brown hands dancing. Shadow puppets. Copperplate.

> No Dogs or Indians
> Pigs Welcome!

Still, they were happy in the stuffy room which once had been the landlady's husband's during the long, flat years between the Wars when the Empire had sailed clean and silent, a brilliant white prow, through deep, blue waters. The room had still smelled of this big artisan and his rolled tobacco and of the sleepy sickness that had killed him before his time.

But now it was the Commonwealth and the South was becoming too busy with Hindustanis and Pakistanis and Jamil and Rashida wanted to escape from the clutches of memory and judgement. So he took a job at the opposite end of the island, in a city of which he had never before heard. He reasoned that, if he hadn't heard of it, then others would be likely not to have either. It would be safe from prying eyes, ears, tongues. See no evil. The twin fusts. Pillars, loincloths. Wisdom and knowledge. Hermeneutic lives.

```
I                    S
Z                    H
Z                    A
A                    R
T                    A
T                    M
```

People in London had warned Jamil that Scotland had never been properly civilised, that he would get there and find himself surrounded by savages clad only in sporrans and brightly patterned woollen skirts. Either that or he would instantly be attacked by lupine, unintelligible gangsters sporting darkened eyes and long silver blades. Beads, crosses and tea would do no good, they insisted, since the natives were irretrievably hard Calvinists who believed only in damnation.

◉◉◉◉◉

Zaf shuddered as he remembered. That had been the beginnin. But, no, he thought, the beginnin had been when his father and mother had run away from their country and had rolled, in a tin chariot, slowly overland, like old-style vanquished conquerors. Such a journey carried with it a burden of finality which those, who had emerged from the big white ships and, later, from the bellies of toothpaste-tube jumbos, had never had to bear. It was a journey in blood. They had trundled through Afghanistan, Iran, Turkey and half the countries of Europe and, in the process, the whole thing had become solidified into some kind of myth. Emi-grants, he thought, can make only one journey because it might be their last. Everythin must go into it. But, then, in a static land, what comes out? The effects last for generations. Centuries mibbee. Zaf had been almost an only child, conceived – whether by accident or through design, he had never been certain and, probably, would never know – some ten years after the couple had emigrated and he had seldom been (back) to Pakistan.

Mukesh wis on the way out. Things were slidin an Zaf didn't know how to stop it. Only now he realised that he had just played that song about forgotten memories twice and the realisation made him gut himself. Not only that – he'd allowed the track to play over and over so that the listeners must've thought that the groove had become stuck, fixed at a single point in time, and mibbee they were right. Mibbee some of them had finally switched off or over in disgust and those would be the last of the sane ones. From here on, only the mad, the fools, the desperate were on the ship. Ahoy there! *HMS Junnune*. In some ways, he even welcomed it – this loosening of the music of age and death.

The moon wis shinin and the rain had finally ceased altogether. Thank the Lord – whether He be Muslim, Hindu, Sikh, Buddhist, Christian, Jewish, Zoroastrian or a Rangers supporter or even a woman. What the fuck does it matter? Zaf could smell the grease of the auld iron rakes of the smelters and welders and the stainless steel of the needles that Zilla, dear, precious soul, Zilla, had used to pierce the skin of her eyeballs and the thirteenth floor techno-rave wis pourin in from down below and he happened to glance across at the next room where, just for an instant, he thought he heard laughter and there were no shadows on the blank wall, no *Asian Babe* sex show for all to see, an he wis disappointed an he wanted to go downstairs and merge himself in the beat of the sewers which Lahore, the City of Loh, had never built and slowly to become demented in the ancient, swelterin darkness. He felt light-headed. The room began to sway. He slapped himself twice on the cheek. Hard. Fuckin get yersel thegether, he said aloud, but it wis too late. Elevate, elevate, elevate.

Awright, jukeboax heids, this is *The Junnune Show* an ma name's Zaf – that's zed ay eff, – an, in case ye've already forgotten or mibbee jist joined us (lucky yous!), we've cruised like a dream through the Great Mukesh's 'Chal Ri Sajni Ab Kya Soche?', the Cosmic Rough Riders' 'The Gun Isn't Loaded', then more 'Chal Ri Sajni Ab Kya Soche?' (those beloved soangs jist nivir go aweye!) then 'Bhooli Hui Yaadon', another Mukesh humdinger, then aifter that we hud The 13th Floor Elevators an 'Rollercoaster', then, tae finish up wi . . . weel, we'll see! Mibbee we'll huv a track by that wonderful an underrated Glasgae band, the goldenhour, with their version ae 'tonight becomes tomorrow' (weel, so far it's the only version cause it's really quite new – it's almost as though it's bein laid doon as we speak or as Ah speak an you listen) an then last, but definitely not least, Jimmy Page an Robert Plant redrawin the map ae Kashmir. Dangerous work, that. Aye, that's whit we'll do. We'll redraw aw the maps an, whun we come oot ae here in the mornin, we willnae recognise the waruld, we willnae know oorsels. No one said this show would be safe, *samaaen*. If it's safety an caution ye're lookin fur, then mibbee ye'd be better tunin elsewhere. Radio Clyde mibbee. An these few tunes huv brought us oan this rockin boat ae sune that we like tae caw Scoatlan, tae the hairt ae darkness, the quietest time ae the night, the period whun thur's only braith an thought an daith. But we'll be expressin it aw through music an soang cause that's whit we're aboot. That's whit Ah'm aboot. Ah'm a disc joakie – Ah ride the horse ae the moon across the black arc ae the sky. Ah'm like that guy in the poem, 'Tam o' Shanter', ye know the wan, the *mahmoor* that almost spun wi Auld Nancy the Witch an then gave his name tae a *topee*. Aye, *yeh raat*, this is that howlin, tavernous darkness that can only be driven through music. Nae wurds can stretch tae those heights, nae clivir phrases, no even Rabbie Buruns could do it – he left aff whun Tam croases the arched bridge. The thing is, Nan the Witch gets a wee bit ae Tam's mare's tail an ye nivir find oot whit happens aifter that. Remember that a practitioner ae *kaala jadoo* can cast spells usin only the tiniest wee bit ae a person's boady – a strand ae hair or a nail clippin or a weel-used scarf even. An we aw know aboot those dark, Soothside gatherins, now, don't we? Up among the gentle hillocks ae suburbia. That's the modern weye. Nae deserted, deconsecrated kirks up the broad driveways ae *apna shehron*. Naw, nowadays, *kaala jadoo* is perpetrated by the maist holy ae holy wummin. Aye, they may be holy but they like gettin thur revenge oan onywan prettier than they are – or mair wealthy or mair lovin. Aye, it's the auld Schadenfreude hard at work. We loang fur some harum tae come tae those we think are mair fortunate than us. Be honest, *samaaen*, be honest. In the mornin, those dames wi time oan thur honds are aff tae *milaads* while, in the aifternoon, thu're speedin thur boadies roon the pentangle ae dark forces. Weel, whitivir turns ye oan, *samaaen*. But ye shouldnae be harmin other people now – that's no right. No that Ah'm some great big angel, mind you. Ah'm no stonnin oan a pillar ae light an lookin doon at all ae yous.

Yes, I am, Zaf thought. Fuckin hubris.

Ah'm no judging onywan. All Ah'm sayin is thur's always mair tae a person than meets the eye. Deep in the night, no one knows whit's goin oan in another person's heid. We're aw human beings an we're aw trapped in oor solitude. Wow! We're gettin heavy oan this show! OK, that's the philosophy ower. Time noo fur a wee bit ae light. Nae mair cryin soangs. At least, no fur the next wee while, onyweye. This is the goldenhour, the title track fae thur first album, *Beyond the Beyond*. A Glasgae band, these lads, aye, an if ye listen closely enough ye'll hear them blastin oot thur magical stuff fae garages all ower the suburbs an hillocks ae the Soothside. This is the happy time, folks, *yeh hamaray sunehreh lumhe hai*. Sit back, relax, close yer eyes if ye like – jist do whit ye wanna do. Cause naebdy's awake except fur us *Junnunies*. We're like Tam an his horse an Auld Nancy aw rolled intae wan. Run wi the soang, then, an dream ae the beyond that lies beyond the beyond. Got that? Beyond the end, thur is no end. Ach, shut up, Zaf! Turn life intae music, that's yer joab. Turn lead tae gold. Go fur it, boays!

He'd already filled Deck B with the CD and now the night heaved with the sounds of the beyond.

Lopin, Midwestern vocals, rejoinin harmonies, solid rock riffs, tender lyrics – this wis what it wis all about. This wis the reason he did this. This wis why he loved music. No, it wis more than that. It wis because music defined him. His identity lay not in a flag or in a particular concretisation of a transcendent Supreme Being but in a chord, a bar, a vocal reaching beyond itself. A harmony wheelin out there, beyond the beyond. This wis not the time fur movin. This wis the time fur just listenin – just floatin with the songs. For a couple of tracks, he would sit and pretend to be a listener. He would imagine that he wis out in the emptiness, in the darkness, and that whatever need he had wis fulfilled by these songs. The singer wis goin on about the quest for happiness in stormy weather, he wis scryin lights in the fog – aye, this wis it. Bein a listener again wis suitin Zaf. God, recently, his head had been so full of schemes, he had forgotten how to just live – to exist in the physical and not just as disembodied words. This wis why Lucifer had erred – this wis why the great fuckin archangel had burned with envy of *Hazrat* Aadam. It wis because Adam had been built of dun stone and cow dung. Zaf massaged the muscles of his thighs and shoulders, he moved his neck slowly from one side to another in an attempt to relieve the tension that had massed in the fibres. At this time, if he did that too fast, he would get dizzy – not for long but long enough to make him feel as though the earth beneath his feet wis shiftin. Even a slight movement would be massive. The day would turn black, the night red. The sun would blow cold – and life would be absolute solitude. Everythin wis a compromise, he thought. It wis in the nature of our being never to be wholly happy, always to sense insecurity or worse. Up by Dunnet Head, the seas heaved with whales and selkies and the sky reddened toward the music of *Burzakh*. The songs of Purgatory. His parents had done the best they could be expected to do. And, now, he wis doin the same. Someday, in the dense coldness of space, he, too, would be judged. And how would the lyric of his life pan out? Even the prophet who had been swallowed by a whale, even he, had not found all the answers. If he had, then the story of his devourment would have been spurious. This song, 'beyond the beyond', would not have been sung.

Its lyric, its joyously melancholic harmonies, would have sunk into perpetual silence. Purgatory wis filled with the sound of music but it wis not the pleasin hum of choirs. These songs were all about sunset, loneliness and love.

Without Zaf realisin it, the machine had moved on to the next track or, rather, its laser beam had jumped six tracks, half the album, to 'west sky picture show', a slow, complex number with subtle, disturbin lyrics about the places where words fail, the vistas out west that span the broad Atlantic, the celluloid of past and future and the deserts where tears won't come. He hadn't intended to let this song on, he'd told the listeners 'no more sad songs'. Well, that lasted exactly five minutes and twelve seconds, didn't it? Right. The song had changed without him willin it – at least, consciously – and now it wis this slower, softer and yet far weirder number. He couldn't get the weirdness out of his brain. So he ran with it. So, beyond the quest for happiness wis sadness and beyond sadness wis nuthin. Denim joy. Nuthin. Once you'd realised that, Zaf thought, either it made you strong or it cracked you up. Aye, it made you ready for whatever the night would bring. Aye, there wis a line of silver that stretched through changin times from The Poets to The Sensational Alex Harvey Band to the goldenhour. It wis raw, it wis freaky, it wis subtle, it wis drawin down deep and it wis unafraid of breathin, of livin, of bein imperfect. If you couldn't weep, you could sing. Somethin like a trumpet (but he knew it wasn't) blew through the words, the drum wis beatin a pensive rhythm around which dollops of electric hard-bop organ rolled and writhed. Dirty, dirty spirits. Ghosts of the Mods. Not scooters, this time around, and not truckin, Greyhound bus or convertibles. Nah, this is a motorbike, a sleek *asmani* lover, and it wis ridin the *baad-e-saba*, the west wind.

But it wasn't music – not at first. Zaf hadn't played this track before – he'd barely listened to it himself. Over the past three months, he'd had so little time on his own. He wis alone in the cubicle but without solitude. And, now, there wis no music – just words. Zaf turned up the volume to try and make out what she wis sayin. Some crazy, Carinthian dame from the limbo time between the Wars. She wis goin on about a garden, a river, polishin a mirror. She wis a bloody liar. A femme fatale. A killer. A man wis howlin and cursin in the background. Zaf thought he recognised the woman's voice. Somethin from the other side of the glass, from the darkness. No, it couldn't be. She wasn't from Carinthia or Bohemia or any of those places. But then, he thought, she wis daith, she could do anything. The howl grew louder. She could be anywhere. It turned to a scream. The music exploded. Guitars, electric organ and hammer drums – it wis sweat 'n' blood, a great riposte, at three-forty-five in the mornin, to the flabby Kingdom of Philly that had ruled for too long.

Zaf did what he had suggested his listeners do and closed his eyes and tried to let the music take him to high places filled with light. The only way to combat those *kaala-jadoo* fanatics wis to engage the forces of love. Zaf sometimes wondered whether his family might have been the victim of one of those spells. Mibbee someone back in the old country had enlisted the help of a black witch in order to try and get revenge on Jamil Ayaan. His first wife perhaps or one of her relatives. That kind of thing happened all the time in Pakistan and also in Glasgow. Curse and damnation. Or *Burzakh*. Well, it had worked, hadn't it? It had sent him down the mine. Worse than the mine – the sewer. His father had come all the way to Alba, the land of whiteness, and had spent most of his life there, down in the darkest places imaginable.

Who would wish for that? Someone who had it in for them all. Ach!

He opened his eyes. He ran his finger along the surface of the console. Gazed at the thin layer of white dust. God! Did no one ever clean this place? Wis everythin always left to him? Not that he had . . .

The vocal wis bein belted out as though it wis the singer's last will and testament. Zaf had the odd impression that, beneath the hyper-rock, below even the immanence of abandonment and sorrow that defined the lyrics, the white-faced woman wis intonin some kind of spell, some pagan incantation or other. Down in the street, tall shadows shifted along the walls. Zaf clamped his hands over his ears but still the voice continued. Tonight, he could hear it, burned into the silver, runnin down under the rhythm section. Tonight, Layla wis a poisoner. He wiped the perspiration off his forehead but all he got wis a mixture of dust and iron. It wis all breakin down and, in the mix, nuthin wis sure any more.

What wis he thinkin? Instead of allowin the song to take him to high places of light, he wis lettin his imagination run away with him. And his imagination lived under the earth. It thrived there, in the clammy darkness, where it listened keenly for the sounds of rats copulatin. Sick bastard, he thought. Sick fuckin bastard.

Love in the summertime. Ferocious harmonies. Joyous betrayal. A psych freak-out. Aye, those guys in the goldenhour had been kickin around the city for years, playin here and there, doin gigs in seamy dives where the audience was more interested in stuffin as many chips into their big *boothes*, before findin a screw for the night, than meldin with the music. The band had been lookin, always, for the big break. A modicum of failure, year after year, could make you really talented but it sapped away at your soul. Nonetheless, the band hadn't let it get to them. In Glasgow, either you got the gleamin skins of The Sensational Alex Harvey Band, rantin and ravin and makin masterpieces, or else it wis dreamy Californian harmonies. It was a place best defined either in the wild depths of the night or else at noon, when the light was brightest and when the borders, the edges of things, the ends of the notes, were diamond-cut. In spite of everythin, the songs of the goldenhour were filled with hope. This wis not saccharine fantasy, this wis the mud 'n' slime 'n' spunk of the earth. Skin, muscle, broken necks. Sunlight on a tenement, raisin spirits, breathin life into the mouths of the dead. Ah, goldenhour! Spin it! Spit it! Make it real! Kabbalistical rock by the *Darya* Clyde. On good nights, the whales swam this far upstream. Zaf could feel their haunches sweep past his skin and, in their slipstream, he went down, right down. *Hazrat* Yunus, spin me a tale, *yaar*, beneath the watery sky as the moon rises once again. From out of the dark tunnels of despair, always eventually a light will shine. 'tonight becomes tomorrow'. Yesterday becomes today.

○◎○◎○

And the moonlight made the land seem less ponderous somehow. Because he was able only to make out the few hundred yards around their vehicle, Jamil Ayaan felt less afraid than during the day when the entire country had seemed to swallow them in its barren vastness. He'd heard that the valleys were filled with orchards of plums and apricots and that the streams flowed with clear water that could heal the soul. But he hadn't seen any of that here. Perhaps it had just been the effect on the Old Travellers of strong Kalaash wine. They were in that part of Afghanistan now called Nuristan which once had been known as the Land of the

Kafirs. The people hereabouts – though, deep in the whirling dust of the night, Jamil found it hard to imagine that any human beings might actually be able to eke out any kind of existence on these desolate slopes – had worshipped stones, sky and wooden dolls. Their shrines had perched on small plateaux, high among the peaks. But they had been converted a hundred years earlier and now were all bone fide *Musalmaan*. There were still a few thousand Kafirs living deep in remote mountain valleys further east but the only pagans here were the ghosts. He shivered. Then he rubbed his eyes. Then he saw the light.

To his left, from far up, from beyond the limit of his vision, Jamil Ayaan thought he made out a faint light. It glimmered for a few seconds and then vanished, then reap-peared only to disappear again soon after. He assumed the moonlight had caught on a rock or that perhaps, somewhere up on the mountain slope, some goatherd was returning home for the night. Not that he'd seen any herders or even any goats for the last few hours they'd been travelling. There seemed to be no living thing in this place. Then he heard the music. Like the light, it eddied through the night air so that he was never really sure whether what he was hearing issued from outside of his head or from some *dastgah* caught in his brain and resurrected by solitude. Yet there was no melody or, if there was, then it was one which Jamil could not decipher.

He glanced across at Rashida. His lover slept soundly, her body exhausted by the journey, by its strangeness, its length and by its gravity. It was madness to leave her there, unprotected, unaware even of his absence. Yet, tonight, he was mad. In later years, when he had gone over the events in his mind, he had never been able to comprehend his actions on that night – any more than he had been able to delineate the onset of his love for his boss's wife. He'd had to admit to himself that there were things that were beyond the compass of even science and that these things were not fixed, repeatable or literate. Perhaps, in the furthest wastes of Nuristan, the skins that separated one world from the next were thinner than elsewhere. Perhaps, here, on this windless night, a seepage of one existence into another might occur.

Flipping his edge of the blanket over Rashida's huddled form, he got out of the car and quietly closed the door. Following the light and the music, he began to climb the mountain. The ground, at first rocky and hard, gradually became softer as though he was walking on powder. Then, when he looked down, he saw that the grey powder had swirled up around his shoes, some of its particles sticking to his trouser legs. The incline grew steeper, the higher he climbed, so that soon the rise and fall of his breathing was making an inordinately loud noise in the darkness. In spite of the night's coldness, he felt beads of sweat break out on his brow. At length, he found that he had to stop. Perhaps, up here, the air was thinner. He was feeling a little dizzy – not exactly a spinning vertigo but just a sense that, at any moment, things might fly out of kilter, the ground shift, as it were, beneath his feet. When he turned to look back at the car, it had vanished behind an outcrop. He guessed he must've been climbing in a diagonal direction. He made a mental note of where he was in relation to the immediate terrain – the outcrop, the gullies to his left, the scattered rocks just below and to his right. However, the landscape seemed, in many respects, quite similar all around. On many slopes, other than the one on which he was standing, it was as though, in this denuded place, there was only a limited number of possible juxtapositions and Jamil began to doubt whether he would be able to relocate himself on the way down. He gazed up and wished that he had learned to read the stars and then he laughed – the idea of a boy from the *shehr* memorising the positions of the constellations or the span of the moon through the heavens somehow struck Jamil Ayaan as hugely comical. His laughter echoed against the stone and then the echo echoed against the echo and so on and, with each dilution, the noise was losing its individuality, its humanity, until, at last, it faded into silence. This alarmed him. It meant that the narrow valley in which they were trapped – and, for the first time, Jamil Ayaan found himself admitting that they were lost – was far larger, ran on for far longer, than he had at first thought. He still could not make out the summit of the mountain that he was climbing. Yet, from time to time, the light shone out – its strange, intermittent gleaming accompanying the distant, siphoned sound of the music. He was unable to make out any melody – not even on the level of assonance – but, somehow, he felt that it was this, the music, that was hauling him on, up the mountain. It had taken hold of his brain so that the thought of returning to the car and his lover did not even occur to him as a realistic course of action. It was as though the madness that had drawn him to Rashida, the lunacy which had induced him to betray his *maalik*, his wife, his son, his life, had now possessed him again and was giving power to his limbs which, only half an hour earlier, had seemed utterly exhausted. Indeed, now, his head felt light and he began to feel a little elated. It was the same emotion as when he had met Rashida in the back-street hotel except that, this time, there was no sexual element to his sense of anticipation. When he had got his breath back, he resumed the climb.

At length, he rounded a rocky outcrop and here he found his footing much surer, the ground almost flat. His eyes had grown so used to the starlight that already he felt as though he had dwelt here for months. He wondered whether perhaps this deserted place was his natural home. Perhaps this was what he had been searching for all his life. Maybe they should stop here. Perhaps Rashida and he could eke out some kind of living from the rocks of this undefined land. They were far away from any villages, even from the tribes whose only philosophical system seemed to be based around endless blood vendettas. If his *maalik* had been a Pathan, Jamil thought, by now, both he and Rashida would either be dead or else would have a hefty reward on their heads. They were lucky that Rashida's husband was a Upean. They were generally two-faced, over-cultured cowards, Jamil thought, and, if they did exact revenge, it would be through *kaala jadoo* and the law courts and not via the gun and the blade. Punjabis lay somewhere in between those two extremes, existing neither on a crude Old Testamental level nor on any *vakili* chessboard. Punjabis were straightforward – loud and emotional rather than violent. Aggression in the land of the five rivers, which they had just forsaken, generally tended to manifest through expletives.

The music up there on that plateau was more defined than before. There was a melody – Jamil could hear it now. It was issuing from a violin or a viola or else from the Arabi version of one of those instruments. It had no echo, which led Jamil Ayaan to suppose that it must be emanating from an enclosed space. He walked slowly in the direction from which it seemed to be coming. His shoes made a crunching sound on the earth – the slower and more carefully he moved, the louder his steps seemed to become.

The entrance was around twelve feet in diameter and he couldn't make out the back wall. The music was definitely issuing from deep inside the cave. He paused but only for a moment. His desire to seek out the source of the music was greater than any cautionary voices in his head. He had expected the interior to be pitch-black but, as he walked on, Jamil found that, as the starlight faded, another, still dimmer, luminescence began to take over. The bowed instruments had given way to a nasal, almost whining voice – possibly that of a woman but Jamil was not certain. He knew that the tribal women did not vocalise in the falsettos of Hindustan but rather in the dark, sweeping alto of the Middle East. *Habibi, ya habibi!*

It was warm in this cavern and it grew warmer the further in he went. His skin began to stick to his clothes and he removed first his scarf and later his coat and sweater. Then he bent down and took off his shoes partly because of the heat and partly because, somehow, he felt that it was the most appropriate thing to do. This place was like a shrine though Jamil was not certain to which deity it might have been dedicated. The air smelt fresh not musty at all, as he might have expected in such a place, and it blew up around his shoulders which now were bare since he had peeled off his shirt. And the air was cool as though it had risen from some underground stream and Jamil felt refreshed by it and by the music which was growing louder with each step. He couldn't define the words of the song. Although they seemed to be in English, the rhythm was unlike anything he had ever heard before – wild and yet, at the same time, intense, focused and elegant. He closed his eyes as he walked. The song was rising and the wind from below billowed all around his body while the light was growing brighter. And, barely pausing, he allowed his trousers to fall around his ankles. He stepped out from the skin of everything that had gone before and went towards the light. Then he tripped over a rock and fell headlong. He came down with his full weight on the dusty floor of the cavern so that, for a few seconds, he was dazed and winded.

The temperature in the cave was similar to that of Lahore in midsummer, during the period just preceding the onset of the monsoon. It was a dry heat and so was bearable. He was aware that his whole body was covered in sweat and also that he was completely naked. The heat made the blood pulse through his head so that it became difficult to distinguish between the drum beats of the song and the contractions of his own heart. When, at last, he was able again to rise, having checked that he hadn't injured himself, Jamil saw that he was close to the rear wall of the cave. The wall was almost flat yet it was scored with the marks of a sweeping, curved blade as though the stone had been cut using a scythe or a scimitar. About five feet from the ground and completely flush with the wall was a small oval window. Jamil went up closer and peered through the glass. He had to go up really close to be able to look directly through the window which was small – about the size of a human palm. He pressed right up so that he was able to feel his breath rebound, cold, from its surface. But all he saw was his own face. The window was a mirror.

He tried to look behind the mirror but it seemed completely contiguous with the surface of the wall. He lifted the index finger of his left hand and gingerly touched the glass. He shuddered and withdrew his finger. It was as though he had touched a block of ice. He repeated the action. This time, he did not remove his finger. When, eventually, he could bear the burning sensation no longer, he drew back. The tip of his digit appeared flattened and was white. When he looked back at the mirror, he saw a trail of dark liquid run down across its surface. There was a green rust around the edges of the glass and this hue seemed to run right through its substance as though it arose from a somewhat deeper layer. Then Jamil realised that the *sheesha* was made not of glass but of Kasperia copper and that, therefore, it must be a very old mirror. The tip of his finger was tingling and was still pale and cold. He raised his left hand again but this time he placed his thumb and the tips of all four fingers against the frozen surface. The tingling sensation streamed through his body in waves that grew more powerful the longer he held his hand against the metal. He flattened his palm, pressed the skin down against the copper. The flat, polished metal was shimmering like the surface of a *jheel* in the moonlight. It was as though it might, at any moment, turn to water. The music thudded through him – violins, bass guitar, clarinet, voice – and it was rising to a climax, he could tell that much, and it lifted from the surface of the subterranean *darya* that flowed from some far, northern place that lay beyond even his dreams and, just before he passed out, Jamil found that, at last, he could make out the single word that comprised the whole song and that was being repeated over and over and that word was 'Kashmir'.

◉◎◉◎◉

Zaf killed the decks and moved towards the mike.

Ahhhhhhhhhhh . . .
  Whit a swirlin sune! Makes ye want tae live yer life in a dream. Kashmir, those cool northern lakes, the houseboats, the wondrous aromatic flowers. Aye, an the blood, the soajers, the bombers, the daith, the wholly unnecessary waste ae life. Some day, it'll end and, then, like wi aw wars, ivirywan will forget those who died, will curl their memories up into just so much flesh and stone, while the livin will transfer their hate on tae some other object an will wonder jist why it aw happened an jist

222

whit it wis aw fur. Weel, Ah'll tell ye whit it's fur. It's
tae determine who rules, who gets rich, who can jerk aff
the people best. Aye. An that Led Zep soang will still be
playin, refashioned via the skin an sinew ae Le Royaume
du Maroc. *Arey*, Jimmy, *yaar*! Pluck us some ae they
guid vibes. *Arey*, Rabbie, howlin wi the swellin revolution
that ye are, let us rise upon yer braith tae the peaks an
caves ae the moontain lands, the Dunnet Heids, the
Heilans ae Kashmir. Ah'm goin aff tae pray fur that puir
country and fur its crushed people. An ma prayer will be
a soang.

Khabr aur Mausum. See yous later.

FOUR A.M.

It wis four am. N 'n' W. K 'n' M. Asians loved *mukhafaf*. *Khabr, khabr, khabr sunaye*! NWFP. ISI. BJP. PPP. Jesus, it wis a fuckin code! A great bloody Enigma Machine. The whole system had probably been invented by some constipated British *babu* with a hyper-declensioned brain (there had never been anything remotely romantic about Latin) who had been unable to cope with the swelterin dance of Hindustan and its holy genitalia quills. Abbreviate the DJ! Decline it, boy! Bo, bis, bit, bimus, bitis, bunt! Tawse! Tawse! Tawse! It wis definitely not a legacy of the Mughals – Farsi wis not an abbreviatable language. No, the whole monstrous series of dots and capitals, the whole pompous culture of indecipherability and wilful obscurantism had arisen from the collective mind of the grey men. Probably sometime soon after the death of the gouty Slut King, George *Chaar*. OK, it has evolved somewhat in the hundred and eighty years since Georgie Porgie had breathed his portly last. It had changed from CPR Charles Burton Esq., DPMB, Acting Deputy Assistant British Resident in Poona and his *chai*-sippin, quinine-guzzlin, tight-bodiced, pig-iron chastity-belted mem-sahib, to MBBS, LLB, BAcc, R 'n' R, R 'n' F, Z 'n' B, Z 'n' Z. Truncation. Prick names. Like fellation, it made people easier to swallow. And, like some ancient river god, Zaf had swallowed everyone that night. He had subsumed the whole fuckin world. Past, present and . . .

Ivir stood oan tap ae a tall buildin an gazed doon at the street below? Eighty-sivin floors up, the waws shimmerin silver in the light ae the perfectly roon moon. Ye've hit the sky an thur's really only wan thing ye can do. Only wan action ye can take.

SWITCH. DECK A. A slight rattle. The mechanism wis tirin. The view fae above.

'The View From Below'.

Remember this wan . . .?

Pregnant pause. Expert mute.

Naw?

Another.

OK. Ah'll gie ye the answer aifter the song hus played oot. Ha! Who said thur wisnae ony suspense oan Radio Chaandni? Madness is aw aboot suspense. *Arey, yaar!* Ah'm a mean dudie-wudie, am Ah not? Tae keep ma audience hangin oan, at four in the mornin. Unforgivable. But the answers are always like blasts ae cauld wind. An this is a hoat summer's night, dark, aye, dark, so it's aw big queues, big questions. Or mibbee it's wan big question.

?

Shadows on the wall. He could see inside the room below just by drawin his finger down the pane of glass – he could trace out the faint shadows from the radio station reflected on to the walls of the buildings on the opposite side of the street. Freaky. Must be the music.

The party wis in full swing. Bhangra-ragga-hipper-hopper beat ruled the day and girls and guys were dancin like in a club, separate-but-together, orgasmic twitch, lune-light fandangoes pirouettin on the black wooden floor and Zaf thought he could make out Harry an even Raj/Taj, fuck, even him, dancin maniacally to the beat. Harry's earring twitched like a golden clitoris while his head swayed from side to side like in a rock video. The music wis by some Asian techno band whose name Zaf had difficulty rememberin at first even though he had segued the damned CD himself. But, then, he recalled they were known as The Wind Machines and it wis their song, 'The View from Below', the reference bein to Marilyn Monroe and her famous, wind-blown white skirt. From somewhere, a white light flashed off and on so that, one moment, the dancers would be hyper-illuminated and, the next, they would fall back into darkness and then the only things in the room were the drum 'n' bass and the great, hauntin wails of the lead singer. It reminded Zaf of an older track he'd heard around the start of his time wi Zilla . . . in the beginnin . . .

. . . that slide

They were usin the same chord changes, the same crazy trumpet. Then he had it. It was the same song, man. The Wind Machines had sampled a section of the middle eight into their own thing. What wis the song called? The old song . . . ?

There wis the word – almost buried beneath fifty licks of bass – Damascus. Yeah, that wis it – 'Damascus' by Richard Strange and the Engine Room. He remembered now. Zilla had got up and danced a sinuous, *doomni*-style dance like the one Helen did in *Sholay* and everyone, *everyone*, had been transfixed by her. In those days, Zilla had still worn *shalvar kamises*. Yeah, Zilla could've been an *Asian Babe* if she'd wanted. She might as well have made some money from her quest for self-destruction – the murder of her children and of herself. The music and dancin had moved on light years from the white-suited electric bhangra of the late eighties and had merged with club sounds and Brit Pop and slush Latino and more and the ravers themselves had altered too – long nights in the clubs had transformed the weave of their muscles and their lives had begun to dance out a new geometry. Funny how people changed – the anonymity of a club had always made Zaf uneasy. Mibbee that wis why he had become a DJ. He wandered around the dark room amidst the sweatin bodies which he couldn't help bumpin into. The dancers were unrecognisable – occasionally, he made out a face or a hand but then the lights went out and, when they flashed on again, the space had become empty. He liked samples, felt comfortable with them. He was a sample of Pakistan, thrown at random into Scotland, into its myths. And, in Lahore, he had felt like a sample of Glasgow in the ancient City of the Conquerors. Yeah, the journey from the Clyde to the Ravi wis a voyage through time, space and spirit. It required a leap of faith, a sword dance but with scimitars instead of claymores.

Even though he wis just watchin shadows on the wall, Zaf felt himself drawn in by the wheelin dance. His limbs began to move and his body swam through the thick night air and, with his fingers, he sliced the whorls of cigarette smoke into crescent moons and the strobe slowed everythin so that the dancers moved with total grace like the fishes in a deep dark loch.

Oh, fuck, now they were back in the cubicle again, in his cubicle. Ruby, Fizz, the lot of them. How could so many people cram into wan wee room? It wis so bloody hot! And they were still dancin as though they were intent on extendin the party right through the old buildin, as though, like cats, they were determined to claim its stone as their own. But it would never be theirs. Or his. He needed air. To try and cool himself down, he tugged at his T-shirt, almost snapped the neckband. He wis expandin.

One day, Babs began to bleed from her head. Zaf had never been able to figure out just how it had started. He thought he'd seen her rub her nose, her ever so slightly retroussé *naak*, just moments before the bleed began but it wis one of those things that the more he thought about it, the less he felt able to know, the less capable he wis of delineatin in his mind exactly what had happened. Perhaps it wis just the muddlin effect of memory, of the act of rememberin, or mibbee it wis the fact that, the moment blood started to flow, everythin seemed to go provisional, like it wis a reminder of old mortality and of the fact that death can affect even the young. And it wis then, as he helped her press on one (was it the right or left?) nostril and as he watched the blood swirl beyond the untidy yellow mop of her hair, down into the sink outlet, Zaf realised that, in spite of his more cynical moments when he and Babs were jist a toxic mixture of self-interest and physical revenge, actually, he did feel quite protective of this being with her fragile back, whose bones seemed to abut the skin painfully closely. And then he thought that the very fact that he had thought these thoughts must mean somethin – the way she snorted the water in the shower, the particular cadences of her love-makin – and, all the while, echoin in his brain, echoin against the clean tiles of the shower cubicle, whale songs from beneath the fall of the water, and it wis a *gana* he either loved or hated or, sometimes, both.

Spirals of red congealin, liquefyin, then congealin again.

Washin away the shit from her head. And, when, after what seemed like half an hour had passed, it stopped, Babs said that her brain felt lighter, as though whatever pressure had built up had needed to be released. Yet it was the first time it had ever happened to her. So she'd said, anyway. He imagined what it might be like to kiss the closed lids of a completely unknown woman, to feel, against the texture of his lips, the porpoise tip of her nose, her lips murmurin some words from a dream, the smooth, surf-wave of her forehead . . .

Her eyes would open, slowly at first, and she would be unsure whether or not she wis still dreamin but, then, as arousal would turn to fear, startlement, whatever, the lids would flicker more rapidly in an attempt to clear away the subconscious from the eyes. Babs's face. Infidelity. He felt that, by havin this unknown woman, this motorcycle girl with whose brain he held no common ground save that of the roads which ran in loops, outside, all around them, he wis betrayin somethin but he wasn't sure what.

'I'm not sure what,' he said aloud into the strobe lights and the deafenin music and it was as though he wis mimin.

It wis burnin in the room – there wis too much human breath. The window had slid shut again and someone had tried to open it but they had lacked the necessary technique or mibbee they had just been too drunk and so Zaf shoved his way through the dancers. Their bodies were skinned, burnin, raw. In the glarin, almost ultraviolet light, everyone wis white. By the time he reached the window, Zaf could smell women's perfume on his skin. *Chumbeylee.* Jasmine. Damascus. He felt kind of woozy. Swayed back on his heels. Grabbed on to the bar at the bottom of the window. Tried to stare into the blackness but the flashin lights from the room below bled silver on to the glass. He needed air, needed rid of the strobe. It had filled the whole street with its shameless revelations. With all his strength, Zaf yanked the window up. Almost ripped his chest apart. He leaned out into the night and breathed – deeply. The music faded behind him and, slowly, the dizziness subsided. Zaf felt an achin in his belly. Should've gone fur a *sannie* or a *cairry-oot*, he thought. Too late now. Everythin would be shut. Even the *Bangali cairry-oot* would be closed, their workers gone to bed or to *chirpaies* or into nightmares of Partition. Not the Partition everyone still talked about even though it had been over fifty years ago, not the Romantic one between India and Pakistan with Jinnah and Nehru and the great Big Soul dressed all in white. Naw, the *Bangali* night workers would be dreamin of the carve-up that no one ever spoke about – the one between the two halves of Pakistan. Nineteen hundred and seventy-one. Thirteen hundred and ninety-one. When the great army of the Motherland, the Land of the Pure, had marched into East Bengal and massacred everythin that moved and turned the Ganga Jumna red. And, later, that great, fashionable Maharishi-pishi guru land, India, had mucked about with the rivers and so, except for the burgeonin call centres, the place was now a permanent fuckin disaster. Bungle-desh. But that wis what all those Punjabi types had told him and who could ever believe what they said? How come they had all those call centres in Dhaka if it wis such a disaster zone? Dialin tone. It wis almost a song. The perfect elocution-English of Directory Enquiries: 'Can I help you?' Purveyors of facts, of mathematics and underwater cables. Fish dances. The truth wis there wis no truth. You had to make up your own version of everythin. Every day, you had to be a wee creator. And, all the while, different versions of the absolute fought over your corpse. Pretentious rubbish! Fuck all that. Here, in Scotland, they were all one big happy family. Enemies-become-brothers. Here, all the wars were civil. 'If it gazes at a mirror for long enough, hate will grow into love.' Zaf remembered readin that somewhere – probably in some book of wisdom or other. The words which had made no difference. The world wasn't ready for the prophets. All the revelations. Futile. Damascus. Makkah. Il Papa. Futile. He began to feel the sensation of a woman's fingertips creep over the surface of his back.

◎◎◎◎◎

In the days before the slum clearances, Glasgow had been a city of tall buildings and dark tunnels, narrow *mohallay*. People lived on top of one another in looming dark structures called tenements and many of these four-storey, Egyptian-style constructions had only outside toilets – tiny, freezing huts stuck in some far corner of the backcourt beyond the wash house, the drying green, the rough, scuffed bits of ungrassed earth. Much of the time, only the top floors were able to catch the wan sunlight . . .

This was how Jamil Ayaan pictured it. This was the in-formative and definitive newsreel which he had constructed scientifically to fill the gaps, to lay down some kind of narrative for what they had done and for the way they were living now. Govan was not a place for the faint-hearted. His heart had been vibrant – once. When he had dreamed his lover into another, better, life, when he had taken hold of the arc of the steering wheel between the soft cushions of his palms, he had been both driver and navigator. When he had faced down the whitened stone expressions of the thin-lipped ladies-of-the-land, their muscles bound with the twine of all that history, from skin to brain to bone, the heavy, the frozen, cosmesis of Empire, Jamil Ayaan's heart had swelled, had grown enormous and, like some mythical cartoon heart, its plasticity had become infinite. Those thin lips, two streaks of paint, set hard as cement, biting off the words, holding back love, burying it beneath the tomb of two centuries or more of received wisdom. Denying internal complexities. Nowhere was as complex as the sewers. From the third floor of their tenement, through the netting of the curtains and over the wooden lip of their valve radio, in the blue dawn light, Jamil and Rashida could see half of Glasgow open up beneath them, with all the convolutions and intensities, the shadows and light and ineffability of a Victorian city. Tall at the centre, the buildings tended to flatten out as they moved towards the outskirts. Every morning, the sun would flood into their flat as it broke, a perfect orange disc, over the clean line of the horizon. The windows, glinting amber fire into the sky, seemed to project such vibrancy that, at times, Jamil had wondered whether, in fact, it was the big plate glass of the tenements that caused the sun to rise and not the other way around.

Those ferocious landladies, the mothers of Teddy boys, and their Orange-and-Green, dance-floor husbands, the heavy men who single-handledly, heroically, in a glorious mess of fire and light and polished wood, built those great white ships that cruised off towards the wharfs of Bombay and Karachi, the old shores, warmed by dreamy sunset strolls down by Clifton Beach, now long evanesced into dream. They were like *djinns*, those men – spirits who had become blind to their powers, even though they held that strength right between their hands. They had all been in the Forces, they had fought in the War – some of the older ones had even been soldiers in the War-To-End-All-Wars. With their Gatling-gun fingers, they had killed and died in their millions and they were called lions. And, somehow, they seemed to have already relinquished this heroic role and to have allowed themselves to be subsumed into a different narrative, a tale of boozy Saturday nights and fast, dry sex. And muscle-dancing, with one another and with their apron-bellied women, fist-fighting through the rain and slime. Sometimes, Jamil would notice that, especially around the eyes, the women's complexions had altered overnight, from pale pink to dark mauve. Sounds through the wall, disordered songs, their scores cut from the dark hulls of unmade ships. The swaying miasma of football crowds, singing through the night. Red, white and blue heavens, hard-blown skies, winter, summer and the spaces in between. A different country, another religion, a separate *maghas*.

But not everyone was cold and distant. There were some among the heretics of the town who smiled and befriended the young Indian couple (which is how everyone saw Jamil and Rashida – no one, it seemed, had ever heard of the Land of the Pure whereas almost every person had either fought over, sweated through or knew someone who had 'served in' the massive and inscrutable land of Hindustan). A couple of Jewish families, who lived further along the street, had arrived some decades earlier, having been pogrom'd from some part of that even more vast, and possibly even more inscrutable, continent that lay to the east of the Dnieper, and Zaf had learned that their name had been shortened at every border crossing. These people seemed to understand what it felt like always to be on the outside, never to quite fully comprehend the totality of a country or its people or the timbre of its humours. Borysthenes. The old kosher shops of the Gorbals. The garment district, woven tightly around Cathcart Road. East European music, fading, twirling mazurkas. Kahn, Cohen, Susskind, Sandler – identities defined by occupation, function, purpose. And then, downstairs, lived a Roman Catholic family from West Belfast, who had been well used to feeling the tracks of a Harland and Wolff work boot on their foreheads and who fried absolutely everything – even bread – in order to make the food palatable. The stench of old guilt, laden heavily across the net curtains. At times, it seemed as though the whole of Ireland, past and present, had moved, en masse, across the sea. A sort of reverse migration. In the history of the world, no one had ever gone east, except maybe the Crusaders and then, much later, the capitalists. Oh, and the victims of Stalin. Such a movement was against nature – it turned time the wrong way around, sunset-to-sunrise. Apparently, their genealogies stretched thin beyond the Great Famine, these people, from Donegal, from Galway and Cork, had intended to sail to America but, by mistake or else in desperation, they had jumped on to the wrong boats and, when they'd woken the next morning, expecting to see open ocean, what they'd got was Yorkhill Quay and Irish Fever. But, in whichever direction one travelled and from whichever direction one had arrived, the work was always the same. Heavy, stinking, bottom-of-the-heap labour, a symphony of broken promises, of dreams cold-burned by inevitable rejection, forged in wrought iron by the strident, dismissive oligarchies of white Anglo-Saxon Protestantism. Such people, the cold doyens of the Presbytery, whose eyes seemed perpetually narrowed against some kind of blinding sunrise which they would never see, also seemed to have forgotten that the Temple of Solomon, that piece of musical architecture which they worshipped above all others, had been built in the East.

But dwelling on such frustrations could drive one crazy and so, bit by bit, day by day, Jamil allowed such painful awarenesses to sink into darkness, into the moments when

Rashida's sleeping body would half-turn away from him so that the angle of her shoulder, suddenly exposed between strap and thready neckline, would be bathed in the metallic light of the docklands moon. He felt the desire to stretch out his hand and touch her skin. It was not a sexual desire – it was hardly even human – it arose from some deep region which Jamil could not place, let alone name. Time and again, he would imagine this small movement – his hand flitting across the *chaandi* of the bed – yet, every time, he found himself paralysed as though trapped in the kind of dream that would overtake him during the moments before waking. The sight would make Jamil want to cry. Why had he brought this woman to this place? Why was he subjecting her to this life? These smells? This elemental hopelessness? And there was no way back. Their boats had sunk in the broiling confluence of the waters of the Ravi and the Clyde. That part of their lives that had gone before now belonged to the ghosts of themselves. Yet, here, in the night's cold heart, tightly bound between the white cotton sheets, her skin bore a luminescence that was like the blood of God. Once, early on, Jamil had traced the tips of all five fingers down one of the rectangular blocks of stone that went to make up the dwelling places of the city's souls, of his soul. He had been somewhat surprised (though his surprise had been tempered and, to some degree, mediated by the electric, the constant awareness of the unfamiliar in which the immigrant per-petually must dwell) that the stone had crumbled, that the tiny grains, some of which glittered as they caught the sunlight, had slipped away from the building into the whorls of his skin. He had raised his hand to his lips and, glancing around quickly in case anyone should see him and think him insane or else possessed by the mythic and unchangeable need for inscrutable and purposeless, for cunning and sleazy, ritual,

Jamil Ayaan elegantly partook upon his tongue of the finest wheaten Giffnock sandstone available to Edwardian masons. Later that same day, he ate the red Ayrshire tenements, too. The twin faces of Aadam.

A smile, a tiny piece of advice, the recognition of a common humanity – such things assume an importance, for the totally receptive immigrant, far greater than can ever be imagined by the giver of the gift. Indeed, Jamil and Rashida's world had turned into one defined on the point of a needle – each sensation, each discovery, every microscopic detail, was a diamond-and-gold icon to be studied, argued over, weighed carefully on the superstitious and impossibly taut dialectic of unfamiliarity. The act of betrayal had been shared – she had left behind house and husband and he had abandoned wife and child – yet, now that her dream, their dream, had been realised, the only possible role for Rashida was that of dutiful, aproned wife. Amidst the ponderous, brittle fragility of Bakelite and lard, such was the way of Britain, such was the way of the world in those days.

The stink of alcohol rose through the air and, as it rose, it became concentrated, deadly, so that up there, on the top floor of the red-stone tenement, it was possible to become lightly intoxicated on the breath of the previous night's drams. Rain on the morning cranes, the chains swinging big in the wind, wide arcs wheeling against the white, to a dissonant, yet comforting, dream music. The flowers of this northern land bore no aromas.

A sari, swishing along the cold wet streets of the Parish of Govan, was apt to make heads turn but it was not always an unpleasant feeling to be marked out in this manner – it made an exciting change from the state of near anonymity one bore in the palace gardens of Lahore. And, yet, it seemed that, in Scotland, one might do almost anything so long as it remained within the bounds of essential probity – bounds which had been set sometime during the period between the death of His Royal Highness, Prince Albert, the Prince Consort, and the nineteen-hundred-and-forty blitz, when Kenya, Uganda, Tanganyika, Zanzibar, Australia, Britain, India, Northern Rhodesia, Southern Rhodesia, Malaya, Nepal, New Zealand, Canada, Somaliland, Cameroon, Muscat and Oman, Guyana and all the princely states of Hindustan had stood alone against the bulging codpieces of Il Duce, the dominatrix-obsessed Nazis, their fellow travellers, the fashionable Fascists of France and the less chic, but dangerously psychotic, loonies of Budapest, Bucharest and Zagreb. The dead German prince had been resurrected and magically transfigured on to the smooth, cylindrical haunches of cheap biscuit tins, upon which he ice-skated, and, always, his head was graced almost casually with a gleaming black silk topper. His dissolute son had given his name to the Teddy boys, the rock 'n' roll Brownshirt lumpenproles who plagued street corners and who imagined themselves as skulking micro-Presleys. They would shout insults at anyone who was in any way different. Yet, by the time Jamil and Rashida arrived, they were already dying out or moving on and were frantically exchanging their silly long coats for leathers and jangling silver chains and then leaping on to the hard saddles of stallion-black motorbikes. It was a natural move, really, for these sons of the warrior Tommies. They would never have been seen dead on an Italian scooter though! Such things were only for those effete middle-class Jew-lovers who worshipped French haircuts and black music.

None of this, of course, in the least concerned Jamil and Rashida. As immigrants, they existed well outside of any indigenous tribal social dynamic. They danced outwith the music of the folk. Or, rather, they did not dance at all. No ballrooms with globes spinning and glittering for them. They were of this material world and they had left any *djinn* dreams at home. Now they were the *djinns* become flesh. They lived on the top floor of the abode of souls. The night they had escaped – or, even before, maybe even right from the day they had first met – their time had petrified. Even before they had known of it, their blood, their breath, had turned to red stone.

It was into this strange complex of bruises, biscuit tins and the pristine painted hulls of ocean liners that Jamil and Rashida entered in their almost moribund Ford Popular. When he sold the vehicle for scrap, Jamil kept only one threadbare blanket, the woollen one with which they had covered themselves during the long nights of their journey, and, down the years, this *qaaleen* remained with them, hardly washed, never used, flying like some bum magic carpet mysteriously from one store cupboard to another, remaining always on the verge of being tossed into the garbage. Perhaps it was a symbol of something though Zaf had never been sure exactly of what. There wis nuthin fuckin magical about anythin. He needed somethin wild, somethin angry. Catharsis, sailin a boat down a river of fire. Burn the past slowly in his head, the darkenin past that wis Charonic, Pharaonic, pointless. A cult of the dyin. Those guys that slammed all that as bein a 'culture of complaint' hadn't got a fuckin clue. Or, rather, they had which wis worse. The politics of knowledge, the philosophers of ignorance. Playground bullies. Teddy boys. Biscuit-tin emperors. Fuck em all! Eat them all. Sing them into the ground! Power chords. !!!Wham-bam-bam!!! Lucid skies. Save Our Souls!!!

◉◉◉◉◉

The mechanism had switched over to Deck B and it wis now playin a far more strident, aggressive song – Kula Shaker's 'S.O.S.'. Zaf wis clutchin his playlist as though it wis the last *surah* of a sinkin book. The music radiated all around him – it seemed to fall on him from above and to rise up through the floorboards and to seam into the lines of his bones, his flesh. Good music wis like that. It filled your world, it completed you. It replicated your soul and turned you to gold. Durin the ninety nights of his sojourn with Radio Chaandni, deep in the aureate darkness, through the walls and the floor, at times Zaf would hear two completely different pieces of music, just muted enough not to be able to make out the melodies or words. In places, the notes would merge and, from somewhere, there would arise a third tune, one that nobody had ever written but which sounded better than either of its component parts. Here it goes. Here it comes. Cold turkey shock – jump forty years. Before its time. Before time.

> Sometimes I feel that the world
> Isn't ready for me.

Glasgow hadn't been ready for Zilla. Its vein hadn't been broad enough. It had burst and blood had covered everythin. Red, black and the moon.

He heard voices down in the street. Some kind of a commotion. Christ, it wis three thirty in the bloody mornin. Even the wild boys had to sleep sometime. Then he re-membered that they didn't get up till after twelve noon – at which time, they would leave no shadow. He craned his neck to get a look. Down below, someone wis batterin on the door which was the back entrance to the community centre. It wis like they had a fuckin batterin ram. The dancers would not be able to hear it, Zaf thought. The music wis too loud.

Blood transfusion, revolution . . .

What the fuck . . .?
There wis a group of lads, all Asian, gathered in the
narrow street that wis really a bin lane and several of them
were launchin at the door. One looked up. Saw him. Hate.
Fuck. Zaf pulled back into the room. The music wis deafenin.
Someone had turned it up. Rome before the Fall. Last Night
in Dhaka. Frantically, Zaf tried to locate Raj or Harry or
anyone who might have had any kind of authority. He
shoved his way through the song.

> This is the age of decay and hypocrisy
> Sometimes I feel that the world
> Isn't ready for me
>
> Every time I turn
> A microscopic worm
> Is telling me he's it
> Dressed in robes of cosmic ego
> Crawling round in shit

The perfume had died on the dancers' skins.
Once, he thought that Raj had bumped into him but then
he saw that it wis just Fizz. Fuckface Fizz. Then, in the
middle of the crowd, he saw Ruby twitchin like an epileptic.
He forced his way over. Grabbed her arm. Caffeine buzz. Or
coke mibbee. Where Zilla had been, Ruby would follow. Or
mibbee not. Mibbee she wis stronger than that. At Ruby's
centre wis a core of iron. He felt it there, burnin beneath the
skin of her forearm. Molten iron. Like the earth. She stopped

dancin. Glared at him. He screamed in her ear. Pointed downwards and then at the window. She didn't understand. He pulled Ruby through the crowd which somehow seemed to part far more easily now that he wis with her. Melted, just like ghee. He and Ruby both stuck their heads out the window. Her arm pushed up against him and he could feel the softness of her skin, already cool in the night air.

'What is it?' she asked, irritably.

'I don't know. A gang, it looks like.' He paused. 'The Kinnin Park Boys, mibbee.'

'Fuck.'

'Yeah.'

'What're we gonna do?'

In spite of the situation, he felt a flutter in his chest. Felt her arm shift, just a little, against his, in a delicate friction.

The gang wis bangin on the door, regularly poundin like some kind of medieval army. A pulse beneath a pulse beneath a pulse. Across the street, Zaf made out the figure of a man. Sharp suit. Shades. The narrow type of shades, like Malcolm X's. Power vision. Even in the darkness, he recognised Zafar. Not the boy in the old photograph – this wis the other, the third, Zafar. This wis the gangsta man, the Shark ae Kinnin Park. Zafar, too, had been there always. He wis a year or so younger than Zaf but, even as a kid, he'd had the face of an auld man – the way some kids do, especially the ones that come from houses with no hope. Their lives are slashed across their faces like the marks of some black elemental, charred deep into the skin. They know when the exact moment of their deaths will be. Zafar's face wis sandpaper – the rough side. The scars had been there from the day he wis born and mibbee from before that. But it wis his eyes that marked him out from all the rest. They were blue-green, underwater marble. Not that Zaf'd ever really looked into them. He felt that, if he did, he would be lost forever. But you didn't stare at Zafar. Zafar's reputation went before him. The rumour went that, once, he'd cut off the end of a guy's finger, just because he'd felt insulted in some obscure way. Fuck sake. He had come from what they called 'a mixed marriage' – as though all marriages weren't mixes of one sort or another. Zafar's father – Faisalabadi like almost everyone else – had hooked up with this slag from the East End (or, at least, that wis how she had always been described – Zaf had imagined a straw-haired woman with curlers everywhere and the legs of a dog) but the liaison had lasted only as long as it had taken to get a divorce, after which, his father had turned to drink while his mother had run off to the chip shops back east from where she'd come. A fittin end, Zaf thought, to what, in the mid seventies, must have seemed like a Bonnie 'n' Clyde adventure except that there'd been no lead to end it all. Mixed marriages, in those days, were nearly always enacted between men made tall with platforms and women whose only attribute wis the fact that they were able to wear miniskirts without lookin like hormone-injected chickens. The relationships were formed on the lighted floors of discos or in the darkness of dirty flick-houses and, when both crazes fell apart, so did the marriages – killed by punk and videos. Sex 'n' spit 'n' rock 'n' roll. His papa had occasionally talked about some of his mates who'd fallen into that one. Not like him – he'd fallen into the nearest sewer and never crawled out. There were worse fates.

Down in the street, the crowd had swelled and now seemed to consist of twenty young lads, some in suits, others in gangsta gear and all with greased hair. Brylcreeme'd or gel'd mibbee. These were the sons and grandsons ae the *kisaan* who had powered the buses, the underground trains, the machines of the sweatshop underwear-manufacturers. The whole of Glasgow had walked in their footsteps and worn their clothes. With bare soles had they trodden out new, hard paths along the Clyde and they had clothed the lily-white bodies of whole generations of Scots and then, later, they had filled their stomachs too. You eat what you are. If that wis the case, then Glasgae wis Faisalabad a hundred times over. But their sons and daughters had gone in the opposite direction and had become Scots. Right down to their gangs and their dancin and their chip-bhatti *sahib* footba tops, they had sipped of the waters of the Clyde and had become cold killers. And they were swearin at him and Ruby in a mixture of Glaswegian and Faisalabadi.

'*Maa di pudhi*!'

'Fuckin *gandu*!'

'Oh, *chholae*!'

'*Teri maa di lun*!'

'Mibbee we should call the cops,' he suggested, not too loudly.

She did not reply but her arm removed itself and she was back in the room. He followed her, feelin stupid.

'Whit're ye doin?' he asked as he trailed after her.

'Lookin fur Harry.'

'Ah couldnae find him before.'

She gave him a look, just a brief, derisory glance, which reduced him from the status of bein stupid to that of bein a fool. It wis OK bein stupid. There were lots of stupid people about – most of the world wis basically stupid – but bein thought of as a fool implied some kind of Westernisation which, like sensibility, might only have been acquired by associatin with too many arty-farty types up the West End. Zilla had been right. He wis a coward. In spite of the cold air that billowed through the window, he felt his cheeks begin to burn. Fuck. Anyway, he thought, what could Harry do? Look what they had done to Raj. The dancin continued and the rhythm wis faster than ever. Couldn't they hear? Or mibbee they thought the bangin from below wis just another sample from some old song. Some crap eighties' thing with an unimaginative, explodin beat an gratin Springsteen vocals. Constipated denim. He went over to where Ruby wis talkin to Harry. She'd seemed to know just where he wis. She had that kind of instinct. A sureness of herself. Like Babs. But mibbee he had just nipped out somewhere for a moment. That made Zaf feel a bit better. A bit. Harry wis frownin and his face, like that of everyone else in the room, wis covered in perspiration. You had to be pretty fit to be able to dance like that all night long. Yeah, OK, 'All Night Long'. Like Springsteen, Lionel Ritchie wis a hugely talented guy but the song wis a load of crap. Like all really bad tunes, it relied solely on its ability to insert itself, like an advertisin jingle, into a loop of your brain and then to be unremovable no matter what you subsequently did, regardless of how many decent or even brilliant songs you might immerse yourself in. Zaf had a long list of bad songs. They were like viruses: Phil Collins's voice; Adam Ant's entire repertoire; Wizzard; Bucks Fizz; ninety-six per cent of Elvis – a-haw-haw; one hundred-and-ten per cent of Meatloaf (on grounds of taste and sanity, Zaf thought the existence of that outfit would, in itself, justify the reimposition of state censorship); Elton John after nineteen seventy-two; Dollar; Mud; Showaddywaddy; Boney M; Bobby Vee (he may've had rubber balls but his music just didn't bounce); all those daft, clean boy bands and girl bands; Sidney Devine; Daniel O'Donnell; most soft-focus Philly Soul; classic pops; Engelbert Humperdinck – the singer not the composer; nearly all of Whitney Houston; the Bachelors; the Carpenters; Lynyrd Skynyrd; Level 42; Haircut 100; Haysie Fuckin Fantaysie . . . it went on and on and that wis because it wis no respecter of time and because there wis far more terrible music than there wis good. It wis like life, really.

It wis a personal thing, OK. But there had to be some kind of aesthetic, even if everyone disagreed with what that meant. Zilla had introduced him to the joys of good rock music, of pop art and psychedelia. Once he'd tasted the good stuff, he'd let all the crap sink away. She'd had her own mind and he'd swum around in it for a while and had indulged himself in her obsessions. Once, she had been quite somethin . . .

He couldn't hear what they were sayin – Ruby 'n' Harry. Sounded like a comedy act or a love story mibbee. American. North-west coast. Up where it rained sometimes but where the rain and the high-rises, gleamin in the darkness, were seen as somehow romantic. Like in Indian films. Not in Scotland though. Fuck sake, not here. After all, when all wis said and done, Harry wis half white. Halfway to Paradise. Ha! He craned his neck to try and hear. A pricklin sensation ran along the skin of his spine. It definitely gave you an entry, one foot in the door, either to be part white or else to marry white. You became an honorary person. No longer a Paki, nigger, wog, now you were a good trooper – basically a foreman, the kind of person who might be relied upon to make the trains run on time. The Grand Trunk Fuckin Railway rollin on straight-and-narrow silver across the slow, burned plane of existence.

He felt a vague sense of havin been cheated. This had been his thing – he had noticed the gang trying to get in at the door and he had told Ruby about it. But now he felt well and truly out of it. The usual. It bugged him that he had never been at the centre of anythin. Instead, he would always seem to find himself spinnin further and further out like that astronaut in *2001* – except that the spaceman's had been a graceful exit. A waltz. No Elton John there. Zaf, on the other hand, would be bouncin along in the darkness of space, totally out of control . . .

'Harry,' he said. 'Harry.'

The Station Master glanced at him for a moment but Ruby wis still talkin, her mouth wis goin like a fuckin locomotive. He could hear sounds but he couldn't make out their meanin. It wis like he wis listenin to a foreign language. Punjabi mibbee. He'd never learned his own mother tongue – not properly so that he would have been able to converse in it, to construct meanin from chaos. He knew how to swear in Punjabi and, boy, did it not have the best expletives this side of hell. Things that would have made a hardened criminal wince. *Maa di pudhi* – 'mother's vagina'. *Chholae* – 'You are a clitoris'. *Teri maa di lun* – 'Your mother is a penis'. Aye, in the expletive wormhole, mothers had it hard. But Ruby and Harry were talkin English. The music – his music – was so bloody loud that no one else in the room had even sensed there might be somethin wrong. But Zaf could hear it. The knockin on wood. The bangin. Then he wasn't sure. But he could feel it vibrate through his feet like that deaf drummer he'd heard of – some red-headed woman or other . . . But, then, women were like that. They could feel through walls. Sometimes, he'd thought that Zilla had been able to hear his thoughts. When she wis stoned, that wis. Babs wis telepathic too but in a different way. He hadn't really been able to work out how it wis different and he wasn't sure that he ever would. Some things about women remained mysteries, even when you had lived with them for years. You could never feel completely secure. Sex wis just a temporary thing, an arc of energy. But, once the moment had passed, you would stand apart from each other, separate as ever. No matter how hard you tried, you could never hide inside their bodies, you could never feel the rhythm which the blood made as it tanked about in the darkness. And now he felt the rhythm of the poundin from below slide up the long bones of his limbs and smash into the case of his skull. It wis like someone wis readin his mind. Fuck. He gripped his forehead. He wis standin by a table. He must've circled across the wall of the cubicle without realisin it. Slid along the axis of the wall. There wis a bottle filled with a greenish liquid and, beside it, a single glass. The light glimmered through the substance of the bottle and the effect wis oddly hypnotic. Zaf reached down and picked up the bottle. There wis a label on the front and across the label, in black letterin, wis a word he had never seen before. He mouthed it.

Absinthe

Christ. What the fuck wis that? The bottle felt warm against the seat of his palm. Warm and green like Old Swamp Jazz or the Sargasso Sea. He unscrewed the top, filled the plastic cup he'd used for the red wine and stared at its exotic green colour. Out of the bottle, the green somehow looked even more intense and he wondered if, like some highly-coloured posonous insect, it wis trying to warn him off. He sniffed it and glanced over the rim at Ruby and Harry who still hadn't stopped talking. What wis that smell? Aniseed or liquorice mibbee. God! His senses must be entirely and exquisitely fucked. Even the bestial wis seamed with imperfection. There were no first principles. Black liquorice. Hog brain. What the hell? He took a swig. Swallowed. Then another and another until the plastic cup was empty. This wis certainly different from the cheap red wine, swilled from some pig farm in the Upper Balkans, that he'd been drinkin earlier. It didn't burn till it hit the very pit of his stomach. A bit like whisky but more piercing. His papa had never drunk alcohol. Not even once. It wis against The Religion. *Sharaab*. Not that his father had been that religious but, still, there were limits. He had a distant uncle (everybody was uncle but this one was for real) who wis a heavy drinker – no, actually, he wis an alky. When he wis sober, he wis the nicest guy you could've met but, once the drink'd got a hold of him, he was a fuckin *deo*. Big, black 'n' nasty. Zaf had never figured out why his wife still took all the crap. Literally, the crap. Stupit bugger. Zaf drained the very last of the green liquid from the plastic cup and he began to feel the *subuz sharaab* smoke like a *djinn* up into his head where it started to pulse malevolently. He looked up. Exhaled. Male – volent. Latin, probably. Latin had been a long time dead by the year he'd reached secondary school. Shawlands Academy. Shaw – lands. The ends of the world. Not Latin, never had been. Akademos. A Greek demigod. Yeah, right. The ceilin wis off-white or cream, perhaps, and shadows flitted across its surface and danced through the cracks, the peelin plaster . . .

Old school ceilins were like that. Integuments crackin slowly apart. Yellow stains. Dead kids. The ones from the photos. Platoons of legs, half of them in varyin shades of brown. The rest, pink and not seemin to vary at all. Chewin-gum desks and gratin noise and untrained, unformed egos constantly bashin up against one another in a chaotic music that, at times, had seemed like a form of terrorism. Zafar the Victori-ous. It wis life, his *maa* had told him. Mothers were merciless. For centuries, they had pushed their sons into battle as though it wis only through unveilin the immanence of death that they might perceive the reality of their own lives. No wonder 'mother' coalesced into a vocal centre of rage. But, then, Zaf thought, what do I know? I'm just a coward anyway. That's why I needed a white woman – to make me strong.

It wis such a fuckin joke really. In London or in the US, Babs 'n' Zaf would've raised no eyebrows whatsoever – it wouldn't even have been an issue. In some respects, Glasgow wis livin in some kind of Dark Age. Change in this country would occur painfully slowly, by infinitesimal degrees, and would happen only after another generation, those who currently were infants in arms, had reached maturity. They would be the ones who might break the bonds, the mental chains, once and for all. Of course, the old generation, with their elegant heroism, their unfathomable villainy, would be long gone – their ignominies and broken dreams snapshots, merely, in some mental heritage museum. Through sound and light, it would be possible to reconstruct their narratives along a series of lucid trajectories. No roulette wheels, no driverless trains. No words that bamboozled with their lack of certainty. But that wis for the future, for a place which seemed to Zaf to be as tremulous and provisional as the onset of mornin. Right now, there wis no museum. Everythin wis rabid, painful, out in the open – people were freshly cut from the lands of their fathers. The sex deprivation, that terrible need to feel a female body sculpted around his, that mindless, brute urge to ejaculate into another person, it could crush your brain to nuthin. Its power defined your responses, your thoughts, your prayers – if you had any. Sex between consentin adults wis a contract. It held unseen clauses, twists and turns, whorled deep in the small print, and such things could return to haunt you for the rest of your life. You were like a blank piece of paper upon which every interaction, emotional, physical, whatever, wis inscribed, over and over, in blood, semen and in words, voice. The whole thing got so dense, so bloody intricate and convoluted, that you couldn't tease out one strand from another. Sometimes, the pressure of all these notes would become too great and cracks would begin to appear – fissures in the quiddity, bum notes that were not bum notes, like in a Coltrane piece, radical changes in direction, tone, life.

They were still talkin. God! How much could there be to say? The poundin in his head wis even stronger but now it seemed like it was comin from inside of himself and he let it flow through him, thinkin that mibbee he would be able to ride the wave, to hold it steady, rhythmical, sequenced – like he did with the console, with the mike. Voice, breath, music. The gang would be in the music – the beat of their fists on the door would be its lifeblood. He'd never had any trouble with the gangs – he'd kept well out of their way. Growin up in the Shiels, he'd learned well how to do that. How never to meet anyone's eye. Just in case. The gangs created their own clouds of paranoia and, even if half the time it wasn't real, even if there was hardly any danger to the average person, the effect wis the same as if it there had been. So it wis real.

He went over and grabbed Harry's arm. Harry turned.

'What are we goannae do? They've already smacked Taj about and now they've come tae smash up the station, tae shut us down.'

Harry gave him a dismissive look. Shrugged him off. Said somethin but Zaf couldn't hear it.

'What?' Zaf leaned closer to The Station Master – so close that he could smell his sweat. He wis aware of Ruby gazin at the side of his neck.

'Ah'm goin downstairs.'

'No!'

'Yes. Ah know these guys. Ah watched them grow up.'

'It disnae matter. They'll be high on somethin. Crack mibbee.'

Harry sneered at him. 'They'll be high on themselves. And

250

that's not much to be high on.'

Zaf admired Harry's courage – it wasn't easy to face twenty guys in a deserted alleyway in the middle of the night. He wis either very brave or else very stupid. Or mibbee, Zaf thought, mibbee he knows somethin I don't. 'Ah'll come wi ye,' he said quickly. But he had left it a moment too late. Just one fuckin semicolon too late. Fuckin yuni-boy. Harry spun round. His face wis a snarl. 'No, you willnae. You'll stay here an run the station.'

Zaf stood transfixed, not knowin what to do.

As The Station Master went down the narrow stairwell that wis really the fire escape, Zaf began to wonder what the fuck he'd been thinkin of. But the left side of his neck still felt warm in the place where he had felt Ruby's breath. Where the pulse was. The poundin grew louder as the music faded. Kula Shaker had given way to some esoteric guitar solo thing. He thought it might be one of Junoon's instrumentals. 'Talaash' perhaps. Quest. But the music seemed muddled and it wis difficult to distinguish the separate notes, one from another. It wis as though the sound wis issuin from underwater or through a dream. Zaf tried to make out who it wis. He had the crazy thought that mibbee the console had acquired a mind of its own and wis now playin whatever the fuck it wanted. The scribbles on his paper had become completely illegible – almost like some kind of lost blue music. Etruscan perhaps. Or Kafiristani. Or John Coltrane's 'Ascension'. Mad music. He remembered that he'd left the voice-control set halfway-to-maximum . . .

Harry tramped down the stairs, all the way to the bottom. He could feel the creakin vibration of his shoes on the wood. He could see the gang all right but only by leanin, somewhat precariously, out of the window. Behind him, the cubicle still seethed with flesh. They were drinkin their own sweat.

The door wis a cartoon door. It bulged inwards every time the weight of bodies pushed from the other side. Bulged, red. Why was this fire door red? Zaf wondered. Mibbee it wis in the vague hope of scarin away the flames – like some kind of gargoyle, totem thing. That's what you got from doin an ethnology degree. It came in really useful at times like these. He felt the salt run into his eyes. He could tell that Harry wis fumblin with the bar which ran horizontally across the middle of the door.

'Fuck sake,' Zaf whispered. He wiped away the sweat. He felt very small.

The silence and the night hit Zaf full in the face. Rottin lemons and expensive aftershave. Brylcreem hair gel. And somethin which he thought smelt like iron until he realised it wis blood. Ruby wis there. Even from up there, he could feel her breath. Christ! He wis a fuckin Geiger counter for human secretions. A psychic junkie for ectoplasm. He hadn't noticed her goin down the stairs. What's she doin out there? he wondered. Didn't she realise that, in the presence of a woman and given the option, a man will always kill? Mibbee she did. She kept remindin him of Zilla. He felt it. His words, his thoughts, were slippin. Fuck that.

A lad wi a face like a *mouli* tried tae push in through the doorway but Harry shoved him back. Zaf had a full view ae the tops ae their heids. It wis like he could see through the thin case of bone and right intae the substance ae the *maghas*.

'Oi! Watch who you're touchin, ya fat bastard!' Harry was not overweight but the guys in gangs tended to refer to anyone older, richer or more intelligent than themselves as a 'fat bastard'.

'Away fae ma door, ya fuckin arsehole!'

'*Behen-chaud.*'

'*Maddar-chaud.*'

The Station Master wis good at that – exchangin insults. Zaf wisnae panickin – no wi aw that booze in his belly an the wee man at his gate. Expletives were a way of demonstratin respect. If ye didnae reckon someone enough tae feel the need tae swear at them, then it meant that ye didnae respect them and that would've been the real insult. The lad moved back, his pride assuaged. Then three or four of them pushed up, screamin, 'You owe us money!'

'Ah don't owe yous nuhin.'

Stock phrases. Could've come straight out ae a crime film. That wis the way they talked. The sons ae peasants, not knowing what mask tae wear, had acquired those of East Coast Gangstas. Wee men, angry. Harvey Keitel – 'You wanna cuppa kuofee, you wanna cuppa kuofee?'

'Aye, ye do. Aye, ye do.'

'Who told you?'

A pause but not a silence – there were no silences in their lives.

'The Big Man.'

'Whit big man is that?'

The lad, who now seemed to be the voice of the gang, wis pointin his finger at Harry and his mouth looked like a cunt. They couldn't see Zaf because they never looked up – never. Zaf began tae hear the music fae the party. Someone must've turned up the volume. Very professional. They've nae idea, he thought. Nae fuckin idea.

'Don't you fuckin laugh at us . . .'

Harry dismissed the *phuddi* wi a wave ae his hond. 'Go home. If The Big Man wants tae deal wi me, then The Big Man'll huv tae get up oot ae his bed, away fae his white whoors an come here tae do business.' He looked them up and down, derisively. 'An no send you bunch ae pissheids.'

The gang, which had seemed so threatenin from the upstairs

window, now appeared to have lost momentum. It wis as if, havin been cheated of the orgasm of smashin down the door, they didn't seem to know why they were there or quite how to proceed. The song, 'Talaash', wis drawn from the sweepin boulevards of Islamabad, from the studious bookshops with their hermeneutic titles – theses on the neuropsychology of *djinns* and the para-theology of *afreets*, long out of print treatises authored by old British Resident-types whose graves slumbered in some sleepy corner of Wiltshire or else on a gentle slope in the South Downs. Like T E Lawrence of the *Seven Pillars*, those guys, all starch and buckram and Hindoo-stanee, were spies, mystics and travel writers rolled into one, a strange *qawwal* indeed. And Junoon, the rock band, drew on all of this and more and took the music somewhere else entirely – out over the breezy Atlantic or up the spirallin road to where the air began to thin, to the hill stations of Muree, Bhurban and Nathiagali. A wild singer, a lunatic guitarist, a bass player whose notes danced together in a swayin curtain of sound. 'Talaash'. A quest, indeed.

'Eh, Ruby!' wan ae them shouted – a guy without a neck. 'Eh!'

'What're you doin here wi these *khuseray?*'

The neckless head nodded towards Harry, his lip curled in disgust. '*Phoodulanah!*' Everything stopped.

Suddenly, Zaf felt as though he wis on the set of some method-acted crime movie, the sort where, if you freeze the frame, you can see that all the action scenes are set pieces – dances almost. He felt like he wis a dancer an it felt fuckin good.

Zaf remembered that Rubina hailed from one of the close-knit families who ran Kinnin Park. Obviously not close-knit enough. Outside of Faisalabad, things had begun to fall apart. *Shukur-al-Hamdulillah*. He saw her shrug down by

Harry's shoulder. She didn't look round though. Never turn your back on a gang. Never.

That wis a challenge. Callin someone a poof wis a declaration – if not of war then at least of skirmish. You could call them, motherfucker, sister-fucker, cunt-face, black fuckin bastard, you could exhaust any dictionary of insults, but, if you once referred to somebody as a *khuserah*, then they would be fully within their rights to chop off the end of your pinkie and no apology. To call someone a *khuserah* might infer that they had fucked other men but, worse than that, it suggested that their life's ambition wis to be like a woman. To be a *phoodulanah*. A cunt-prick. And, just as the gangs were caricatures of New York gangsta gangs, so too were the *khuseray* caricatures of women. There were lots of them in Pakistan, especially in the big cities like Lahore and Karachi. They paraded about, wearin perfume and lipstick and flowin robes, an they formed a community all of their own. Among the sophisticated city *lok*, the *hijeray* were a long-running joke, a kind of quaint hangover from Mughal times – spiritual descendants of the court *doomnis* who'd escaped the blades of the British after eighteen sixty by pretending that they were women and so, instead of being murdered or sent to Eton, they were thrown out on to the streets to sell themselves. The ultimate insult but, for them, the highest salvation. But in Glasgae, the only good *khuserah* wis a deid yin.

The strings buzzed electric – that guy, Salman, wis a fuckin spider. A wondrous, shimmerin screen of notes, dancin peacocks, singin dragons and that bird whose beak wis touched by *Hazrat* Suleiman's glance. Zaf looked up at the sky. The *hud-hud* wis disappearin in a spiral of smoke. He could feel it rise through the chords, through the bodies of the Kinnin Park Boys. This band wis live. Then, feedback, silence.

TALAASH FINITO

Zaf felt somethin move beside him. Before he realised whit it wis, Harry wis oot in the street an had his airm aroon the guy's throat. The fucker wis doon on the groon an his face wis turnin blue. And, while this wis goin on, the sound of dub reggae thudded out across the darkness. Deck B. 'Charge'. Music without words.

Zaf shuddered with excitement. The thuddin had moved intae his muscles an noo he felt like he could take oan aw twenty ae the pissheids an smash them tae fuck. He felt like that guitarist in ADF who sweatit an scissor-jumped his weye acroass the stage. His legs wur pure punk but his heid wis aw blood. Bharat. Holi, Holi, Holi. In an instant, all his years of carefully avoidin confrontation had fallen from Zaf like the worn-out robes of a *hijerah*. For the first time in years, mibbee for the first time ever, he felt like a man. And it felt bloody good. Almost as good as screwin Babs. Better mibbee.

The gang stood aside, didn't join in. This wis not because of any false sense of honour but because, in the half light of the alley, Harry seemed to have expanded somehow so that the entirety of his bulk filled the darkness. He wis like a nightmare. Unstoppable. From the corner of his eye, Zaf caught a slight movement on the opposite side of the street. Just that – nuthin more. Just the slightest alteration in the pattern of shadows on the other side of the wall. He knew it wis Zafar. Then he realised that no one else had seen Zafar. Not Harry, not Ruby, not the gang. With his blue eyes, he had slipped through the darkness and had come to this tunnel of half-night where the radio waves fought with the barefoot stink of Fenian immigrants. Zaf wondered why had he come – just to look, to taste the time before dawn when anyone might kill or be killed and when most of the big deals took place at the lowest ebb of the city which, for him, would be its peak. Him an Zaf, both. Aye, he felt himself slippin into the body of Zafar, into the scars which he had instead of birth lines, into the hate that he had for everythin an especially for himself and into the black-and-white of his blood, the streams which had never mixed, could never mix, no even after he wis dead and cold. Muslim graves were meant to be unmarked – the trials of this life were not carried over into the next – but Zafar wouldn't have a Muslim grave. There wis no escape for Zafar. He hovered around trouble like a fly around dead meat and now he wis leavin – not runnin away, leavin – because the trouble here wis comin to a resolution and it no longer fed his need. Or mibbee, Zaf thought, he wis leavin because he wis no longer required.

The lad sued fur peace and Harry let him go. The gang were already headin off, lookin rather dejected. The moment had passed. For a short time, there had been the real possibility of serious violence but it had come to nuthin. Zaf felt disappointed. Cheated. The top half of his body wis tremblin. It wasn't cold out there in the street, not tonight – he wis shakin with the rush. Harry's face wis flushed and his eyes stared at somethin no one else could've seen. Like Ruby, Zaf thought, back there in the booth. Harry turned round, pushed past the remnants of the gang – and past Ruby too – and began to climb the stairs. Zaf glanced down again at Ruby who returned his look. It shook him and he almost fell out the window – had to grab the sill and almost snapped the bones of his fingers doin it. A lizard reaction. He must have been goin up in the scale of things. He followed her movements as she turned and disappeared into the darkness of the

stairwell and he wis tryin not to gaze at her bum. He felt
Harry pull the door shut behind them.

Zaf hauled himself back into the cubicle. He wis pantin
like a dog but he felt more like an automaton. Simple movements were tortuous, stiff, like he'd forgotten how. He'd
been poised over the crotch of the window sill for too long.

OFF MUSIC
UP SWITCH
TALK, FUR FUCK'S SAKE, TALK.

OK, jinns an *jinaabon*, here's me again.

His neck ached. He rubbed at the muscle.

Thought Ah'd fallen asleep, did ye? Thought Ah wis
deid tae the waruld? Ye cannae get rid ae me that easily!

He tapped his finger on the console top, firmly, rhythmically,
in tune with the metre of his words.

A wee poem.

> Ah'm here fur the duration, friends,
> Midnight tae six.
> Dinnae despair,
> Ah'm in wi the bricks.

Right. Fuckin Shakespeare. Ads. Go. Ads. Buy! Buy! Buy!

Back in the cubicle, the party wis in full swing. Drink wis
bein passed around like jibes and the strobe seemed to flash
even more brightly than before while the music blasted from

the giant black speakers in a mess of beat and bass. No words. Somethin very, very Black. On one level, the level that ran beneath the commercials, Zaf knew it wis ADF again and that their dub thing, 'Charge', and that it wis mergin, bar by bar, into 'Assassin'. Udham Singh. Nineteen thirty-nine. The Motherfucker of Parliaments. Colonel O'Dwyer's come-uppance. But he watched Ruby go over to Fizz, fuck-in Fizz, and he watched her grab him by the arm, even though he had done absolutely fuck all, nuthin, durin the fight, and he began to feel the notes pounce on to his back and they forced him down on to the floor so that he could taste and smell the stone of the old church which, in spite of all the dust and the cleanin fluids and the parquet, he saw now had retained imprints of those who had gone before. Footprints of the dead. The soldiers, the seamstresses and, before them, those select few of the worshippers who had made it up here from the pews. The damned. The saved. In all the three months he'd been workin here, he had never sensed the past of the church even though, at times, in spite of himself, he had sought it out and, now, tonight, when he really didn't need the complication of all that, he could feel the sensation against his flesh of a creepin, invisible thing like the radio waves or like his own voice or like the music which he played over the air – yet different. He felt it rise from the stone into his palms and he felt it press like ice against his temples. He wis dizzy and his head wis poundin. Everythin he had gained in adrenalin, in spirit, durin the almost-fight, had ebbed away on to the floor and now he saw it. He watched as the shadows on the walls, on those parts of the walls which lay above the line, danced and flowed and changed and he watched the shadows entwine and kiss and mingle their forms as though they were those bushes which folk used to plant over the graves of dead lovers. A spring death, in the garden. Jallianwallah

Bagh. Grand Cemetery of the Raj. His life laid out in a metrical psalm across the old stone of the kirk. ADF spat out the song as though each syllable wis a bullet.

!BANG! !BANG! !BANG!
LEAD-HEAD
YOU'RE DEAD

Fuck sake.

Fuck. Sake.

He let his head rest in his palms and he stayed in that position until the thuddin had eased off.

'Whit's wrong wi you?' someone asked.

Zaf looked up. It wis Raj. Taj. Whatever. 'Nuthin. I just felt a bit faint. Must be that drink. That buggery blue stuff – green, I mean. Mean I green. Whatever.'

Raj looked around. 'Where's that?'

Zaf nodded in the direction of the small table. He couldn't see the bottle from where he wis sittin but he knew it wis there. It wis almost like he could smell it. Aniseed poison. The noose, the hangmen's foetid breath. Thick black liquorice sticks. Nuthin special. Bulk buy from one of those *pukka* Musalmaan off-licences. A crate to smooth the path to hell for the *goras*. I don't think so.

'It's over there – on a table. What is it, anyway? It's not like any booze I've ever had before.' The skin of Zaf's face felt like the surface of a mirror. 'Have you ever tried it?'

Raj laughed and the wrinkles around his eyes made him seem suddenly friendly.

Zaf remembered the time he'd been sittin alone in a pub one evening. It had been some time after he'd left Zilla but before Babs. He'd not had any real relationships during that period. Just the odd one-night stand with some sleek, practised shop girl or other. Cold feet and freckles. Checkout contraception. Nuthin to write home about. Nuthin to hang yourself over. Anyway, that evenin, Zaf had been sittin on his own next to a wall that had seemed to be hollow. Some stranger, some guy, had glanced across the floor of the public house and smiled at him – not in a gay kind of a way, not like that at all. And he'd nodded back. It had been comradely, like two soldiers on the night before battle. That kind of thing. A connection, an intimation of shared mortality. Later, Zaf had realised that he'd been sittin right next to the snug where he imagined that dodgy deals would be done and unwritten contracts taken out and the thought of this had laden the whole thing with a heavy significance. That had all gone once Babs had come along. When you fell in love with a *goree*, you abandoned everythin else. Philosophy, friendships, angst, everythin.

Zaf decided that Raj/Taj's face looked better the way it wis tonight – all puffed-up with the beatin he'd had. He wis liquid, he wis high-tech! The Kinnin Park lads had done somethin which, in thirty years or more, music had never been able to do – they had done him a favour and he didn't even know it.

'The Kinnin Park Boys . . .' Zaf began.

'Eh?'

The smile had fallen off Raj's face. Suddenly, it wis all punched out. Black and blue.

'They were here. Tonight.'

'When?'

'Just now. Didn't you hear them?'

Raj wis dishevelled. His shirt wis undone to the level of his collarbones. He's comin apart, thought Zaf. Black and blue. Aren't we all?

'Aye. Harry fuckin squashed one of them. Sent them

scurryin away like rats.'

'They're full ae crap, right?'

Zaf disgusted himself. So what wis he, Harry Singh's fuckin fan club or what? The lowest lion in the Chaandni Pack. Zaf had been there. Oh, yeah, he'd been there. No pride. He seemed to have spent his whole life, searchin for heroes. Tryin to fill the night with music. The drum 'n' bass thudded relentlessly through the buildin. Piledrivers. Demolition men. Zafar.

Raj looked petrified. He stood with one foot in front of the other as though he were about to begin a game of hop-scotch.

'He did . . . what?'

Zaf shrugged. He could see the eyes of the strobe reflected in the sweat on Raj's face. What wis this guy like? 'He beat one of them up. They deserved it, man. What wis he supposed to do?'

Raj's face had turned to stone. Then the stone spoke. Like an oracle. 'Do you realise that now they'll be back and that, this time, they'll be lookin for me?' He wis breathin heavily and, through the inverted pyramid of his splayed shirt, Zaf could see that the hairs on his chest rose and fell like seaweed. Driftwood. He wis fallin apart. Couldn't stop.

'Ah don't gie a shit aboot you or aboot Harry Singh or aboot ony ae these *chooTiyay*. Jist remember that, withoot me, nane ae this would ae happened. This radio station owes its existence an continued functionin an financin an jist aboot iviryhin else tae me – an me, alane!' Raj wis stickin his index finger into his own breastbone.

What wis he talkin about? He wis ravin. Symmetrical sweat marks had seeped through the cotton of his pinstriped blue shirt. Crescent moons in his armpits. Symbols of love, Zaf thought. *Ishq. Mohabbat. Wahdat.* I have to get these *bundhay* out of here, he thought. Now.

In a single movement, he stood up and, even though the room wis doin some kind of a starboard sway, he herded the crowd towards the door. It wis surprisinly easy – they were in that pliant state which a certain level of drunkenness can confer. Happy boozers. Or mibbee it isn't just drunkenness, Zaf thought, judgin by the smiles.

'Where are you goin?' Raj asked. He wis still standin over by the window. His voice sounded thin, weedy. Suddenly, Zaf realised that Raj had nobody. Not even the stranger in the pub. No one. He stopped. Half turned.

'I've got to get back to my chair. The segue will end soon. This is the last track. ADF. You know it?' He knew that Raj wouldn't know the song. Perhaps not even the band. Unlike Harry, who had leapt forwards out of his own generation, Raj Khanna had dressed himself back in time.

He called out to Zaf, 'You're not meant to mix red wine and spirits. Not that kind. It changes colour if you do. It changes to something else altogether.'

As he returned to his seat, Zaf thought he heard a noise from the next cubicle. The sound of a door closin. Oh, fuck, he thought. They're at it again. What wis wrong with them? Not enough adrenalin? Was the booze not cheap enough? Not green enough? Two sips and it would close off your throat. Open up your brain.

OK, that wis wild. *Jungalee, jungalee, jungalee.* Zaf here on ninety-nine-point-nine meters FM. Radio Chaandni, *Junnune Show.*

His words were truncatin, abbreviatin. Soon, he would begin talkin in code. Like the stuff on his playlist. Semiotic. Hermeneutic.

Ah think that mibbee we all need sumhin tae calm us doon, *hai ke nahii?* Ye reckon? Ah think so. This is calm, calm, calm, cause it's deid, deid, deid. Slip ower the waves ae the seas ae the past. Four-thirty in the mornin, New Year's Day, nineteen hundred an two. Anno Domini. Twenty-first ae Ramadan, thirteen nineteen. Twenty-second of *Teventh*, five thoosand sax hundred an saxty-two. Iliventh ae *Dey*, twelve hundred an eighty. Eleventh ae *Pasusa*, eighteen twenty-three. Eleventh ae *Nivôse*, year wan hundred an ten. Aye, right. Time's a funny hing, no? It's like a lover. Aw in the mind. Slips away when ye think ye've grabbed a haud ae it. Ohhhh!! Risky wan, Zaf! Close tae the edge. That's where Ah live.

S-E-X. M-U-S-T-T-E-E.
JAMA

Yes, he must.

Nah, don't worry yer chaste boadies aboot that wan. In the Sooth Asian Subcontinent, naebdy hus sex. We jist multiply like amoebas an sponges, right? It's totally pristine an it happens ten thoosand fathoms under watter. A-million-pounds-per-square-inch. That's why the whole place is a bloody pressure cooker. Money an sex. Or the lack ae it.

The room wis dark again and Zaf found he had to blink a few times before he managed to adjust to it. The music playin now wis a very old song. It was somethin he'd picked up, years ago, from a market stall in a town in the East Midlands. Middle England, for God's sake. It wis some concubine singin out for custom. In those days, in India, only the whores had been allowed to sing. If you were a woman and you sang, it meant that you would open your legs for coin. And someone, back then in nineteen hundred and two, had sat down in this particular *rundi*'s morning room, her *divaan-e-zanaane*, and had put a big, brass horn before her and enticed her to sing. Perhaps he hadn't had to entice very hard. Mibbee it had been one of her English gentlemen clients, all puttees and whiskers and buttoned-lip *purdah*. Tea-on-the-lawn. Lots of *punkha-wallahs* and *chabri-wallahs* and *chai-wallahs*. A porcelain life. Love among the teapots. A distracted mad hatter of a husband who had preferred to spend his spare time layin down singin hookers for posterity. Singin kettles. Boil one for me, Cecil. Anyway, he'd managed to catch Janki Bai on tape. Well, it wouldn't exactly have been on tape – not in those days. Wax cylinders more likely. The eccentric mustachio who'd recorded her would be long dead, Zaf thought. So would his wife, his children and all of the *wallahs* and their children. Their eyes had been dyin even as the song wis bein recorded. Like the wax of their music, they had melted away. But she had not died. Janki Bai Allahabadi lived on through her voice and, on the CD case, there wis even a picture of her sittin surrounded by a group of court musicians. A smile played around her lips, just the faintest line of a dance, as though somehow she had known that, one night, after a hundred years or more, her disembodied voice would twirl and stretch and spin, deep into space, far into a blackness of which her time was only beginning to dream. Mibbee she had known, back then, that some other eccentric would be playin her song again. 'Play it again, Sam . . .' But that had been later. Cinema had come to India a few years before World War One. After Janki Bai, before Gandhi. The sound before the image. Her voice wis oddly mellifluous. He turned the CD case over in his hands. Some-how, he had expected that she would sound shrill, that her voice might lack depth, partly due to the age of the recordin and partly due to the fact that, when all wis said and done, Janki Bai had been merely an elegant whore. An A1 hooker for top-class punters. Ten piercins per ear, gold everywhere. Teeth betel-nut red. Spittoon-carryin bearers, Calcutta car-riages. Three hundred rupees for the evenin. And, after each song, a muscle dance. She had been reserved for Maharajas and Englishmen. And her voice had just been an arty stimulant in foreplay. The Raj's equivalent of a Blue Lagoon or a Black Russian or the moment before a shot of coke. 'Rasile Tori Akhiyan'. Most of it wis in Braj-basha, the old language of the north of India, but, every so often, she would sing a verse in Urdu – somethin to do with the encitin, drunken eyes of her lover . . .

The song curved and danced around him in the semi-darkness of the room and, though he had heard it countless times before, like waves against a cliff, its power lay in its repetition. And, every time he listened, he would hear the same phrases bein iterated over and over again until Zaf would feel himself begin to sway in the undertow.

> In the darkness of night,
> Will a ship come
> O'er the waves?
> Its prow will be golden
> Its sails black
> And its deck will be awash
> With my love's blood . . .

She wis singin in difficult, semi-archaic Lucknow Urdu and the words might've meant somethin quite different from what he'd imagined and yet the feelin that they evoked in him went far beyond the sequences of letters. Like the best of Rafi, Kishore and Mukesh, it stretched beyond the lyric. You could never get that with rock music, Zaf thought. It wis like the difference between Zilla 'n' Babs. The one half-crazy, restless, eternally rebellin, the other breathin melody every moment of her life. Well, OK, it wis an exaggeration but so wis everythin else. He found himself smilin and he glanced in the direction of her photo. Needed her to smile back at him. That's all those Angraise *sahibs* had been lookin for back in the old days. A gesture of human kindness. A connection which they hadn't been able to get from their bodiced, thin-lipped wives because the wives had been trained from birth to withhold it. 'Bridge, sixteen annas to the rupee.' Like the porcelain of their tea sets and the starch of their sheets and the whiteness of their god, its power lay not in its strength but in its ineffability. Theirs wis a totally transcendent universe. Except when it came to empire-buildin. Then, God wis pulled down into the mire along with all the rest – the poets, the Greeks, the heroes, all of them. He would never be able to give himself completely to her. Even his soul wis finite.

The wall was blank. Grey. Dark.

Blank.

The photo was missing.

It couldn't be, he thought, panickin. He thought that mibbee he wis in the wrong room again but, no, the console wis his for sure and the bloody music wis his as well. He could smell himself in the room, for God's sake – all three months of him. A hundred years. He wis on both sides of the line. Zaf rushed over and inspected the area carefully. Ran his palm across the surface of the wall. It was the only place, apart from the two windows and the corner where the sockets entered, where there were no cones at all. No pyramids to hold in the sound. He had put up a photo of the woman he currently loved so that she might dance the melody of her bones and so that he might hold the golden blondeness of her skin in his head at all times. 'Harmony in my Head' – Buzzcocks. Brilliant song. Long gone. Not as long gone as Janki Bai but long enough. What the fuck wis he thinkin? Babs! He felt a great hole open up inside of him. The line had run straight through her face. Every time he had turned, during his *Khabr-aur-Mausam* interludes, on each of his anti-clockwise whirls around the room, Zaf had made sure he had avoided her photo. He hadn't touched it – not even once. You didn't provoke your deity – not even if you had really been an atheist all along. Instinctively, he looked towards the window that separated the two cubicles. The shared window. He saw no shadows in the other room. He wondered whether perhaps Ruby 'n' Fizz were playin some kind of joke on him. Pullin a fast one. If they were, then they'd be sorry. Totally fuckin sorry. He'd had enough of this. It wis past four in the bloody mornin and it wis the last night of the run an Zaf had decided that, at last, at fuckin last, he wis goin to stop runnin. He wasn't goin to be like his father. Chasin down channels of crap after pipe dreams. He wasn't sure yet what he wis goin to do. Not in the long-term, anyway. You couldn't just stop your life in mid-flow . . . 'crackin up is easy, it's livin that's hard'. Yeah, right. You could listen all day to wise songs by ex-junkies but you couldn't live your life by songs either. They weren't meant literally. Sometimes they weren't even meant sincerely. Mostly not, in fact. You had only to depart from your teens to realise that and, in any case, nowadays, teenagers seemed already to have tumbled to it. Music wis for money. And it wasn't as if his life wis exactly in midstream either. There wis only so much you

could do with a degree in ethnology. Join some think tank
or other. Or the sort of community project where the lack
of cash made people scramble about like dogs and bark at
one another. No thanks. He wis dog-tired with gettin the odd
bit of work through the City Council, the Community Friend-
ship Forum or the Glasgow Institute for Ethnological Studies
. . . He'd felt, for a while, that it would be time, soon, for
a major move in his life. And tonight – this mornin – would
be the start of it. That wis the theory, anyhow.

All this couldn't hide the fact that he wis fuckin petrified.
There wis no one else in the buildin or at least there shouldn't
have been – if Ruby 'n' Fizz were still somewhere about, then
they were there illegally, so to speak, though mibbee it would
be just such a thing which would drive them to remain in the
old kirk, to fuck each other among the detritus of fallen
farishtas. He knew that the party had ended a while ago. It
had kind of trickled away quite rapidly – the way most crap
parties did. The guys had left the stuff – the amps, the
turntables, the cablin an all that – and would probably be
intendin to pick it up, plus what had been left over from the
runnin of the station, sometime late the next afternoon. It
would need a fuckin truck to lift the whole lot. Anyway, he
figured Ruby 'n' Fizz would've more or less pissed off after
they'd played their joke on him. They would probably now
be sittin in some public house or other, gigglin over a couple
of drinks, while some shite Rod Stewart song farted and
grunted through the night and a coterie of Marks 'n' Spencer's
girls cackled away in the background. That wis Fizz's style,
you might have said – not Ruby's – but she wis obviously
goin along with everythin the wee man did. He still couldn't
figure out why. Fuck that. It wasn't worth it. Ruby wis a pale
imitation of Zilla and Fizz wis a pale imitation of himself.
Well, not exactly pale. But, then, Zaf reminded himself that

it wis four in the mornin. He looked at his watch. Four thirty one, to be exact. Speakin clock. From East to West and from North to South, almost everythin would be shut. Throughout the whole city, the only places that would be open at this time would be a few holes and dives and spaced-out clubs an, of course, the twenty-four hour shops and all-night cafés where bleary-eyed waitresses, who were really out-of-work actors, would be stumblin through their orders, unsure of whether or not they were in the middle of someone else's role. That wis more Ruby's style than Fizz's. Her motif, you might say. And, right now, the music wis circlin around its own particular motif. Strings, strings, strings. Jarrin, atonal.

He looked through the window into the next room.

Darkness.

Just darkness. Converging into fugue.

⊚⊚⊚⊚⊚

A quarter of a century after arriving in Britain, Jamil had managed to get together enough money to purchase the lease on a small shop in Govan. The Opening Day had been an afternoon of bunting and streamers – as though it was some kind of ship that was being launched. The local councillor had cut the red ribbon which had then come loose and fluttered away over the tenement rooftops. It was the usual kind of place – sold everything to everyone – and, quite soon, their faces became perhaps too familiar to the locals, along with the gleaming surfaces of the new glass counters and the store's freshly painted metal-and-wood skeleton. It had been a retail outlet since the First World War, apparently – Zaf had looked into the deeds – but, before that, it had functioned as a drinking shop for navvies. He pictured it, there, as the multicoloured bunting flecked like the words of an illegible

270

script across the overcast sky – the grizzled, Dún na nGall peasants, so recently escaped from the sinkin famine and poverty of Lough Swilly and so recently delivered from the worship of the potato, slappin down quarts of dark beer brewed thick by long-defunct companies and cuppin their broad, leathery palms over the tired buttocks of some tousled, peely-wally tenement whore. The songs still slunk about the walls – they had been intoned so often in strange, polyphonic choruses that their notes had become inspissated into the grains. 'Rosie O'Grady', 'The Fields of Athenry', 'The Sash My Father Wore' and others that were no longer sung save by the odd dement, festerin in some distant, milky-tea nursin home. Even though they had finally achieved their dream, his parents' faces had seemed tired that day. Some dream, he thought. Talk about lowerin your sights. Everyone lost their mind eventually. *Bhooli hui yaadon.*

The shop wis called, rather unimaginatively,

CORNERSHOP

– a title that wis emblazoned in big red letters across a *haldi* background. But, then, Zaf mused, it wis situated in a part of the city where imagination had never been at a premium. His father, at last, had achieved his life-long ambition of climbin out of the sewers but, by the time he'd got there, he wis exhausted and so it wis simply a corner shop with no frills and even fewer illusions.

Those lucid sunrises over Govan, over the roofs of disused crane sheds and the crests of arid trees, mornins when the air wis clean and still and fresh. *Subahs* after long nights of drinkin red wine. Walkin along the deserted pavements which bordered the Elder Park and its bare, melancholy green squares. The smells liftin off the skin of the river – scents from far upstream, from the country and from beyond the north bank, from the slopin, slate-coloured mountains. On days like those, Zaf had felt his body, the tissues of his being, begin to dance and flow with the waves of the Clyde and with the breezy gusts that rose, every so often, from beyond the cranes – he would begin to get the feelin that his bones were of this land. He had felt light as air, as music, a Beethoven quartet, a twelve-string guitar solo – his mind *saaf*, uncluttered. But, every time, underneath the elation would run the dark seam of knowledge that this wis just a fiction, that, in reality, he wis some kind of interloper, not just in Govan but also now to his parents and to the life he had had before. The cracklin sound of the old valve radio as it came to life, as, slowly, it warmed up. He had grown up and away. He might as well have been in Australia if the government there would have let him in. They wouldn't let him in, he knew, because he wis British and nowadays they were lookin for Asians. And, yet, as though the radio held, within its Kashmiri copper, the notes of songs that had not yet played out, melancholic songs – say, those of The Poets or The Dream Police or The Sensational Alex Harvey Band – those mornins seemed to promise somethin more than the tired arc of another day in the corner shop. The whirlpool of failure. The same faces, the same inevitable reiterations of despair. A thousand false dawns. And now this one.

It had happened gradually at first – just an old man forgettin things. No one worries about that. For God's sake, Zaf himself would often put somethin down and then not be able to remember where he had put it! But you didn't forget where you lived – not if you'd lived there for twenty-odd years. Twenty-five sweatin years. Jamil Ayaan had specialised in the efficient recyclin of waste. In this, as he had often said to his son, he was most definitely ahead of his time – since time, like sewage, moves through the body only very slowly when one is merely living – and, most probably, ahead of Zaf's time as well.

And then, in the night, Jamil had begun to dream of rats – big, black Norwegian monsters, mutants of the dark waters – and Rashida had shaken him out of sleep and doused him in the bath since that had been the only thing which had convinced him that the rats weren't going to get him. Zaf could still remember the screams and the sounds of runnin water in the middle of the night. And, gradually, his father had slipped down some kind of invisible slope into an almost stupefied state where nuthin and no one had been able to reach him. He would sit for hours, mouth drippin saliva on to the broad orange tie that he had still insisted on wearin, even in the evenin (he had worn it beneath his protective clothin, down the sewers) as he had watched children's programmes on TV while Rashida and Zaf had tried somehow to keep the business goin. He remembered his father's smile turned to mush in his face. Tried not to remember his voice as it had been before. The memory wis too painful. His eyes glistened the way they always had but, behind the gleam, there wis nuthin. Presenile dementia – that's what had struck down his papa and turned him into a walkin vegetable. Yep, Papa wis ahead of his time all right. Zaf closed his eyes, shut in the tears. Oh, fuck. Why am I playin this stuff? he thought. He fished in his jeans' pocket and drew out a grubby hankie. Blew his nose. 'It's all them rats,' his *maa* had said. *Haraam zaaday chuhay*. He lived his life among *pakhana* and was too proud to borrow money. 'Look at all those *jahils*,' and, so sayin, she would indicate, with a dismissive sweep of her arm, the ubiquity in the Shields of the uneducated ex-peasantry. 'They took the money and now look at them. They knew how to survive, *beyta*. Your father didn't.' At this point, his *maa* would strike her breast, sigh and add, 'It's all his fault and now we are being punished.' Rashida would say that no one in Pakistan had that disease. 'It's an English disease and he came to England and he got it. It comes from breathing in them *haramis*. Rats an pigs too. *Sooers*.' If he wis not too tired, Zaf would sometimes point out to her that they had been livin in Scotland for the past three decades or more but she would wave him away, sayin, 'English, Scottish, Pottish – what's the difference?' Zaf had heard this tirade or endless variations of it a thousand times and he had come to be unaffected by it – or so he had told himself. He found he had constantly to resist the temptation to stereotype his own mother. The thing wis Rashida wis a walkin pillar of guilt. It wasn't that she carried it on her shoulders, it wis far, far worse than that – with time and too much patience, Rashida's guilt had become invisible. To anyone who didn't really know her, she would appear completely cheery or, like those folk fae th'Islands tended tae say before departin, 'Cheerie!' On rainy days, she would breeze about, cleanin everythin up as though tomorrow must always be brighter than today. She had become the court jester to her man's fallen hero. Zaf remembered her, three months earlier, almost to the day, laughin as they'd wheeled him away to the nursin home. Some hero. He'd fallen into the sewers, for God's sake. She'd always managed, somehow, to see the funny side of things. Zaf supposed it wis some kind of a blessin but it could lead you to hell, that attitude. It had probably got her there and back on more than one occasion and now she trusted it as she would a faithful old banger. Ford Popular. You wore the masks that allowed you to get by but the skins of the masks seeped into you, changed you. You had only yourself to live with and that wis more than enough. Livin with herself had sharpened Rashida, had made her harder than marble. Like

274

a diamond, she wis almost indestructible. The thing wis Zaf knew that, beneath it all, beneath all the silly jokes and the endless use of the word 'should', his *maa* blamed herself for everythin. After all, it had been she who had dragged Jamil Ayaan away from his *qanuni bivii* and his young son and it had been she who'd led him across nine borders and several subcontinents, not to mention the oceans, seas and rivers . . . And, finally, it had been she who had driven away her son. He had become an *avara gurd* and, as far as she wis concerned, he probably slept with a different *goree* every night. Runnin the business had not been easy and she had done it single-handed with no *baratherie* and, effectively, no husband until she could do it no longer and she'd had to give up the lease on the shop. She'd had only her religion, her humour and her son. And, now, she had only her religion and her humour. Zaf wished he had her strength. He'd not been to a mosque since he wis twelve.

His father had become incapable of drinkin on his own. Yeah, he thought, Papa's become permanently intoxicated by life in Britain. Like in that Pulp song, he's never come down. Probably, in his mind, he's runnin in slow motion through a field of rapeseed, singin, at the top of his voice, of great, unfulfillable longings. Zaf's father had never raised his voice in song – not even when he had seemed most happy, which had been on his days off. Even in madness, he had never sworn. His journey had been too great.

And Engineer Jamil Ayaan had ended up in the madhoose. The loony bin. Or, to put it more politely, a nursin home called, fur fuck's sake, Tree Tops, where he had the distinction of bein one of the youngest residents. They'd had to put him there when he'd begun to shit into the chest of drawers, though, meticulously, he would always close the drawers once he'd done. And that had been another source of guilt for Rashida. She would visit him every single day. Zaf had opted out of that one and he felt so fuckin awful about it that, sometimes, he wished his own life would end. If he just dropped dead, he reckoned, then everyone would love him again, unconditionally like they had when he wis a child. The touch of his mother's lips on his. The warm, strong palm of his papa upon his back or wrapped around his fingers. Safety. Warmth. Love. It's what we all crave for, Zaf thought, it's like a drug. And, in those moments, he would gladly have died for love. Then he would be venerated forever.

His father still dreamed of the rats. They were always comin to get him, edgin on their bellies through the slime. Durin the long days, which were punctuated only by the squint wheels of the drugs trolley and the rattlin of well-used teacups, his father had taken to chasin the nurses up and down the corridor, enticin them to don Punjabi cotton, to lower the lids over the glistenin blue arcs of their eyes and to marry him. They loved him. No, Zaf thought, it wasn't love. They pitied him and, at the same time, they found him amusin. They saw him as a kind of a cross between Peter Sellars and the jokey Indian who used to wear a belt round his head which he would touch in deference to the loud-mouthed sergeant major in that old TV series. He never chased nurses when his wife wis around. He still had that amount of savvy. Jamil knew who Rashida wis but he steadfastly refused to recognise Zaf. Or, rather, he did recognise that Zafar was his son but he called him by a different name – Qaisar. Very strange. But Zaf had kind of grown used to it. You could get used to anythin after a while. Not that it rested easy with him. On his last visit to the nursing home, his papa had stroked his cheek and called him *beyta*, 'son', but, in his father's eyes, Zaf could make out the reflection of another, earlier *beyta*. Qaisar. Caesar. The

Emperor. Zaf had heard third-hand, as always, that, when he had run away with Rashida, his father had left behind a young son. That had been almost forty years ago but Zaf supposed that, somehow, now, his papa wis seein his firstborn son in the face of the man who came to visit him on rainy Sunday afternoons. The ghost in the face. And, now, to his papa, Zaf wis dead. Worse than that – he had never existed. In his own mind, Jamil wis livin all the lives that he had failed to span. He was redressin the imbalances that he had been unable to redress. Perhaps, Zaf thought, there is some justice in that. He pulled at the skin of his cheeks, tested the elastic, checked it wis still him. Perhaps, after all, Ah wis a mistake, he thought, and now Ah have been rectified. He sighed and thanked God that he had escaped when he had. Like his father before him, Zaf had run away. He'd had to get way from the madness, the miserable neuroticisms and the suffocatin immanence of the guilt. He'd felt that, otherwise, he would have exploded. And then he'd managed to get a place in a university almost as far from home as wis possible, without actually leavin the city. If he ever did get into religion, Zaf thought, it would be in some other, deeper way. Guilt would never be a reason.

And, now, the old Indian song had gone back further, a hundred and fifty years mibbee, long before the recordin of music had begun, and wis chimin baroque on a harpsichord. Dark London vocals. Bill Sykes, Dickensian Baroque – it wis too early. A hundred years too early. It wis an impossibility and it could only have happened through opium. Aye, that guy's vocal cords had been blasted away by the dragon's breath so that, now, all he had left wis a paean to his lover. Dust from angels' feet. Risin through the funnels of *karubiyyun* pipes.

◎◎◎◎◎

The Stranglers. 'Golden Brown'. He had lost count of which deck wis playin. He just let the machine decide. Mibbee the sequencin wis out, mibbee the lights were deceptive. Who cared? As long as music played, the world would go on.

Fuck. He had been right. They had pissed off into the night. Ruby 'n' Fizz. The lovers. He leaned his elbows on the glass, pressed his face up against its coldness. His lips. Watched the shape of his breath. In. Out. In. Out. In.

A face appeared at the window. He leapt back and the face did the same. 'Christ! What's that?' His voice had frayed at the edges as though he'd smoked a hundred cigarettes and he felt like he'd barely survived the shudder that had passed through his body. He wis in a bad way. Runnin from his own reflection. The sense of unease didn't seep away and Zaf found himself whisperin a quick couple of *kulmas*.

Laillahah illallah muhammad-ar-rasulallah,
Laillahah illalah muhammad-ar-rasulallah.

He could pull the words down whenever he needed them but it had been so long since he had been to a *masjid* that the movements of prayer, the elaborate dance of gnosis, had begun to elude him. He had thought that perhaps, given the right situation, his limbs might remember but, even then, there would be no unity between his body and his mind, let alone with his spirit, and, without such a unity, there would be no fugue. Talkin to God was a symphonic affair and Zaf hadn't even grabbed the melody. The harpsichords were goin wild, the bars of their music loopin into one another. He gazed through his reflection, searched in the grainy darkness beyond. There were no shadows on the wall in the other room. Just more blank grey. His palms hurt and Zaf realised that his fists were clenched. He released them and breathed

out but he felt as though he wis walkin on his toes. Like a
cat. A lion. A *singh*. He wished that he had just one ounce
of the courage that Harry seemed to possess in tons. At some
point in his life, Harry, the actor, had stopped wearin masks.
Zaf had never known where his own reality lay. That was
why he'd left Zilla. Because she had dived into the depths of
herself, only to find that there wis no end, that her soul wis
a form of hell. Mibbee that wis what had attracted him to
her in the first place. A common bond of horror. He had got
out just in time. The near escape had left him empty. And
then Babs had come along and had been his salvation.
Hallelujah! Amen! She had run the tips of her fingers over
the surface of his body and had turned him white and she
had whispered, 'You've got such a sleek body, Zaf. You're
like a panther.' He ran his fingers over the bit of wall where
the image had been. And now someone had ripped away her
photo, leavin not even a trace of the tape that had held it in
place. Not even a stain of where it had been. Like a dead
love. He would leave Babs. He had got everythin he needed
out of her so he would dump her, too – not because he wis
an evil bastard or a misogynist or a control freak but simply
because it wis in his nature to move on. Because, if you didn't
run, you'd be pegged down and shot. If not with a gun, then
through betrayal or, worse still, by love. Like his papa had
been betrayed. Sold out, to the immigrant dream. Bein an
immigrant, Zaf thought, or bein the son of an immigrant,
meant you had to live along both sides of a double-edged
blade. Either everything you did wis an act – the way you
arranged your hair, the mannerisms which you acquired, the
pictures you cut of yourself and of those closest to you and,
most of all, the ideas that accrued to your skin like so much
dandelion fluff – all of it wis mediated, guided and fulfilled
by imitation of that which you thought wis real. You modelled

yourself on the ways in which they, the natives, the locals, the *goras*, lived. The alternative to that wis to reject as much as you could of white society and to join one or other of the religious groups that seemed to be breedin like tannin salons, pet shops and massage parlours. Money-launderin. Two ways to hell. Compared with that, anythin else wis life. And the fact wis most people had to live somewhere between extremes. Only no one talked about the failures, the ones who didn't make it to the big stone mansions at the good end of Pollokshields with their delicate, pink blossoms in spring and their golden brown leaves in autumn. Harpsichords. 'Golden Brown' . . . Hawwa, basically, right? Snake goin west. Or like his *maa* who'd left behind so much and who had been payin for it ever since. The voice of Janki Bai reminded Zaf of his *maa*'s voice. That wis it! He'd never figured it out before. *Khuda-ke-liye!* His mother and a whore. Sick or what? And the more he listened – and he did listen there as time stretched across the windows and the walls and the floors of the building that once had been some kind of church – the more he felt the face of his *maa* upon him, watchin him even before he wis born. Before Glasgow had trapped him into bein just another act. Him 'n' his papa, both. Women were imprisoned in their bodies, men in their minds. He felt time elongate invisibly – just as, occasionally, over the course of the ninety days, he had felt the gentle lap-lappin of the radio waves as they had carried his voice out across the emptiness of space. A ship in the darkness. Black sails. Golden prow. Destined to sink before it reached the edge of the sunrise. No sunlight had got to the photo, he reasoned, not even durin the day when he hadn't been around. That wis why it had left no square mark on the wall. Ruby 'n' Fizz will leave nuthin of themselves in that room, he thought. A flashback of Ruby's face, terrible in its ecstasy.

Women were frightenin. Icebergs. They could float up, across a hundred years of darkness, and destroy you. He glanced through the window into the other cubicle. There wis a shadow on the wall. Fuck! He wis on his toes, ready to fight, and his heart began to pulsate wildly. He wis capable of anythin. The courtesan wis dyin with a smile on her face. The shadow wis different. Its shape – different. The harsh voice of old Stranglers' London, of the Ripper's East End, of dark white chapels and huddled, headscarfed hookers, had split and broken into a mess of bloodied organs, into countless echoes. Black monks spinnin among the stucco and mirrors of the Sun King. 'Golden Brown'. He strained to get a better view. His eyes kept blurrin over. Damn that *sharaab*. Green bastard booze. Or mibbee it wis just the time. He didn't dare glance at his watch in case, when he looked up, the shadow would have vanished. Like the photo of Babs. Fuck. He needed her now. Needed her smooth, golden white to fill out his darkness. But the music had changed again. Now it wis somethin orchestral. A single clarinet. Christ! How had he let that slip in? He couldn't remember having segued any classical stuff but, since he had made up the tape and disc sequences at various different times over the past three months, anythin wis possible. His order wis all screwed up, the slip of paper dead in the night air as those Wisdom Scrolls secreted for millennia in bone-dry Levantine caves. After tonight, anythin wis possible. He wondered how he could've put the radio station before Babs. It wasn't as if he wis bein paid for it. God, how stupid could you get? If it had been a test of some sort, a loyalty test mibbee or a battle of wills, then he wis losin the battle. In which case, the test didn't matter anyhow. No music wis comin from down below. Aye, the party wis definitely over. Good riddance. He'd always hated parties anyway. They had never made him feel comfortable or even human. He wis vaguely aware of people fallin out into the street. Fallin off the edge, into the darkness of the earth. Deep in his belly, he had a strange but irresistible feelin of anticipation that wis neither good nor bad but just powerful. In itself, it wis not sexual – yet the power of the emotion wis comparable. He wis drawn to the shadow as he had been drawn to the *sharaab*. He moved towards the window. A noise from behind made him stop.

He spun round. Nothing.

Turned slowly back again. The shadow had gone.

He blinked. Nothing.

Zaf saw that the thing had vanished yet he felt its presence all around.

> I seen him, man. I seen his face.
> Looked me right in the eye . . .

But it wasn't Kula Shaker. It wis classical – Western classical. Some kind of polytonal thing. Modern. Well, not more than a hundred years old, at most. That wis modern. The clarinet had been joined by other instruments – horns and strings – and the whole thing wis growin louder and yet, somehow, it did not seem to move at all. The same note, played by whole sections of the orchestra, would be repeated again and again, with only slight alterations in the accents and the phrasin. It could've been the background music that had played while the eccentric aristocrat had recorded his exotic concubine. Potted her for posterity. A jardinière. White gardenias. Babs. But, no, this wis not background music. The swirlin wind produced by the instruments would have been strong enough to have blown the iron needle right out of its groove, even the strongest of the dancers off the stage, the night clean out of its time. He didn't dare go into the other room. The adrenalin wis ebbin away like coffee does when it starts to rain. He felt the need for some kind of security. Wanted to be a rat in a wheel. A white rat. Wanted to do things and to live as though nuthin had ever happened to him in his whole life. A blank page. So he went over and sat down. The music stamped in his head – it moved and yet did not shift – it wis black like flamenco, a dancer slammin on the spot. It wasn't a clarinet, that instrument at the start, it wis a bassoon and it had been playin higher than wis physically possible. He spun his chair twice and leaned over the mike. Then he realised he had left the thing full on. Just as well he hadn't said anythin into it. Fuck sake. He leaned back. Inhaled. Licked his lips. Leaned forwards.

Remember me? Ah'm yer host this mornin. Zaf's ma name an Ah'm still broadcastin oan ninety-nine-point-nine meters on the FM waveband. Ah huvnae moved an inch fae this seat. This is Radio Chaandni an ye're listenin tae *The Junnune Show*. An we've hud some pretty crazy things oan the show thenight, huven't we? What ye're listenin tae, right noo, is cawd . . .

Just strings, very low and pulsin, like the run of blood through a vein. He turned over the cassette case but, since it had been recorded ages beforehand, its track listin had become blurred. Shit.

Well, as it's the last night, let's make up a name, shall we?

He paused. Leaned back. Breathed in. Closed his eyes. Shit.

Let's call it 'Ode to My Father'. Yeah. How aboot that?

Ah dedicate this piece tae ma papa who'll no be listenin since he's asleep in a hame – no his ane hame, a nursin hame – but mibbee someone doon there hus the radio switched oan and mibbee it'll reach him in his sleep. Sweet dreams, Papa.

Two-man ambulance to the Tree Tops Nursin Home. White metal in the sun. The community lookin on, powerless to help. Dream flowers. A modern ritual. An abduction.

He pulled the switch down. Leaned back. Closed his eyes. Spun. The music swayed heavily between two tones and he felt their weight press down on his chest.

E Major. E Flat.

He fought with the knot in his throat. The piece had quietened but the discord within it made Zaf uneasy, as though, at any moment, quite unpredictably, it might explode. He spun round and round and round till, even with his eyes open, he could no longer make out the contours of the room, the walls, the glass of the windows. The window on the inside – the window on the outside. Ivirythin wis slippin an slidin an, this time, the slope wis steep, real steep, an it wis impossible to keep stonnin, impossible, even, tae sit doon an he rolled, he fell, he tumbled but he wis a blind man flyin.

He couldnae bear tae go an see his papa. Tae see him try tae walk acroass the room an barely manage. The man who hud taken Zaf tae the park an taught him how tae play cricket. The art ae spin bowling, the science ae keepin yer eye oan the baw, even as it flew an rotated like a planet. If you could keep yer eye oan the baw, you would be able tae keep a grip oan life. Iviry time he hud goan tae see his papa, Zaf had wantit tae ask him wan question. 'So whit happened, then? Why did you take yer eye aff the baw, Papa?' How could a man, who hud travelled acroass continents an lived between lives, end up wettin himsel an not bein able tae even recognise his ane *beyta*? Life wis a drug. It goat ye hooked oan the guid bits, the sex, the new babies, those moments oan the taps ae moontains or at the end ae a guitar solo whun ye felt as if thur wis, after aw, a scheme tae things or whun ye wur whisperin intae the mike like ye wur moothin stuff tae a lover . . .

Nuthins.

But then it betrayed you. And its betrayal wis relentless, metrical an withoot mercy. It made ye watch the people ye loved maist grouw auld an faw apart an no even know ye an then it wiped them away like dust aff a flaer. It made the people ye loved stick needles intae themseles. Nuhin wis too low. Life wis heroin. Junk, shit, smack. People wur junkie dancers, twistin thur souls intae impossible shapes, jis tae survive till they died. An Goad, if there wis wan, wis jist a pusher. How else could ye explain it? Why gie someone the ability tae see that they wur livin in a pile ae crap and then no give them wings tae be able tae rise up an fly oot ae it? The animals wur the lucky ones. Zaf pushed his foot doon oan the rim ae the chair an spun roon harder, faster until he wis like a planet, a sphere, a molten globe, spinnin fast and silent through the darkness. He felt his boady slump oot in aw directions, his insides wur oot an his ootsides wur in. Ivirythin rolled into wan, grey blur. Ye danced, ye died. Ye stopped dancin, ye died.

Trumpets, drums, silence. Trumpets, drums, silence.

And in the middle of the blur was a figure. A silhouette. Not a shadow.

He spun faster, tryin tae dispel the image. Tryin tae replace her. Tae bring Babs back. But the photae wis goan an he could nae longer form her face in his mind. He would huv hud tae huv built it up fae memory, like a photaefit. He wis gettin dizzy an his legs seemed detached fae his brain. That drink wis spiked, he thought. Either that or the night. He tried tae stoap turnin but it wis too late an his foot slipped oan the rim at the bottom ae the chair an he fell sideways aff the seat. A lang faw, still spinnin like he wis fawin off a merry-go-round. Fuckin merry . . .

Big violins, cellos, everything.

He felt the side ae his heid hit the waw near whur the sockets wur. Sparks flew oot aroon his hair. He felt the static dance ower his scalp and arc doon his airm whur it held fur a microsecond. Then it died an he crumpled intae a mess. The room continued tae whirl an he closed his eyes but that jist made it worse. His heid wis a bomb explodin in slow motion and a searin pain came fae somewhur tae his left. When, at last, he opened his eyes, he foon that they hud sumthin tae anchor oan. The figure ae a wumman stood in front ae the windae. Behind her, the windae wis hauf open an the night swirled intae the room an it wis black as ivir but, behind the darkness, thur wis sumthin else . . .

The strings were slidin, louder and louder, as though they were buildin up tae some thing. The piece seemed familiar but still he couldnae place it. He could make oot the strands ae her hair ootlined against the buildins opposite. Fae whur he wis, it looked as if she hud wings grouwin oot ae the sides ae her heid. Fuck sake.

Zaf struggled tae focus. Tried tae get up. He hud twisted his knee an ony attempt tae rise sent a loang needle ae pain right up through his thigh. Involuntarily, he rubbed at his elbow. Funny bone. Ha-fuckin-ha. The sunes in the room wur disordered, frantic, as though time wis runnin oot. That wis it. Behind the darkness, time wis escapin like sand through a glass. The figure wis grouwin larger. She wis comin ower tae him. He hunched back against the waw, tried tae occupy

the space between the waw an the flaer. Nae space at aw.
'Ye always wur a coward.' The voice. The hair. Nightmare.
Zilla.

'Zilla?'

She wis stonnin above him, close, so that he could smell
her jeans. The threads, denim black. He had tae crane his
neck tae look at her face. Even if he'd been able tae get up,
it wouldnae huv been physically possible. His heid hud
stoapped spinnin an he looked aweye fae her an back oot the
open windae. The smell ae burnin flesh an cigarette smoke.
He began tae shiver. The music swelled tae a crescendo, then
fell back again intae almost silence.

'How did you get in? He hud the sense that she wis smilin.
God. 'Ah thought . . .' he stammered.

She knelt doon an he felt her braith oan the skin ae his
face. The smoke fae her fag swirled elegantly intae the
darkness. She'd always smoked like that, wi wan hond held
above her shooder. Kind ae tramp style. Tramp-vamp.

'Ye thought, whit? That Ah wis deid? Aye. Ah can see
that. Ye're pissin in yer pants. Fuckin DJ. Fame an fortune
gan tae yer heid or whit? Aye. Ye're a coward an a liar tae.'

He didnae dare look. Swallowed. Thought very fast. Fast-
forward. Furst wurds that came. 'Ah thought ye might be
listenin tae the show . . .'

She stood up again. Laughed – that cacklin thing she used
tae do. Hauled him right back. Five years. Rewind. The
strings wur now bein accompanied by woodwind an drums
wur in it somewheres. Whitivir ye do, don't ask her aboot
the photae. 'Help me up, then. Ah think Ah've hurt ma leg.'

She didnae move – just stared down at him. He wis aware
ae her gaze burnin a hole through the tap ae his heid. His
wisdom wis total. He looked up. He needn't have because
her face hud nivir really goan away. Like the drums that

pumped oot thur rud beat, Zilla hud nivir left his brain. There it wis. Her lang face seemed even langer than before – as though time or gravity or wan ae they bastards hud pulled the features downward in some kind ae prelude tae her becomin a skull. Her hair a mess ae black, slightly wavy. Her skin the colour ae dry sherry. Very dry.

She moved her lips. Her voice wis in wi the music. 'Why should Ah do onyhin fur you?' She turned away. Went ower tae the windae again – this time wi her back turned towards him – began tae draw patterns in the steam which hud formed oan its surface. He couldnae see the patterns she wis drawin.

'Ye jist walked oot oan me. Jist left.'

'Zilla . . .' he began but she didnae hear.

'Ah don't need onywan. Ah nivir needed you. It's always been number wan wi me. Ah've aye been the ootside. An you couldnae take that.'

The slow logic of madness. The music wis breathin.

'Zilla, ye wurnae oan ony kind ae "ootside". Onyweye, whit dis that mean? Ye jist left wan hoose ae oppression an ran intae another. The drugs . . .'

She spun roon. Puffed hard on her fag, again an again, until he thought it would bleed. 'Don't fuckin talk tae me aboot drugs. Ah've seen things you couldnae even huv nightmares aboot. Boadies rolled up in carpets, disused barns in the countryside, yon dealer wi nae knees . . .'

He waved his arm at her. 'Ah don't want tae know.'

'Naw. Ye nivir did. That wis always the problem – no the drugs.'

'Whit, then?'

She moved rapidly towards him. He flinched. Couldnae help himself. The pain shot through his knee. She knelt down an grabbed his hair, yanked his heid back against the waw.

A sickenin thud. Dizziness. A reprise.

'It wis that white bitch.' She wis close. Very close. He could feel iviry exhalation. He inhaled. Hud nae choice. He tried tae shake his heid but couldnae. 'Naw. That wis aifter. Lang aifter . . .'

The back ae his head thumped against the waw. Ricocheted tae the sight ae a glouwin fag end. 'Don't fuck wi me or Ah'll burn a hole in yer fuckin face. You don't know whit love is.'

He tried tae avoid the fag end but aw he goat wur her eyes which seemed a streynge shade ae electric blue. He blinked an looked again. Still blue. Real Anglo-Saxon-Celtic sparky. His surprise must huv shown.

Her smile wis coquettish, ludicrous. He could see the cracks in her make-up an, beneath them, the fissures in the skin. It wis as though her face hud become jist a mess ae elastic but he knew that, underneath, her bones wur steel.

'Ye like ma eyes? Some ae the punters prefer blue. They like the mix. Kind ae exotic an twistit.' She wis almost singin but there wis nae tune.

'Kiss, dance . . .'

Aw ae a sudden, she wis an actress. Curvin and twistin. Dancin.

'Ah put these in fur you. D'ye like them, sir?'

Her skin wis the colour ae the earth oan a burnin hoat day. Zaf felt his heid begin tae spin, as though his bones wur followin her movements. He felt the vibration in the hollow ae his skull.

With her free hand, one at a time, Zilla gouged out her eyes.

'Christ! Whit . . .' His voice sounded lame, ridiculously bourgeois.

She smiled and stared at him. Then flicked the lenses into his face. Her eyes wur black, the weye they used tae be. Aw he could think ae wis how she hud aged. Mair than five years. She'd spent too long as someone else's fantasy. Someone's else's oil paintin.

'And noo, Ah've taken them oot.'

Black.

She stared intae him, filled him wi her music. Her adoration.

An despite his fear – or mibbee because ae it – Zaf found himsel rememberin. Thur first days. A college romance. Kind ae. Aw flowers an mulled wine. Chilli con carne. Festival ae Meat. Those red beans that could kill if they wurnae heatit properly. Shamen, The Catherine Wheel, Primal Scream, The Stone Roses. Bands wi elegant, brainy names. Sons ae the Sons ae Champlin. Soangs ae lang-haired ladies, floatin slowly doon oxbow lakes. Blue eyes, ae course. Sapphire sky. But the watter wis deadly. Paradox bands.

'Spirea-X'. 'Cocaine Arabic'. 'Happy Days'.

'Ω Amigo'. Cary Grant's smile. Here we go. Wwhhu-Up!

Crimson moment, chosen time
Here and now, forever mine
Ω Amigo, for you, I will always have time

Lucid visions, sight sublime
Seeing, hearing, feeling fine
Ω Amigo, for you, I will always have time

The Catherine Wheel. 'She's My Friend'. Roon an roon an roon an roon

The girl with flowers,
She don't care.
I could say
She makes no sense.

Her dreams are drawn on a knife edge
She's my friend
Till the very, very end.

'Crystal Crescent'. Sweepin trumpets, Pre-Raphaelite vocals.

I'm falling, I'm falling, I'm falling, I'm falling
I
  N
    T
      O
        the tail end ae the eighties. The start ae the clubs.
Barns filled wi house. Auld aircraft hangars. Big cigars. Acid.
Es. Freakin oot gently in the Municipal Park, lyin thegether
in the heat, tryin fur a tan. Ha ha ha. Children's laughter.
Sunshine days. Fuck.

Through the black leather ae her jacket, he could smell her
boady. That acrid stink which he hud never smelled off ae
ony other wumman. Sulphur. Jist beneath the skin, he could
make oot scars. Or bits ae paleness fae which the pigment
hud vanished. Christ, he thought, insanely, Zilla's turnin
white! Almost said it, then wondered whether he hud said it.
Spoken or not, words hud power. He wis jist the conduit.
Zilla hud always been mair than that. His scalp wis beginnin
tae hurt. She thumped his heid against the waw wan last time
an then let go an stood up again. This time, she didn't go tae
the windae but, instead, sat oan the chair whur she proceeded
tae turn jist a little, first this weye an then that, so that he
hud tae follow her like some kind ae eejit. Like a child. As
she spoke, she tinkered wi the things that wur lyin aboot,
close tae the console. She seemed distracted – occasionally,
she would glance at him but, maistly, she seemed tae be in
a waruld ae her ane. He wondered whether she might be

stoned but she wis probably so far goan that it would ae been difficult tae tell. Some ae them, he thought, got tae the stage whur their normality wis bein stoned an, if they wurnae stoned, then ye would think that sumhin wis far wrong. It wis yer shadae that kept ye anchored tae the waruld. Withoot it, ye wur guid as deid. He checked his ane shadae. It wis pathetic, crushed, but it wis still there, in the early mornin amber darkness. He hud forgotten tae check hers an noo it wis too late – the weye she wis sittin, it wis impossible tae tell. Deep in his gut, sumwhur beneath aw the music, he knew the answer – that Zilla's shadae hud escaped fae her that night five years ago whun the moon hud been fu. Perhaps that wis the weye ae it. If someone's life hud become too awful fur thur soul, thur soul would slip aweye an hide sumwhur. Doon the narrow, dark streets – perhaps those that wance hud been the main thoroughfares ae the city but which noo wur basically ootdoor brothels. He felt an auld sorrow wrench up fae the pit ae his stomach. It hudnae aw been bad. There hud been guid times whun they had acted as though thur might huv been a future. If only she hud been white. Or if he hud been. That would ae made aw the difference. But noo, whun it wis far, far too late, finally, she wis cheyngin colour. She hud loast her shadae an so she could be ony colour she wantit. Or ony colour onywan else wantit. Why couldnae he huv been like his fuckin faither, his papa, his *abu*, who hud nivir, nivir screwed onywan aifter he'd met Zaf's *maa* because she hud been his only reason fur livin, the wumman he hud croassed continents for, fur fuck sake, he should be a fuckin legend, The Man who Croassed Continents an Times wi his Lover, the man who hud immersed himsel, Orpheus-like, in the sewers ae hell because he hud imagined a better life fur the wumman he loved, the man who hud nivir wance goat drunk, who hud nivir spent even a farthin on onyhin unnecessary so that the endless thrift an the foul watters ae the *cludgie* pipes hud finally driven him soakin mad. Doon the drain.

An this music wis risin fae deep in the earth, fae the stane and metal ae its core. It wis so irregular, it could assume ony shape, ony form in his mind. Its dance wis untrammelled.

Then he laughed an, in the funnel ae the sewer, his laughter sounded hollow an the pain which hud begun in his airm moved up an spread ower his chest.

'Fuck. Ah'm goannae be sick. Let me be sick.'

'Fuck you.'

He felt his head bein yanked back again an then she let go.

He tried tae get on tae his knees but couldnae lever himself up. His faither's legs, aifter late nights doon the sewers. Bone an jelly. The watter hud softened his brain.

He puked all ower his shirt. 'Fuck sake. Ye could ae helped me. Fuck . . .'

She wis over at the windae again. He wondered whether that wis how she hud got in. Like some vampire. 'I wouldnae help you if you wur dyin in the street. You left me tae rot.'

He breathed deeply, fished fur a hankie, tried tae finger the sick oot ae his nose. He disgusted himsel but it wis too late fur that. Things wur too far oan. His voice wis tremulous an uncertain ae itself, like that ae an auld man. Ivirythin he said or thought wis circular – it led nowhere. Whereas she . . .

'Zilla, fur Goad's sake. You wur oan heroin. Ah hud tae leave. Can ye no see that? It would ae been me next. Ah hud tae live. Christ! Ah tried . . .'

'Oh, yeah! Ye tried. Ye're forgettin sumhin.'

He shook his heid slowly. The orchestra hud grouwn louder again, poco forte, and Zaf felt the music slip intae his boady but it didnae soothe. The wounds wur too auld.

'Ye dinnae remember? Ye're a liar – as well as a coward.

Ye gave me ma first hit. Ah coughed for ten minutes aifter. Ye must remember.'

She moved towards him slowly. The music wis dancin aw ower the place. It wis crazy – polytonal. He tried tae get a hook oan it but couldnae. He felt out ae time – like some guy who'd been moved suddenly fae the eighteenth century tae the twenty-first. Unnatural.

She spat in his face. 'You arsehole! You goat me oan the shit. Said it would bring us together. Hah! That wis a fuckin joke. Ah hud run away fae home – Ah wis vulnerable, fuck sake, – Ah wis jist a girl and ye swung me roon the joint ae yer dick. Ye swung me aroon yersel. Oan a fuckin silver aluminium foil plate!'

He wis still shakin his heid. Felt unable tae stoap. 'But, Zilla . . .'

'Don't patronise me! Don't say ma name.'

'Whit?'

'You're OK – noo you're wi that white cow.' She nodded tae whur the photae hud been. Then wheeled back slowly. Smiled. Fuck. Her face cracked. He could see she wis fawin apart. She wis far thinner than he remembered and she hudnae been fat then. Still wore black leather an denim though. Style wis the last thing tae go. He remembered her breists which wur unusually small fur an Asian girl – dark nipples wi rud in the centres like targets. Bulls' eyes or bruises.

'She's clean. She's no on onyhin.'

'An she's white.'

He would ae shrugged but it wis too sair. 'So? Whit's that goat tae do wi onyhin?'

'Don't fuck wi me. Ah can read yer fuckin mind.' She wis borin holes in his heid. Fuck. He glanced away, hopin that she might do the same. The music wis nivir endin. That classical stuff jist went oan and oan. It held nae relation tae life. It wis jist a delusion. A fond lie. Like thur love. Naw, that wis the lie.

He looked back at her. Black. Felt sumhin warum run doon intae his eyes. Rud.

Her voice wis a wire oan the point ae tearin. 'Ah loved ye. Ah killed ma babies fur ye.' It wis like she had goan oot – right ower the edge ae the cliff whur thur wis only darkness an gravity. The loang faw. 'I . . . loved . . . you.'

There it wis – the axis ae the music. He could feel it. But it wis mair, much mair. It shook every organ in his boady. He said nuhin. Turned his face away. He thought he heard her sigh but perhaps it wis jis the night air. He wiped away the blood. It tasted ae iron. Auld swords.

'But you love her – that white bitch. Whit's her name? . . . Babs.' He flinched. She spat oot it like it wis some kind ae expletive.

'How do ye know her name?'

'Ye think Ah'm stupit. All you Asian men think yer ane wummin huvnae goat a brain. Ye'll treat the *gorees* like they wur goaddesses or prufessors – even if thu're jis cleaners – but ye treat us like shite – nae matter whit we are. Ah listen tae the radio, Zaf. Ye dedicate hauf the stuff ye play tae her. The nurse. It's no exactly a secret. But she disnae know ye – no like Ah know ye! She disnae know that ye feel nuhin fur onywan an that iviryhin, ivirywan ye touch goes straight tae hell. Ye jis use people. The wee nurse disnae know that yet.' The masks wur aff. She wis a gargoyle. 'She'd better get oot soon or she'll end up the same as me. Ah give her two years – three at the maist . . . Mibbee Ah should warn her – be a *behen* tae her. Sisterly solidarity. An together, her 'n' me, we'll fuckin castrate ye. Hey! That sounds like fun.'

Her face. Her inner child. Glory, glory, glory.

'Ye're no exactly an open book yersel.'

She turned oan him. The music hud exploded intae bellowin transparency. It wis like he could see through Zilla's boady as she wheeled aroon. 'You don't know the hauf ae it. Ye nivir did. Stupit bastart. Ye're jis like them other wankers. The wans wi the bits ae paper. But, behind it aw, they huvnae goat a clue.'

Ivirythin aboot Zilla's life hud always been secret. *Anjaana*: her engagement, a lifetime ago, tae some guy fae the *gao* near Faisalabad; her escape fae a forced marriage; her pose as liberated wumman; her vampin it up as chic junkie; her disappearance; an, noo, finally, her reappearance oan the very last night ae the radio station's run. She wis a fuckin actress. Either that or she wis real but Zaf couldnae handle that. Like the babies which they'd nivir talked aboot aifter. He couldnae huv handled it – no right noo. No noo she wis appearin afore him like some avengin ancestor. They hud always been two poles but, ower the years, they hud been cast far apart an noo thur meetin would be explosive.

'Look . . . life goes oan. Ah met someone and that's that. Whitivir you think aboot it, Ah cannae cheynge the weye things happened. Look, ye've goat tae stoap hatin ivirythin – ye've goat tae stoap hatin yersel. Ah used tae hate masel . . .'

She spun roon. 'An then ye goat a *goree*. And noo ye love yersel. And ye'll keep lovin yersel as long as she stays wi ye. Tae you, Zaf, wummin are jist stack-ups fur yer heels.' She smiled cynically. 'But she's goan an you've fawen.'

He panicked. 'Whit?'

'Ah tore her aff the waw. She's in ma poaket. Her face is right next tae ma fuckin cunt.' She paused, then smiled. 'Cannae live withoot her, eh? Well, noo ye know.'

'Oh, fur Goad's sake, Zilla . . .'

'Goad's no here. He's no onywhur. Neether's love. It's aw jis trade.' She slipped her hond intae the tight, square pocket ae her jeans. Pulled oot the photae. The edges hud goat crumpled, whur the loch hud been an the sky. She looked at it. Squinted. Smiled again. Then she tore it up quickly and tossed the bits oot the windae. They disappeared like confetti intae the darkness.

'Are ye proud ae yersel?' His voice wis sandpaper in his throat. He could underston, noo, why people goat murdered.

'Who're you tae talk aboot pride? Look at ye. Puke all over ye, blood in yer eyes. Ye're pathetic. Ah could kill ye and naebdy would know the difference. Ye'd jis be wan mair boady in the night. Like that guy in the hotel room . . .'

The roof ae his mooth felt dry. He tried tae get up. Made a real effort. Managed tae get wan leg oot fae underneath. The music hud fawen tae a whisper. He couldnae recall whether or not it wis endin.

She laughed. 'Ye're pathetic.'

'Can ye no help me? This is no achievin onyhin. Look, Ah'm sorry if Ah hurt ye. But a joint isnae the same as stickin needles intae yersel. Thur's the whole waruld ae difference.'

'That's no the point. You took me when Ah wis doon and you put me intae a car wi nae brakes and nae steerin. That wis oor "love" – a fuckin dragster. All because it wis fun fur ye. Ah wis livin it. And, noo, ye play yer fuckin music and ye dedicate it to yer white whoor.'

'She's not a whore.'

'Naw? Ah'm the hooker cause Ah take money. But her price is invisible. Ye cannae feel it but it's there aw the same.'

She yanked the windae full up. The music billowed oot intae the street. Zaf could hear it curl aroon the deserted buildings – he could feel it take the shape ae the city. He wis surprised at her strength – she had seemed so thin. Aye, he mused as the blood trickled doon intae his eyes again, she hud always been far stronger than him. But, noo, aw the spurious bits hud wasted away, hud been blitzed 'n' burned by the dope an noo aw that remained wis the core. White an gauld. It wis like she hud become pure metal. That an hate. She wis talkin intae the street, lookin acroass at the empty windaes whur no one lived or died ony mair. Her voice, the music, wis low, taut. A thick wire. Iron.

'Ah loved ye. Ah love ye. Ah hate ye. Ah pushed oot ma children and then Ah murdered them. You were ma heroin, ye fuckin bastard. Ah gave up iviryhin fur ye. Because Ah thought ye'd be wi me. Ah thought that mibbee you would save me. Draw me back fae the darkness. Raise me fae the deid. Ah thought ye wur fuckin Jesus. Then, aifter, Ah tried tae forget ye, tae push ye away like Ah pushed oot those weans afore thur time so they nivir even hud a chance tae breathe . . .' Her voice trembled. She swallowed. He could see that she would be capable of onyhin. 'But then ye popped back an ye wur oan the radio. Right in ma face again. In ma ear. All ae ma efforts tae escape wur buggered in wan night. Again an again, fillin the waruld, suckin the air oot ae the darkness. There it wis – yer *Madness Show*. *Junnune*. The madness wis always mine, Zaf – no yours. You took it fae me an ye used it. Listenin, night aifter night, tae yer voice, no bein able tae touch ye yet knowin that ye wur oot there, sumwhur in the dark, in the rain, dedicatin yer soangs tae someone else. Ah hatit ye fur it. Ah hate ye.' She paused. Her face wis ashen, the colour ae the sky up north in the moments before a storm. Her accent wis much broader noo than it hud been when Zaf hud been her . . . friend. It wis as though she hud imbibed stuff fae the streets – fae the dust an mud ae the back streets whur boadies slipped oot ae doors only tae visit the corner shop fur another boax ae fags or a turbo

298

lager six-pack or mibbee the local doacter's tae hang aroon, mibbee tae spin a tale or two, tae try an cadge some yellas or blues or vomit-meths. Bent noses, bruised foreheads, lang-runnin lies. Thick make-up, smacked oan wi honds that hud done iviryhin an mair. Deid eyes. It wis as though Zilla hud become those streets. She hud descended tae this. It wis historical – it wis aye the weye. Suddenly, she wis wistful.

'Sum ae those songs we listened tae thegether . . . remember? The Catherine Wheel. 'Damascus'. 'Saeein'. 'Khilona'. Ah nivir had ye – you wur always jis playin. But you wur playin wi ma life.' She gazed up and doon her airms, inspectin them. 'Ah shoved the shit intae masel, intae this body ae mine, because Ah could nivir huv ye. Yer soul, yer aw. Ah would ae geen masel, ma life. Ah did. Ah thought you were ma *masih*. Ma goad, Ah would ae goat through it. The drugs, the shite, ivirythin.' Her voice trembled. 'But you wur a fake – like aw the rest. In these five years, Ah've sunk low . . .' She paused. Wrapped her airms aroon her chest. 'Goad, so low. Onywan can huv me onytime – fur almost nuhin. Ah'm a cheap East-End whoor – rough an ready. Noo, Ah'm injectin intae ma neck. That's the end. Ye can fuck up yer brain doin that.'

She clutched the left side ae her neck an turned aroon. The breeze caught oan the notes ae a flute solo an made the ends ae her T-shirt tremble jist a little. She let her hand drop tae her side. She wis cryin. Her face hud fawen apart altogether. Iviry time she spoke, her voice wis like a dagger in his boady. Twistin. 'Ah tauld ye Ah would come back.' An she wis here, bendin ower him, pullin oan his jeans. Iviryhin wis happenin so slow but iviry sensation wis doubled. It wis a reprise but, this time, it wis really happenin. She bent doon further and she hud her honds aroon his windpipe an she wis whisperin, 'Ah'm back, Zaf.'

The touch ae her honds oan his cock, the way she worked it – she'd hud lots ae practice, hard bags ae experience. The palms ae her honds wur calloused and so wur her lips. 'Ah'm back, Zaf.' And it wis as though her lips, her neck, her breists, her belly, her thighs, her knees, her calves, the spasmed arches ae her feet an the music, that wis no longer music but a livin, breathin being, an assault, an ancient ritual, were aw sayin wan thing:

Nae surrender

Her love-makin hud always been terrifyin, animalistic – the imprint ae which Zaf hud been incapable ae forgettin. It had been quite different fae any other wumman he'd known. There hud always been sumthin ae a last stand tae Zilla's sex – a reek ae fire an Kiamath – an Zaf hud imagined that bein made love tae by this wumman wis what bein possessed by a *djinn* would be like. An, yet, at the end, he hud always sensed an emptiness which, even in the middle ae a winter's night oan the street-wi-nae-name, hud become transfigured intae light. Nae wonder, he'd thought, nae fuckin wonder the *djinns* hud followed the burnin wings ae Iblis, doon, doon, intae the spherical regions ae hell. But that hud been then. Oan this night, this broilin summer's night, Zaf hud been taken by surprise an assaulted in a place he hud thought might be safe, right in the middle ae *The Junnune Show*, in a madness which he hud imagined might be his alone. An the moves hud cheynged, too. Her physical being hud altered. She wis thinner, aye, but it wis mair than that – it wis as though iviryhin that wis unnecessary, aw that hud made her human, hud been burned away an noo aw that wis left wis pure form. Her iviry action wis unconscious and that terrified him – the thought that thur would be nae appeal tae rationality, tae logic, tae pity. Iviryhin wis lucid, almost transparent. He could smell the dank *pathaRi* ae stonnin stanes. He could even coont the stanes – thur wur forty-wan. If she wantit tae kill him, there oan the flaer ae the cubicle, then she would do it withoot even the remotest possibility ae remorse. The music hud billowed intae ear-splittin cacophony again an, this time, the distinctions between the different instruments wur becomin hard tae make oot – it wis as though the whole orchestra wis a percussion section. There wis nae major an nae minor. There wis nae melody, nae duality. Jist rhythm, rhythm, rhythm.

Wi her right hond, she grabbed him by the throat. He could feel the blades ae her nails break the skin – streynge that she hud kept those sharpened in spite ae iviryhin. Mibbee it wis self-defence or mibbee the punters liked it. An it wis equally streynge that he wis able tae think like this, given that he wis in the honds ae a human beast and that she wis compressin his windpipe, each finger an iron vice, muscle-an-bone-an-hate. Wi her left hond, she grabbed his cock an began tae pull the skin up an doon like she wis haulin him fae the grave, her lang blades diggin, rough an smooth, intae his earth, intae the furze ae his crotch bone. Aye an it wis as though Zaf wis no longer man or wumman but sumhin undefined – sumthin in between or doon below, a hindbrain ae a thing, a purely physical entity that would jist shudder an die an leave nae imprint.

The music hud slipped intae an arrhythmic orchestral movement that Zaf couldnae recall huvin been there the last time he hud listened tae this stuff. Her palm wis cupped aroon his baws but thur wis nae tenderness in the furrows, nae calligraphies ae onyhin resemblin love. Deathlines. End signatures wi nae possibility ae redemption. She wis oan tap ae him. Her hale boady wis formin a hide ower his, a skin that stopped him fae movin, sweatin, breathin, a darkness that engulfed him an turned his boady, his mind, his essence, intae music, intae a single, howlin note ae despair. An that note wis the shape ae their boadies, once again become wan in the *junnune* ae the night. Wi her teeth, she peeled back his T-shirt so that she wis like a tiger, rollin back the skin ae its victim's belly. Iviryhin wis claw, tooth, saliva. The weye she fucked him, the weye she raised the dark leaves ae her swollen cunt mooth ower his *tadger*, hard as stane, its seam stretched neothilic, the smooth, yet tremulous, movement her boady made as she lowered hersel on tae him as, wance again, aifter the millennia ae lang nights, she took him intae her belly, but deep, deep, beyond onywhur he had ivir goan afore. Her grip tightened. She hud nae face.

Zilla hud always been a Celtic supporter but she should ae been a Bear. She hud the hate. It poured oot ae her cunt, the hate, an she wis sittin on tap ae him, ridin him like he wis a fuckin pig or sumhin. She hud the strength ae four wummin – she wis insane. Iviry vestige ae other wummin wis bein gutted fae his body – his mind wis a stane bein blasted by a ferocious wind. A mad duchess ridin a pig. A *sooer*. Great Britain. She hud the strength ae a thoosand. She wis aw muscle an steel an blood. She wis a river movin intae a delta, expandin intae an ocean. An, aw aroon her, the night sky an its gleamin moon enveloped him, smothered him, so that he couldnae exist an he felt himsel sinkin doon, doon intae the blackness . . .

Zaf tried tae focus. Blood kept seepin intae his eyes. He blinked hard. Forced oot the rud. As she moved ower him, like Goad ower the watters, he noticed that, oan the left side ae her neck, jist above the collarbone, jist whur the bone dipped, thur wur two identical puncture marks. Love bites. The same oan baith sides. She wis runnin oot ae veins. The marks oan the left side wur fresh. So fresh that he thought fur a moment that he saw blood seep fae them. Stigmata. Fuckin great hosannah! But it wis his ane blood, runnin intae his eyes. He blinked. 'The flute is the instrument closest to God.' Some Sufi thing he'd heard wance, lang ago. Before Zilla. A rush ae dizziness. Iviryhin became blurred. Her spine wis a long, hollow flute. Nae shadae, nae substance, jist air an pain an howlin – a scream that nivir ended. *Ney* music wis comin fae Zilla's cunt, the sunes ae the broken reed that she wis pourin intae him. The end ae the end ae the end. Her fingers tightened aroon his throat an he began tae fade. He felt her braith burnin oan his abdomen an then further up, between his breists. The nipples hud sprung taut long before her lips, her bulbous *kunjeree* lips, hud reached them. Her tongue wis rough – a big cat's tongue – an it tore him as she flicked it up an doon the skin. It wis alternately broad wan second – a heavy, suffocatin, flat-bladed broadsword – the next an épée stabbin an penetratin the pores. Her skin wis ripplin like the surface ae a loch – a boady ae watter molten like it nivir wis in Scoatland but like it might hae been in the hills above Taxila. The hills ae Alexander – Sikander's *pahaR*. Even in the night, when the moon wis cookin an the land burned like the inner waws ae a tandoor, even then, the watters swayed an trembled an turned the roon *chaand* tae elephant's mulk. Even as Zilla rode him, the single note elongated, deepened, drapped beneath the physically possible tae a place whur only long-extinct howlin beasts could hear – beasts like Zaf or Zafar or Qaisar or the serried legions ae fake violinists who played only the descendin notes which wur really landscapes, dioramas. And Zaf wis the fuckin land. His boady an his feet, which somehow hud become dirty, wur bare an his bones, which hud been sharpened by these months ae lunes waxin an wanin, and that wisnae

303

coontin Ruby 'n' Fizz or Raj/Taj or Harry Raam or mibbee
the anonymous bespectacled accoontant who, Zaf now knew,
wis really wan ae Zilla's clients, wan ae her regulars. Not
that it meant onyhin. Wan cock-an-bull wis as guid as ony
other – as Rabby Buruns, the transsexualised taxman version
ae the great Tartan Tin bard beloved ae North Amrikans fae
Baffin Island tae Florida Keyes, would ae said. Expand the
human heart, said Rabbie, an it would *skite* ower sax continents an it would end, like Zilla's womb, the bag bulging wi
so much *nafrat* – the red sack, which he hud filled wi hate
an which noo, oan this nicht-tae-end-aw-nichts, he could feel
richt at this fuckin (fuckin) moment abuttin, heid-buttin,
Glasgae-kissin, Punjabi-*kisaan*, Rabbied-Burnin against the
very empired state ae his glans penis, the saft-heidit pink, his
only truly white part – how proud he wis ae its tumescent
magic trick that it wis an instant, sivin-second *masjid* dome
cawin the faithful tae prayer, summonin the zillions who
denied the divil, the Grand Imperial Shaitan who resided,
hot, pulsatin an purple an focused like a candle flame, inside
iviry saint, iviry martyr at the very ermine-turnin moment ae
martyrdome, whichivir weye it might happen, the penitenti-
ary secret, the long-held, baw-sweatin, cock-suckin arcana
alphabet ae urbane whoredome that, at the very moment ae
cricoid crushin which may or may not be simultaneous,
synchronous, the weye truly guid and guid-an-true climaxes
should be wi back-necked, odontoid orgasm, the genitalia
springin intae action an searin a hole in the fuckin sky, the
auld black firmament, the sivin layers ae heavin hivin, an
only the condemned wans know this but, in that moment
which remains unmeasurable, even the most degraded an
mundane criminal attains a level ae illumination significantly
higher than that ae the great, quillin scribe ae Auld Firenze,
that doyen's doyen, that great furry-collared mascot ae the

West, Durante Alighieri. The cosmos ae the flesh. Ponderin deeply thus upon the machinations ae the *Safaid Guelfo*, Zaf began heretically, depolitically, anti-dialectically an definitely post-chauvinistically tae enjoy the process, the dynamic, the lifespan, the immanent mortality, ae the seduction. Ye see, as he said tae the Great Fartin Judge in the huge, baronial, marquisal, ducal, regal hall ae the sky, a kind ae an Ellis Island in the outer circle ae Alba Hivin – in Islay, say, or Kintyre – but, naw, it hud always been in the Scouser part ae Liverpool or in the soundless dreams ae Eel Pie Island, in the days afore guitar heroes, pre-Jeff Beck an electric Telecaster Paradiso, ye see, Yer Honour, he enjoyed this violation, this invasion ae his radio show ae Madness by a greater madness, a dwam that simply couldnae possibly be expressed in music, let alone in words.

INANOOTANINANOOTAN-SHAKEITAWABOOT!!!

He enjoyed the massive splayin act because part ae him hud always been Zilla, right fae that very first time that mibbee wisnae the first, back in the days ae the bushy puss park, in the ridiculous, grand-mulleted nineteen eighties, wi its powdered hip-hoppin leaders, when she first hud turned his flesh. Ivirythin that wis inside ae him wis Zilla. Take the human heart . . . Thur dance wis a ritual wan. Aifter a while, his boady moved withoot the involvement ae thought. He hud become the music. Wan note, carved in stone, firin aff tae the farthest corners ae the universe.

An, noo, she wis pullin his skin in impossible directions, his circumcised (His Holiness) phallus, her broken ivory teeth peeled back the husk, peeled it back doon, up, tae a place where, fur decades – mibbee for centuries – only its poor, holiest ghost hud been lain. A testamental land. 'And Aah huv seeee'd the promised land!' It wis like wan ae those superchip simulations ae ancient ruined cities whur they extrapolated upwards an constructed mighty temples, fuckin ziggurats ae skin an muscle an fat an blood. Zilla wis resurrectin his flesh right, left an centre – she wis a fuckin archangel. Black wings an aw. Her wiry broon airms were ootstretched – the long, lean muscles seamed through wi the hard white lines ae heroin or mibbee cocaine. It wis a geological thing – eighty per cent genetic, twenty environment but wan hundred-an-fuckin-wan per cent archaeo-paleo-geologico-poetic an she wis balancin oan some invisible uplift, some jet draught music that siphoned up fae his skin, like the pyramidal rock above a dust cist, an she wis dancin horizontally, shiftin ower him, defyin gravity an aw the faces ae the multiverse – her hard wee bilberry breists, the nipples plucked fresh fae the burnin furze ae the Trossachs, they wur hardly hangin at aw but painfully, excruciatinly, pennin lines in his hide, drawin pictures in the broon earth ae his skin, like some crazy, choreic wurum, an noo aw fifty-sivin hectares ae his skin wur risin an comin, like the auld Alexandrian (or possibly Seleucid) peaks ae light. A reunion ae nightmare, a conjunction beyond flesh, beneath music, beneath even his music – nae wavelengths could express whit Zaf wis feelin at that molten moment, whit he wis bein wi iviry inch ae his impossibly-stretched, wan-dimensional boady. His mind hud contracted tae a point ae darkness, his soul held nuhin at aw. Deck A. Deck B. Soangs withoot breath, music withoot frequency. Love sans love.

Now he wis up oan the ceilin, watchin. Bat. Spider. Blind. Leggy. But mibbee he wisnae actually watchin – mibbee it wis mair like he wis feelin through the lang-disused radar ae his spine or his pelvis, against which she had ground, grind,

grind, grind, a crushin an rollin ae tissues. Zilla hud always known whit it wis aboot – right fae the heavin, gruntin nights ae those bull-an-spear cave painters tae noo, in the dawnin darkness ae the polyfuckinwhatsit square ae Radio Chaandni, broadcastin oan ninety-nine-point-nine meters FM, ivirthin hud been nuhin mair than the beatin ae a bone oan a drum. Noo, which archangel wis that?

There wis only wan.

An, as he watched-withoot-watchin, Zilla (also bone-naked) removed a loang, silver cylinder fae her arsehole an plunged it deep intae the base ae his spine. Mush, mush, mush. De-cortication – a lowerin ae his state ae being.

Watchin people hovin sex fae sivin feet above is a *gey* streynge experience. A karmic undertakin, ye might say.

Creakin ships, aye, they blackened, burned wooden boats wi golden time signatures oan their prows, ridin oarless ower the watter, deid-eyed Charon ships, billions ae them, all heidit in wan direction. Midnight tae sax. Radio Chaandni. *The Junnune Show.*

Daith wis a river an oan the river bed thur wis a face. He rose, he rose, he rose. His spine arched – he felt it bend like a longbow – but the force wis Zilla's. It wis the tense, reptile tendons ae her groin an the hardwood muscles ae her buttocks that wur pullin his body up towards the ceilin – even as his heid wis sinkin intae unconsciousness, the skin ae his scalp an the strands ae his hair, heavin intae the rough timbre ae the flaerboards. Nae memory. Nae braith. Nae bein.

Radio Madness. Static. Silence. Iviryhin wis pure.

Noo she wis aweye – aff ae him. His hairt wis thuddin like an eighties' bass against his ribs. He could hardly breathe fur it. Gradually, it subsided an he felt his braith comin back. There wis a stickiness aroon his thighs an a risin smell ae rottin leaves. But it wisnae over. She moved towards him –

blood streamin fae her neck – an in her hond sumhin gleamed. Silver. A sword, he thought. She's goat a sword in her right hond. She's an avengin angel. Wan ae the fawen wans. Black, rud and siller. The colours ae evil. The colours ae love. Whit wis the colour ae money? Fuckin nineteen eighties' soang. Before Zilla. Crap. He tried tae move but his boady seemed tae weigh a honner tons. The weight ae the waruld is oan ma shooder. Ah'm a sad soang. The classical stuff hud ended. Someone wis pullin oan his airm. The *farishta*. Zilla. He felt his face smile. Tomorra nivir knows, right enough. Neether dis yisterday. Deck A. She'd pushed it in. The soang.

Aye, guid music. The Stravinskies, the *Shahzaday*, Hare Hare. Iviryhin wis black an red.

He didnae feel the needle. He did hear the stuff roar up his airm an, at first, it wis the sune ae a thoosand monks chantin, 'Om- om- om- om- om- om- om- om- om- om- om- om- om- om- om- om- om- om- om- om- om- om.' But, then, whun it goat tae the base ae his neck, it wis screamin like a lion ae Judah, a great gaulden *singh*, an it ballooned in the middle ae his heid an began slowly tae explode.

And at the end of the world,
The Messiah will come
In the form of a lion . . .

Ah must huv veins like rivers, he thought, as he popped his mooth above the watters. *Paanch aab*. Punjab. Vast watters movin so slow acroass the plains. Green an broon an the shiftin shades ae the day. The smell ae love an cow dung. Fecundity. Shadaes. Taped music. Heat. Horns. Lust behind shutters. The shadae ae Janki Bai, in the mid-afternoon heat, flittin acroass the boadies ae sleepin lovers. Sweat. Blood. Daith. Love.

Sweat   Blood   Daith   Love

The sewers here are aw open, Zaf thought, an he dived in an swam. It wis warum an green – not hoat, not the skinnin, rapin heat ae Lahore but jis comfortably warum like oan a Glasgae summer's day. Sausage dugs in the park. The slim boadies ae young wummin shinin like candles in the pure light. Funny that. Doon here, he could see his feelins, he could touch them an run them beneath his fingers. Bags ae blood. He wis loang, loang as a snake, an the blood shot through him at the speed ae light an he wis flowin doon towards the river and the river wis flowin doon tae the sea, as they used to say in the auld days. The guid auld days before . . .

Zilla. Zilla wis here. Zilla wis there. Zilla wis ivirywhere. Jis like in the soang. The soang tae end aw soangs. The journey tae end all journeys. Dust. Moontains. The final frontier. A lone piper. Rud face oan the mornin. Soldier's warnin. 'A Scottish soldier, a Scottish soldier . . . '

Fuck that. Oan second thoughts, don't.

Nae underwear, man. Jis kilts an stanes. An drains. An Ferris wheels. Paddle steamers up the Clyde. 'A-roll, a-roll, the Waverleeee. Nineteen hundred and eight.' Fourth Annual Trip.

Ladies and gentlemen, the train leaves St. Enoch at 8.20 a.m. for Princess Pier on the Clyde River thence per G. and S. W. Railway Steamer to Corrie, via Dunoon, Rothesay and Tighnabruaich, arriving at Corrie Lochranza where a dinner dance will be followed by a séance with Mistress Angelina Yeoward, lately of Erevan and Calcutta, hosted by the Glasgow Theosophical

Society and at the behest of the honoured guest-in-absentia, Doctor Arthur Conan Doyle. Home from Lochranza per Turbine Steamer, *Queen Alexandra*, at 3.45 p.m., calling at Fairlie – 4.50, Wemyss Bay, Rothesay and Dunoon, arriving at Greenock at 7 p.m. St. Enoch at 8.12 p.m.

TEA ON BOARD *QUEEN ALEXANDRA.*

TICKETS (Lady or Gent.), 15/-

Deck B – 'Migra'. *Auliya* Hanna. Santana. Reverse conquistadors, modal progression, lyrics in *español mejicano*. Peyote music. Bandannas, tom-toms, hot *picote*. Columbus hud made a mistake an thought that America wis India. Well, there ye go – mibbee he knew mair than we hud thought. 'Migra' crawlin up the cracks in the waw ae the waruld, 'Migra' seamin through the earth, fae the bedecked votive *mandirs* ae West Punjab tae the howlin black stane ae the Wee Free kirks. 'And The Lord Thy Goad will ride wi' thee wan ae these days. Nivir forget, sinners, he is hoverin oan thy shooder – his cauld braith shifts o'er the integument ae thy brow – He is transformin thee, He is drawin thee oot . . . fear, sinner, for thy end is nigh! Thy end is thy beginnin! Thy boady will be broken 'pon the rock ae the angels. Loth Angheles.'

Other watters. Lahore, Faisalabad, Battle Field . . . deep in the green shite ae the sewers whur Jamil Ayaan beavers away, Migra Polis, the deepest layer ae hell. An he makes his hame here – he breathes it, he lives it. Migra Polis. And, iviry evenin, doon against the dank slime ae the auld stane waws – doon whur no one except Jamil an the black rats dare venture – there Zaf feels himsel huggin the waw. He feels its cauldness, its wet, sink through him. Migra Polis. But, between himsel an the waw, he feels the contours ae a boady – the

310

boady ae a white woman, a hooker, the lowest ae the low, the wan that no one, up there in the waruld ae the streets an the red lights, will touch because she's drapped so fuckin low. And Jamil Ayaan, Migra Polis, is screwin her against the waw ae the fuckin sewer an he's really enjoyin it an Zaf is too an, fuck, if ye cannae get a bit ae white pussy doon here where no one can see ye, where ye cannae even see yersel, where the watters are so black that nae light can ivir escape tae form a reflection, a reality, then where can ye get it? Jesus fuck, Migra Polis. Aye, she's ugly as sin. Uglier. Aye, she's crawlin wi mites an crabs an Goad knows whit else but that isnae the point. The point is she's

WHITE.

And that cancels oot ivirythin. Migra Polis. Ye huv tae live the myth because thur is nuhin else. An onyweye, *Chueco*, ye cannae see her face – no doon here among the shite an the piss an the emigrant dreams. The lost wans. Oh, Migra Polis, ye can feel her boady though, ye can feel the bones ae her hips diggin intae yer sides, ye can feel the muscles oan the insides ae her thighs tighten aroon yer back where the kidneys are. Ye can feel her crush ye again, Migra Polis, an this time it's yer spirit that's bein flattened, abbreviated, nullified, but ye dinnae care cause it's whit ye've wantit aw these years, it's whit ye've been dreamin ae acroass the centuries. An Zaf sees his faither beaverin away like a rat and he feels his back curve and straighten an he sees his faither's mooth open like Ruby's did – the face a rictus ae desperation, the teeth shinin, dryin, in the whistling, Alban wind, an then, oot his mooth, he breathes rats. *Chuhay, Chuhay, Chuhay. Chueco.* Five an a hauf seconds ae pure, unadulterated joy.

Grace. Beatification. Loth Angheles. *Migra*, *Migra*, Migra Polis. In those five an a hauf seconds, Jamil Ayaan an Zaf, both, are saints ae the sewers, conquerors on the moral plane. And Zilla an the *goree kunjeree* wur great, swollen Beatrices, points ae light in the midst ae darkness, points ae darkness in the midst ae light, which he wantit tae merge wi, needed tae be a part ae. An mibbee screwin the *goree* whore, night aifter night, had finally chewed up his brain. She wis invisible so it wis like humpin yer fantasy, *Migra*. An there wis nane better. In the hairt ae hell, there would always be five and a hauf seconds ae *Migra* Hivin. The only thing wis which wis worse? He wis in the deepest layer. Naw. There's wan deeper than that. A blacker one, whur Shaitan the Black Bastard sits upon his *takht* – he who wance wis Iblis the White an who hud great wings ae *siller* that stretched across the boady ae the earth. Rud. Black. Love. Daith. *Migra*.

Rud. Black. Love. Daith.

Rewind.

'Migra' hud ended. The journey hud concluded an he hud arrived. But she hud gone, through Deck B, she hud slipped back intae the mechanism and he wis split intae two or mair pieces. He stumbled tae his feet – he wis movin on auto or less. Wi the leaf-shaped thing he cawd his hond, he jammed in 'The Grace' by The Colour of Memory. It wisnae intentional – it wis jist the disc that hud lain nearest his hond. The pure instinct that drove his movements also compelled him tae add tae it the playlist. It wis these things, physical things, that hud kept him sane – until noo. Tonight, they hud driven him ower the edge and ower the edge wis not interestin, wis not cool – it wis totally fuckin empty. It wis pain, it wis a circle, it wis an unendin scream withoot braith, a howl that arose not fae the throat but fae the belly, fae the spine, a *quejío* that nivir ended. Zilla's soang. He dared not speak its name. Remnants of its disc still hovered in the cubicle. The air wis thick wi the smell ae sex. No jis human couplin but sumehin much aulder an stronger. He saw a man in the windae an stepped back a couple ae paces so that his back came intae contact wi the rough surfaces ae the cone points. Then he realised that it wis his own reflection but he knew that nuhin would ivir be the same again – that he would nivir be able tae look at his own boady in the same way as before. As he gazed at himsel, his *nunga* form seemed tae recede intae the blind windaes ae the buildin opposite. He wis almost crouchin, like some kind ae pre-human thing. He wis also reflected in the side windae, in the plane ae the glass that separated an yet joined his cubicle wi its mirror image. Deck A. 'The Grace'.

Jump, fly, swim upstream. Salmon-leap.

Rivers intae streams an streams intae watterfaws. Watterfaws intae glaciers. Icebergs. Zilla. Babs. *Maa*. The lot ae them.

An, up there, ivirythin wis white. The snow, the rocks, the sky, the people . . . an, in the sky, Babs's face wis gleamin, milky-white. Smilin, beatifically like Beatrice. Santa Beatrix. Descend, ma love, an lift me up tae the empyrean whur Ah might meet aw the heroes ae Christendom, aw the people who massacred ma people, an whur Ah shall be able tae eat Whiteness, tae partake ae its *siller* draught an tae bathe ma black boady in its clear, jewelled waters an then Ah'll be ready.

Past Ladakh, rise, rise, rise, ower the Himaalyas an intae Tibbet. The big, fat Buddhist glaciers. Mahayana or mibbee Tantrayana. A silent clarity – solemn almost but no quite. Meltin in the small sun – drip, drip, drip – an, in each drap ae watter, the whole waruld, wi its high lands an its I lands an its wan-track roads. Drivin up tae the tap ae the island ae Albion, perfidious Albion, leavin behind the piss-green grass ae the city an its fairms an slidin up intae the loch face ae the land ae moontains an sky. Babs, her gleamin white airms takin the judder fae the bike as, fur three honner years, she hud ridden the judder ae the waruld, the nearside ae her cheek wi the bone hidden beneath aw that paddin. Not that she wis fat – naw, quite the opposite – but her bones wur big an heavy like those ae the auld farmers an seawummin, the bothy peasants an fushwives ae the north. Norwomen. The touch ae her fingers wis gentle. Tapestries. Long fingers wi coarse ends but gentle. The udders ae cows. Mead. Honeyed skin. Time. Stane. Stonnin. Stonner. Hauf a blue iris. Babs. Barbara. Strange. Foreign. Her ae the three windaes. Tenement windaes or bathhoose wans. Santa Barbara. Patron saint ae miners an sewage workers. An fourth-century Syrian baths. The princess in the tower. The pillar ae his phallus. Fuck. Like Zilla, she hud calloused honds. Martyr's honds. The palms ae a whoor, collapsin in oan him like the twin leaves ae a giant cunt. Zilla-Zilla. Then he wis up, out ae the watter an intae the funk, intae the black tar ae the night. Intae the lang whoor's cunt. Intae Zilla. The Wan. She wis turnin roon, grabbin his cock again. The tattoo ae the moon – that shape stamped blue oan his brain – but there wis sumhin different aboot it. Aye, it wis fuller than before – it wis almost a full moon an it wis burned on tae the wrang thigh. The left yin. Then he wisnae sure ony mair. Mibbee it had been oan the left all alang and mibbee it hud been almost fu. Or mibbee it wis the sort ae thing ye only see if ye want tae. Like sin or betrayal. Or love. He felt the tight muscle ae her arse grip the sides ae his pillar ae blood, he felt its warum, cavernous waws engulf him like silk, like velvet, an the colours wur black an rud, blood an shite. Steel an bone.

Calcium, whitenin in the earth. Grave-fuckin. Necro-music. He closed his eyes an shut oot the fu-ness ae the moon an the music that wis still fuckin playin – nae matter that the DJ wis doon oan the flaer bein fucked by some vamp or succubus or mibbee jis by some twistit piece ae song, some fugue ae undefined music that had run out ae line sumwhur alang the line . . .

Babs wis back. Behind it aw, Babs, the motorcycle lassie. Goin fae Glasgae up tae the Heilans. The Heilanman's Umbrella. Unfoldin, ootside ae Central Station. Dark, stinkin. The anal umbrella.

The further north they hud gone, the bigger she hud grouwn. At Loch Houm, she hud become enormous, fecund, an wis glouwin like the moon. Her angular body, her pellucid skin, half-buried in the *siller* sands ae deserted, northern beaches. It hud seemed, fur a moment, as though Zaf an Babs might exist ootside ae society, divorced fae their tortuous pasts by the glistenin blade ae sky oan watter. Reflected light, the strongest kind. A stane hut, grey. Summer by the loch. Two bottles ae rud wine. Norman French. Hard, sharp. The ends ae spears. Shields, lang like hairts. The Queen. Deid Harry. Babs. The light streamin like tears up fae the watter. Milk tears. The place wis an auld dovecote. Nae doves but they'd gan up tae where the birds hud used tae settle – up close tae the roof fae where they could see the sky. An they hud made love up there, whur wance the doves hud made love, and they hud done it gently, like quiet jazz, takin thur time because life, as she'd always said, wis too short by hauf. An her boady hud tastit ae salt an moonlight an Zaf hud known, in that moment ae daith, that thur loch wis tidal. An, aifterwards, they'd watched the stars come oot, wan by wan, until the whole waruld wis fired up wi the light an she'd said wisn't it amazin that thur wur so mony mair stars oot here than thur wur in the toon – it wis jis like a traffic jam in hivin. And he'd rolled over an kissed her an that hud been that. And, then, aifter they'd filled themselves up wi wine an starlight, she'd run aff an he'd chased her roon the sleek, luminescent frame ae her motorcycle, followin the regular dance ae her white calves against the holy black ae the night an he wis thinkin that, out ae the city, it wis jis him an her an he liked it that way. Two naked, wine-filled gourds. Layla and Majnoon, Yusuf and Zuleikha, Barbara an Zafar wur runnin doon the slope ae the *beinn*, through the gorse an the tangleweed, the thorns tearin their skin but they didnae care cause the drug ae lust protects fae aw that an then they wur treadin saun an he could feel the warum, broon grains roll, like unrefined sugar, beneath the skin ae his *baries* an then he felt the watter lappin aroon his taes, caul an delightfu, an they wur leapin an jumpin intae the moonlight an swimmin through the dark watters ae the loch whose depth wis unknown an thur white limbs, white, *shukur Allah*, thrashed aboot in the black sea. *A' mhuir dhubh*. He caught glimpses ae her shooders an ae her lang gaulden hair as it wafted ower her back, the wee, square bones formin a delicate curve like the spine ae a crescent moon, slidin in an oot ae the seethin, black body ae the loch. 'The Grace'.

> With forever stone worn smooth
> Sleep eternal

An she wis a better swimmer than he wis an, stroke by stroke, she began tae pu away fae him an, before he knew it, she wis miles in front and aw he could see in the distance wis her heid, bobbin up an doon, an her hair, silvery gauld against the black ae the loch. The watter wis cault. It's so stupit, he thought. We might easily drown. But, at that moment, it wouldnae huv maitered. They wur right oot in the deepest, maist silent part whur the fushes dream ae deserts an the air is unmovin ower the surface ae the watter. Ower his boady. He could feel her darkness, arch ower his corpse – silent, like the daith – could feel himsel sinkin intae emptiness. A perfect, quiet moment. *Huu. Tattva.* Alleluia. Doon intae the black watter, drownin, joyous. Her *goree* body washed in the ancient darkness ae the *jheel*. Her whiteness turnin tae black. Becomin Zaf. Zafar the Victorious. Becomin Wan. *Om Shanti Om.* No like the Other. No like Zilla. She hud always existed in fragments. Broken mirrors. Shattered glass. Sivin years ae bad fortune. Zaf is swimmin doon, doon intae the caud watter, tryin tae get tae Babs, tryin tae get tae the place that lay between the insides ae her honeyed thighs – he wantit tae feel the muscles, like lion's sinews, grab him an no let go, he wantit tae feel the twitch ae the *singh* thighs as they clamped ower the sides ae his boady in the rictus ae conjunction. Wantit tae reach fur the perfect nexus. The big Y. But he hud loast her there oan the loch-wi-nae-music, he hud loast his great, white soul an aw he could see, aw he could feel, wis Zilla. The perfect wan. The Shadae ae Goad. Wi her deid weans oan her back, she wis comin up through the fush. The fush music. Country-Joe-and-the-. 'Eastern Jam'. Deck A. Hubbly-bubbly, here we go again. Wordless songs. Anti-war. Uncle Peace. *Salaam alaikum wa rehmattallah barakat-a huu.* The moon wis still there, hangin in the sky, but its power hud waned an noo it wis trapped between the parallel lines ae a windae. The last thing he saw, in that weird, circular state in which he'd found himsel, wis the kitchen table in his flat. Everythin aroon it hud been smashed up, as though the place hud been broken intae. The wee notelets, the big prints, the sivin-by-sivin postcards advertisin Radio Chaandni wur aw torn an hangin an the calendar hud been hauf-ripped fae the waw – its dates scattered at random across the flaer. And, in the midst ae chaos, he wis drawn tae a place ae order. A rectangle. Oan the table wis a wee piece ae paper. He knew it wis a note – he couldnae read it but he knew it meant that Babs hud left him. Aifter three months ae this shit, aifter two years, she'd hud enough. She'd broken oot.

You're a whole person, now. You don't need me. I'm not your fucking mother.

You can take your bloody radio station and shove it up your arse.

Go and stay with your friends. I've had enough.

It wis unsigned. Whunivir they would ride back doon sooth again, back tae Glasgae, the illusion ae unity would evaporate mair quickly than dew aff ae granite. Even as they rod doon the craggy west coast oan the power bike, the nineteen-ninety-nine Kawasaki Vulcan 1500 Classic, the contact between his honds an her waist, though separated by only a few millimetres ae cotton, would seem tae alter subtly yet overwhelminly, like the June simmer breakin ower the flattened, southern bank ae Loch Lomond. Through the clearin mist, a phantasmal vision ae elm beacons oan the distant shore. A landscape sunk deep intae prehistory. He felt sadness sink like a dead snake intae him an he wantit tae die, there an then, oan the flaer ae the auld kirk, he wantit tae be burit there an tae join the legions ae plague victims, the seamstresses, the soldiers, his papa, Zafar-the-child-in-the-photae . . . the faither an the son. Heresy. Glorious infidelity.

When he awoke, his body wis soakin and he could feel the blood caked over his forehead like the imprint of a mantra. His back felt stiff but the pains in his knee and elbow had disappeared. Cautiously, he got up off the chair and tried to move his limbs. A bit stiff, that wis all. She had gone. Her body, anyway. Only now, two songs on, could he really be sure. He still felt her, everywhere. In the music, in his head which was no longer dizzy. And, especially, he felt her inside him. Smelled her dissolution as it dissolved through his skin. It wis like she had jerked off into him. Seeded him. Fuck sake. The window wis full open and the room wis freezin. The sky beyond wis still dark with moonlight but, behind the darkness, he made out a pale glow. It wis this glow, he realised, which had sapped the moon of its strength. He looked at his watch. Four forty. Christ! He must've been trippin for half an hour. He couldn't remember it all – it wis in bits and pieces, it wis like flippin stills or old photos. He began to shiver. Needed to pee. And to wash his face, his hair. Cautiously, Zaf levered himself up. Tested his leg. It wis fine. The music wis still playin. 'Eastern Jam'. The old, psychedelic number from the sixties. Country Joe . . . that guitarist wi the blond Afro. The F-U-C-K song. It had all happened long before Zaf but, somehow, he'd always felt closer to that time than he had to the icons of his own life.

But it wis time for patter. The News, the Weather. Reassurin solidity. But the limpin agony in his anus told him it had not been a dream.

He gripped the microphone as though it wis a steel rope hangin from a cliff edge. His voice came out differently, a full octave lower and tremulous like that singer who hovered like a buzzin fly and then killed himself.

The time is four forty-three in the mornin an it's almost light oot there.

He screwed up his eyes and peered towards the window,

though he hardly dared. The rain had stopped but it wis still dark. Absolute silence reigned.

Somethin wis playin around the tight, inner pocket of his jeans. The one nobody ever used. Except mibbee wiry guys at parties, secretin extra-thin, rugose-ridged, red-wine-flavoured, touchie-feelie condoms. He reached in and yanked out the slip of paper on which he had scrawled the playlist. Then, carefully, as though aware suddenly of the fragility of such a thing, he opened its folded leaves. There seemed to be lots of songs on the list which he just couldn't remember addin. Some of them had already been played while others were yet to come, but these latter were indecipherable. It wis as though the songs would only reveal themselves to him when he played them to the entire bloody city of Glasgow.

Something red was dripping on to the console and it wasn't wine.

And Ah'm Zaf – that's zed ay eff – an this is *The Junnune Show* an it's been a pretty *junnune* kind ae a night, husn't it, here oan ninety-nine-point-nine meters FM? The station broadcastin tae ye fae the moon. *Mare Frigoris*. Right. Here's Tim Buckley, the deid faither ae the deid son. Sing oan through the night, holy, holy ghost. Papa Tim. 'Starsailor'.

It started off with a cacophony of howlin, yodellin, ululatin – backwards voices like somethin from a bad dream. Discordant madness, turnin the voice into a reed pipe, a wailin siren. Wolf music, good for the brain or the soul or somethin.

He went to the bathroom and bent down over the sink and ran the cold water tap over his hair, strainin out the blood. His fingers found a cut, the length of a penknife blade, just above the right temple. The injection site on the inside of his left elbow wis bruised, a mottled purplish red. Goddam bitch, he thought. She didn't even press on it. Buckley's voice wis spirallin through the runnels of water – he wasn't sure whether the guy wis singin backwards or forwards. It wis like Zaf wis standin in a waterfall, listenin to someone chantin up on the hill. That wis when he knew for certain it hadn't all just been some kind of crazy dream caused by the booze and the bang to his head. You didn't dream bruises. He wouldn't be able to wash down below though. That would have to wait till he got home. Oh, Christ! Babs. Howlin fuckin Buckley in the background, makin the shiny white tiles shimmer and almost vanish. He wouldn't be able to wash at home either. Women could always tell if you'd been with another woman. Like cats, like screamin banshees, they could smell the sex. Dead subtle. The thoughts flew through his mind like early mornin thrushes. Aye, he wis definitely singin forwards and yet now the song had grown even weirder. There wis hardly any music, just a solitary horn on acid, floatin somewhere in the background. Sometimes, Tim B wis a wrinkle-faced White-Russian crone livin far beyond her allotted span in a musty, spaniel apartment in Menton. At other times, he wis a florid schizo. Every word wis stretched beyond possibility, beyond humanity – he wis fuckin Tarzan swingin from bough to bough, he wis the fuckin Duke of the Lizards (not the King though – that title belonged to another dead rock star; Paris, not Provence. God, those Farishta City Singers were a weird bunch).

Then he hit on it. The Central Station. They had showers there. They would be openin soon and, when he'd finished here, he would make his way to the Central Station and wash himself. Mibbee he would take a train out to the coast. Stay with a friend. He would need clothes and a bit of money though. Better check, he thought, before Ah go. But then he remembered that she had already left him. She'd seen the writin on the wall. The quill screeches and then moves on . . . And he'd seen the note on the table. She wouldn't be at the flat. But that wis just a bad trip, he thought. A bum sample. A hallucination, like this growlin, barely human track. Put it on to wake em up! To wake him up, more like. He wis the one who'd been sleepwalkin through life. That whole album, Zaf thought, that entire conception, wis the most way-out piece of music that the folk genre had ever produced. It wisnae folk, rock or jazz yet, at the same time, it wis all three and it achieved this nexus not by reachin some tepid compromise that rendered the music meaninless but by pushin all the forms beyond themselves. *Starsailor.* It wis a fuckin work of genius.

He suddenly felt intensely hungry. Usually, sometime during the long night, he would've had a takeaway but, tonight, it had gone completely out of his mind. Hadn't seemed important somehow. He wanted to eat somethin but didn't think he'd have enough money for both a meal and a shower. So he'd have to choose. He could always have a cup of black coffee with lots of sugar in. It would keep him goin. Runnin. Breathin. Wah-wah-wah.

Then, as he stared at his newly-clean face in the bathroom mirror, somethin else happened. Somethin he wis just not ready for. It hud been such a long time since he'd last had a hit. Five years. That last night wi Zilla. The night he'd seen that she hud nae shadae. He'd stumbled, hauf-stoned, doon the street-wi-nae-music, tae the jeers an jibes ae aw those guys who lived an died in doorways. Hauf ae them, by noo, would be jist ashes in urns in some forgotten corner ae the bod gairden. The bad hoose. As he gazed intae the glais, he saw, behind his ane face, not a reflection ae the back wall ae the toilet but, instead, the studio cubicle, the windae, black with night, an, comin through the Buckley soang, flashin up in the swingin hollows ae the notes, from the closed, deid eyes ae the singer, he heard the music, 'Om Shanti Om', ae Madonna oan a mantra. Wee Louise Veronica. Aye. Sounds like wan ae those diminutive East-End bad Catholic girls who've goat a man up iviry skirt. Waitin by the gleamin van fur a perfect cone. 'Om, om, om', goannae gie's a ninety-nine-point-nine, mister? The wan wi the big, broon dick stuck through its heid! Or it might've been Kishore Kumar. Different soang, same sentiment. Loud fry-up down-winders. Brawlin *luRkees* whose screechin anthem wis 'begin an end in the East End!' Nipples tracin oot the hoops ae green acroass the white. Alpha, omega. Rough an ready! Hey-hey-hey. Randy tan, lipstick 'n' nae knickers. 'Gimme the bag-cocked Bhoys, *maa*!!'

Jesus, that Buckley song wis weirder than he'd thought. Starsailor, right enough. He examined his fingers – they were drippin with water. Deck B. Deck A. The way the amphet-amine guitar played against the alto flute, it wis enough to send you to Counterpoint Heaven. But this title track, this 'Starsailor', wis more like the first flourish of 'Fugue Hell'. An epiphany to a lost spirit. For a moment, he thought he could see through his own skin, right down to the inordinately white bones. He splayed out his fingers before his face. The notes of the song turnin to waves, to shiftin points of darkness, behind his hands. An the room wis cold, fuckin cold, an Zilla wis standin there by the glass window. Oh, fuck-oh-fuck-oh-fuck.

She wis smilin and then she climbed out of the window. Just threw her leg over and climbed out. She sat on the outside ledge for a moment. Then she let go. She didn't jump – there was no leap into oblivion. She just dropped into blackness. A flutter, a whoosh. Then nuthin. Silence. 'Om

323

Shanti Om'. He blinked.

He realised he wis gripping the taps. He twisted his hands and turned them, hot and cold both, full on so that the water splashed up and hit him in the chest. He closed his eyes, bent down and pushed his head below the water. Kept it there. Then he sprang back up. Gasped. Didn't open his eyes. Then down again. He felt the water seep between his lids. Did the same three or mibbee four times. Lost count. When he'd finished, he pulled the plug out and watched the water spiral down the hole. A magnetic shape, a circle, an ellipse, an eye, swirlin, shrinkin, disappearin into nuthin. He tore himself away and left the bathroom quickly. He avoided glancin at the back wall in case it wasn't there.

When he got back to the booth, the place wis flooded with light. A pale blue luminescence streamed in from the open window and the sounds of the first birds broke through the silence. The song playin over the console wis a quiet number by Kaleidoscope. 'Taxim'. He slumped down on to the chair. Didn't spin. Just sat and gazed at the window which wis growin brighter every second. She must've slipped into the buildin through the fire escape door when someone had nipped out for a minute. Harry, mibbee, or Raj/Taj. The rest had all been hallucination. A combination of the bang to his head and the drug that she had given him. Injury and insult. There were many ways of getting bruised. She could've left even more easily than she had entered. The window thing wis a load of crap. The dream of a fevered mind. The sex too. He let his eyes sink into the lightening sky. It wasn't yet blue but he knew that, as the mornin emerged, it would turn slowly azure. As he looked up at the indeterminate sky, as the notes of the *saz* plucked themselves free, from where he wis sittin, Zaf felt he could've been anywhere in the world. 'Taxim'. It wis a lopin instrumental, a Turkish-American modal piece from the California of the late nineteen sixties that turned on a single, repeated phrase. He could've been by the banks of the Bosphorus or behind the walls of a high Anatolian *khanaqah*. Or else in some strange hinterland of hillbillies where, like log-cabin luminaries, the down-homers carried not rifles but musical instruments and a copy of Hafiz Shirazi's *Divaan*. He might've been anywhere.

The heroin had probably just given him a wet dream. The sex, the degradation, the manner in which he had been turned almost into an animal. Hallmarks of unreality. But he had never lost awareness. Right through the whole thing, his body had remained totally sensate and his brain had possessed a hard lucidity. Came from swimmin in too many lochs. Drownin slowly in the cold black. Babs. The strange thing wis Babs would've been alone at home, in bed, and she would've slept completely unperturbed, right through the night. She hadn't come to the party. He wondered why. She'd said that she might. Hadn't seemed that committed, right enough. It wasn't her radio station – it had meant nuthin to her. Worse than nuthin. For the past three months, it had been his life and all she'd done wis carp and moan. But subtly, the way a woman would. Especially a white woman. Like the way they applied make-up or contraception. They had rights and the most basic right of all wis the fact that, whatever happened, whatever arguments might be brought forth about somethin or whatever facts might emerge to refute their case, beneath it all, there would be a tacit understandin, a two-hundred-year-old foundation stone which said that they would always be right. Dead subtle. And they had argued about his life so many fuckin times. Like why didn't he get a job – any job. OK, she'd accepted that he might not have had to use his nut – there were precious few jobs goin that a graduate in ethnological studies might aspire to – but it would've brought in a few extra pounds. And they needed them badly. She wis the breadwinner. She won the bread and he ate it – that wis the way she wis beginnin to make it seem. She sweated blood through her nursin to make ends meet, she worked all the hours God gave and yet, still, they were stuck in a one-bedroom rented flat on the wrong side of Woodlands. And, the way he wis goin, they might never get out, might never move on up. 'An whit wis this radio station business?' she had said. 'Dis it pay? No! Mair ae yer crap. Ah've fuckin jist aboot hud enough.' Yet, still, she would sleep well. He would lie awake beside her and he would hear her deep, satisfied breathing. There wis obviously a bowed instrument, a violin mibbee, on this track. It wasn't a classical violin – there wis none of your Stradivarius stuff up on the verdant slopes of these *pahaRi*. This wis a different beast altogether. This fiddle, at times, sounded like a *kemance*. Even as it played, Zaf could feel its body stretch and change. When she slept, her face wis like that of an angel. She wis suffused with light. Peace. A state he had never known. The work she did wis physically tirin but it wis more than that. The thing wis, Babs knew her place in life. She did her job and, in spite of everythin, she liked it and she brought home her pay and they shared the cookin an cleanin but she wis better at it than he wis so he let her do the difficult bits and she had no dilemmas about who she really wis – no fractures of the soul. Sometimes, when she wis naked, he would watch her back as she slept, he would study its contours in a way in which he never felt able to do durin their love-makin, which wis always tender but frantic, imbued, as it wis, with the dancin, *maqam* shadows of former lovers, and he would become fascinated by the manner in which the tiny bones moved, one on the other, and by the way her skin gave off a pale light like that of the moon and it wis at those moments, as she slipped beneath consciousness, that he would feel most at one with her. He would feel as though they were still up there in the dovecote, gazin at the stars and feelin themselves rise like dead gods towards the empty sky.

The music wis speedin up – the same notes were bein played, the same motifs bein enunciated, that wis the *taxim*, after all, that wis the whole point – though, of course, with every loop, there were slight variations in timin and style and now the drummer wis joinin in, his taut skins turnin black and risin from their chrome trammels, risin and foldin over the land, the light runs of snare, the underpinnin of bass, encompassin the frenetic, flyin fox of the *saz* – aye, the drum kit wis scorin out notes in a yurt sweep across the great whale continent. In music, in 'Taxim', the divisions were all artifice, unity wis reality – in life, it wis the other way round.

And they must've had somethin good otherwise it wouldn't have lasted for as long as it had – especially in the face of all the dagger glances that they'd received from Zaf's *maa* – an he didn't want to lose it but, like Zilla, he felt that his life wasn't in his control, he felt like a salmon tryin to leap but always seemin to fall, to drop back into the dark, swirlin waters of the sea. He had carried Zilla's shadow with him through his life and, even now, all these years later, it haunted his every thought. And he wis sure that Babs could feel the presence of the other woman, tattooed deep in the moistness of his skin. Leathered to his soul. Mibbee he would never reach the glacier. His promised, frozen land. His Sea of Cold. Mibbee that wis why he had agreed to do this insane radio thing, the graveyard shift, the slot no one else had wanted. For four years, Zilla had given him a high and he had balanced on the edge of her cliff. But Babs still made him feel big. When he walked alongside her or when he rode behind her on the big blue bike or when he saw that the washin

327

instructions label of her favourite cardigan had flipped, in that blissfully uncool, homely way of hers, out over the rim of her neckline, stupid pastel, plastic buttons and all, he felt twice as tall, he felt accepted, loved or, at least, not hated. He had felt part of her world though he had always remained unsure, really, of what that world might be – like some secret college of alchemists, he felt he'd never really gained admission and that all he'd got wis the illusion of a door. But, still, he had needed more. Fame, freedom, whatever. The track alternated between fast passages, when the whole band joined in, and slow, complicated, improvised sections, when only the *saz* and flute would play. There was no written music for these slow sections. Every time would be different. Each performance rose from the darkness like a dancer and began to turn and swoop and trip across the wooden floorboards of his twenty-by-twenty cubicle and mibbee it wis Zilla and mibbee it wis Babs – the dancer had no face, just form and sound. 'Taxim'. His voice goin out to millions (well, hundreds) of people, all over Glasgow and beyond. A captive audience. It wis like some bastard or other, who might've treated him like shite, would twiddle the knobs of his radio set, lookin for amusement or whatever it wis those guys looked for, and, sittin there, smilin, balanced on the ninety-nine-point-nine meter Frequency Modulation waveband among the *saz* notes and the reed pipes, would be Zaf, the King of the Airwaves. Kind of like Orson Welles. Or Mohammed Rafi. Or Doctor Goebbels. 'Taxim'. It wis the last rush of all. The one before the silence. But now he'd lost her. Babs. She wis the sort of woman who would never go back on somethin once she'd made up her mind. She wis stubborn that way. She'd told him once that, out there in the Galloway peninsula, you were quite cut off – it wis like bein in the American Midwest. 'Ye had ta do what ye had ta do,' she'd said. They'd laughed at that, at her fake Yankee *gae*-girl accent, and he'd kissed her and he had been full of wonder. Wonderful. Aye, it wis one of the things that first had attracted him to her. Her strength of purpose. Her refusal to take bullshit. Motorcycle girl. But she'd swallowed his bullshit for two years and, tonight, or this mornin mibbee, she'd finally had enough. It wis the end. He wondered whether she might have met someone else. Some big white man who would share her strength and not feed off it as Zaf had done. Some guy who would be capable of holdin his own with her like Zaf had never been able to. How could you ever feel equal to someone you worshipped? Mibbee that had been why, without discussin it with her beforehand, he'd agreed to do the radio slot. *The Junnune Show*. How to break up your relationship in three easy stages. Madness. Madness. Madness.

A moment of inchoate jealousy writhed through his mind but he killed it. Babs wis a one-man woman, he thought. An Ah'm . . . But mibbee that had been part of the problem. In his fear of her, he'd taken her for granted and you should never take any woman for granted. And especially not a *goree*. They didn't live their lives in hock to a man, the way his mother had with his papa. Not if they had any self-respect. And Asian girls were gettin the same way. Mibbee that wis why they seemed to prefer to go with white guys. Because they thought they would get some respect. Or mibbee, Zaf thought, it's just that we're all fascinated by difference. That wis why men an women got together in the first place, wasn't it? Because they were opposites. God, that wis right. Well, now he'd well and truly fucked up his relationship with Babs and he hated himself for it. But it's because Ah hated myself that the thing got screwed up in the first place, he thought. But there wis nuthin he could have done about that. He couldn't change the way things happened. Everybody wis a fuckin nomad and the borders were all closed. The hate lived inside of him an it burned like desire so that, sometimes, he found it hard to tell the two apart. Hate and desire. That wis lust. There's no love in me, Zaf thought, and he felt like cryin. But he'd been through too much tonight. To cry would have been impossible. Instead, he did somethin which he'd never done before – not in all his three months of broadcastin. He turned up the volume, turned it right up to full, and then he went over to the control panel and he boosted the signal. That wis illegal – it would have got the station shut down for good but he wis beyond carin. He wanted to let everyone within a twenty-mile radius hear *The Show of Madness*. Wanted to share himself with the whole of Glasgow. The moon wis fallin over the edge of the world. He did it coolly, with no emotion. At least, none that showed.

'I'm the real prostitute,' he said aloud. But he couldn't hear his own voice amidst the mess of strings. The plucked sounds of the *saz* from 'Taxim' strummed through the room, fillin it with their sonority. Kaleidoscope. A wonderful, wordless song. It would build slowly, like good sex, and would mass in waves toward a climax and would then subside again into silence. He didn't announce anythin into the mike. He saw that it was still switched on – she had left it that way. Silence had been her final requiem. No words. He went over to close the window. Put his hands on the brass knobs. He had intended just to shut the thing and not to look out at the buildings opposite, nor to gaze down at the street. But he couldn't resist the temptation to lean out. To lean and swing like hot jazz. Brass skin trumpet. The long windows were still dark but they seemed to have lost some of their mystery. Down on the road, he half expected to see a body, lyin crumpled and broken, blood and brain released finally in a pool around the head . . . But the street wis empty. This wis the quiet time. That period in the very early morning when no one wis about. The night shifts would not yet have ended and the day workers would still be asleep. And both would be in the final, vivid stages of dreamin. An entire city of the not sane. He inhaled. It smelled clean. Like the first mornin.

Originally, he'd planned to do a kind of a farewell thing over the airwaves. A sort of 'Goodnight 'n' Good Mornin tae Glasgae' only hipper – sampled, punched out, like ADF might've done it.

> You know the night has ended
> An the day has just begun
> But you 'n' me, pal
> We go on an on an on an on

Jah!

He smiled. Not to be. Mibbee it wis better that the good folk of Glasgae, the good, upstanding *lok*, had been spared the misery of hearin that just as they were wakin up.

Ah'm walkin, folks. Walkin an wakin. Ah'm pacin oot the cartogram ae this toon. *Theen* steps – *Aik, dthow, theen.* Boom! Creation fae nuhin. Music fae silence. *Kun!* Let it Play! Want tae come wi me? Suit yersels. It's aw the same tae me.

He shoved in 'Taxim' by Kaleidoscope. And then he realised that he had already sequenced the same song on Deck A. And the two decks hadn't cancelled each other out. Somethin wis wrong. Deep in the heart of the machine, somethin wis rotten. So now, the two tracks would play out of synch with each other for another seven minutes. Or at least for as long as they overlapped. Oh, shit. So, now, the song wis playin in quadruped or quadraphonia or whatever the word for a sound wis. It wis runnin on four legs, *chaar* strings, twice over. Spider song, climbin up the walls, crossin the line. Anyway, it wis too late now, he couldn't go back and de-sequence the plastic. So, now, the city of Glasgow would get two *sazes*, an encampment of drum skins and a whole bed of reeds, all playin at ferocious, wake-up speed. A *maqam* sky. A swirlin dancer. Fuckin brilliant. An, as he leaned forwards out the window, he had another flashback. Flash forward. Oh, no, oh, no, oh, no.

He walked past the deserted buildings which now, in the half-light of early morning, seemed merely empty. They no longer held any threat. He aimed his foot at a stone. Kicked it from a perfect angle so that it flew in an arc and hit the wall of the empty building. A small sound. The street smelled of emptied bins, of detritus, uncovered and removed. As he drew closer to the far end of the street, Zaf was startled by the figure of the man with the stick. He wis half-leanin against the wall of one of the buildings and his hair was bound back in a silver ponytail. The band must've been tied more tightly than the night before or mibbee it wis just that the wind had dropped. He didn't seem quite as tall now or mibbee it wis just the angle of the light. His leg wis splayed out behind him. Some kind of deformity, Zaf thought. And, last night, he had seemed so sinister. Perhaps he wis sinister and it wis the mornin that lied. He wis feedin the birds. He seemed to watch Zaf without really lookin at him. Zaf could feel the man's eyes move across his body like those of a starling. From far off, the sound of the occasional car sharpened the silence. He did not acknowledge the man as he drew past him but he found his gaze drawn to the man's hands. He watched as the hands tossed breadcrumbs to a clutter of pigeons. His fingers made repetitive movements – tiny flicks like those of a jazz guitarist. The fingers were long, tapered. The nails had been polished with pink lacquer. Zaf looked away. The pigeons, suddenly disturbed, fluttered up around the figure and then settled back down again. Blue, grey and pink. He felt the man watch him until he was out of vision.

Back in the cubicle. Darkness. The mike. Breath. 'Taxim', the second version, wis drawin to a close. It had run differently from the first time. It had been as though the musicians had been playin live from some secret chamber deep in the iron mountain of the console. The track slowed towards the end, slowed impossibly – you couldn't hit those gut strings that slowly and still make them resound. But Old *Hazrat* Suleiman Feldthouse wis doin just that. And, then, a mess of all the instruments, a fanfare as the ship leaves harbour. The sound of breakin glass. 'We bless this ship and all who sail in her. We name her *HMS Chaandni*.'

Nah, it's no aw the same tae me. Ah care – Ah really do. Ah'd like ye tae come wi me. Aw the weye. Ye've come this far, *samaaen*, ye've run an danced wi me through over four and a hauf oors ae this night an it's too late noo fur yous tae climb up the rail an leap aff the side ae the ship. The watter at this time ae the mornin is very cauld. So Ah invite yous aw tae remain oan board till the end. Ah insist.

Sonic addiction. The ones still listenin would be unable to

prise their ears off the loudspeakers of their digital radios. They were stuck to the mesh. They were his. An he wis theirs forever. Lovers on the ayre. Tra-la-lee. Ha! Elizabethan tights and all. *Wa-wa*! Now, Zaf wis a real poet. No longer a jockey – words his horse. Black, trusted steed. Lyin *goRah*, in a hurricane. Battened down, Shaitan ears. Knight on a white . . .

But the night wis gone. And, in its place, the risin, raga-rock arpeggios of 'Why'. Auld Roger ae The Byrds, younger than yesterday, King of the Psychedelic Midwest, cowboys on mushrooms, balancin twelve-string sitars on their saddle-packs, smilin into the face of the lightenin sky and askin that one big question.

Giddy-up!!

He wished he had given them a wake-up call. The goodies, the respectable folk of the town whose only aim in life wis to own a Merc or a BMW or to have children who would be as pale as possible. They worked God-awful hours not because they were, in some way, virtuous but simply because oppression back home and in Scotland had taught them to keep their eyes and their heads down, down, down and because, somewhere, in the *canaals* of their minds, they imagined that they might float, on the sweat of their backs, up to the higher level which lay on the other side of the rusted, closed-off lock gates. Turn the world to liquid. Meantime, all they saw, slippin in the other direction, goin downstream, were the detritus and perverts of the land with their stoned phalluses and their gleamin Venus flytrap cunts – the godless, dancin hordes of pagan Arabia returned now to plague the good, risen, petit bourgeois Punjabi folk of Glasgae. They would not have tolerated people like the man with the stick. No way. Not if they'd had any say in it. In a land where nuthin had ever been equal, the losers fought for solace among the weeds and the crumbs and the stones. Meanwhile, the kids, whom they'd filled with dreams of the work ethic, were goin off an screwin an gettin screwed in all directions. Sex, heroin, gamblin, prostitution – the lot. That wis the stuff you didn't read about in the rags. That wis the stuff you never saw on TV. Would've been too sensitive.

An those good *sharif* people had produced Zilla. They had made Zaf. *Aashiq*. Mibbee the story about her forced marriage had been true all along and she really wis just a victim. No one had offered to step in when her folks had disowned her and tossed her out ae the *ghaR* like a used tampon. Mibbee if there had been or mibbee if her parents had been just a wee bit mair sensitive to what she'd been feelin . . . But, then, he thought, I'm more to blame than anyone else for the way she is. It had been her crazed love for him that had driven her to do the things she had done – to prostitute herself, to mutilate her own body, to run with the dogs of Possil and to eat with the rats of Barlanark. The whole thing had been some kind of a slow, deliberate killin. A suicide. And he'd given her that first, adulterated joint and, with it, the fake love.

He sighed and his breath wis a jet of steam in the cold, morning air. But wasn't everybody a victim of some sort? That wis just a cop-out. The easy way. You got your deal in life or you didn't but, somehow, you had to make it work. Because nobody else would. There were no safety nets – there were only wolves and rats. *Sooers*.

Soangs ae the pigs, *haraam* soangs. Whit can Ah say? Ye can wash yer honds aifterwards. Say a wee prayer. Pumice-stone the adulterous *sooers*! Drive the hogs ower

335

the edge ae the cliff, send them aw gruntin intae the white sky!

Dream snort.

He fingered the song-list which now resembled an eighteenth-century map of mid Argyllshire. Faint, blue lines runnin across the world. Hills and rivers, *beantann* and burns. Boswell and Johnson. Sammy not Binyamin. Scrawled diaries runnin on and on into a high-tech, paperless eternity. All madness and flashes.

By mistake, the side of his left hand touched a switch.

'Pepys peeps. Peep, peep, peep. The lights huv jist goan oot!'

Fellatio Mike.

'Mibbee they'll no cum oan again in oor time.'

Nice guy, that Mike. If ye were that way inclined. Zaf wisnae. Right? Jist to make it clear. OK? 'Fight them oan the beaches.' Wage war wi Cuban cigars. Fidelio. His wis oot again. Oot ae this world. Thank Goad. Next track.

Deck B.

'This Land Is Our Land'. 'Ce Pays'. Les Negresses Vertes. *Maajoun*!! Here's a night tale in the mornin: Follae the distant sound ae a bee, buzzin in the desert, intae a cool cave whur ye faw intae some tom-toms or mibbee intae the big, spherical cheek ae a *duf* drum. A poutin, rai trumpet, the plucked strings ae an 'ud, *ce pays*, Pachomian, Serapic monks, Middle Dynasty or mibbee even before, buried in the grains ae white sand, sweepin up fae somewhur, ye cannae see whur, an noo it's a quiet dust storm an night is fawin an the stars burn invisibly behind the cloak ae the dust music an ivirythin's jist a pulse an in the back ae yer heid whur it aw began – the continuous sound ae an auld, auld horn.

Breeeeeeeeeeeeeeathe

Papyrus. The playlist. Ancient fingers. Trumpet bones. 'Ce Pays'.

DRINK

He inhaled and felt the coldness penetrate his chest and spread outwards along his arms. He stretched and it wis like he could almost touch both sides ae the street. He felt larger than life – as though, durin the night, he had died and wis now invisible. Ineffable. God only wise. Some hymn he remembered from long ago, in school. Early mornins always reminded him of school. Habits die hard. Wisdom never dies. Yeah, he had got wisdom but what had Zilla got? And what about Zafar the Gangsta? Well, who knows? Mibbee, in a few years' time, his namesake would be playin golf wi the provost or mibbee he would be the provost. And then he would've graduated from a Porsche to a Rolls. But Zilla wouldn't be at his side. She wis headed down the dark tunnel of herself and it wis a one-way trip. It transcended politics. He laughed. It was outside any dealins she might have had with other people. She had had him there in the fuckin studio but, to her, it hadn't seemed to mean anythin. It had simply been another hit. One of ten or mibbee twelve she would need every day to get by. To breathe. To feel. But, no, she didn't feel. Not really. That had died a long time ago.

He came to the end of the street. From here, he could see right across the city. An orange fire burned along the eastern horizon and had begun to cast pink streaks across the sky. The sandstone of the city glowed salmon and russet – the palette of a god. Somewhere between Zaf and the dawn, the River Clyde curled like a scimitar pointin westwards. He breathed slowly and closed his eyes. Let the smells of the mornin sink into him. Daisies and disinfectant. He went in the direction that his legs took him. Just let himself walk across the city. Mibbee it wis the smell comin from a mobile sandwich bar of fried eggs and hot dogs and very basic coffee or perhaps it wis the pull of the flowin water – Zaf wasn't sure – but, either way, after he had spent the last of his money on a roll-and-sausage and a cup of polystyrene tea, he found himself headed towards the Botanic Gardens.

It wis a lie. He wis aimin at goin back to the flat, for a shower and a change of clothes. And mibbee a sleep. North Kelvinside or South Maryhill, dependin on which social class you wanted to impress. The sort of shiftin, uncertain place where a nurse might just live and thrive, somewhere along the backbeat of the Kelvin. Goin through the Gardens wis a bright idea. A kind of a short cut. The place had several exit gates. And, yet, even though he knew this, Zaf felt that nuthin could ever be certain, that, if the stones and the trees could move, then perhaps people might too. Under the mornin skies of Scotland, anythin wis possible.

Absolutely anythin. Ivirythin. It's aw here oan this show which is unlike any other show ye've ivir listened tae in aw yer born puffs. Ivir been in two places at wance? Like Auld Rabbie Burns. He slept in twinty beds, in twinty different toons, between forty pairs ae thighs, aw in the same night. Here we go!

THE TARBOLTON LASSIES

If ye gae up to yon hill-tap,
Ye'll there see bonie Peggy;
She kens her father is a laird,
And she forsooth's a leddy.
There Sophy tight, a lassie bright,
Besides a handsome fortune:
Wha canna win her in a night,
Has little art in courtin'.

Gae down by Faile, and taste the ale,
And tak a look o' Mysie;
She's dour and din, a deil within,
But aiblins she may please ye.

If she be shy, her sister try,
Ye'll maybe fancy Jenny;
If ye'll dispense wi' want o' sense —
She kens hersel she's bonie.
As ye gae up by yon hillside,
Speir in for bonie Bessy;
She'll gie ye a beck, and bid ye light,
And handsomely address ye.

There's few sae bonie, nane sae guid,
In a' King George' dominion;
If ye should doubt the truth o' this —
It's Bessy's ain opinion!

Tell me more, Rabbie, tell me more. *Mujhe bathao*!

How sweetly bloom'd the gay green birk,
How rich the hawthorn's blossom,

As underneath their fragrant shade,
I clasp'd her to my bosom!

The golden hours, on angel wings,
Flew o'er me and my dearie;
For dear to me, as light and life,
Was my sweet Highland Mary.

Wi' monie a vow, and lock'd embrace,
Our parting was fu' tender;
And, pledging aft to meet again,
We tore oursels asunder;

Jesus! Quantum bard.

The shades of the wall behind him assumed the form of
the old taxman. Ah, Zaf thought, revolution in a mouse. Zaf
sang into the mike.

Meri zindagi, mera jeevan!

But his voice came out like that of Marlene Dietrich, ten
years post-mortem. Croakin and fatale.

We're where we shouldnae be, ye realise that, *bundhay*,
an you're comin along fur the ride. Fae the Sahra Desert
tae the filthy auld river. Swingin Londres. We can go
onywhur oan this show. Onytime, ony place, onywhur.
Ma face. It's jist like in the movies an Ah'm the hero! Or
mibbee Ah'm the villain. Or mibbee jist the clown dancin
oan the fag ends ae the celluloid. A *muskhaira* spinnin in
the dawn, totally alone. Ye know that feelin when, aw ae
a sudden, the big universe is blowin around ye. Where
are all yer friends goin? The wans ye talk tae all day
lang, through those cuts ae plastic that play at bein souls.

Lips an ears. Ye want tae find oot? Then listen tae this.

He glanced over his shoulder. The shades had vanished. Slip another piece of music into the metal machine. Grin an die!

He scribbled somethin on the playlist and then threw down his pen and scrunched up the paper into a ball and lobbed it at the partition window. It bounced off the glass and flew straight back into his lap. He spun round once, the full three-hundred-and-sixty-five degrees, and the playlist flew off again.

The swamp metal chords of 'See My Friends' clanged out through the mornin air. An end-of-party song howled from the burned, broken tail of a pier. Gay, Gangetic-Victorian romp. The kinky time, in the hours between dawn and sunrise, when the day seemed not quite real. Velvet suits-and-ruffs on the grass. Double entendres. Illicit smiles passin across a crowded room. Songs in wrought iron.

Zaf stooped but the room kept on rollin. Round and round and round and round and

Jump aff! Noooooo!

It wis unstoppable. The music, the raga-rock. It wis the howlin universe.

Intae the gairdens, folks. *Firdaus. Paridaeza. Jannat.* Thrawn. Glais hooses. Ghost hooses.

The park gates had just been opened but the place was empty. There was no wind and everything was in a state of glistening silence. The leaves had assumed that shade of mature green which they tended to acquire towards the height of summer and the park seemed poised on the edge of something. The Winter Gardens in August. His legs felt light and his trainers bounced over the asphalt as though he wis on another planet. The sun wis unusually warm for the time of day and the sky had cleared except for a few harmless bits of fluff over to the west. It was goin to be a sunny day. Zaf smiled and then wondered why. He had just walked out of the radio station where a bunch of thugs had done their best to cause mayhem. He had been drugged and then technically raped, his father wis demented and his girlfriend had probably left him. And, as she had been in the habit of reminding him, he had no job. What's there to smile about? he thought. But he kept smilin anyway. Didn't care if it wis the drug. Might as well enjoy it while it lasted. He stretched his arms upward, pushed the joints out as far as they would go, then let them fall back again. Took off his jacket, slung it over his shoulder. Just like ole Dick Whittington, he thought, and then he laughed. Turn again . . .

The glass palaces looked like stage scenery out of some old sci-fi movie. Victorian futurism. Gentlemen in space. Top hats. He passed by the huge tropical houses with their big glass plates. Caught a glimpse of the strange plants inside. The giant specimens which had been uprooted from far-off countries and which, like caged aliens, contorted and seeped their way across the insides of the windows. A tiny piece of Pakistan in every Scottish field . . .

The park wis so quiet he could hear the sound of rushin water and he went down towards the river. As he descended the path, the noise of birds erupted from far above. He gazed upwards, through the highest branches of the trees, but the birds had already vanished into the mornin and all he could make out wis the uniform pale blueness of the sky and the tiny, almost imperceptible movements of the leaves against its surface. When he looked again, he wis already right down by the river's edge. The water flowed fast and clean over flat stones and the sound it made reminded Zaf of his own past and of the pasts which he had never lived through but which were part of him. The stories of his parents' childhoods, of their journey, their exile, their struggle and, now, their decline. And of Babs's life before him. Her photo which, like ashes, had been scattered across the city, their love-makin up in the dovecote by the great dark loch, the strange conjunction of need that had drawn them together and, now, their imminent separation and exile from each other's lives. Sympathetic strings. But they would always be part of the same past. Nuthin could change what had happened. He gazed into the water, watched as it flowed over the grey stone of the river bed. The Kelvin here wis very shallow but, further on, it got much deeper and, there, the water wis black and you couldn't see the bottom. That wis where people committed suicide. Prayed for oblivion, for an end to pain and then jumped off the bridge.

He broke into the song. Kinky notes.

Ivir thought ae committin suicide? Now, don't get me wrong. Ah don't mean tae suggest that ye go aff an top yersels. Ah'm jist askin the question. Cause it seems tae me that so many guid people huv taken that way oot. Exoterically or esoterically. Wan weye or another. Ye huv tae ask yersel – why?

Here comes the litany of saints:

Tim Hardin, Tim Buckley, Waheed Murat, Walter Benjamin, Phil Ochs, Guru Dutt, Jackson C Frank, Primo Levi, Nicholas Drake, Nanna the Comic Actor. An whit aboot the stars that died young, eaten away slowly by the claws ae the Big C? Nargis, Nautan an Mina Kumari –

tragic, monochrome heroines all. Oh, an Rehman, the guy wi the *surma* eyes. Scion ae the Sadozais, the Royals ae Afghanistan. Oh, Merciful Son ae Abraham. 'The King is dead! Long Live the King!' Long live Qaisar.

Ach, there ye go. Jist life, eh? Ah guess. Wee optimisms at four sumhin in the mornin. Hard tae come by. Mibbee suicides are jist optimists that wake up. Insomnia fur this life. Shoot me doon but it's very Scottish, that, isn't it? Very Glasgae. Wallowin an maudlin. C an W. Ah, well, cow-people, time fur some mair *saaz*. This is a music station, aifter aw, an Ah'm a disc joakie. Ah tell bad jokes. Ha! Nah, it's whit Ah dae. This . . .

Zaf tapped the surface of a compact disc twice.

this is why Ah'm oan this earth. Why are you here?

In with the silver! Deck A.

Profound questions for insomniacs like me. Bad jokes, bad rhymes. *Sumjhe?* Rock 'n' rollin majestie!
Aff wi their heids!

The closin notes of 'See My Friends'. Ray-diation on a good day. Sunlight and alchemy.

He had reached the big red sandstone viaduct that crossed the river. A road ran along its top but the road was quiet. Zaf paused for a moment beneath the arch of the bridge. He could hear the sound of his own breathin echo against the stone. Graffiti had been scrawled in white paint across the rough blocks and, in the middle of all the personal messages, a smooth, blood-red rectangle announced that the bridge had

344

been opened on January the seventeenth, nineteen hundred.

CORPORATION OF GLASGOW
KIRKLEE BRIDGE
MEMORIAL STONE
LAID BY
COUNCILLOR JOHN McFARLANE
CHAIRMAN OF THE STATUTE LABOUR COMMITTEE
17th JANUARY 1900
THE HON. SAMUEL CHISHOLM JP
LORD PROVOST OF THIS CITY

The other side of the same stone block, bore the inscription:

WILLIAM WILSON
CONTRACTOR

All these people were long-dead, Zaf thought, and even their memories had been forgotten. No one knew what they had looked like or the way they had talked, no one still livin had heard the sound of their laughter. They were as dead as the Mughal courtiers of Lahore or the *doomnis* who had sung to them of unfulfilled desire and of love unattainable. The servant's dark eyes as he sways the fan from side to side, the stretch of the singer's slender arms across the emptiness of an eighteenth-century *divaan-e-zanaane*, the sound of her voice, a disturbance of the air . . . music.

He leaned forwards and whispered into the microphone.

This song is a hundred years old. Aulder than yer granny's granny. *PaR paR nani.* Let it fill yer ears, let it take ye tae long-forgotten places. Bow Bazaar, haunt ae courtesans, *zamindars* an *babus.*

345

The impossibly distant and yet somehow knowing voice of Gauhar Jan, singer-songwriter and polylingual diva, lasered out from Deck A, through the twisted metal of the Radio Chaandni Community Asian Radio Station, out into the cracks of the dawn and beyond. 'Bhairavi'. The vocal cords of Erevan transplanted to Kolkata and the brass horns and thick wax of the Gramophone and Typewriter Company.

Miss Angelina Yeoward, being the daughter of dry-ice engineer and Armenian Yehudi William Robert Yeoward and a certain Miss Victoria Hemming, aka *BaRi* Malka Jan, wishes to present her tableau of songs and physical dance. Four-horse buggies and several hubbies and *bhajans* and *thumris* and *ghazals* and *billies*.

Miaow!!

And Zaf might as well have been a cat because the song wis almost impossible to decipher. It seemed as though the words were issuin from several of Gauhar Jan's eleven languages at once. But, more than that, the singin style wis archaic, open throated, somethin from the deep past that lay beyond livin memory. Voices which only the insane could hear, issuin from the trees. Voices strainin with the bonded freedom of words and convention. Wild voices.

It was then Zaf noticed that, beneath the bridge, just above the uppermost level of the water where the reeds stopped and the grass began, there wis an openin. He would normally never have looked there and it wis only because he wis leanin over the metal fence and gazin at the water that he saw it now. Carefully, he climbed over the fence and let himself down on the other side. It wis more difficult than it seemed because the river bank wis steep and slippery with the overnight rain but, eventually, Zaf managed to angle himself opposite the opening which wis fringed by long weeds and a discarded car tyre. He peered into the darkness but couldn't make out the back wall. On hands and knees, he crawled through the weeds and into the opening. He almost banged his head on the stone roof but, after a while, he got used to it and kept his head down – did not look ahead but only down at the ground immediately in front of his fingers. What the fuck am I doin? he thought, but, like the rest of the mornin, this side trip seemed somehow inevitable. The passageway smelt dank, rotten, and he became aware that he wis crawlin over more than mud. It wis so dark he couldn't see what it wis and so he pushed the thought out of his mind and kept movin.

After a while, the sounds of the park faded and he realised that he was in a large chamber. He wis able to stand and turn and it occurred to him that he should have brought a torch. But then he laughed. As if I'd planned this, he thought. He could no longer see the entrance. The tunnel must have curved somehow and he would now be beneath a different part of the park altogether. He must've been crawlin for longer than he had imagined. The drug again, he supposed. Or mibbee it wis just like that. Mibbee the park was intoxicated or the whole city . . .

Gauhar Jan's powerful yet plaintive voice (that was what they'd liked about her, those starched, white gentlemen – the strong whore broken is a good reed to ride) danced across the cubicle in the dawn light, so like the glimmer of the Bombay sky on the pink Arabian Sea – or was it the shimmer of the Calicut heavens over the Bay of Bengal? Well, anyway, this Armenian Indian moved her muscles that had given birth

to seven children – three dead, three living and one escaped
– and the shape which they formed in the old park resembled
the shape of a crescent turning a wheel. Hanover vinyl. Roll
'n' roll.

Ye're watchin me, folks – Ah know ye are. Ye're listenin
tae ma iviry breath. Tae see if Ah make a mistake. Fart
oan air. Nae weye. Ah'm too clivir fur yous. Ye can hear
ma brain tickin ower. Tick-toak, tick-toak, tick-toak. Ah
go back a lang weye. Beyond yer granny's granny's
granny. Ah'm an unexploded bomb an Ah'm in yer ear.

Take cover, bombardier!!

The Great War. Trenches, khaki buglers, men of dust astride
putterin, black motorcycles, gas. He sniffed the air. An odd
smell which he couldn't quite place, seemed to lead him on,
deeper into the tunnel. His eyes had become accustomed to
the darkness which no longer seemed complete. Shafts of
light trickled in from far above. He could tell, from the echo
that his voice made when he tested it and from the way the
light diffused downwards, that the roof wis some twenty feet
above his head. The walls were wet, cold and slippery and
they seemed to be covered in some kind of moss. But there
wis somethin else as well. Not just the dampness but somethin
mixed in with it. He could feel it beneath his fingers.

This city is a great auld city. Iviry brick, iviry slice ae
stane wis carved in the shape ae equality. Iviry block wis
cut wi a soang.

He paused.

D'ye believe me? You shouldnae believe iviryhin ye hear oan the radio.

Another breath. Wait . . . Wait . . . Go!

Songs in the gravel
Poets in the stane.
It's the very last mornin
And Ah'm aw alane.

Arey, yaar, auld music. The root, the source, the best. Jis wan string. *Ektar.* Mystical metal. Miraculous gut. Ah go wanderin fae hoose tae hoose, fae border tae border, wi ma gourd-an-bamboo. Nae fush suppers. News 'n' Weather comin up, eventually. Retch, retch! Not all over me, please!

He thought he heard the plucked notes of a single mandolin. He wondered what he wis doin, down here in this dark tunnel, this suffocatin cubicle, when he could've been up an out in the light of a summer's mornin. He wondered why he had a predilection for dark places, moonlit lochs, old churches, East-End streets . . .

Mibbee there wis more to him 'n' Zilla than he had supposed. Mibbee darkness wis his heroin.

A sudden force against his head.

He felt himself reel and the light spun around him. Just before he blacked out completely, he wis engulfed by the sweepin sound of violins. The *Light Empress* wis ridin the rails and time wis going backwards, one bead after the next . . .

A hundred years ago, trains filled with seamstresses and soldiers and small children had steamed through the tunnels beneath the Botanic Gardens in a network that had spanned the undersurface of Glasgow. Zaf felt himself stretch out and touch the invisible metal-and-stone skeleton that was neither part of the official metro nor yet of the surface lines. And where had all those stations gone? All that rushin air, the hubbub of voices, the intoxicatin stench of coal steam and old metal? Zaf held out his hands and felt the slipstream of the iron carriages pull him into the darkness. Deeper and deeper, through the puddles and the oil and the years, until it wis so dark he wis like a worm and could only touch and feel and smell. He felt the soft cotton of the turban on Zafar's head and, beneath it, he felt the skin of a living child – he wis in the notes of Gauhar Jan's voice, as she streamed into space. And he wis there, at the Afghan frontier, in the deep brown eyes of the border guards as they allowed through a battered black Ford Popular, containin two runaway lovers. And he wis in Zilla's vein as it pulsed with the blood of poppies an he wis in Zafar's hand as he pulled the trigger of a long-barrelled *pistole* aimed at his own right temple. And he wis in the tears of his *maa* as she went on, songless, from day to day and he wis in the lost songs, the ones which would never be sung.

◎◎◎◎◎

Jamil Ayaan stared up at the ceiling until his eyes filled with pools of water and the front of his brain began to throb. The moonlight was burning up the air and was causing the ceiling to peel off in thin white strips. When his lids closed, rivers poured from the skin. In the distance, a police siren. A night bird. Some ancient song was playing from somewhere. From where he lay, Jamil couldn't quite make out the melody but he felt he had it almost within grasp. As she approached the bed, Rashida's naked body swayed a little in the moonlight. She had pulled open the heavy outer curtains so that, now, only the nets and the wooden radio that sat in the window recess protected her modesty. The radio was switched on and, from its glass front, its valves and the lists of its stations glowed the colour of bright Kashimilo emeralds but the volume had been turned to zero. Under the soles of her feet, as slowly she walked, lay the golden sari she had donned in perfect sweeps and then allowed him to peel off, to unwind from her frame as though, once again, he were removing her skin. There was hardly any breeze – just occasionally, the lower hem of the net curtain rippled and wafted inwards over the glossed wood of the radio as though the cotton was dancing to the archaic cadences of the music. She was smiling. Her whole body smiled. She was open to him like the full moon to the sky – she was Layla to his Majnoon. She was his night dancer. As he lay there amidst the mess of sheets, his body rising like some old god from the white surf of the waves, one hand still gripped the edge of the sari. The cloth was smooth and soft in his palm. Its rich satin sheen and the smell, that rose from its thread, the aroma of his lover and of old field *rooi*, almost made him swoon, almost caused him to forget the darkness that surrounded the world. The scurrying of rats, the calluses on his fingers, the *rundi* of the sewers. This was meant to be, he thought, this illicit love beneath the cranes of Govan. The journey had made it licit. They had merged their individual selves into each other – their existence outside of this life no longer held meaning. On this *raat*, he would take his wife not like a whore in the gut of the night but, once again, he would enter her body as though they were the same lovers whose eyes had met across the filtered, cooled air of the *haveli*, all those years ago. Once again, in the deep dream of the song that lay beyond words, their seed

351

would meet and form and, perhaps, would begin, at last, to dance. The song rose and fell with the pull of the breeze and, as Rashida came within reach of his hand, Jamil let the sari fall in a mess of gold on to the floor.

◎◎◎◎◎

When he came round, there wis a thuddin in his head where Zafar's gun had been and caked blood wis mixed in with his hair. He stumbled through the tunnel, followin the sound of runnin water. The noise grew louder and louder until it wis deafenin. He knelt and cupped his hands. The water wis cold but not as cold as he had imagined. He slipped off his T-shirt and splashed the water over his chest, his back and over the place on his scalp where the wound was. And, though it made him shiver, it felt good and fresh as though it had gushed, unbroken, from a silvery *alltan* in the black peaks of the Highlands. He stepped out of his jeans and lay down in the flow and he let the cold water wash over his body. He felt the blood and sweat and spunk of the night slip from his skin and he wis totally alone. The thuddin in his head gradually eased. Then he sat up and bathed his feet, massaged the soles. No wonder the old prophets set such store by the washin of feet. Nah, he thought, they never really got Gauhar Jan. With her six hundred songs and her eleven tongues and her sleek racin horses and the manifold loves of her life, she had cracked even the strongest vinyl. He dressed and waded through the water, feelin his way upstream. And, as the last song died, Zaf began to make out a faint light. He stumbled towards the light which grew steadily bigger until it surrounded the tunnel and he let himself be blinded by it and he let it fill him and he lay down on a patch of grass and fell asleep.

Ye're listenin tae *The Junnune Show* oan Radio
Chaandni, ninety-nine-point-nine meters FM an this is still
Zaf – that's zed ay eff – an Ah'm yer host in the auld
caravanserai sense ae the word. Come in an huv some
mai. Put yer lips tae the rim ae the *jaam*. *Accha, hai ke
nahii*? Now put yer ears up an listen tae the silence in
the sky. Listen tae it, *meray bundhay*. Ye're up oan a
moontain tap an ye're jist breathin. Jist livin. Nae wind.
Whisper it – *tu hi tu*. Ah'll no die fur you.

> Tae sleep, tae dream . . .
> *Haraam* Hammy
> 'Satrangi Re'

When he awoke, the sun was burning on his face and he was
lying in a bowl of leaves, just outside the opening of the
tunnel. He glanced back at where he had come from and he
saw that the tunnel entrance was virtually completely blocked
except for some broken stones that lay in heaps at one side.
He realised he must have crawled through this narrow opening
like a cat burglar or a masochist – yet his skin was unmarked.
He'd vaguely heard about these tunnels that coursed through
the earth beneath the old city but he'd never thought that he
would crawl through one like some kind of mendicant on his
way to attaining redemption. Mibbee they should consecrate
these dark places. Make them Houses of God by default.
Somewhere, down there, would be the skeleton of a nun who
had never got out or an illegal immigrant who had never got
in or an escaped slave who had never got free. But he wis
too tired to ponder on such things. Too tired even to shiver.
The ground wis dryin fast and his back wis stiff and sore.
It wis the mornin and the things of the night were past. There
were no mysteries, no incense-swung delusions – the calli-

graphies were etched clear in the burnin summer light. A shrapnelled fate, splayed out like an Ordnance Survey map.

It must've been the other end of the tunnel because he wis on the far side of the Botanics, up close to where the hills began. The foothills of the foothills. The West End. More trees and windows and endless sandstone columns. Infinity in a tenement. He wis stiff but wis almost dry. He reckoned it must be mid mornin at least. The rumblin of traffic came from all directions. He liked that. He longed for the here and now, for the transient realities of the moment. He stood up and stretched his spine, right from the stem of his buttocks to the hang-bone of his neck, and his whole body rose on to the tips of his toes. And then he extended his arms upward, locked the joints, medieval style, at shoulder and elbow and wrist so that his fingers reached so far into the bright light that he could no longer make them out and, through his exhaustion, Zaf felt like the diamond on a stylus, ready to sing.

Sing, sing, sing. Ah'm back, folks. It's me. It's mornin an the sun is shinin. Get rich quick or, if ye cannae, then at least get warum. Mibbee that wis why that dervish in *Dil Se* wis spinnin oan moontain snow. *Baraf* dancin. Huruf *baraf*. Here comes a playlist fur ye jist in case ye lose track – an tae prove that Ah huvnae lost track. Onywan still listenin tae this show must be clinically insane. Join the club! OK, that wis 'Anjaana' by Lata Mangeshkar, 'Taxim' by Kaleidoscope, The Green Negresses' 'Ce Pays', 'See My Friends' by the Kinks, 'Bhairavi' by Gauhar Jan and 'Satrangi Re' by Kavita Krishnamurthy and Sonu Nigam. Now it's sax meenuts tae five o'cloack in the mornin and soon we'll huv yer auld pals, the News 'n' Weather, otherwise known as 'The *TaileT* Break'. Oops! A BMW: A Bad Middle Word.

Zaf sang, mock-Sinatra style.

> Auld friends,
> They nivir go away.
> They linger roon yer heid,
> More's the pitaayyy . . .

An it'll be the same as before, guid listeners. Same as it
ivir wis – it's the wan thing in this waruld that nivir
really cheynges. War, famine, lust, greed, extinction, the
News 'n' Weather plod oan an oan, flat and joyless – a
bit like yer auld granny, frownin beneath the specs. But
don't knock grannies. Think about what they've hud tae
go through . . .

A pregnant pause. He wis gettin good at this. He went over,
bent down and retrieved the playlist. Got back to the mike.

If you hud tae live as they have lived, then you too
would be emptied ae spirit. Thur's always a granny in ma
heid, suckin at ma brain, drainin me away intae the past.
Sing, *maghas*, suck oan this wan. K L Saigal.

Deck B.

> I'm crazy
> From peace I am far away
> How do I entertain my heart?
> When do I show my word?
> Even my tears, they listen to my lament
> And they laugh.

'Diwana Huu Diwana'. Died at the height of his fame, aged

forty-two. Like Rudolf Valentino and Harry Houdini. Escape artists escapin. Crazy, crazy.

Saigal's song wis court poetry. Every line wis repeated twice and the second time it bore a slightly different emphasis. Zaf had seen old film reels in which the singer, dressed in period costume of the Lodi dynasty, had stood in the middle of a palace garden, stock-still save for his right hand with which he had choreographed the loop and dive of the words he was singin. Saigal's black-and-white eyes had been full of emotion but it wis not the uncontrolled, shambolic, emetic emotiveness of a Kishore or a Lata at her most maudlin. Beneath his every gesture, behind every nuance of expression, lay three thousand years of Farsi and Sanskrit poetry. No wonder he didn't move across the studio garden – the weight of all of those words must have been heavy indeed.

> What a sad tale am I.
> The spring didn't come
> So let it stay autumn.
> Let it remain as an unfulfilled desire
> In my broken heart.

And Zaf felt that same heaviness – the turns, in stone, of Kufic script, the twenty-volume collections of the old masters, some lost in the Mongol fires, others moulderin in fake palace libraries where the light, filtered through thick mouth-blown glass, still shone faint and monochrome. The dawn had turned the cubicle walls a shimmerin grey, the colour of a luminescent, cloudy sky when the sun is somewhere behind, tryin to break through. Some very old men still maintained that Saigal had always been the best but then there were other, yet older, men who asserted that Master Nisar, who had been a wind-up gramophone superstar in the nineteen

twenties and who had ended his life, like a Romanov
Grand Duchess, beggin for a crust on the jewel-in-the-coronet
platform of the Great Trunk Railway, had, in fact, been
considerably better. It wis a competition of tragedy. These
same *booDeh* were also convinced that the child star and
incipient guru, Master Madan from Jullunder, had been
poisoned by the envious supporters of older, more powerful
but less talented vocalists. Like the moats of a medieval
castle, the grooves ran with blood. It wis almost decreed, Zaf
thought, that Saigal himself should die young – a fate lifted
off the vinyl. You could never go back the way you came.
The song would always run in a single, classical, preordained
direction, each loop echoin and yet defyin the one that had
gone before. There would never be another sunrise in his
father's brain. In Jamil Ayaan's limbo world, there wis no
longer any distinction between night and day, good and evil,
sound and silence. On this last night, the points where
these opposites met had been sharply defined – even as the
boundaries between them, like the fake garden walls enclosin
the world of Kundun Laal Saigal, had shimmered and fallen.

> I wonder what am I.
> Is there any life in me,
> Or is it barren?
> I am wounded. I am far away from you.
> I have burned my wings and I am helpless.
> Candle, come and kiss me
> For, after all, I am a moth.

A lang generation. Leap years leapin.

Somewhere, his mother and father were living a different
life. Perhaps, in some place by the sea, they moved in long
robes, languorously, casually, through Clifton, past huge,

ice-cream flavoured houses where gardeners clipped at the delicate purple flowers of the burgeoning bougainvillea. Karachi beaches – as they might have been if there had been no despots, no mullahs, no I-S-I-C-I-A-M-I-6-6-6. Perhaps it might have been a place where drivers and street cleaners were protected by unions and pension schemes and where engineers could work as engineers, no matter who their fathers happened to be. A place where the words that had assumed the forms of golden asses could be challenged and broken. At the centres of the marble palaces of the dictators, for a long hundred years or more, there had stood an idol, carved in hard nine-carat gold, of a naked Nordic woman, into which successive waves of rulers, bearded or not, had screwed themselves. Even the *djinns* had fled their jars and now were pulling minicabs through the streets of London, Manhattan and Toronto. A land bereft of *djinns* is like a body bereft of music. 'Pakistan *Zindabad*!' A whole nation whose subconscious wis dislocated. In the pure land of Zaf's imaginings, there would be no idols. The fields and the cities would not be crushed beneath the sway of swaggerin, feudal *jagirdaars* and bloated factory owners with offshore accounts. No torture chambers, no heavy water, no Kalashnikovs in the classroom. But the ends became a product of the means – you couldn't divorce the two. Look at all those school-teachers who had become revolutionaries and ended up monsters. So, from his grey, evolutionary cubicle, from his felt and wood sound box, Zaf would take the good things and make them grow. Simple things. That would be his motto. No more *ghoonda* government death squads. Street cops would be paid enough to feed their families so that they would be less gaunt and emaciated and wouldn't have to arrest people on spurious charges and demand on-the-spot ransoms for their release. And they wouldn't have to

wear those dreadful synthetic jumpers in order to direct the
psychotic traffic in an ambient temperature of one hundred
and twenty-five degrees Fahrenheit. Holes in the road would
be repaired quickly and children would get vaccinated so
that they wouldn't die in their millions to finance the building
of yet another fake *madrasah*. Ordinary women would get
to rise up from the ditches of illiteracy and reinterpret the
texts.

It would be a Pakistan less hot, less dangerous. It wis
a longin that almost every powerless person, from those
countries south and east of Suez, had had at some point in
their lives – it wis about the only thing that united the
diaspora with those who had stayed put. Nah, that wis
wrong, Zaf thought – it hadn't united them, it had split them
into many pieces. It wis not a clash of civilisations – those
were just the kind of thoughts someone had when their brain
wis turnin to shite an could regurgitate only Mystery Plays,
smoke 'n' mirrors, surface reflections – civilisation had never
been a hermetically-sealed, pure item. Most of it, includin
Athens and Sparta and all the rest of those gleamin, aniseed-
pillared cities, had come, originally and essentially, from
Memphis, Susa and Moenjodaro. It wis really a clash of
wealth distribution, of guns versus everythin, combined with
a lack of imagination. A deadenin music. Everyone knew
this, really. It wis just that some didn't know that they
knew it. Others were too feart to admit it and, for some, it
lacked the eschatology necessary for hate. Ha! Right enough,
Zaf thought, there were some positive aspects to doin an
ethnology degree.

Ethiopia!!

The Eye, the Pyramid, the Zero-point. If you stared into

the *annkhey*, really gazed into its dark centre, you would see that, ultimately, we all came from the same wee green hollow in East Africa. Deep down, we were all black. Our souls were wrapped in a black blanket and we lived on a *kaala* rug and saluted a *siya* flag. We were all singin swans – we danced alone and the only way we could pierce the moonless water wis through the *jondo*. In our hearts, we were all Glaswegian, we all belonged to the night. To Layla. Even Madame Planta-genet, the Queen of England. The Four Kings of Song – Rafi, Mukesh, Talat and Kishore. Lata, Asha and Maria Callas. Enrique Morente and Crispian Mills. Um Kulsum and Jacques Brel. Socraat, Aristu and Hypatia. John, Paul, George and Ringo. Everyone. Even Babs. Hawwa, Lilith. The Colour of Memory wis black.

But the jar of knowledge had been broken into many pieces and the pieces scattered to the winds. Some had been sucked into the vortex of monosyllabic, psychotic faith while others had bought cheap replicas of the golden statue – breasts, voice, cunt and all. But most folk had just cut everythin down to its most irreducible form as though, instead of food, they now preferred to ingest the nutrients of words in the form of initials, block-shaped capitals. It wis a region where there would never again be the delusions of poetic ecstasy. In this world, everythin wis Qaisar. In this world, Zaf did not exist. And so Saigal, Suraiya, Ambalawali, Hemant Kumar, Kanan Bala and the rest had given way to struttin male singers who thought that emotion wis best communicated through coarse ejaculations and to women who crushed their throats until they sounded like five-year-old children. A fake innocence. If the land had not been abbreviated and initialled to non-existence, perhaps there would have been no need for blood epiphanies and then the light, no longer searin all year round, would have been tremulous in its possibilities. Perhaps, like Z-A-F, Z-I-L-L-A, J-A-M-I-L and R-A-S-H-I-D-A, the singers, too, led quantum existences, lives split and burned through invisible mirrors. Show and illusion. Radio dreams.

Five o'clock, folks. News 'n' Weather. Haud tight tae yer mind and it will haud ye in its coils. Ride the *saamnp*. SSSSSSSSSSSSSSSSSSSSSSSSSSS!!!!!!!!!!!!!!

FIVE A.M.

Mornin, people! *Salaam alaikum, namaste ji, sat sri akaal.*
It's five o'clock, bright 'n' breezy, Greenwich Standard
Time. A mean time, *samaaen*, a mean time. This is Zaf –
that's zed ay eff – an wu're broadcastin this fine August
mornin oan ninety-nine-point-nine meters FM. We bein
Radio Chaandni. Well, actually, it's jis me, noo. Ah'm the
last. Ah'm the end-beyond-the-end. OK?

Zaf fiddled about on the console with the various companions
of his night – pen, paper and the bones of his fingers. You
had to trust at least the unseen frame of your own body.
Christ. Lose that and you'd lost everythin. It occurred to him
that, in order to think that thought, he would have had to
have lost it already. Big fuck. He wis kickin out, ridin upstream, breast-strokin the rhythm. An the water wis burnin
– it lifted the skin of his ribs, his thighs, it tore the linin off
of his vocal cords. Ragged songs of the movin flesh of the
nations. He cleared his throat, wrote the words. The two
were one. Voice and letter. Flesh and spirit. Ganesh Panto-
crater. Big, black Byzantine mouths all around, elephant
trunk heads, and he wis fallin down every one of them.
Down Ganapati and up Maya.

Fae the nineteen thirties' Gramophone Company ae India,
we're movin right up tae loud London noo, courtesy ae
deepest Australia. Awwroigh? Well, as near tae noo as ye
can get withoot tippin aff the sharp edge ae the waruld.
Hindustan tae Londonium by way ae Oz. That's no very
geographically bright, is it? But people don't always

362

follow the latitudes. Life disnae trek alang parallel lines.
Ye no agree? Think aboot it, auld-timers. And you,
who've been wi me aw this time, can only be considered
as oldies. That's no an insult, mind, it's an honour. Tae
be a *booDa Junnunie* is wan ae the greatest honours
Radio Chaandni can bestow. So be bestowed. Please
accept oor invisible medal. Ye goat here, ye survived an
that's enough. That wis yer role in Creation. The Great
Archangel ae Politics an *Pesay* chucked ye all oot ae the
gairden an then ye came here, tae these ultimate islands,
as far as ye could go withoot cheyngin continent, cause,
as all you buddin geographers oot there'll know fine well,
Asia an Europe don't really exist. They're part ae wan
big land mass, aw joined up. Right? OK. So, you be-
medalled wans, wi yer chests aw decked oot in gauld an
siller, ye're a wee bit like Adam an Eve. Hawwa an
Aadam. And ye'll aw live tae be a thoosand an wan. Be
ancient, then, as the turnin earth, dig deeper than ye ivir
thought possible an let this wumman in yer grey matter.
This is Susheela Raman fae her *Salt Rain* album. Two
tracks, back-tae-back or heid-tae-heid, ye might say.
Cause this is heid music, right. Telegoid hivin, blown
through Smyrna reeds. Sway, folks, sway an dance – it's
wan meenut past five and we're aw born again. Rise, rise,
rise!

Deck A: 'Ganapati'.

The Sanskriti blues, Louisiana, Ghana in Udhagaman-
dalam. *Gana*. Pati. Slippin, slidin violins – *neela* chords,
slow, hypnotic bass and funk drums, swirlin, heavy silk
vocals, sing to me, Susheela, sing those songs of the
Indian Deep South all night long, and time will stand still

like ice in a glacier. Deep, south, deep, south, deep,
south.

He let his head sway in the river of the rhythm and he wis
away again. Thinkin, feelin, reelin.
   Down to the river.

> Big, elephant chords
> Swan guitar
> Lilith
> Love-frets
> Mad violins
> Ganapati
> Ganapati
> Ganapati
> Ganapati
> Ganapati
> Ganapati
> Ganapati
> Ganapati

Carnatic ballet. His route. That wis it! The path he wis
followin, that night, that mornin, wis not linear – A to B to
C – but wis more akin to the pattern traced out by the body
– the arms, the twirlin fingers, the broadened, stampin feet
of a Classical South Indian dancer. Pondicherry, Kochi,
Chennai, Alappuzha . . . it wis a voyage in more than three
dimensions, the points of its trajectory defined yet invisible
and transient. And, yet, he felt that he had no choice – or,
at least, that any choice he might have in the matter wis
mediated by boundary conditions, the nature of which he wis
barely aware. Breezy Rhineland quartets or waxed Carnatic
dancers – it wis all the same. A thousand strings, a parrot

face. There were rules you couldn't break because the rules constituted the fabric of your being. They had drawn you up from the bubblin mud. They had formed you. You were like a *mela*, inseparable from the *raag*. Those old, clappin, wavin dance mistresses of Carnataka had known this – for thousands of years, they had lived it. It wis sculpted in the stone of subterranean temples, it wis embedded in the *ragam* jackwood of the *sarasvati vina*, it spun and sang from the skull of its gourd. The knowledge of the beginnin and the end.

All around, he thought, we see the ends of ourselves and we try to run, to remain in the centre of the wheel so that our runnin might keep us from spinnin off into the oblivion of our own space. Intimations of mortality. They're in the bricks. They're everywhere. So he walked back to Pollokshields, the place of his beginnin. The end of himself. And right through him, waxin and wanin, the sound of the *sarasvati vina*, the music of the swan. If they were Aadam an Hawwa, the listeners, his father, his mother, then he wis Cain.

Varanam.

It wis safer stickin to major thoroughfares, busy places where your past and present got mixed up and copper coiled and drowned out by the sheer funk of life. He wis on a second, or mibbee a third or fourth, wind and his legs felt light, the joints, the muscles, looser, a bit like he'd feel when he wis really, really fit. The oxygen slipped into his body and went right down to the tips of his toes – he could feel the air shoop out from the far ends of his trainers and the sun wis shinin right into his hardened wax eyes but he felt he could stare it out, all ninety million miles of it, all twelve billion years of it. Aye, the music wis buzzin in his head an he wis lighter than light. Up there, somewhere beyond the sun, invisible in the mornin light, wis the constellation of the beginnin. Nada, mother of all *raags*. The cosmic hum. And Zaf felt this hum, this vibration, there, on the burnin street – he felt that his body wis an instrument, his life a certain music. A Californian accent, deep, guttural, Manson-esque yet, at the same time, comical, especially when filtered through rud malt Finniestonian. And when you have reached that point at which you are lighter than light, at that moment, you can gaze at your Creator and be one with . . . whatever-it-is!

'Maya'. There had been no division between the two songs – at least none that he could hear. It wis as though Susheela-*jee* wis cleavin him from Kanyakumari all the way to Alba, via the Bulkhans. Virgin territory. Zaf laughed into the mike. *Hurufi* flute, drawn down alchemically from a mountain top in Anatolia or Bulgaria or perhaps from one of those mounds of the dead in the wooded hills overlookin the old city of Sarajevo. Runnin, Bosnian drums. Elevated observations. His journey, wheelin back and forth, through the stations.

Bhava.

It's the journey ae the Celts, friends, the auld voyage acroass the fields an steppes an rivers. An Ah'm bathin in aw the *daryaon*, Ah'm bein cleansed by the watters ae Amu *Darya*, Dnieper, Don, Clyde.

It wis his parents' route westwards – from the *haveli* to the backstreet hotel to the wastelands to the cold northern guest house to the sewer to the corner shop to the nursin home. 'Maya'. It wis the stuff of this world, risin from the world beyond.

He wis goin with his gut. There had been no logic to his direction. Zaf smiled. But, then, there had never really been any logic to his actions, his loves, the cracks in his soul. If there had been, he wouldn't have stayed up all night, rantin like some loony into a long metal cock, bein screwed by the ghosts of his past and the saints of the entire fuckin city. Even Kentigern had changed his name, had lost himself in the arched music of white stone chapels. He'd hidden beneath the great black swan's wings of his mother. Saint Thenew, the Forgotten, the Buried. So, like a coffee fish, he bounced along Byres Road, listenin to the samples of music emanatin from every third retail outlet, every second first-floor window, the cafés 'n' delis, with their slim-waisted servin folk lookin like they'd just stepped out of a rock video, the estate agents, banks and buildin societies, that seemed to be locked into some complex, century-long, sub-Masonic collaboration, the ancient pubs, which once had been inns but which somehow had managed to avoid the glossy idiocy of so many suburban drinkin holes that fancied themselves as English village taverns. It wis a film set buzzin with the joy of a summer's mornin, the joy. Joi.

Bani!!!

A manic Levantine lute swellin and pulsin over a 'Street Fightin Man' bass, balanced on the top ridge of the dead Aaron and, at last, after several hours of bein right out of it, on the far edge of sanity and beyond, Zaf felt like he wis back in the groove.

Deck B. He broke in.

The last fifty meenuts. We're movin tae the music ae Joi. We aw need that, friends. A proclamation of victory. A wee bit ae happiness. It's whit it's aw aboot, right? Fifty, forty-nine, forty-eight, forty-sivin . . .

If ye're wonderin who this voice belongs tae, rest assured, *samaaen*, that Ah'm back an Ah'm no the same. It disnae maiter, though, cause ma time is noo, ma time is *durmyani shubb ko chay bajeh*, aw the weye fae tall *Aleph* tae big *Yae*. Ma name's no *Hazrat* Mikhail and, if it's no him, then Ah must be . . . aweye wi ye, enough ae aw that! Dawn hus broken the night but the night husnae broken me. An since ye're still listenin, it husnae broken you neether. Nae cracks in your souls. You lucky listeners that ye are. *Yaar*. How many are ye, Ah wonder? Let's take a guess. Mathematics wis nivir ma strongpoint but, aifter thenight, Ah feel as though Ah could calculate the likes ae pi doon tae a million an three decimal places.

Zaf rummaged about for his pen and paper. The process wis a ritual, as important to him, during this night, as the fast or the charity or the *kulmas* recited again and again. Heretic! Recidivist!

Don't worry! Joi'll be back soon, Ah'll jist huv tae press a wee red button, Back-Tae-Track-Ilivin, Ah'll do a Lazarus oan yer favourite son. Rise, rise, ye lovely wan! OK. Let's coont yous – heids oan the table, Ah mean, honds oan the table. Mibbee if Ah turn this here microphone intae a receiver . . . let's see . . . it's easy enough done. Aw ye do is turn the magnet roon. Told ye Ah wis a scientist, a master ae matter an energy, an alchemist ae the radio waruld. Do the magic, Zaf!

!!ABRACADABRA!!

An, then, wan million – joke!! – wan hundred – ae yous
party people can whisper sweet nuhins intae ma *kaan*.
Sweet stereo nuhins.

A very pregnant pause. Zaf put his left ear to the tongue of
the mike and cupped the palm of his left hand over it.

Where are ye, folks? Ah cannae hear ye. Speak tae me
noo or furivir haud yer silence. Ah pronounce ye . . .

Another pause, this time caused by Zaf yawning off-mike.
Ahhh, still the pro.

Weel, since ye willnae speak tae me, Ah'll tell ye a wee
story which may or may not be true, *zaroorat*. Nah,
that's a lie. Stories are nivir true. That's why thu're cawd
stories. That's why we're drawn tae them. The glossy
trails ae Glasgae – it's almost like Bombay, oh soarry,
Mum-*bai*, Mum, Mum, Mum-*baiii*! Mibbee we should
rename this great green hollow ae a city ae oors aifter the
auld, Pictish bog brothel that used tae lie oan the site ae
its dear, bleedin, sacred hairt. Ye goat there an ye jist
sank intae the circles ae bright green grass. Or mibbee we
could call it '*Chaand* City'. '*Shehr* ae Loons'. 'The City of
the Moon'. That's Kinnin Park, a course. Aw! Too fast as
usual. An, onyweye, Ah'm biased. Up the Shiels!!
Pollokshields *Zindabad*!! Nah, but wu're still pacin oot
the wondrous trajectories ae Woodlands, Finnieston an
aw that. Wu're still jivin in the name ae the Joi.

Undo, reverse the act. Pull out. Impossible. A French

AIMPOSS-IBLUGH!!!

OK, cut the crap. Deck B: 'Joi Bani!'. Sequenced, initiated, dream on. Back to the serious business of Joi. It lasted all the way along Argyle Street with its mixture of druggies, arties and Asian men who'd been born middle-aged with pot bellies and pastel-patterned cash-'n'-carry jumpers. Zaf had worn plenty of those in his time – until he had come alive and stretched and burst through the fabric. Right now, this mornin, Zaf wis all awareness. Walkin down to Finnieston and the river wis like unwindin threads. Where the flyovers now stood, Zaf heard the scratchin sound of *barfit* Irish immigrants – illegals – as they crept up dark, unknown tunnels which led them from the newly dredged, widened Clyde to the shifting O'Neill hovels where they would live, twenty to a room, and from whence the roads, the railways, the canals, the flyovers would emerge. Yeah. Drogheda violins, hey, Spanish Armadan eyes. Curly hair. The Black Irish. The Morrocan Hibernian. Nowadays, you couldn't smell the river but Zaf could smell it, all the way from that really interestin county of Lanarkshire and the Ballencleuch Law. Except that, now, the lithe body of the water wis perfumed with the *Amitabhian* odours of *methi* and Faisalabadi *pulaow. Pattach*!!

He felt the river water fill his lungs so that standin there on Bell's Bridge, in the windless mornin sunshine, he became almost transparent. It wis as though the entire story of Glasgow lay, like some dead hero, along the horizon. Zaf wheeled around, afraid that someone, some element of that thousand years of drowned horses and pulsin hearts, might leap out and knock him off his feet, send him tumblin into the cold river. To the east, behind the frenetic but inaudible Kingston Bridge and the dirty white towers of the risen Gorbals, there piped a long plume of smoke. Multicoloured luxury flats, with elegant, continental balconies and windows too small to see through, had been built in tiers along the south bank. The hangin gardens of Babylon. The wolf king of Pacific Quay. Across the middle of the muddy river were two thick metal columns, each topped with a plastic light – one red, the other blue. Flood beacons. Along the north bank, the sleek silver walls of the City Inn and the battleship grey of the Clydeport crane sat uneasily alongside the redbrick North Rotunda – once a port buildin but now a gamblin den of some notoriety.

Everywhere he looked, to east and west, were buildins that were deceptive, their shells done up to look as though they were somethin else or else to create the impression that nuthin had changed in the course of two centuries: the Bilsland Bakery that no longer wis a bakery yet which still sported the gloss-white letters across its tower; the sleek red cranes that punctuated the line of the river and whose chains hung, unmovin, in the air; the glass and grey metal of the Skypark which was neither sky nor park; the concrete breath of the Clydeside Expressway, risin and fallin in an arc from nowhere to nowhere; the miniature armadillo of the imitation Sydney Opera House where no voices ever sang, except through celluloid and light; the Science Tower risin, like an unrequited Shivling, into the blue sky; the muddy site intended for the BBC buildin, which was right bang on the place where, two hundred years earlier, Zaf figured, mibbee someone had planted a forest or else mibbee slaves had shivered in the rain as they waited to be bought and parcelled off, either to some drafty Presbyterian household in Ayrshire or else across the sea to the killin swelter of Cuba; the space in the sky where, for a lifetime, the monstrous twin Clyde Port Authority buildins had sprawled like Gog and Magog; the high masts of a sailin ship which no longer sailed; a ferry that, for the past twenty years, had ferried no one; the broken clock of a clock tower whose attached buildin had been lost somewhere; and the mysterious scaffolded structures in mid river, crawled over by Masonic-lookin men in hard hats. Perhaps it had somethin to do with the constant movement of the water, some hundred feet below, but everythin seemed to be regressin – not so much into the past as into essences, sensations, concepts. The cuboid shapes of the Moat House; the Hill town; the Queen's Mother and the Royal Hospital for Sick Children risin, orange, from a plague pit; and, everywhere, in rows, like great stone chess pieces, the red and white sand bodies of tenements, abodes of the soul. The city seemed to be shiftin constantly – not just in that sense of the frenetic automobile turbulence which confers to a place the illusion of excitement but in the slippin of time through brickwork and concrete, the filmin of dark days across stone-broken windows, the erosion of layers of paint and somethin more than that – a feelin which Zaf couldn't pin down, a frontier sense of exhilaration, of ridin the west wind on the back of this city of light and dark where everythin was an illusion. Even the river had been artificially widened and no longer knew itself. Zaf liked that. He closed his eyes and let the breeze blow across his face as though it would lift off the dirt of that night, of those years. He stayed like that for what seemed like minutes, oblivious to a group of gigglin teenies who scarpered across towards the big hotel.

Now here Ah am, up oan Bell's Bridge. Nae bells though. Nae hunchbacks, neether. Dancers mibbee. An the breeze is blowin lightly across the face ae the city. An Ah'm blowin lightly across the face ae the breeze.

He closed his eyes.
They must think he'd totally flipped. A guided tour of

Glasgow like from one of those open-top tour buses. 'And now, on our left, mesdames et messieurs, we see a housing estate, one of zee poorest in Western Europe, and, if you look to your right, up zer, between zee trees, you will be able to make out zee genuine Victorian walls of zee prison, commonly known to good and bad alike as zee Bar-elle.'

A loud noise shocked his eyes open. The jungle sound of a motorbike revvin. Back to the bridge.

As he was about to leave the river, to cross over to the south side of the city, somethin caught his eye. He stopped and gazed once more over the metal rail. At the base of the Science Tower, where the river bank fell into large, rectangular tunnels, a solitary swan moved slowly upriver, the elegant hull of its body slicin a large, inverted V-shape through the Clyde.

He leapt across and landed on the other side, not breathless but dizzy. The river wis flowin inside his head – the stream of Kinnin Park where the Changezi Family ruled like the villains in *Sholay*. That fat-Elvis baddie – what was his name? Murderer of orphans and defiler of virgins, scourge of innocent, troubadour, Southside love. The lithe and curvaceous Helen, Mata-Hari of the *Bunderbunds*, belly dancin in the double-barrel darkness of the camp fire. *Mehbooba-a-Mehbooba, Mehbooba-a-Mehbooba!* Wonderful yodellin corruption. Definitely not Graceland. The Kinnin Park Boys were the test-tube babes of that clan. Genetically modified so that they would have ears which acted as mobile phone receivers and greased number-three haircuts (three wis a magic *hindsa*). Big shoes, bhangra boots, markin out territory. The pavements hereabouts were all Punjabi. As he lingered by the window of a shop sellin silver plastic everythin, Zaf caught a whiff of Kashmir – 'Satrangi Re'. The palindromic song wis back, this time on Deck A. A reprise, a revamp, a variation on a *dastgah*. OK, in this weirdo *raag* whose title wasn't the title, everythin rode on a *taal* of love 'n' dust – frozen love, lust, petrified into emotion, the double spinal arc of beasts in the *baraf*. Red-hot snow beasts. Led Zeppelin, the Sufi, Manisha version. From the heart, a spinnin chorea, an avalanche of red notes in the snow. Glacier dancin, female dervishes. Death, the sky. Zaf shuddered, just a little, as. underneath the sunshine and warmth of the risin mornin, he remembered the crap of the night. He hurried on in a south-easterly direction. He wis headin for the Shiels. He wasn't certain why he was goin where he wis goin but, then, nuthin really made any sense when you looked on it that way. It wis all just a big Country-and-Western lament – Glasgae-style. The Grand Ole Opry where grown men played with toy guns and fancied themselves as John Wayne or Gary Cooper. Zaf smiled to himself. Alan Ladd more like! Standin on a milk crate, tryin to snog his leadin lady!

Nae mair C an W. The Wean Yahya an the Lad Alan are deid an buriet. Nae C an W, please, we're British. No unless it's spiked. Am Ah promotin drugs? Ah plead the Fourth Amendment. Or should that be the Fifth? Now, where did Ah put that Joi CD? Ah jist took it oot the machine.

He scrambled among the mess that the console had become. 'Mess, mess, mess,' Babs would've said.
  'Mess, mess, mess,' Zaf said.
  His playlist wis almost black with the various stains of the night. Wine, blood, spunk, vomit . . . skin, bone, flesh, brain . . . Zaf had emptied his body on to the clean white surface of the paper. But that wis the way a map should be. Used and crumpled, like a person. Aye, Zaf had used most people

in his life. He wis what they called 'a user'. He laughed. Zilla wis right.

He found the CD. Back into Deck B.

It's time tae laugh, *meray bundhay*, time tae laugh an forget. An remember. Joi. Music fae a deid man's mooth. Or 'A Deid Wumman Gazes at the *Chumbeylee*'. Shoooop!!

ANIMA
GO CEEDEE
GO MEEEEEE!!

Doon the plastic road tae ma hame. A phantom band, in Kinnin Park. Wush, wush, wush, wush fur fush, fush, fush, fush. *Mutchlee*, *aajao*!!

And Zaf wis there. A wish come true. The realm of the dreamin gangs. Love, blood an music. Asian Vibe, dig the tribe!

Maather-i-maa

In spite of the new luxury flats and the gleamin river-walk steel, Kinnin Park clutched its slum credo close to its hairy chest. There had to be an obscure council regulation that a pub should stand every thirty yards along the Paisley Road West. The sort of place where recoverin alkies could wrestle with their demon. Aye. Rustum and Sohrab trapped inside a used green boa'ul. The tops of mountains gushin forth from brass mouths on Judgment Day. Munkar and Nakir. The twin angels. The skins of Auld Govan stretched eastward like black bible leather across the bones of the bonnie banks. Aye, thumpin, humpin trumpets. The swoonin blast of Israfil.

The Bolly, where Hindi films blasted daily on to the risin face of Orange 'n' Green. The Bombay Cinema stood right opposite the Lorne Street Orange Lodge – the two hovered in a Giffnock stone harmony that could exist only in Kinnin Park, just down the red road from white Ibrox. Drums, drums, drums . . . beyond the final whistle, miracles could happen.

Over the expressway, under the motorway, past the zoomin cars . . . and he wis there. The Shiels. The Big U. Hame. The Shiels wis different from Kinnin Park or Finnieston or Woodlands. All of those places had been built along ancient trunk roads – Paisley Road West, Argyle Street, Great Western Road – which had been slippin an slidin since before the city wis a city and which had been taking folk in and out and in and out, like the pulses of a bull's heart, from Kentigern-who-became-Mungo onwards. The Shiels wis different. All the houses there faced inward, away from Pollokshaws Road, and into quadrangles and culs-de-sac. Streets which the city fathers had built to be blocked off. Oxbow roads. In the Shiels, it wis possible for someone to live and die and never venture over the railway lines which cut off the main part of Albert Drive from its fag end. There were people who lived behind closed windows and who emerged only occasionally from the flat stone and, even then, it would be heads buried behind glossy magazines as they rolled in big, silent cars which took them to weddings, funerals and the elephant cities down south (where they would slip into other *haveli* quadrangles much like the ones back home).

On that warm day, children were spinnin games around puddles which had been created by the *dhookandaars* cleanin the dust off their shop windows. When Zaf had been their age, the Shiels had been Pollokshields and had been the residence of tweedy, middle-class Presbyterian types, who were probably very nice people underneath it all, but the problem wis you never got to see what wis underneath. Not if you were separated by a wall of skin and a cold, blooded Cross. In those days, walkin up and down the street in the daytime, you felt like an old Roman werewolf. The sun burned on his bare arms, turnin the skin. It was gettin really hot. A water-bucket day. But this wis not Roma. Here, his skin would never burn. By the sea mibbee. The Ayr beach, with Ailsa Craig shimmerin on the horizon. A dream within a dream. Growin up in the Shiels in those days wis purgatorial and, for years, Zaf had existed in a state of unrequited life. Stale, uninterestin video stores, crap warehouse clothes and fag-end, fast-food music. Nuthin whatsoever of interest had happened in Pollokshields since Mary Regina had lost a battle up on the Queen's Park hill which had not been named after her. Thank Christ that'd changed!, Zaf reflected. Now, at least there wis some kind of a buzz, a *joie*, the incipient kind of electricity that came from a sense of community. Call it a ghetto or a *jhopar putti* or whatever – there wis somethin almost musical in amongst the shite. An Asian vibe, right enough!

Eh, *loagon*, grab this! Ah'm here in the wee studio, ye know the wan, though Ah'm no tellin ye whur it really is in case ye might want tae come up an peye me a visit. Ah've hud enough visitors thenight awready.

Zaf looked around, just to make sure.

OK, so here Ah am . . . here, in the cubicle ae *The Junnune Show*, ae Radio Chaandni, broadcastin fur only forty-five meenuts mair oan ninety-nine-point-nine meters FM. And, yet, at the same time, Ah'm roamin aroon the streets ae this magnificent city. How d'ye figure that wan? Well, let me ask ye this: Whit happens tae a particular wavelenth aifter a radio station hus stopped usin it? Where dae aw the wurds go? Eh? Does it jis fade away or does it refuse tae disappear? Does it grab the invisible air an take oan a life ae its ane so that, even aifter the radio station's door hus been closed an bolted, the voice goes oan? An the music? Think aboot that, guid people. Now here Ah am, oan Albert Drive, *dil ka dil*, and here's Joi. Ah love those guys. 'Fingers'. *Ji haa*!

It wis a double-edged sword. There were at least two sides to everythin. Like those Pakistani weddings, where people would just scramble over one another to get to the plentiful food, not carin who had young children with them or who wis in wheelchairs or whatever. It wis every woman and man for themselves. It wis that irritatin habit folk had of lookin over your shoulder and then just walkin away while you were in the middle of a sentence. The terrible weight of opprobrium, of bein flung outside of the collective, karmic, *dharmic, ummic baratherie*-hood. And once they'd stuffed their plates to overflowin, they would just stand there by the big steamin trays and eat their fill, periodically restockin their cornucopias so as never to run out and so that they would effectively block everyone else's access to the grub. Clearly, they must think they were already in Paradise. And the respectable oldies were as bad as anyone! And this, Zaf thought, wis really what wis wrong. But what wis right wis what happened when there wis a crisis, a death in the family, say, when everyone would come together – not just blood or marital relatives but friends as well and even acquaintances. He hoped that this would not be lost with the passin of generations. They had tried to do this with Zaf's papa but, whereas, by definition, death wis an end, dementia wis jist the beginnin. It wisnae their fault – it wis life and that wis just more difficult to get a handle on. The person wis dead but their body lived on. It wis like the Antichrist had arrived and perfused the soul. It wis a Dajjal situation and there were no stock formulae for salvation.

His soles began to burn on the asphalt and so he accelerated his pace, faster and faster, until, before long, he wis almost cyclin through the air. A bhajan-woman with a long voice, swingin, lopin scales, hard, Damascene guitar. *Sa-re-ga-ma.* Joi, new buzz foot soldiers on the empty, white plain. *Sa-re-ga-ma*, blood flowin through an artery, newly opened. Joi. Ye had to take the bum notes to reach the pure tone. Only the good die young. Joi. For decades, the people had had to fight for every fuckin inch. But now, it wis theirs. Aye, the Shiels wis a skin of sorts, an armour against the scaldin winds of an all-white Alba. To avoid hittin his head off the tartan ceilin, he crept into the stone ovens of Albert Drive and Leven Street. If Prince Albert only knew! Halaal butchers, subcontinental grocers, the ubiquitous video shops crammed with noisy amusement machines, the religious bookshops with their glowerin, bearded Holy Willies whose skins had never been touched by yellow dirt and who seemed to live not on food, music or spirit but on fear of *jahannam*. Blue vans double-parked. Silent churches with no visible congregations. *Masjids* secreted in tenement flats devoid even of Glasgow light. Bearded sisters, ferociously pristine white converts or born-again *phoodulanahs*, the former of whom dreamed, presumably, of a paradise filled with the stereotypically sleek bodies of tall black men and the latter of a kind of garden party *jannat* stuffed with slick-headed, roarin twenties gentle men who were so white they were fuckin monochrome. The only animals hereabouts were the hippocrites. Road hogs, drivin Sequoia SR5 four-wheel-drive people carriers. A hymn to the lost ones.

Up oan the pavement, up they go!
Watch them marchin wi thur souls!

Those things were never in the Books. Come to think of it, neither were the Jolly Jelly Brigade. The FBI: Federal Bureau of Islamisation. Mullah Hoovers. Have you ever been, have you ever known, have you ever touched, have you ever even thought of, a strand of hair? 'Yes, yes, yes. I have revelled in Afro-style barnets, I have slid down shiny seventh-century Sassanian, I have ploughed along the wavy furrows of Anglo-Saxonian blonde! I confess all! I confess that, above all, I have desired human beings! I have loved! Mea culpa.' Whoops! Wrong religion. Still, it's all the same, really. Down in the grave, that is, it's all the same. The purveyors of fire 'n' brimstone had turned a faith into a fashion statement. An egotistical ride on the wild side. They must actually get a finger G-spot sexual frisson from sailin down the street, beards and bunnets waftin a little in the rough trade of the Scottish winds, all eyes rakin up and down their heavily armoured bodies. Fingers undoin buttons an belts, pullin down long zips. They secreted their humanity. They ditched their humility – it wis just another form of cross-dressin. It wis a cover for all kinds of sins. No, in the grave, there's no one to enclose your fuckin head in a *hijaab* or a *jellaba* or an Armani suit or whatever the current fashion is – cause no one, except the worms, is lookin. Right? But even worms have desires so mibbee they, too, should be wearin *sharif* clothin. 'S.O.B. *sharif* businessman and arms dealer, purveyor of bisexual whores and muscle dancers, monetary patron of several *mesquitas* and promoter-customer-pin-up-boy of the minimalist style of hairdressin known as "Fundmentalist Fanny".' Fuck. Well, don't actually. Not if you value your sanity. These people were always right. Everythin they said, every word they spoke and the letter-less silences, too, wis punctuated by a series of t's crossed relentlessly, scored, broken, till the ink had run out. He could feel the nails of their bolted fanaticism, he could smell the blood, it made his head spin with the weight of the iron, with the steel of their sins. Bright blue eyes. A form of lunacy. Some of them were really clued-up though. In the past, and mibbee in some version of the future, they would've been left wing, radicals even, but, right now, the times were not conducive. For a certain generation, a particularly artificial version of Islam wis the only refuge left. Yet, politically, it wis a blind alley. And it wis the opposite of submission. Yet, perhaps, on some deep level, it wis needed – a stage that had to be got through, a station on the path to awareness. The trouble wis a lot of people just got stuck there – attracted by the exoteric simplicity of ritual, the comfortin touch of regulated apparel, the measured negotiation of relationships. They decided that the path ended there, with them and their limited vista of God. *Jazakallah khairan*! Road hogs, right enough.

A certain section of the community were alienated from both the contemporaneous indigenous life and from the various non-diasporic South Asian cultures. In some respects, Pakistan had moved on while they had sunk ever deeper into the stillness of their self-regarding *hijaabdom*. In fact, one of Zaf's Pindi *doston* had joked that the Shields had been renamed 'Hijaababad' by the council and one of its suburbs had been designated 'Long Johnistan' on account of its many chaste techno-gymnasia. The real joke, Zaf thought – the killing joke, you might say – wis that most of this shit had been dreamed up somewhere near London's Embankment and somewhere deep in Virginia's Langley. Yes, siree, whether or not they know it, like their grandfathers, the *soobedars*, they are simply followin orders. Right, right, right, right, right.

Of course, there wis a huge, concrete double standard operatin constantly in all of this. Guys were generally allowed to get away with most things – they tended to be forgiven eventually and, indeed, the perennial celluloid theme of the returned prodigal son wis a well-massaged trope for Asian men. For women, on the other hand, it wis all or nuthin. There wis no such entity as the prodigal daughter. Anythin – a glance, a touch, a modicum of success – might bring on the jackals of malicious gossip and then truth, honesty, honour – all those virtues held in such high esteem by South Asian society – no longer seemed to apply. All things bad were believed. The good wis relentlessly disparaged as bein merely a front – it wis a reflected cynicism that burned deep. For a woman, once she had been branded in this way, there wis no possibility of redemption. And so, by insidious association, all women potentially were seven-veiled Salmahs – if not physically, then in their heads and in their souls. Every time they appeared in public, every time their name wis mentioned, they would be stripped of all their veils, one by one. Hawwa, Zuleikha, Bint Sheikh Lut, Salmah . . . it wis all there – it wis all down in the Book. And real women were not granted even the slim chance of salvation which these half-prophets had been accorded.

But, at least, Zaf thought, those people knew where they were. It might be a cul-de-sac – who wis to say? – but, at least, they had their feet (and hands) firmly on the ground. Aye, they were livin in hidin but still, on some deep level, these people were Zaf's people and they imagined that they were risin to God through love. Whereas Zaf wasn't sure if he wis risin at all. 'Something black in the lentil soup', as the old ones used to say. Things were never what they seemed. He had always felt stifled in these streets. Even though he might have visited no one, he always came away from this place feelin bloated and useless, as though his belly had been filled with a large, porcelain teapotful of *doodh puthee*. Heavy milk, a fuckin nuclear bomb of a beverage. The liquid weight of the *baratherie* pressin down on him all the way to the grave. There was no ease, no sense of plurality. It was not like Woodlands or even Kinnin Park. The Shiels wis a ghetto of sorts, a mental ghetto, and, yet, there was succour and a certain type of strength in that. In returning to the burning arc of its arms. To his *maa*. In the seed, lieth redemption. Mibbee dancin dead Bertie did know. Joi.

Here's a wranklin question fur five thirty in the mornin. Nae prizes. Did ye ivir think aboot who exactly it wis designed pebble-dashin? Ye know – those ragged bits ae rock that rip the skin aff yer knuckles iviry time ye try tae embrace yer ane hame. Not that Ah go aboot graspin at folks' waws. Ah'm not some kind ae architectural pervert! But no, seriously, who invented the stuff? They must've been either insane or else a great humourist. A *muskhara*. And then whit bright Expressionist spark decided that iviry last bit ae grit should be that hugely excitin, wonderfully exotic, dun, tawny shade ae beef vomit? Turned the whole ae Scotland intae some kind ae pill-boax *banjar zameene* straight oot ae Waruld War Wan? Nae laughter. Nae hope. OK. mibbee Ah'm exaggeratin jist a wee bitty. Mibbee some ae ye live in those hooses fae hell. OK. Ah'm not knockin yer homes or the Queen, the flag or onyhin – it's jis the waws. Now, here's ma solution. Ah think that aw these places, these loci ae excitement, should be paintit pink, green, yellae an purple. An, afore that, the rubble they caw 'pebble-dashin' should be ripped aff, stane by stane, fur safety reasons. It could be a European Union directive. Guid auld clean, white Christian Europa. Jist as weel she leapt aff ae that bull. If she hudnae done that, she would still hae been wan ae us. 'Hail! Hail!', as they say in Paradise. The *farishtay*, the Celts. Onyweye, Ah'm ramblin again. Back tae the pebble-dashin. How dis that sune? Ma proposal. Wipe it clean in twenty-five languages. Gie it a try, eh? At wan stroke, it would brighten up the whole city. Mibbee we should aw write tae oor MSPs. Aweye an fush oot yer pen an paper. In the meantime . . .

Zaf searched for his own crumpled sheaf – the book of hours on which he had inscribed the architecture of the night.

In the meantime, let's huv another soang. Fur this wan, wu're croassin the Med, goin sooth, a course. Rai. Aw the *chebs* 'n' *chabas*. Dancin soangs ae the West. Al-Maghrebi. Moutawassetei music. Sunshine quarter-tones, calligraphic stars. Hannibal's gold. Live the night furivir, *Ya Habibi*! *Cheb* Kader, Le Comte du Rai. Hey, wu're multilingual oan this station. Polyethelene ethnic. The United Nations ae the bin lane.

He shot the disc and decked his tongue muscle for the difficult Arabic.

'M'Hainek Ya Qalbi'. A-chugha-chugha-chugha-chugha-chugha-chugha-chugha . . .

Zaf leaned away from the console, swung his body back so

that he wis balancin on the tips of his toes, his body poised in the dim light of the cubicle. He closed his eyes and felt the mornin breeze sift over his face. Easy, easy heart. Hard, hard love. Deck A. The Arabic words jigged around the room, the singer's voice seemin to possess more solidity than either the physical structure of the place or the things which Zaf had left behind durin the long night. The partition window, the soundproofin cones, his regular walk that he had somehow abandoned. Why? Well, now he wis walkin anyway. He wis swingin along an arc – his flesh balancin between gravity and space – he wis on the verge of weightlessness, of bein a thing without being or borders.

Zilla wis runnin doon another, mair distant street. At the end ae the Maghrebi road, a sports car. Lang, white, clean. Open tap. Nae back seat. Jist a space filled wi rectangles. Bits ae equipment – amps, speakers, mikes, keyboards an the like, aw jammed in at awkward angles, a strange tablature of forms behind Zafar the Gangsta, Zafar the Thief, the man who hud always been guid wi his honds an who wis now beginnin the lang climb up the ladder ae criminality which, like the ladder ae *Hazrat* Israel, has nae tap rung. She's oot ae braith by the time she gets there an she jis stops and pants away like an animal. Zafar the Gangsta is sittin in the driver's seat, smokin a lang roll-up. He's wearin sunglasses. It is still dark but the eastern edge ae the sky is a quarter-tone lighter than the rest. He turns tae Zilla. Mooths the words 'Whit ye waitin fur? Get in, ye fuckin whore.' Takes oot two bags an tosses them on tae the seat. Payment fur bein the Trojan horse. Moutawassetei music. Looks away again. Puffs twice oan the fag. Starts the engine. Revs it wi his boot – the weye he would a wumman. Zilla gets wan leg an a bum-cheek intae the motor. The car shoots aff, door swingin. Zero tae

saxty in sivin seconds. An she's wettin hersel no through fear
– she hus none – but simply because ae the G force oan her
boady. But it disnae maitter because she's pullin oot the
pump an needle an it's amazin how she can do this at saxty
miles an oor doon an alleyway but then she wis always
amazin. An she lets her heid faw back intae the rai slipstream
an she's stickin the point ae the metal intae her neck, she's
shovin it in, aw two bags ae it, an thur's a moment, jist a
moment, when she thinks she sees a man, wi a silver stick
an nail lacquer, peerin at her denim jacket which hus flapped
open tae reveal the dark berries ae her nipples an she turns
tae Zafar an she says, 'Aw, fuck, man, look at that.' an then
she's oot ae time–space an, in that moment, Zaf the DJ is in
the car. *Qalb, Qalb, Qalb.* To his right, Zafar the Gangsta
is puffin away as he burns up the road. Zaf's muscles tighten,
his hips clutch the seat. Cauld leather. Snake. He lets his neck
faw back. Feels the saftness ae the heidrest against the bones
ae his spine. His neck feels cauld in the freezin mornin air.
Sweepin love. *Habibi.* His lang black hair billows in the
wind. Saxty miles an oor doon the narra street. Flyin ower
poatholes an grit. The speed makes him clean. His love clean.
Ishq. He disnae feel the jab ae the needle. *Ishq.* The second
bite is the longest. *Ishshshshshshq.* Zero tae a thoosand in
sivin seconds. Wan. Two. Three. Four. Five. Sax.

He feels his face go intae rictus. Two bags aw in wan go.
It's better than ony sex he's ever hud. Better than birth. Zafar
the Gangsta is grinnin. The Holy Fuckin Spirit. Zaf is too
high tae smile. He's flyin. In order that others might live and
walk alang the streets ae Glasgae, Zilla an Zafar must fly.
They died fur oor sins. They wur baith *shaheeds.* Wan day,
they would be venerated as martyrs. Glasgae would be
the new Karbala, the Clyde an the Euphrates would flow
thegether. Sasters. Sumer. A ziggurat symmetry. Sivin thoosand

years. Afore Jehovah.

Thu're oot ae the narra street. Behind them, the sky's gan pink. Blue an pink. Baby colours. Fuckin beautiful. Hivin.

Siven.

Zaf felt himsel faw.

His fingers caught oan sumhin. Air. Nuhin mair.

He saw the street swayin below him. Christ!

A moment of perfect balance.

Harmony.

No breath.

Silence.

In one awkward movement, he pulled himself back in and half-collapsed, sideways, on to the floor.

He had no breath in his lungs but then, the next moment, they were on the point of explodin. Just in time, he realised that he wis goin to be sick but he didn't dare lean out of the window again and instead, crawled over to the waste-paper basket and puked into that.

It seemed to go on for hours and, when, at last, the waves of nausea had subsided and the beatin of his heart had finally slowed, he felt as though he had nuhin left inside. He felt oddly light, as though he might just float away across the city. It wis time to leave. There would be no fond farewells over the air. Let them take their own leave. You didn't get a chance to say goodbye, even if it wis for good. Forever. His papa hadn't had a chance to bid farewell – not to his first family or to his second. He had slipped out of Pakistan, like a thief, then out of air and daylight and finally, *anjaana*, out of Scotland. He had secreted his sins along the hidden byways of his life and it had driven him insane. You could vomit up *munnashiath* but you couldn't rid yourself of your sins. Next song.

Zaf wiped his mouth on the cuff of his shirt, picked up his

jacket and went to leave the room. One last glance through the shared window. No shadows. Love is dead, thought Zaf. Even lust washes away into the sewers. Before he left the cubicle, he threw on one last CD. He didn't look at the cover – he'd hardly ever played it. But he knew what it wis. He'd had it for ages. It went back a long way. Before Babs. Before Zilla. Before even the sewers. It contained a series of songs that would play on even as the radio station itself flickered and died – even as the moon faded and vanished. 'Tere Mere Beech Mein Kaisa Hai Ye Bandhan Anjaana'. Perhaps, Zaf reflected, as the first, tentative notes of the *saaz* hit the morning air, perhaps it stretches right back to the time before all the partitions. The splits across land and the chasms between people. The cuts which had sliced him into many pieces. The scars in his heart. Those were the deepest of all. He had held the music within him always. As he got up to leave the radio station, he knew that he would carry it with him wherever he went.

But the first words of Lata's song stopped him in his tracks. *Anjaana*. That which is hidden. Those melodies were like sinews, they were cemented to your bones, they wouldn't let go. There wis still half an hour left of *The Junnune Show*. One part of him wanted to leave, to walk out through the cubicle door, turn around the wrought-iron head of the stairwell and leave behind Radio Chaandni, *The Junnune Show*, the songs, the patter, the whole bloody welter of the night. EXIT. OFF. SILENCE. But Lata's voice, the strains of the sympathetic strings, the timbres of her syllables, somethin held him there, fixed to the spot, stupidly gazin at the console, at the plastic lights which now, in the mackerel-blue mornin light, seemed more mystical than ever. The reflexive attraction which they held for him seemed almost embarrassin – like the fondness, on wakin, for the intense physicality of a dream. A numinous love. Pollokshields. The place of his beginnin. BOOK THE FIRST, *SURAH* ONE, DECK *BEY*. Lata's song wis the spiritual anthem of the Shiels – its sky wis tramelled by her soarin falsettos, the hearths of Kier Street burned in the terrible melancholy of her undertone. 'Anjaana' wis the *sistherie*, the great spider, the hidden mother goddess of the diaspora. It wis a bosom he would never be able wholly to leave. He returned to the altar of the mike and sat down. Through this dream that wis really a song, he would try to pull away, try to lift off and fly. But the radio waves eddied about his brain like communion wine – his words the transubstantiation of music into flesh.

He inhaled but there wis no real air. The trees gave little shade. He had hardly eaten and it felt like there wis a brick in his belly. Giffnock sandstone. A great emptiness filled Zaf as he walked up the steep hill of Maxwell Drive. It wis afternoon and children, birds and white-hot metal cars ruled the streets. In the distance, from some tinny battery radio, he made out the syncopated dream music of Nitin Sawhney. 'Migration'. Skins – again.

He upped his pace. Speed would banish self-pity. Fuck it. Nuthin he did seemed to possess any inherent logic. He just followed his instincts – even if they were buggered. Tabla, tabla, tabla, tabla, tabla, tabla, tabla, tabla, tabla . . . and *shehnai*. Curlin, coilin, sinuous vocals. A man in a dream. The dream in the man. Snare drums. *Khwab*. Those dark circles under the eyes that came from too many nights imaginin the old country. Years, decades, workin God-awful hours. Of waitin for the boat. The weight of dreams wis heavy indeed. So many women and men were like that – all broken up inside. And there wis no one to hear them scream or sing. On the proscenium, they had been cast as monsters or clowns but the truth lay elsewhere. It lay where truth always lies – in bricks, bones and music. In breath and love and in a language that wis a garden – in words and silence and near perfect arcs that too few seemed able to hear or see or even care about. And, so, all those wonderful, mystical symbols, the elegant, cursive filigree of Kufic and *Naskhi* and *Nastaliq*, the *kalaam* of the heart – each sweepin letter that spanned the worlds wis turned into a single, never-endin, inhuman scream. Standin in the frozen winds of Alba, in the desert of the soul, they had turned into marionettes. And yet they were no more puppets than anyone else wis. They had founded the fuckin city. And now they were broken. Broken by time and by labour. That they had survived at all and were still able to put on *mushairas* and the like wis damn near a miracle. They were the real poets of the city – *raags*-to-riches singin their way through the *mohallay*, singin their way to a better life. 'Migrations'. A thousand laments by the Clyde *Darya* bellowin across the waters – mere echoes now and a shinin beauty risin from the sleek of the waves. Ruby 'n' Fizz and all the rest – the future belonged to them. It did not belong to Zaf or Zilla – they were the chaff. Reality lay elsewhere.

The tiredness wis beginnin to grip at his eyelids and he massaged his forehead as he walked. The bass wis too heavy – this wis amblin buffalo music, the slow movement, within his tired muscles, across the tarmac-and-asphalt of the burnin city. Too much migration slowed you down, held you forever by the river with the swayin boats and the sleepy-eyed water bulls – you became hypnotised by the buzzin of flies . . . Madya Pradesh, deepest India. That wis where it must come from, he thought. It wis like in summer when *doodh puthee* didn't wake you up – it sent you off to sleep. It took a long century to wash through your system. God! His trainers were flies' feet caught in honey. It should really be reserved for crisp, midwinter afternoons in Scotland – it could be a substitute for porridge. The caber men could toss down a tankard of the stuff before throwin around tree trunks. Then he wis swattin flies – those nearly invisible midge things that hovered and circled like Highland dancers and which somehow had always gone for his flesh. Mibbee they sensed his fear or the pulse of his blood. Even if he were to raise his hand to the damn bastards, they would elude him. The more you slapped, the faster they danced. Wankin insects. Transparent fuckers. A loud buzzin noise filled his head. Barely perceptibly, the song had turned from dream to swayin para-Latino slush. 'Market Daze'.

Off to his left lay Maxwell Park where, from time-to-time and usually under cover of night, quasi-gang-fights would take place and where, long ago, his father used to take him to play on the swings and generally muck about. He would avoid it – too many memories. Too many Asian vibes. What had really freaked him out wis somethin else though. It wasn't just Nitin Sawhney. He had heard someone's voice over the airwaves. Radio Chaandni. *The Madness Show* had gone completely mad. It wis out of control. He wondered whether perhaps he wis still hallucinatin but he knew that he wasn't. Even though it had been years, several lives in the karmic wheel of things, the sound of Zafar's voice had remained inside him, as unmistakable as the taste of his own exhaled breath. Turned skin. Zafar the Gangsta wis in control of the radio station. The nutcase had taken over the asylum.

Now that he wis leavin behind the Shiels and headin north again towards the river and its bridges, he felt lighter and fitter again and his trainers slipped over the surface of the asphalt like hot lava over rock. The anger seemed to give him a new and energisin sense of escape. He walked so fast he wis back near the big river in no time at all. The crazy thought of Zafar sittin in his seat and breathin into his mike, gazin into his pristine plastic CDs and starin at his own face reflected in the gleamin silver of the mornin, with the holy ghost of Babs's photo at his back and the racks of frozen music beneath his palm, aroused Zaf sexually. Fuckin loon body, he thought, and he put it down to the sleep deprivation. God! No wonder they used it as a form of torture. After you'd been awake for a certain length of time, you'd believe anythin, you would do anythin, no matter how surreal. You'd be willin to believe that it wis winter in the middle of August or that it was night in the afternoon. Or that Ailsa Craig really existed and that you were a bird seekin paradise. Or that the world wis just a toy – a plastic globe set spinnin by the hand of a fat, blue Hindu deity. So he took out his mobile, shook it a few times and found that, in spite of its near-immersion in the cold water of the tunnel, its plastic cover had kept the mechanism dry and its cell wis still charged. He dialled the station. It rang out seven times. Then a voice, which he had known for centuries, answered.

'Who's this?'

'It's me.'

'An who are you, ma friend.'

'No yer friend.'

'Then ye're a deid man.'

'Whit're ye doin, sittin in ma seat, Zafar?'

'How d'ye know ma name?'

'Ah know iviryhin aboot ye.'

Then the voice moved closer to Zaf's ear so that, involuntarily, he held the handset away from his head. A snake coiled on a lotus leaf.

'Listen, wanker, Ah'm sittin in yer seat an Ah'm playin yer music an Ah'm whisperin intae yer mike an Ah'm screwin yer wummin – baith ae them. The *goree* an the Paki!'

Zaf wis confused. Wis Zilla wi Zafar in the studio? Were they both stoned out ae their minds? An whit did he mean 'baith ae them'?

'You're no on air!'

The Unseen One laughed – a strange, cacklin laugh – and then Zaf thought he heard breathin.

'Turn oan yer radio.'

'Oh fuck!'

Then Zafar was addressing his new audience. 'Let's play the next track, folks.'

For a gut-twistin moment, Zaf wondered whether Babs might be listenin. Or his papa.

'That wanker that wis here last night . . .'

And then the sound of a woman's laughter. He knew the voice. It wis unmistakable. But the echo, as it died away, sounded like Babs. Then the noise of a plastic CD case bein rapped on the desk.

RAT-A-TAT-TAT

'Whit the fuck's this? Some fuckin spider song. Ma wumman's goat eight legs! Hey-hey!'

Oh, shite. Deck A.

The cantilever'd, buzzin, fragile sounds of Alessandra Belloni's 'Agur Iziarko' juddered through the afternoon heat. Sicily over Bell's Bridge. Zaf felt waves of nausea grip his abdomen, his chest. He leaned over the rail and boaked, twice, into the fast-movin Clyde. *Doodh puthee*. The breeze wis goin west. The mobile sat just inches from his left cheek. Its pale-blue metal body shimmered in the unremittin sunlight. He could feel its heat burn the skin. Tarantata. Spider dance. The Clyde wis blue and it wis nivir blue. That wis where the

393

buzzin had been comin fae. Zafar had Babs's shadow captured
on the wall behind him and Zilla wis on his knee. Now he
wis spinnin discs far too fast – a spider on speed – screechin
hairy legs in Zaf's ear. This wis the Omega. Now his alter
ego wis whisperin intae his ear even though the phone wisnae
anywhere near his jawbone.

'Know why Ah've goat yer wummin? Know why Ah've
got yer radio station, yer *Madness Show*? Know why Ah
hold yer music, yer soul, in the palm ae ma hond?'

The Clyde *Darya* had no sound as it flowed past – the
waves seemin to go eastward as Zaf's eyes tripped over their
cold spines.

'Ah can feel ye as ye slide yersel intae yer wee white
whoor. Ah can feel iviry inch ae yer corpse. An ye know
why? Cause Ah'm better than you in iviry way. Ah'm inside
ye.'

A cold sweat broke out on his skin. He wis an insect
caught in webs of light and there wis a point of unbroken
darkness movin towards him. And the darkness spoke slowly,
like God.

'Ah am you.'

The 'Agur Iziarko' smashed intae the 'Canto di Sant'Irene'
– the song ae the sirens. Calabria oan the Clyde. Songs ae
the bandits. A dark face came up at Zaf an he fell backwards.
Landed oan his bum. He sat wi his heid between his thighs
and began tae rock back an forth. But the music went oan.
Oan that day, as the sun flew westwards at Kiamath speed,
playin the waruld like it wis a silver disc, Zaf felt as though
the music might nivir end an that he an ivirywan he hud
known would be swept up in its hoat wave an be drooned
in its deep chant. Wan note, a high-pitched scream, a face,
contorted beyond the architecture ae the physical, beyond
bone. He wantit tae stare intae the eyes ae the gangsta, tae

droon in the fuckin azure ae his soul an tae yell, '*WaR oi!*
Khotay ka lun!' But he couldnae draw the words up fae the
darkness. An, noo, the tarantata songs hud moved into
'Omega', the high-tension punk flamenco ae Enrique Morente
and Lagartija Nick. Auld Nick. The bearded, wan-legged *lul*
wi the lizard skin, the kirk hobbler, the tub-thumpin, skull-
poundin *Phut Gai Gand* Wan. Fae the thoosand white towers
ae Glasgow, the deafenin, Andalusian *azaan* swept him intae
action. Wi aw the strength left in his exhausted boady, Zaf
rose tae his feet, swayed. 'Ah am you,' the voice kept intonin
as though it wis a spell. A soul spell, a dark lake, black
swans. The reflection ae a face. *Cante jondo.* The face wis
interchangeable – wan moment, it wis Zilla, the next Babs,
then his *maa*, then his papa, then it wis Zaf an he wis Zafar.
There wis nae separation – iviryhin wis wan note. Impure,
broken-winged, 'koo-koo-ka-choo', the Divil's Note. A bangin,
bone drum, a retchin trumpet. Israfil-Raphael, King ae the
Seraphiel. It wis issuin, cartoon-like, fae the phone an wis
swallowin the universe, the big iron crane, the glass tower
hotel, the enormous silver armadillo ae the Science Centre an
the hypodermic hivin ae the Space Needle. Thur wur some
people mountin the northern end ae the bridge, American
tourist types, wi their bulky paranoias, whom he thought
might be watchin him, but he wis beyond carin. He stumbled
ower tae the rail, picked up the phone and flung it owerairm,
fast-bowler style, intae the sky. He thought he'd let go a
moment too soon an that the wee blue bastard would land
oan his heid. Knoack him oot cauld. Send him spinnin intae
yet another hallucinatory spiral. But then the soang exploded
intae discordant rock an he watched as the mobile arc reached
its peak an then dopplered gracefully intae the Clyde River
at the place where, at the end, the liquid city would sink aw
intae nuhin. A splash, a ripple an the music wis gone. Zafar,

Zilla an aw the rest . . . Mibbee they were deid already an their voices jist barks fae *jahannam*. But thur wis still Babs. He still had to deal wi her. He couldnae leave the city withoot that final act. An his papa. Whitivir wis left. His bones felt like cartilage. He brushed doon his claes tae gie him time tae get his braith back an then he walked oan, headin north once again. 'Omega' hud ended.

Good mornin, *sat sri akaal, namashkar, salaam alaikum*. It's five-forty-wan-an-two-an-a-hauf seconds an this is Zaf, King ae *The Junnune Show*, Grand Master ae Radio Chaandni, the trumpet angel, the last wan left stonnin as the lights go oot. When the real waruld ae the mornin strikes ye like the *tarrd* fae Paradise, it's ma voice ye hear. It's the music ae ma soul, the story ae ma life. But ma life is jist a *raag* ae aw your lives. Ah'm like a bloodied banner ae war – iviryhin ye've ivir thought, done, aw ae it hus happened through yer host thenight, *nazim-sahib, mushaira ki malik, cheb* Zaf ae the gaulden glitter-suit. Ah wear stars in ma bones. Ma eyes are rings ae light. Gaze intae them an hear the sune ae yer ane hairt!

He drew up the playlist. The surface of the paper wis almost completely covered in ink. His biro had been leakin for some time now and the ink had spewed out, thick, blue and sticky. It reminded Zaf of one of those archaic ballpoint pens made of angular scholastic plastic. During the course of the night, the blue had smudged and spread so that, now, the song titles were partially obscured by irregularly shaped blotches. Letters faded into pools of ink and the meanings of the words had grown less distinct with each note of every song he had played. Liquid into music and music into air.

This is a wake-up call. Wakey-wakey!

Oh, God, what was he becomin? A Butlins' redcoat? Hi-di-fuckin-hi. A full, lifelong and permafrost member of the Whitecraigs Golf Club? A big shiny bouffant four-wheel driver? Wakey-wakey, that wis a Babs thing – that wis what she would say, sometimes, when she rolled towards him, wantin sex in the mornin. Her eyes, still closed, her lips movin, smilin, pullin him from dream to flesh.

It's a quarter tae sax an, soon, the signal will be switched aff – mibbee fur guid. But Ah think ye know that the *junnune* will go oan intae space, intae yer heids, an that thur will be nae end tae the music. Ye're aw comin wi me intae eternity. Scary, eh? Then cairry them wi ye. The soangs ae the soul. Soon, we'll huv Nusrat Fateh Ali Khan singin doon fae th'ither side. Wait fur it. Stay oan air. Sock it to us, Nusrat! *Qawwal*! A divine utterance from auld wee Deck A. Wakey-wakey-wakey-wakey.

Like all *qawwals*, the song began real slow as though lyrics and instrumentation, both, were risin from deep inside the earth. And that wis how they worked, these songs – they circled around you, they reached down inside of you and they lifted you up slowly, slowly, so you hardly knew it, and then the music, the hand clappin, the swayin from side to side, all of it began to turn a little faster while the closed sound of the harmonium opened, just a little, just enough, and, before you knew it, you were soarin with the larks, up into the sky. The *qawwal* wis a *mi'raj*, the singer wis the magic winged horse. And now Zaf began to sway from side to side and, with each movement, the wheels of his wheelie chair sent him skatin across the wooden floor. He let his arms splay out and his head fall back and, as the music accelerated, he began to feel like a dervish spinnin round and round. 'Mustt, Mustt'. The enunciation of the words grew more truncated until each ejaculation lasted no longer than the sound of a finger tap on a drumskin. Zaf felt the swing of the chair against his back yet, simultaneously, it wis the turn and twist of a bull skin resurrected by the alchemical magnetism of his rotation so that, with the next circle of the song, he wis trippin lightly before the steamin, snortin face of a full-grown bull. 'Mustt, Mustt'. All night, every night, for three months, he had been avoidin it and now it had come to get him. Nusrat Fateh Ali Khan, dead these past years, had risen through the music, like some Orphic Messiah, and wis after him. As Zaf moved across the floor, as he circled around the walls, his arms splayed full so that the fingers of his right hand were just touchin the tips of the cones, as he drew his skin along the line that separated the worlds, he saw Nusrat's face, his giant form, and it moved with Zaf's movements as though Nusrat wis there with him, physically stompin around inside the twenty-by-twenty cubicle. The *qawwalis* were singin in total unison so that their voices were as one voice and their words were unintelligible – they no longer held any meanin. Round and round Zaf went, faster and faster, somehow miraculously avoidin the wires, the plugs, the adaptors, the accoutrements of Radio Chaandni broadcastin on ninety-nine-point-nine meters FM. He wis movin anti-clockwise, the way space moved – though it had no breath – the way it danced and sang. And now the bull wis chargin and Zaf wis circlin around an invisible point of stillness and then, suddenly, he stopped and wis still. He could not move – he stood fixed to the spot as the giant bull of *qawwal* charged straight at him. He could smell its earth breath – it siphoned the air and burned his skin. He felt the weight of its muscle as it hulked over the ground and he just stood there, in the place where old blood had stained the earth brown.

The light wis streamin in through the long glass. Zaf could feel it ripple beneath his eyelids and the *qawwal*, 'Mustt, Mustt', wis buildin to its climax – a peak that would last for minutes, hours, centuries. The bull wis almost upon him – its nostrils flared, the tips of its horns glistened in the light of the new morning. 'Mustt, Mustt'. At the point of contact when the hard ivory touched the skin of his belly, at the moment of revelation when he knew that his soul would unfurl like the petals of a flower, Zaf opened his eyes. The music stopped. The cubicle spun silently around him – its walls shimmering silver. The air swirled around his face. Everything stood poised.

Then it hit.

One, single scream.

Nusrat, the disembodied Nusrat, screamed the longest note Zaf had ever heard. It had gone beyond the song. This wis live. And the entire ninety days, all the years of his life, were impaled on to that end *quejío*. The music exploded into the morning but Zaf closed his eyes so that he didn't have to see Nusrat's face. He wis not worthy.

The bull lifted him on its horns and he wis ridin on its back. He felt, beneath him, the rough, buckin arc of its spine. He felt the air pulled before him in a tunnel and he wis headin for a blue light. The leather wis hardenin beneath his pelvis. The discordantly rhythmic gallop of the bull's hooves turned to the smooth *taal* of rollin wheels and now he wis on the path, Vulcan blue, and he wis Babs.

But the figure on the motorbike, the figure assumin the shape of the letter B or ꓭ – whichever shape wis possible there, in that early mornin phase where things kind of shimmered and never truly gained fixed form. Babs or B was speedin along, rubber screaming off the tyres, at ninety miles per hour, goin either north to the Heilans and Orkney, Shetland, the Faroes, the hot, smoky springs of Iceland or else she wis headin down to Galloway, Cumbria, Cymru, Cornwall, Gaul, Galicia, Galatia, the lands of the Celts. To go either north or south wis to travel back in time, ninety years, nine hundred, nine thousand. *Aleph-bey*. Back.

And why not? If Zilla wis speedin beyond the light barrier, jettin with her lover-pimp, with Zaf-Zafar, the double-headed, mortal deity, if, in her vengeful victory, she wis transcendin time, sex, song, men, then who, really, wins the resolution? Who clutches the *siller* cup, the *jaam* ae narrative queenship? Zilla didnae mairry the glossy magazine mate selected fur her by her family and nor did she follow Zaf intae whitivir self-referential journey he wis heidit. Why should she? She hud loast enough through the loang, narra vacuum ae his love. She'd goat her strange kind ae revenge and wis nae longer a victim. And her pin-up?

Really, listeners, *samaaen-jee*, ye shouldnae be so naive, in the endless voracity ae yer consumption, tae think that Zaf wis ony different, at core, fae Zafar or that eether ae them – ae us – were – are – real. We exist only oan air an that is nae existence at aw. Each ae us lives only between midnight an sax, ma freends. At five fifty-five an fifty-nine-point-nine, nine, nine, nine . . . seconds (Did Ah no tell ye Ah wis a dab hond at the mathematics? But, then, Ah wis bein economical wi la vérité.), wu're well and truly balancin oan the thin metal metal ae the cloack honds.

400

So, mibbee Babs ends up in España an mibbee, eventually, she meets a short, fair stranger, a wumman, who is filled wi duende or *taraab* or, at least, wi a measure ae Kabbalistical wisdom an who speaks in tongues through a mooth cast open in wonder. An mibbee the mooth belongs tae a face which belongs tae an eternally unnameable deity. Of course, that's why she bought the blue nineteen-ninety-nine Kawasaki Vulcan 1500 Classic in the first place – because, sumwhur in her subconscious, in the strange, barely known regions ae her bio-anatomical axonic interaction, she (Barbara, Babs, Barabbas, The Nurse or whitivir the hell her name is this time aroon), this wumman, the one Zaf thought he could fuck aroon (and fuck aroon wi), hud known, even then, that, wan day, she would leap on tae her steed an would speed aff intae the *surat* ae the sunrise. An she's ridin fast, fast, faster an the air is billowin aroon her, like she's a seal in the sea, an she's tryin, tryin fur the rush, when her *naak* suddenly begins tae bleed like stink, tae swarm an draw fae her face, but she's no goannae stoap noo – nivir again will she stoap an rest her dreams in a man's belly – and, finally, she takes the torso by the horns, the gleamin, chrome horns, an, with blood streamin gloriously, heids either wanderin magnetic north or fixed due sooth, the difference between the two bein drawn in a straight line acroass the land, exactly wan honner an eighty-eight-point-eight-eight-eight-eight degrees apart – or twice ninety-nine-point-nine. Ha! The joyous, bloody borders ae synchronicity! Ah telt ye Ah wis a numbers conjuror. How else would Ah huv been able tae sit here, like some stylitised saint, oan this spinnin chair, fur ninety days? Nights. Or even tae pace oot these *gurrum* streets. The hoat, white paths ae Alba. Think aboot it, *samaaen*. Wanderin soangs, a narrative ae the night. Turn the knob, a wee bit tentatively (Are ye, perhaps, a wee bit hyper aifter aw ye've been through?), an pause yer fingertips aroon the ninety-nine-point-nine wave-length. D'ye hear onyhin? Jist white noise, probably. Alba music. Beyond the ends ae the wurds, thur hus always been music. So, in a honner or a thoosand years' time, Zaf's voice, ma voice, will still be circlin, conjoinin wi the magical, geometric dance ae the spheres. Stick a magnetic receiver in the right place an ye might jist catch it – although thur's nae guaranteein that ye'll onnerston whit ye'll be hearin. The voices ae the angels. Radio Chaandni, *The Junnune Show*, broadcastin oan . . .

Madness as a means to sanity. Or madness simply as a means to a greater madness. Zaf and his papa. And his *maa* with her plants. Babs with her bike and Zilla and the heroin dream of which she was a part. A terrible madness, *munnashiath* love, a lunacy of the will. Deck A, Deck B.

The revvin of the motorbike outside grew louder until it began to give Zaf a headache. Fuck sake. In the middle of a *qawwali* song as well. But he hadn't really heard it again till now – just as the song wis fawin silent and as the scream that issued from his mouth wis endin. He wis all out of breath. All out of music. Well, almost.

Deck B.

ETERNITY

His throat wis like graphite – the muscles were knotted tightly together. A cadeceus.

Ah, ecstasy! Ecstasy!! Nusrat's voice is deep, deep an strong – it goes back a long weye, *samaaen*, right back tae the Auld Parsee fires ae the Mazandaran Sea. Aye, Nusrat, that man ae victory, wis singin alang the shores ae the almond-shaped Caspian. He supped oan pomegranate seeds wi the Perfect Master an he sipped *mai* wi the thrasher *qawwals* in the black fields ae Kentucky and noo he's blastin oot his great voice aw alang the shoreless ocean ae Faraakh-kard. Put yer ear tae the groon onywhur in the waruld – here, in Pedlar Glasgae, whur life is sweetened by the Kentigern songs ae the deep past, an there, in Lahore, whur the Mosque ae the *Djinns* appears only wance a year an, each time, in a different *mohalla*. Even in the maist desperate torture chambers an the deepest, darkest prisons ae steamin, millipede dictatorships, ye'll hear the music if ye can. Goodbye, Nusrat, fare thee weel!

A pause for respect. And then,

An noo we're movin oan cause we've got tae – right, ma friends? Time waits fur nae *bundha*. No even fur the *Hazrats*. An certainly not fur Zaf!

He realised that his voice wis growin louder as he tried to battle against the rattlin of the motorbike. He half considered scootin over to the window and pullin it shut but his legs felt too weak to bother and, then again, he didn't know who or what he might see out there. The light was almost full now and there would be nowhere to hide. A sense of regret welled in his chest – sadness that the last night wis finally endin, that this phase of his life wis now almost over. You could develop affection for even the lowest dog of a thing. Perhaps, one day, he would learn to love himself. He covered himself in words.

An, as ye'll know, the time right noo is . . .

He glanced at his watch, no longer trustin the clock on the wall. Anythin attached to this place wis mutable.

Five fifty. Ten tae sax. Whitivir turns ye oan. Before Ah put oan the next soang, Ah want ye tae think aboot whit ye'll be doin the day. Wurkin mibbee? Or prayin? Or takin a trip? Or jist dreamin. Ah don't know whit Ah'm goannae dae. It's been *theen maheenay*, ninety days. Ah've been ridin alang . . .

Out there, the bike was reaching orgasm.

ridin alang beside yer ears fur too loang. Noo it's time fur me tae sink back intae the total obscurity from whence comes oor only reality. It's time fur me tae get real. Mibbee Ah'll saunter doon tae the west coast an jump on tae wan ae those auld fake paddle steamers. Or mibbee Ah'll jist steep aroon right here in this hoat city ae oors an set ma fins dancin tae the jugular beat ae some darkly ecstatic club or other. Whit d'ye think? Mibbee we should open the lines noo an huv a phone-in wi suggestions. Or, then again, mibbee not! Ye might aw tell me tae go an jump in the river! So Ah'll dae jist whit Ah'm hauf good at an that's bein a disc joakie. Ah'm The King ae the Disc Joakies! The Amir ae the Pendant Wavelength. The Qaisar . . .

He paused. He realised that he'd been shouting. The bike had roared off and now Zaf was almost screaming into the mike. Its mesh was covered in flecks of saliva. He pulled out the belly of his T-shirt and wiped it clean.

The Caesar ae Sune will put oan the next track.

One foot after the next. It wis the only way.

This is the point in the mornin whun we aw turn intae fushes. Fins, scales, gills, the loat! In the light ae the mornin sun, slowly we move back up the evolutionary scale ae hings. We nae loanger huv tae breathe that invisible thing they caw 'air'. Noo, wu're livin an laughin an lovin in watter. It's fun, folks! You should try it. Dip yer toes an feel the change. Feel yer bones grow light an hollow, feel yer skin stre-e-e-tch an turn *siller*, feel yer blood run cauld. As ye sink intae subconsciousness, as yer brain shrinks back tae the prehistoric, ponder oan this: from now oan, fur the rest ae yer lives, ye'll nivir touch anither bein, except tae eat or be eaten! Nae mair relationships, nae mair sivin deadly sins, nae mair end-ae-time resurrection. Jist instinct an even that willnae huv a name. How aboot it, eh? Piscanthropy. Such a change demands anither language. So here we go, fushes! Turn intae *mutchlees* an this is whit ye'll hear.

FISH

PLAY

SWIM

Deck B: 'An Emotional Fish'. The Colour of Memory. A salmon crawlin up the hills ae hame.

Gaelic words, the Old Tongue, which Zaf did not understand. He wondered whether anyone out there would know what the woman wis singin about. Her voice wis strong, with just the slightest hint of tremolo, but it wis quite distinct from that of the other female vocalist on the album. If the earlier singer's voice came from the rocks – if it wis a seal cry or a bird's serenade – then this gentler *saaz* wis a spirit swimmin through the ocean and the song wis that of a fish perhaps or a dreamer or a lover. The music piped in from some very deep, murky place, countless fathoms down, where the darkness remained unbroken. A chamber hollowed out in the rocks, a fin palace, where their love, his and Babs's, might yet prosper. And the music, the serenade, would be 'An Emotional Fish', played slow on an echoin, cosmic church organ by Skanderjoss, the phenomenal wizard, King of the Keyboards, the guy who could wheel out whole orchestras on the tips of his fingers. His music issued from the top of a lighthouse and its sound could resurrect choirs of the dead. But the woman's song wis splittin into two, it wis double trackin perhaps or mibbee the voice, the breath, did not belong just to Babs or to Scotland or to the *Gàidhealtachd* but also to Zaf, to the People of Asia. Of course, those rhythms were the *taals* of his bones. It wis a great fin-woman's symphony within him. It wis his life. Even as he realised this, he knew that his love for her wis decayed, its motifs drawn in impossible scripts. They had been pulled from the past and stamped too often on the parchment of the world, they had risen from the deep, dark bellies of bagpipes and from the cold skulls of soldiers' laments and now the echoes of these forgotten songs blew at him in the wind. The metal and skin of battles turned to sand wafted into his lungs. Opium dust. *Munnashiath*.

The nursin home wis in a lush part of the city, not that far from the Botanics, towards the fringes of the West End, up where gentility merged seamlessly into squalor, up near Maryhill. To get there, he had to double back, go eastwards for a stretch and then climb due north. It wasn't far really but, as the road curved, the trees behind him slipped out of vision and he wis climbin a hill. Mary's hill. Zaf wondered who Mary had been. Probably some lassie from the eighteenth century, some flaxen-haired milkmaid from when all this area wis deep country and the land, still unenclosed, danced to the rhythmic stomp of Jacks and Jills and tumblin crowns. As he climbed past the garage, Zaf thought he caught a whiff of the fields that lay to the north. Manure and the hoots of cowherds. Or mibbee it wis just a distant car horn and a fartin catalytic converter. Round the bend and up the hill. On his left, the new terraced houses that had been built to look like semis. Wee suburban deceptions in the middle of the city. On the other side of the road, the small, bright faces of ghost children peeked out at him from behind slender saplings but, when he looked again, he saw that it was only the illusion of light through leaves. At the top of the hill, he turned left on to Maryhill Road. The road to the Wild West. As a kid, he'd always thought that this *saRak* might lead somehow to Randolph Scott and Sunday afternoon TV matinees. Goodies an baddies. White hats, silver pistols. Sunshine through the rain. He walked past the shops, many of which were shuttered and had 'For Sale' or 'To Let' signs nailed to their fronts. Zaf knew that some of them would never open again. Mary wis long gone and her hill wis up for sale.

He walked past the old pubs and his nostrils caught the

whiff of spirits dead in the bottle. The traffic wis pickin up now and, from somewhere behind him, Zaf heard the siren of a fire engine. The noise faded as the engine headed rapidly east. The road's gradient wis still steep and he felt the pull of the tarmac on his muscles but the fresh mornin air fuelled his body so that he felt the tiredness seep away and, instead, he began to feel a sense of weightlessness as though, at any moment, he might take off and fly. He rounded a bend and suddenly, before him, wis a row of brown hills. It wis amazin, Zaf thought, how in this city, everythin was so close to everythin else. Just a breath away . . .

He left the main road and turned into Doyle Avenue where things suddenly got much quieter and where packets of greenery reappeared in the postcard-sized gardens. A haven of tranquillity, Zaf thought. At the end of the street, he turned left and, a couple of hundred yards away, he made out the 'Welcome' sign of the Tree Tops Nursing Home.

The nurses were wearin excessively bright uniforms and the sun shone with an almost nuclear brightness. As he walked slowly along the corridor, Zaf felt a tremor run through his body and his knees went suddenly weak. He pushed open the door. Babs wis sittin by his father's bedside. At first, he wis startled but then he realised that they were both fast asleep and he gazed from one to the other, marvellin at the tiny differences in the way their faces moved as they slept. Her head wis restin on the back of her hand. Her skin looked so pale it wis almost transparent. She had on blue jeans and a little white top which he remembered she had bought from a sale in a clothes shop that had long since gone bust. It had dainty wee frills around the tops of the arms and the sleeves went down only half the way to her elbows. Everythin seemed so familiar. And yet, somehow, the familiar wis hypnotic. He didn't want to break the spell and so he just stood and watched. All our forefathers sleep within us, Zaf thought – they slumber and wait and then they rise up and take us by surprise. And, as Zaf gazed at his father's face, he found that he could make out the brushstrokes of his own features and also those of his long-lost brother. It occurred to him that the picture of Zafar, the child, which lay now in darkness beneath the staircase, might just as easily be that of his grandfather or of his grandfather's grandfather. He looked at Babs. At some point, somewhere in the distant past, Babs and he must've had a common ancestor. He strained to capture a likeness. Words in the form of living flesh. 'An Emotional Fish'. Deck B. Now, at last, he understood.

> The beauty of your face,
> The beauty of your spirit . . .

He bent down and kissed her lips. They tasted salty and her cheeks were covered in a fine layer of sweat. Out of habit, he touched her arm. He felt her body tremble just a little beneath his fingers. She smelt of old perfume. Once, they had been like continents and their edges had matched perfectly. In the mornin, though, it had always been more difficult to span the gap. Her eyes fluttered and she woke up and, for a moment, she wis startled as though she hadn't expected to see him. Then she smiled that broad-lipped smile of hers and Zaf found he wis smilin back. Her eyes were tired and the whites were scored with tiny red vessels. She'd been here all night. She nodded towards Jamil. Spoke quietly as though she wis afraid of wakin the dead. 'It's all over, isn't it?'

For a moment, Zaf thought his father wis dead. It wis a strange thing to say, here, in this place, wherever here was.

It had been a strange mornin. Night. Papa had turns like that from time to time. He went down, he came up. It wis no different from how it had always been. And yet the thought occurred to Zaf that mibbee, this time, it would not be the same. And this thought sent shivers up his spine. What if, this time, he wisnae comin back? What if he wis deid? He felt as though he wis in a scene from some film or other. Or mibbee from some future or other. He nodded slowly. 'An Emotional Fish'. Sleek, silver, streamin through the ocean. Outside, her hard woman's metal wheels lay still and silent as the sleepin earth.

She turned away. Gazed out the window. From the side, her eyes were translucent blue and moist. Lines splayed out across her forehead. Downstairs, bathed in sunlight, her lightnin-blue Kawasaki rested on its side, the chrome of its neck bar gleamin silver with her tears. He hated that. It made him feel sorry for her. It made him love her through pity. Her voice wis haltin, uncertain. The palms of her hands, untouched, shifted slightly, makin her entire posture seem tenuous. A fresco about to crumble.

In the room downstairs, where the party had taken place, the equipment had all been trashed. He hadn't heard a thing – he hadn't even been down there since midnight – yet he knew it had happened. It wis a total mess so that it wis impossible to differentiate between what wis missin and what had just been smashed or dumped. The imprints of disorder lay all over the old wooden boards where, only a few hours earlier, the dancers had tapped out their subtle geometries. Funny the gangstas hadn't found their way up here to Zaf's cubicle. Probably hadn't even noticed the narrow stairwell. They'd have had more important things on the blank phone cards of their minds. He shrugged. What the fuck? The fire door had gone. The Kinnin Park Boys must have slunk back, like rats, across the river to get their revenge. Harry'll go fuckin spare, he thought, and then he smiled at the idea of him findin the radio station in tatters. Any faint hope Harry Singh might still have harboured of obtaining a long-term licence must surely now have gone. Deid lion. So what? More music. It wis the answer to everythin. Because, really, there were no answers. Just echoes.

The last tracks would be done silently – the music would flow like blood. No explanations, no more patter. No words. The last fifteen minutes of *The Junnune Show* would be sequenced in silence, the clicks and flips, the button pressin, Deck B, Deck A, goin back, runnin forwards, skimmin sideways – all of that would happen in some other space. Or, rather, it would occur, as everythin had really occurred, in itself and without reference to anythin goin on around him. Everythin wis discrete – the linkages between people and occurrences were just so much air and smoke, beautiful puffy-cloud bridges like in those mythical Chinese paintings. Lies, all.

A flashback of the sewer wall. Pulsatin flesh. He pushed it away. Radio Chaandni had come and gone – as had Zilla and Babs and his *maa* and papa and now *The Junnune Show*, too, was about to end. The countdown to six a.m. *Bas khutum*. Omega. *Al-nihayat*. Deck A. Nusrat's voice reachin again from beyond the edge of the grave, risin from the corpse face of the playlist. 'Mustt, Mustt'. The fat man expandin in sound, his form swellin an intoxicatin the universe. Nusrat hadn't died – he had just become everythin. That wis the sign of a cosmic song. 'Mustt, Mustt'. It had never ended – it had run beneath the songs of the night and had burst through the bull and the fish and now it would go on forever. The voice would begin slow dancin circles, real slow, and it would build in layers, one layin down upon the next in a great sonic ziggurat. Nusrat, His Sumerian Holiness. Even the dried-up, fag-end scrawls of Zaf the DJ might rise up and become paradisiacal in their frenzy. Set Michael at the Gate! Hand Raphael the music! Drop Azrael into the yawnin grave! Let her gather dust into words. And toss Gabriel on to a nineteen-ninety-nine Kawasaki Vulcan 1500 Classic. Hey!! This is Gospel, man! Halle-fuckin-lujah. Praise the Lord, everybody's shiftin! But today's heretical angel of annunciation wis Babs, her face illumined with the acceleration of the mornin, her straw-coloured hair turned to gold, a long plume streamin behind her at forty miles per hour, forty-five, fifty . . . wings, almost. *Karubiyyun* and *seraphiel. Hazrat* Babs.

The sound of a motorcycle engine revvin, growin louder, closer, until he could almost smell the petrol and feel the dizzyin vibration in the air. Zaf bent forwards, his hands clasped around the stem of the mike. His words came out staccato, his voice wis tremulous. The last words of the broadcast from a world collapsin and expandin simultaneously.

This is fur Babs. Barbara. Yous know her. The wan
Ah've been sendin messages tae fur the past three months,
night aifter night, oor upon oor, midnight tae sax.

He sighed. His words were like hard metal in his brain.

Mibbee it's tae say Ah'm sorry. Nah, that's a lie. Mibbee
Ah've goat nae wurds left. Mibbee the music should
speak fur me. Fur us aw. We aw try tae run away fae
fear ae daith. And whit does a nurse do tae get daith oot
ae her system? She leaps on tae her powerbike an she

revs up the fifteen hundred cubic capacity engine, zero tae saxty in sivin seconds, an she spins the silver wheel an aff she goes!

Zaf leaned back, sniffed. The stink of burnin rubber wis makin him dizzy. His palms had been branded by the metal. But it wasn't over yet.

She rides her sleek blue bike fast, fast, fast an she closes her eyes.

Zaf swallowed but his throat wouldnae work. He blurted.

This one's for you, *meri jaan.*

He jammed the end of his thumb against the button and didn't let go till he heard the music pour out into the mornin light. The harsh, *qawwali* utterances, beginnin in singularity on the point of a laser beam, grew and became manifold and blasted and rocked like a Kawasaki and Zaf held his head between his palms and got up, stumbled over to the partition window and began to bang his head against the glass, in a kind of atonal *taal* mimicry of the bellowin sound of the pump organ. The one imbibed by Hindustan from old Christian missionaries and now, a hundred years later, exhaled by *qawwals*. Go, Nusrat, go! Right through the song, he tried to shut out the sound but it just got louder and more insistent and he wis movin his head along with the rhythm, the thrust of the words. The rise and fall of his chest wis swept up into the movement of breath across a dyin woman's lips. Blue steel in the mornin sunshine. The steam on the mirror gradually fades to clear. Babs had reached her station but Zaf would never reach his. His guilt would be never-endin

– his road tortuous always.

He collapsed on to the floor, still clutchin the *maghas* that had done all this. The music wis in its final seventh phase. Soon, like everythin else, it would die away and he would be left with the terrifyin weight of his own silence. The cubicle had turned red. The glass of both the windows, the inner and the outer, was stained with the figures, the long faces, of beatified saints. Zaf Pantocrator. His palms were covered in blood. He wis clutchin somethin. Zaf stared down at the portrait. It wis not somethin he had drawn by design – he couldn't draw to save himself. But that's what the chaotic concatenation, the blue lines and scores of the song list, mixed in with his own blood, the scribbled arcane words and symbols, had become – a face. Or, rather, many faces. An intoxication with the past, with darkened versions of things. Gaze into a face and see the ancestral lines run back through flesh and bone, through the chords of long-forgotten bass structures. Pillars of light, modes of salt. It's all there – right back to the grinning yowls of the savannah. Lust, avarice, envy, sloth, gluttony, pride, anger – meat for the tigers. It was not so much the physical representation of bone structure, muscle, shadow and so on. The course of Zaf's fractal was not that of the old masters – his was a different kind of visage. It was made up of all the people in his life, all those who continually swarmed and died within him. Thousands, millions, maybe – an unending *silsila* of human beings, bloodied and spunked and covered in the excreta of their own actions, pieces of flesh and spirit pulling back to the mud and lightning of the beginning. And of whatever had been there before. Music perhaps. Or light. But the music was ending.

Trembling and shaking, Zaf got to his feet. He hobbled over to the console and slumped down in the chair. Let his

breath out. Cleared his throat. Bent forwards. Gripped the
mike tightly with both hands, splayed out his elbows. His
thigh was jammed up against the base of the machine. There
seemed less space than before – as though, somehow, his
body had swelled durin the night. Or maybe, in the violence
of the music, the cubicle had imploded. The air was filled
with the stink of iron. *Loha* was streaming down his face.
Some of it dripped on to the metal of the console, mixing
with the older blood – that drawn by Zilla.

Good morning, everybody. Hello. This is Zafar. You
know how it's spelt. It's . . .

He glanced up at the clock. Blinked. Five minutes to six. No
one's listening. Everyone's dead. The one who might have
been hearing this is sleeping.
    He pulled the mike down close to his chest. Breathed a few
times. His ribs hurt.

The music's over – the journey, the madness. No more
Weather, no more News. There is nowhere left to run.
This is where it ends. Here, in this cubicle, before this
mike. Through this voice.

Zaf slipped back one last time – his face, his body, his soul
slipped back into jargon.

In fact (an, as ye aw know, facts are people), Ah am an
intuitive, illiterate expert in the auld Al-Misr discipline ae
Euclidean geometry. The alchemical lore ae the Grand
Equilateral Triangle. So, durin this last soang, brought
oot ae chaos by Yahya, Paulo, Jorge *aur* Ricardo, those
bearded prophets ae the core, Ah would like ye aw tae

close yer *een* an imagine aw the possible ramifications ae sax o'cloak. The end ae a night in the life. OK.

Deck *Aleph*: 'A Day in the Life'. The Beatles.

To George and John. To everyone.

In the Tree Tops Nursing Home, through the tinkling sounds of a piano, the sun was just breaking through the big glass panes of the windows. The first-floor bedroom felt hot and stuffy behind the big, unopenable double-glazed panes. There was a dripping noise coming from the wall by the door, opposite the bed, from the cold tap of the sink. It seemed as though it would cease but, every few seconds, a globule of water would form and grow and then drop from the outlet of the metal. Above the sink and bolted to the wall was a square-shaped mirror, peeling a little at the edges, but the glass caught the sunlight and almost doubled its intensity. Over in the far corner, tucked beneath the window and balanced on spindly, wooden legs, the television was on but its sound had been switched to mute and it must have been tuned between channels because all that played across its screen was an undifferentiated, raging snowstorm. Zaf had always thought that the box had been placed in a stupid position – too close to the window and facing back from it so that, every time you tried to watch a programme, you would almost be blinded in the attempt either by the daylight or else, in the winter, by the glare from the neon street lamps. He realised that it had never occurred to him, until this moment, that he should move the bloody thing. He had never spent long enough, with his whole self, in this place. He had always dreamed of being somewhere else – by the sea or on the motorbike or in the past. It was as though he had been blinded not so much by the sun as by the horror of the present – by the loss of his father's soul.

Babs was slumped in an armchair, her long legs crossed, her ankles in shadow beneath the bed, and Jamil Ayaan was lying on his side with his back towards the sunbeams. His father's dark three-quarter-length raincoat was hanging from a peg on the door, its collar partially obscured by the peak of his flat, cream-coloured cap. The light seemed to catch on the skin of his cheek and temple so that, as Zaf gazed, it was as though the golden light was emanating not from the sun or from the mirror but from his father's face. The way it had been maybe once, a long time back – before the big journey had stripped him of his self-respect. Beyond the window, somebody was already burning leaves in a nearby garden and the vegetation sent up a column of curling white smoke. Outside, the sound of birdsong was diminishing into the sky.

He knelt down, close to his papa's face. Felt the deep regularity of his breathing. The feel of his father's chest – the muscles, once strong as stone, turned now to fibre and dust. *Ishq*, stripped by the violence of time, was just bone and dreams and darkness. His father and him, their faces reflected from the clear glass of the mirror. Jamil smelled clean as though he had just risen from ocean waters. At last there were no chemicals left – the cold, hard, blue water had washed his bones clean.

His eyes still closed, Jamil Ayaan's left hand emerged from beneath the covers. He stretched towards the bedside table, carefully avoiding the cooling mug of milky tea, the nearly empty glass of water, the plastic battery-operated alarm clock, the glossy half-brick of an unread paperback thriller and the square hankie box decorated with smooth-stemmed pink roses, and his hand hovered before the wall and the black and red call buttons. His middle finger protruded downwards, circled, swooped and then descended on to the 'ON/OFF' knob of the wooden valve radio. But he was at a mechanical disadvantage – the pressure was not adequate, his leverage too light, his grip too weak and the machine emitted a squeak or two and then fell silent again. Jamil ran his hand through his silvery hair, combed his fingers through the strands, though still he did not open his eyes. Then he tried again and, this time, the set began to emit a low-pitched hum. A faint green light began to glow from behind the glass of the frontage, began to illuminate the tables that ran vertically over its surface and which delineated the frequency wavebands all the way from Thirteen Meters to Long Wave, from the Light Programme to Tangier to Kalundberg, Ankara, Tel Aviv, Tehran and then back again to the Third Programme. And, unmarked, somewhere out over the dark ocean, the remembered voices of Lahore, Karachi, Dehli, Agra. Most of the stations on Jamil Ayaan's radio were long defunct and the wavelengths, which they once had occupied, were now filled with the bark and chatter, the strange *burzakh* hyper-speak of the disc jockeys with their rhythm-heavy fanfares. As, gradually, the valves warmed up, the hum, which the radio at first had emitted, merged into what sounded like a medieval polyphony coming up through a light blues rhythm. And then violins finning through the ocean, like the spines of whales sliding up out of a dream.

The sunbeams were stronger now and they penetrated right through the room, illuminating the palm-sized photographs hung in oval frames on the wall. And, as the light changed, so too did the music. It seemed, now, to be swaying from side to side like some crazed, intoxicated dervish. Violins, trumpets, clarinets, guitars, everything. And, as it swayed, it rose. Higher and higher, past the line of finger grease, the bloodstains, the dried seed, the dust, the levels that, for so long, had divided and defined Zaf's world, past the summer colour photographs of Jamil and Rashida, with the dark lochs of Dunnet Head looming at their backs, past the un-photographed desolation of Nuristan, the run and pulse of their journey through the darkness, past the cranes swinging in the pink sky, the music ascended and flowed into the morning, notes shaped like lizards and birds and tiny faces coursed through the sleek waves of Babs's hair and over the *chaandi-ki-chuRia* and the silver piercings of the bangles at her crossed ankles and through Zaf's earphones, into his head, and through Radio Chaandni, through *The Junnune Show*, on the ninety-nine-point-nine meters FM waveband, the old valve radio was reaching its station at last.

The wind had dropped quite suddenly and a filtered, golden light perfused the air and held the buildings, the roads, the leaves in silence. Even the birds seemed to have stopped singing. There, in the small room, Zaf closed his eyes and stretched right from the heels of his feet – he stretched himself and he threw his head back so that his spine became an arc and he let the air pour into him. The city seemed poised on the brink of a stillness which occurs maybe once during the course of a day. A day in the life. That last hovering piano chord.

E Major. Perfect. Like the name of God.

Suddenly, one eye opened. Then the other. Both were empty.

His papa looked at him. Recognised Qaisar. The King.

'Qaisar, *mera beyta?*'

Zaf turned the volume up to full, pushed the fade switch back as far as it would go and then some. Leaned forwards into the microphone. Whispered. Sang. '*Haa ji*, Papa. Qaisar *hai.*'

GLOSSARY

Unless otherwise specified, all words are of Urdu origin. Note that, when indicated by capitals L, R or T, the letter should be pronounced with a hard, rolling sound.

A

Aadam Adam [Arabic]
aajao come
aam a mango; mangoes
aashiq the lovers
aba-o-ajdad ancestors
abu a father
accha good; all right; OK
afreet a ghost or demon
aik one
aleph the first letter of the Hebrew alphabet
al-Jaza'iriyah an island [Arabic, the name of Algeria is derived from this]
alltan a brook [Gaelic]
Al-Maghrebi denoting or relating to the western parts of the Islamic world, especially Morocco, Algeria, Tunisia and Libya
Al-Misr Egypt
al-nihayat the omega or the end of the world
al-taqiyya religious dissimulation
Altaqween Genesis [Arabic]
ameyn amen
a' mhuir dhubh the black sea [Gaelic]
Amrikan an American person; denoting or relating to America or American people
Amu the Oxus river
d'Ancona, Iacobbe a medieval Jewish-Italian scholar, merchant and explorer
Angraise an English person; denoting or relating to an English person, English people or the English language
Anha see Hazrat . . . Anha
anjaana hidden or secret
annkh (pl. annkhey) an eye
apna our
aql a mind

Arabi denoting or relating to an Arab person, Arab people or the Arabic language
arey hey
argento saans silver breath
Aristu Aristotle [Arabic]
ashik-e-mashuk (pl. the same) a lover and his or her beloved
asmani blue
ata flour
auliya a saint or prophet
aur and
avara gurd a vagabond
azaan a Muslim call to prayer
azab jahannum perdition
Azrael the archangel of death

B

baad-e-saba the west wind; a zephyr
baara twelve
baat-chit small talk
babu a clerk
Bachchan, Amitabh a male Indian film star
bai a woman
bajayen play it (a respectful request)
balti a bucket or pan; denoting or relating to a type of bath in which a bucket of water is poured over the head and body
Bangali a Bengali person; denoting or relating to a Bengali person
Bangla denoting or relating to the Bengali language
bani a proclamation or announcement
banjar zameene wastelands
baRa (also **baRi**) big
baraf snow

421

baratherie   a person's extended family; a clan [from the same Sanskrit root as 'brother']

Barbarossa, Khairuddin   a sixteenth-century privateer and admiral known as the Lord of the Seas. *Also called* Barbaros Hayreddin

Bardo Thodol   the Tibetan Book of the Dead

barfit   barefoot [Scots]

baries   bare feet [Scots]

barra   a pedlar's cart [Scots]

bas khutum   that's the end; it's all over; it's finished; washed-up

Battuta, Ibn   a medieval Arab explorer and writer

baw'wabaat   the gates of paradise

behen   a sister

behen-chaud   a sisterfucker

Behr-e-Rum   the Mediterranean Sea

beinn (*pl.* beantann)   a mountain [Gaelic]

bey   the second letter of the Arabic and Urdu alphabets

beyta a son

bhai   a brother

bhajan   a religious chant

bhava   a feeling [Sanskrit]

bhookee annkh   a glutton [*lit.* 'hungry eye']

bhooli hui yaadon   forgotten memories

billies   cats

Bint Sheikh Lut   Lot's wife [Arabic]

Binyamin   Benjamin

bivii   a wife

booDah   an old person

booDeh   old folk

Boori Annkh   the Evil Eye

boothes   mouths

Borysthenes   a horned river god; the river named after this god. *Also called* Dnieper

Braj-basha   an old language of Northern India

Bulkhans   the Balkans

Bunderbunds   a neologism formed from the corruption of *bunder* 'a monkey' and *bun* 'a jungle or forest' and pluralised. It is also a play on Sunderbunds or Sunderbuns, the name of a real area of India

bundha   a man or person

bundhay   people; folks

burzakh   purgatory

C

cairry-oot   a takeaway meal; a shop where takeaway meals can be bought; a supply of alcohol bought from an off-licence [Scots]

canaal   a small measure of land area, less than an acre and roughly equivalent to the area of a small house plot

cante jondo   a heart-rending type of flamenco song, often a tragic one [Spanish]

ce pays   this country; this land [French]

chaand   the moon

chaandi   silver

chaandi-ki-chuRia   silver bangles

chaandni   moonlight

chaar   four

chaba   a young woman; a term commonly used as a prefix to a rai singer's name [Arabic]

chabri-wallah   a basket-seller

chai   tea

chai-wallah   a tea-seller

chalo   let's go

Changhez   Genghis

Changhezi   denoting or relating to Genghis

cheb   a young man; a term commonly used as a prefix to a rai singer's name [Arabic]

chehilum   a ceremony held forty days after a person's death

chenar   the oriental plane tree

chholae   a clitoris

chirpaies   outdoor beds

chirya   a bird

chooTiyay   arseholes

chowk   a crossroads

chueco   an illegal immigrant [Mexican Spanish slang]

chuhay   rats

chumbeylee   jasmine, the national flower of Pakistan

chunn-chunn-chunn   an onomatopoeic word for the sound of jangling bangles, especially ankle ones

cludgie   a toilet

D

daakoo   a bandit

daavat   a party

dada   a paternal grandfather

Dajjal (*in full* al-Masih ad-Dajjal)   the Antichrist, the false Messiah

darone khwab   nightmares
darya (*pl.* daryaon)   a river
dastgah   a Persian version of maqam
[Farsi]
deo   a demon
derzi   a tailor
dharmic   denoting or relating to the
dharma which, in Hinduism and Bud-
dhism, is a cosmic law governing existence [Sanskrit, meaning 'degree' or 'custom']
dhookan   a shop
dhookandaar   a shopkeepers
dil (*pl.* dilon)   a heart
dil ka dil   the heart of the heart
Dil Se   a 1998 Indian film about
chance meetings and falling in and out
of love [*lit.* 'From the Heart']
dil toRay jathay ho   you are breaking
my heart
divaan   a collection of poetry
divaan-e-zanaane   a drawing room or
morning room
Dixit, Madhuri   a female Indian film
star
djinn   a genie; a poltergeist; a being
made from fire or energey that generally
lies beyond the compass of the electro-
magnetic spectrum
djinnie   a neologism meaning 'female
djinn'
doodh   milk
doodh puthee   tea made with lots of
hot milk
doomni   an itinerant female singer
doston   (male) friends
dthow   two
dubeez   elegant or graceful
duf   denoting or relating to a drum
played by beating it with the hands
Dún na nGall   Donegal [Irish Gaelic]
durmyani shubb ko chay bajeh (*colloq.*)
midnight to six

E

een   eyes [Scots]
Eid   one of three Muslim festivals
ektar   a single-stringed lute
español mejicano   Mexican Spanish
[Spanish]

F

falsafa   philosophy
Faraakh-kard   the Indian Ocean [Farsi,

lit. 'the many shored' or 'the vast
bordered']
Farangi   Europeans; Franks
Farangoid   European; Frankish
farishta (*pl.* farishtas *or* farishtay)   an
angel
Farsi   the modern Persian language
fauj   an army
filmi   denoting or relating to the
commercial films or South Asia or to
the commercial film industry of that
area
firdaus   paradise; a garden [Farsi]
Francisi   denoting or relating to French
people or the French language

G

gae   cow
Gàidhealtachd   the region where Gaelic
is spoken or where Gaelic culture is the
dominant one [Gaelic]
gana   a song
ganda   dirty
gandu   a bugger, specifically one who
is in the recipient role
Ganga Jumna   the River Ganges after
it unites with the River Jumna
gao (*pl.* gaon)   a village
gee haa   yes
geet   a light South Asian song
gey (pronounced 'gigh' as in 'high') considerably; rather [Scots]
Ghalib and Zauq   nineteenth-century
Urdu poets
ghaR   a house
gharibon   poor people
ghazal   a classical amatory lyric poem
or song characterised by a limited
number of stanzas and the recurrence of
the same rhyme scheme
ghoonda   a hoodlum
golu   an affectionate term for a rotund
person; a fatty
gora   a white men, sometimes used in
a derogatory way
goRah   a horse
goree   a white woman, sometimes used
in a derogatory way
goree kunjeree   a white prostitute
Govinda   the name of a male Indian
film star
gully   backstreet
guRee   a ring
Gurmukhi   a language spoken in eastern Punjab

gurrum   hot
gurrum masalaa   a type of hot spice

H

haa ji   yes [Punjabi]
haandi   a pan
habibi   darling [Arabic]
hai   is
hai ke nahii?   isn't it?; isn't that right?
haldi   a yellow spice
halo ma-tha   hello there [Gaelic]
hamaray chai   South Asian milky tea
  [*lit.* 'our tea']
hamaray loag   our people
haraam   (religiously) forbidden; bad
haraam zaaday   a bastard
harami   a bastard
Hare Hare (an address to) the potency of
  the Supreme Lord, part of a Hindu
  prayer
haveli   an old-style house or houses
  with the floors arranged in a square
  around a central courtyard
Hawwa   Eve [Arabic]
Hazrat   a term of respect applied to a
  prophet or saint
Hazrat . . . Anha   terms of respect
  applied to a female saint whose name
  goes between the two terms
Helen   the name of a dancer and
  actress in Indian cinema
high heid yin   a boss [Scots]
hijaab   a veil both in the physical
  sense and in the metaphorical internal
  or spiritual sense
hijerah (*pl.* hijeray)   a transvestite or
  transsexual
Himaalyas   the Himalayas
Hindoostanee   an archaic British
  colonial term for the Hindi/Urdu
  language
hindsa (*pl.* hindsay)   a number
von Hohenheim, Philippus Aureolus
Theophrastus Bombastus   a sixteenth-century German doctor and
  alchemist, the father of modern
  chemistry. Also known as Paracelsus
hud-hud   a mythical and real species
  of bird, usually identified with the
  hoopoe which was the bird that told
  Solomon (Suleiman) about Sheba
  (Bilquis) and her land of Yemen (Saba)
hunda   a guy
Huruf   an esoteric sect of Sufis
  founded in Iran in the fourteenth
  century. They applied an arcane,
cabbalistic model to the Qu'ran
Hurufi   denoting or referring to an
  esoteric sect of Sufis
Huu   a Sufi word evincing an
  awareness of perfection
Hypatia   the last of the pagan
  philosophers of the Library of
  Alexandria. She was head of the
  Neoplatonist school there

I

Iblis   Lucifer
il muladaad   cosmic numbers
Inglistan   England
Iqbal, Allama   a mid-twentieth-century
  Urdu poet
ishq   (spiritual) love
ISI   (Pakistani) Interservices Intelligence
Israfil   Raphael
izzat   honour; respect

J

jaam   a cup or goblet, especially one
  used in poetic Sufi wine-drinking
  imagery
jadui hindsay   magic numbers
jagirdaar   a person who own a lot of
  land
jahannam   hell
jahil   a derogatory term for an
  uncultured person
jaldi karo   do it quickly
Jallianwallah Bagh   the site, near the
  Golden Temple of Amritsar, of the
  massacre, in 1919, of supporters of
  Indian independence
jama   sex [Arabic]
Jamiat   a right-wing Islamic Pakistani
  political party
jannat   paradise; a garden [Arabic]
jao (*often* jao!)   go on (it can also be
  used in the sense of 'tell me another
  one')
javaabaat   answers
jazakallah khairan   thanks be to god;
  may you be well
jazakallah sharran   may God reward
  you bad things (used as a curse)
jee   a term of respect that is appended
  to a person's name or title
jellaba   a loose hooded cloak worn in
  the Middle East and northern Africa
jhankar (*pl.* jhankarian)   a clanging
  sound, as in a disco beat
jheel   a loch or lake

Jhelum, Ravi, Chenab, Sutlej and Beas the five rivers of Punjab
jhopar putti   a slum or ghetto
Jibril and Maryam   Gabriel and Mary
ji haa   yes
jild   skin
jinaab (*pl.* jinaabon)   a term of respect used to address a single person
jinn   *see* djinn
joie   happiness [French]
jondo   the deep [Spanish]
joothay   shoes
Jumna   a river in India that flows into the Ganges
jungalee   wild
jungle ki kokh   the womb of the jungle
junnune   madness; a trance-like state

K

kaafi   quite
kaala   black
kaala jadoo   black magic
kaala pani   black water
kaan (*pl.* the same)   an ear
kabbadi   a South Asian game in which a player has to touch as many of his opponents as is possible, while not drawing breath
Kabhi, Kabhi   an Indian film of the 1970s and also the title of a song [*lit.* 'Now and Then']
kaboother   a pigeon
Kafiristani   a person from eastern Afghanistan; denoting or relating to eastern Afghanistan [*lit.* 'Land of the Unbelievers' (the area is now known as Nuristan)]
kahve   coffee [Turkish]
kalaam   a poetical work
Kalaash   an indigenous people of the extreme north-west of Pakistan who follow a pagan religion
Kanyakumari   Cape Comorin, the southernmost tip of India [*lit.* 'the virgin']
Kapoor, Anil   a male Indian film star
kapRae   clothes
Karbala   a city in Iraq where Hussein, the son of Ali, was killed and which is a holy place in Islam, especially for Shias
karubiyyun   cherubim
Kashimilo   an old Chinese name for Kashmir

Kasperia   an old Greek name for Kashmir
kathak   a form of north Indian classical dance
Kaukaf   a Caucasian person; denoting or relating to a Caucasian person
kemance   a bowed Indian folk instrument
khabr aur mausum   news and weather
khabr, khabr, khabr sunaye   news, news, listen to the news
khamoshi   quiet
khana   a room
khanaqah   a residential institution for the meditation and training of Sufi adepts
khashkhash   heroin
kha urasan   we got here safely [possibly the origin of name of the old Persian province of Khurasan, a conjecture based on the apocryphal legend that the Afghans were of Hebrew origin]
Khooni Raat   an Indian film of 1991 whose title in English is usually *Night of the Long Knives* [*lit.* 'Night of Blood']
khotay ka lun   you're a donkey's prick
Khuda hafez   God go with you (a common way of saying 'bye-bye')
Khuda-ke-liye   for God's sake
khuserah (*pl.* khuseray)   an effeminate homosexual
khush   happy or content
khwab   a dream
Kiamath   Doomsday
kisaan   a peasant or peasants
kithara (*pl.* kitharae)   an Ancient Greek and Roman stringed instrument, akin to the lyre, with two necks rising vertically from the soundbox
Koirala, Manisha   a female Indian film star
Kolkata   Calcutta
kooni   a bugger where the person is in the donor role
kulma   a phrase in Muslim prayers
kun   be (a mystical Sufi term)
kunjeree   a prostitute

L

laal   red
Laillahah illallah muhammad-ar-rasulallah   there is no god but God and Muhammad is His prophet (a Muslim prayer)

la jota   an up-tempo traditional dance
of Moorish origin, still extant in parts
of Spain, esp. Aragón [Spanish]
Layla   a female Arabic name meaning
'dark beauty' or 'born at night'
Layla and Majnoon   two lovers in a
traditional Arabic story
Le Royaume du Maroc   the Kingdom
of Morocco [French]
loag (pl. loagon)   a person
Lodi   denoting or relating to a dynasty
that ruled the Delhi Sultanate until the
sixteenth century when the Mogul
dynasty took over
Loh   the name of the mythical founder
of city of Lahore
loha   iron
lok   folk
Lollywood   the Lahore film industry
lul   a big, thick dick (penis)
lun   a prick (penis)
luRkee   a girl

M

maa   a person's mum; a mother
maa di pudhi   a mother's vagina
maaf kijiye   forgive me
maajoun   a legendary psychoactive
confection, a blend of dried fruits, nuts,
spices, honey and cannabis
maalik   a boss
maalik-sahib   a boss man
maather-i-maa   oh, mother of mine;
oh, my mother [Farsi]
maddar-chaud   a motherfucker
madrasah   an Islamic religious school
Madya Pradesh   a large state in central
India
maghas   a brain
Maghrebi (also Maghrebian)   from an
Asian world view, Western, esp. North
African
maheenay   months
mahmoor   a drunk
mai   wine
majaaz-i-khuda   a metaphorical god;
also a term for a husband
Makkah   Mecca
Makrani   denoting or relating to
Makran, a region in the extreme south
of Pakistan
mandir   a Hindu temple
maqam   a place or situation. In the
context of music, it refers to the specific
oriental tone scales, of which there are
an enormous variety in Arabic music

due to the vast range of different
'microtones'. It can also be applied to a
special kind of 'suite', consisting of
improvisations based on certain
standard   rules of performance and
aesthetics
Mare Frigoris   a basalt plain on the
moon [Latin, lit. 'Sea of Cold']
Mashriki   an Eastern person (with
connotations of sophistication)
masih   messiah (in Islamic eschatology,
Al-Masih is the Prophet Jesus, Hazrat
Isa)
masjid   a mosque
mata   a mother
maulvi   a Muslim cleric
mausaki   music
Mazandaran   the Caspian Sea [Farsi]
mehbooba   a beloved person
mehman khana   a guest house; rooms
in a haveli for guests to use
mela   in Carnatic South Indian
classical music, a mode; a fête
mera   my (used with singular nouns)
meray   my (used with plural nouns)
meri jaan   my love [lit. 'my life']
meri zindagi, mera jeevan!   my life, my
incarnation!
mesquita   a mosque [Spanish]
methi   fenugreek
Migra Polis   Immigration Police
[Mexican Spanish]
milaad   a payer meeting
mi'raj   the Prophet Mohammed's
night-journey to the heavens
Mirpur   a region in Indian-controlled
Kashmir
mitai   a type of confectionery
Moenjodaro   a huge ruined city dating
from around 3000 BCE, located in the
Indus valley, outside Karachi
mohabat   (spiritual) love
mohalla (pl. mohallay)   an alley or
backstreet
mouli   a type of root vegetable that
resembles something between a carrot
and a turnip
Mounth   a geographical line in
Scotland, extending from Fort William
to Inverness, which separates the north
from the extreme north
Moutawassetei   the Mediterranean Sea;
denoting or relating to the Mediterranean Sea [Arabic]
mujhe bathao   tell me
mukhafaf   initials
mulk   a country; a land

Munkar and Nakir   the angels who meet the dead shortly after death to ask how faithful they were when they were alive

munnashiath   drugs

Murree   a Pakistani hill station

Musalmaan   a Muslim; denoting or relating to Muslims or the Muslim religion

mushaira   a poetry recital

mushaira ki malik   a leader of a mushaira; a master of ceremonies

muskhara   a clown

musttee   naughtiness; sexual transgression

mutchlee   a fish

N

naak   a nose

nafrat   hate

namashkar   the spirit in me bows to the spirit in you (a Hindu greeting)

namaste ji   the spirit in me bows to the spirit in you (a Hindu greeting)

Naskhi   a type of Arabic script [*lit.* 'copying']

Nastaliq   an elegant cursive form of Arabic script commonly used in writing Urdu and Farsi

nazim-sahib   a master of ceremonies; a compère

neela (*also* **neeli**)   blue

neendth   sleep

n'est-ce pas?   is it not? [French]

ney   a flute used esp. in Sufi ceremonies

nihari   a type of beef dish

nunga   naked

Nuristan   the part of eastern Afghanistan that was formerly known as **Kafiristan** [*lit.* 'Land of Light']

O

Octoober   October

Om Shanti Om   Om is the primeval word which stands for the entire universe permeated by Brahman and, therefore, Brahman itself. Shanti means 'peace' (a Hindu religious phrase)

Oudh   an old kingdom in northern India

ouRo!   fly!

P

paagal   mad; crazy

paanch aab   five waters [this is the root of the word 'Punjab']

paan-wallah   a person who sells betel nuts or leaves

Pachomian   denoting or relating to St Pachomius of Egypt, the founder of Christian monasticism, who was possibly influenced in this by followers of the god Serapis

pahaR (*pl.* **pahaRi**)   a mountain

Pakeezah   an Indian film of the 1970s

pakhana   faeces

pani   water

pardesi   a foreigner

paridaeza   paradise [Old Persian]

paridaezical   a neologism denoting or relating to paradise

paR paR nani   a person's granny's granny

Parsee   a Zoroastrian; denoting or relating to Zoroastrians

pathaR   stone (male gender)

pathaRi   grit (female gender)

pattach   bang

pena   a type of bowed Indian instrument

pesay   money

phoodulanah   (*derog.*) a cunt-prick

phuddi   a clitoris

phutt gai gand   fucked

picote   a Mexican dance

Pindi   a short informal form of **Rawalpindi**

pishaap   urine

pistole   a pistol

pukka   proper

pulaow   a rice and meat meal

punkha-wallah   a man whose job is wafting a fan

purdah   a curtain; a veil behind which women might live

Q

qaaleen   a rug

qabaristan   a graveyard

Qaisar   Caesar, the proper name; Kaiser; King

qalb   a heart

qanuni   lawful

qawwal   an utterance; a type of ecstatic song

qawwali   denoting or relating to a qawwal; aperson who sings a **qawwal**

quejío   a lament or cry; the wordless, most extreme, form of **cante jondo** [Spanish]

queu?   why?

R

raag   a pattern of notes in Indian music used as the basis for melodies and improvisations; a piece of music based on a particular raag. Raags convey various emotions – such as anger, love, sadness, humour, wonder, fear and peace – and are classified according to times of the day, month or season. Personalised descriptions of a raag enable a musician to meditate on its characteristics and to unite his or her personality with a particular mood and, thereby, instil the same mood in the audience. *Also called* raga

raat   night

raat ka dil   the heart of the night

raat-ki-raani   jasmine [*lit.* 'queen of the night']

raga   *see* raag

ragam   denoting or relating to the raga

rajarasa   in Sanskrit poetics, the supreme, intuitive understanding of a poem

Rajasthani   denoting or relating to the state in north-west India that borders the Pakistani state of Sindh

Rajesh Khanna   a male Indian film star

Raj Kumar   Prince (used as a title before someone's name)

raq   a dance

Ravi   a river that runs through Lahore, one of the five rivers of the Punjab

Rawalpindi   a city in Punjab

Rishi Kapoor   a male Indian film star

rooi   cotton buds

ruh   spirit

Ruh-Afza   a sweet soft drink

Rumi, Jalaluddin   a thirteenth-century Persian Sufi poet

rundi   a whore

Rustum and Sohrab   mythical Iranian heroes, a father and son who fought each other

S

saadhu   an ascetic

saaf   clean

saamnp   a snake

saans   breath

saaz   music

Safaid Guelfo   White Gulf (For a time, Dante Alighieri was a moderate supporter – i.e., a Guelf – of the Papacy against the Ghibelline faction who supported the Holy Roman Empire.)

sahib   sir

Sahra   Sahara (desert)

Saigal, K L   an Indian singer and film actor of the 1930s and early 1940s

sair (*pl.* sairon)   a particular liquid measure, used in the plural, in the same way as gallons, to indicate a large amount

salaam alaikum   peace be upon you (a Muslim greeting)

salaam alaikum wa rehmattallah barakat-a huu   peace be upon you and God's kindness and grace be upon you (a Muslim greeting)

Salmah   Salome

samaaen   people, used esp. to address an audience

sannie   a sandwich [Scots]

sanu   darling

saRak   a road

sarasvati vina   a south Indian classical musical stringed instrument, named after and symbolising Sarasvati, the Mother Goddess

sa-re-ga-ma   in Indian music, the first four notes of the seven notes in the scale of the raag – the other three being pa-da-ni. Their names are contractions of Shadjam (sa), Rishabam (re), Gandharam (ga), Madhyamam (ma), Panchamam (pa), Dhaivatham (da) and Nishadam (ni). Each note is said to correspond to a particular sound in nature

sat sri akaal   truth is eternal (a Sikh greeting)

savaalat   questions

saz (*pl.* sazes)   a Turkish lute

seraphiel   a seraphim

Serapic   denoting or relating to Serapis, a Hellenic-Egyptian god, syncretised from earlier Graeco-Egyptian gods to unite the Greeks and Egyptians in worship

shaam   night

shaheed   a martyr

Shah Rukh Khan   a male Indian film star
shahzaday   princes
shair   a male poet
Shaitan   Satan
shalvar kamise   baggy trousers and shirt worn in Punjab
sharaab   alcohol
sharaabi   an alcoholic
sharam   shame
sharif   respectable
shayad   perhaps
sheesha   a mirror
shehnai   a flute that is held and played in the same way as the recorder. It is associated with Sufism and is of Persian, Arabic and South Asian origin
shehr (*pl.* **shehron**)   a city
ShielDi   a neologism denoting, relating to or coming from Pollokshields
Shirazi, Hafiz   a fourteenth-century Persian poet**siya**   black [Farsi]
shithers   the shivers [Scots]
Shivling   a phallic symbol of the Hindu god Shiva
Sholay   a classic Indian film of the 1970s
shukur Allah   thank God
shukur-al-Hamdulillah   thanks be to God
Sikander   Alexander (the Great)
siller   silver; money [Scots]
silsila   a chain or succession
Sindh   a province in southern Pakistan
singh   a lion
Singh, Udham   in 1940, Udham Singh assassinated Sir Michael O'Dwyer at a public meeting in London's Caxton Hall. This was an act of revenge for the British Imperial Forces' massacre of unarmed Indians at Jallianwallah Bagh, Amritsar, in 1919. O'Dwyer, Governor of the Punjab region at the time of the massacre, had supported the atrocity. After a brief two-day trial, Udham Singh was sentenced to death
sistherie   a neologism modelled on **baratherie** and meaning women or womankind
Skanderjoss   Alaxander Joss [a Balkanised version of Alasdair Joss, a member of the band The Colour of Memory]
skite   to fly awkwardly; to slip or fall [Scots]
Socraat   Socrates [Arabic]
soobedar   a junior commissioned

officer in the British Indian Army, holding a rank equivalent to that of a (first) lieutenant or captain
sooer   a pig
subah   morning
subuz   green
Sumer   a region in present-day Iraq which, in ancient times, formed the southern part of Mesopotamia
sumjhe?   understand?
surah   a Qu'ranic chapter
surat   a face
surma   black eyeliner

T

taal   a rhythmic element in north Indian classical music
tadger   a penis [Scots]
TaileT   a toilet
takht   a throne
tamas   darkness
tambaku   tobacco
taraab   a state of ecstasy, especially one attained through music, song or dance
tarrd   expulsion, especially from Paradise [Arabic]
Tattva   in Hindu philosophy, the concept of 'that-ness', the real being of anything and an expression of the link between the Godhead and the individual [Hindi, *lit.* 'that-thou']
Taxila   an important archeological site in northern Pakistan, comprised of cities founded by the Indus Valley Civilisation and the Greeks
taxim   a style of Turkish instrumental music in which the musician improvises. In general, it is performed to guide the course of a modal system
Telegoid   a neologism denoting or relating to Telegu, a language of southeast India; denoting or relating to the people who speak this language
teri maa di lun   your mother is a prick
Thar Desert   a desert in south-eastern Pakistan
theen   three
thumri   an Indian light-classical song
Tibbet   Tibet
topee   a cap or hat
trobairitz (*pl.* the same)   a female troubadour
tu hi tu   you, only you
tuu meri dil toR   you broke my heart

U

'ud   an Arabic lute [from Arabic *al ud* a lute]

uloo   an owl; a fool

ummic   denoting or relating to the umma, the worldwide community of Muslims

Upean (pronounced ewe-pee-an)   a person from Uttar Pradesh or United Provinces; denoting or relating to such a person or to the area [from UP, a contraction of United Provinces and Uttar Pradesh]

V

vakili   denoting or relating to a lawyer

varanam   in South Indian classical music, the introduction to the **raag** [*lit.* 'a description']

W

Wahabi   the strictest school of religious interpretation in Islam

wahdat   the spiritual unity of cosmic love

wallah   used in combination to denote a person concerned with or engaged in a specified occupation or business – *see, for example,* **punkha-wallah, chabri-wallah,** etc.

waR oi   fuck off

Wa-wa!   an expression of appreciation commonly bestowed on the poet during a **mushaira**

Y

Ya Ali!   an exhortation to *Hazrat* Ali, son-in-law of the Prophet Muhammad

yaar   a person's friend; a buddy (used as an address to someone)

Yae   the last letter in the Arabic alphabet; symbolic equivalent of omega [Arabic]

ya habibi!   oh, darling! [Arabic]

Yahya   John

yeh   this

yeh hamaray sunehreh lumhe hai   these are our golden moments

Yeh kya hai?   What's this?

Yehudi   a Jew; Jewish

Yunani   a Greek; denoting or relating to Greek people or Greece

Yunus   Jonah

Yusuf and Zuleikha   two lovers (Joseph and Potiphar's wife) who appear in a traditional Iranian story

Z

zabardast   fantastical [from the Prophet David's Book of Psalms, the Zabur]

zameen   land

zamindar   a landowner

zard   yellow

zaroorat   really

zhikr   a repetitive Muslim recitation, often used in Sufi ceremonies [Urdu, Farsi, Arabic]

ziafat   a feast

zindabad   long live

Ziryab   a ninth-century Persian musician and musicologist who settled in Spain. *Also known as* The Black Bird

Zuleikha   another name for the wife of Potiphar, who later married the Prophat Joseph [*lit.* 'the place where a man slips' or 'wondrously beautiful']

PLAYLIST

Asian Dub Foundation   'Naxalite'
The Colour of Memory   'Changed Days'
Asian Dub Foundation   'Black and White'
The Colour of Memory   'Always With Me'
Mohammad Rafi   'Khilona'
Sheila Chandra   'Mecca'
Cornershop   'It's Good to Be on the Road Back Home'
The Colour of Memory   'Rigmarole'
Davy Graham   'Maajun'
Kula Shaker   'Great Hosannah'
Kula Shaker   'Mystical Machine Gun'
Kishore Kumar   'Ye Kya Hua Kaise Hua?'
Cornershop   'Brimful of Asha'
Junoon   'Saeein'
Yardbirds   'Happenings Ten Years Time Ago'
The Byrds   'Eight Miles High'
Mohammad Rafi   'Chho Lene Do Nazuk Hunton Ko'
Lata Mangeshkar   'Mohe Bhool Gaye Saavariya'
Chaba Fadela   'N'Sel Fik'
The Beatles   'Rain'
The Beatles   'Within You Without You'
Talat Mahmood   'Chal Diya Caravan'
Lata Mangeshar   'Chalte Chalte'
Mukesh   'O Jane Wale Ho Sake To LauT ke Anna'
Mukesh and Lata Mangeshkar   'Kabhi Kabhi Mere Dil Mein'
Talvin Singh   'Sutrix'

The 13th Floor Elevators   'Slip Inside This House'
The Beatles   'Helter Skelter'
The 13th Floor Elevators   'You're Gonna Miss Me'
Mukesh   'Chal Ri Sajni Ab Kya Soche?'
The Cosmic Rough Riders   'The Gun Isn't Loaded'
Mukesh   'Chal Ri Sajni Ab Kya Soche?' (reprise)
Mukesh   'Bhooli Hui Yaadon'
The 13th Floor Elevators   'Roller Coaster'
Mukesh   'Bhooli Hui Yaadon' (reprise)
the goldenhour   'beyond the beyond'
the goldenhour   'west sky picture show'
the goldenhour   'tonight becomes tomorrow'
Jimmy Page and Robert Plant   'Kashmir'
The Wind Machines   'The View from Below'
Richard Strange and the Engine-Room   'Damascus'
Kula Shaker   'S.O.S.'
Junoon   'Talaash'
Asian Dub Foundation   'Charge'
Asian Dub Foundation   'Assassin'
Janki Bai Allahabadi   'Rasile Tori Akhian'
The Stranglers   'Golden Brown'
Igor Stravinsky   'The Rite of Spring'
Primal Scream   'Spirea-X'
Shamen   'Happy Days'
Shamen   'Ω Amigo'
Catherine Wheel   'She's My Friend'
Primal Scream   'Crystal Crescent'
The Beatles   'Tomorrow Never Knows'
Santana   'Migra'
The Colour of Memory   'The Grace'
Country Joe and the Fish   'Eastern Jam'
Tim Buckley   'Starsailor'

Madonna   'Shanti/Ashtangi'
Kishore Kumar   'Om Shanti Om'
Kaleidoscope   'Taxim'
The Byrds   'Why'
Les Negresses Vertes   'Ce Pays'
The Kinks   'See My Friends'
Gauhar Jan   'Bhairavi'
Kavita Krishnamurthy and Sonu Nigam   'Satrangi Re'
K L Saigal   'Diwana Huu Diwana'
Susheela Raman   'Ganapati'
Susheela Raman   'Maya'
Joi   'Joi Bani!'
Kavita Krishnamurthy and Sonu Nigam   'Satrangi Re' (reprise)
Joi   'Asian Vibes'
Joi   'Fingers'
Cheb Kader   'M'Hainek Ya Qalbi'
Lata Mangeshkar   'Tere Mere Beech Mein Kaisa Hai Ye Bandhan
    Anjaana?'
Nitin Sawhney   'Migration'
Nitin Sawhney   'Market Daze'
Allesandra Belloni   'Agur Iziarko'
Allesandro Belloni   'Canto di Sant'Irene'
Enrique Morente and Lagartija Nick   'Omega'
Nusrat Fateh Ali Khan   'Mustt, Mustt'
The Colour of Memory   'An Emotional Fish'
Nusrat Fateh Ali Khan   'Mustt, Mustt' (Massive Attack remix)
The Beatles   'A Day In The Life'

DISCOGRAPHY

Allahabadi, Janki Bai   'Rasile Tori Akhiyan' (Your Enticing Eyes), *Vintage Music from India: Early Twentieth Century* (Rounder: 1993)

Asian Dub Foundation   'Assassin', *Rafi's Revenge* (Polygram: 1998)

Asian Dub Foundation   'Black White', *Rafi's Revenge* (Polygram: 1998)

Asian Dub Foundation   'Charge', *Rafi's Revenge* (Polygram: 1998)

Asian Dub Foundation   'Naxalite', *Rafi's Revenge* (Polygram: 1998)

Beatles, The   'A Day In The Life', *Sgt Pepper's Lonely Hearts Club Band* (Parlophone: 1967)

Beatles, The   'Helter Skelter', *The Beatles* (Parlophone: 1968)

Beatles, The   'Rain', B-side of 'Paperback Writer' (Parlophone: 1966)

Beatles, The   'Tomorrow Never Knows', *Revolver* (Parlophone: 1966)

Beatles, The   'Within You Without You', *Sgt Pepper's Lonely Hearts Club Band* (Parlophone: 1967)

Belloni, Allesandra   'Agur Iziarko', *Tarantata: Dance of the Ancient Spider* (Sounds True: 2000)

Belloni, Allesandro   'Canto di Sant'Irene', *Tarantata: Dance of the Ancient Spider* (Sounds True: 2000)

Buckley, Tim   'Buzzin' Fly', *Happy Sad* (Asylum: 1969)

Buckley, Tim   'Starsailor', *Starsailor* (Straight: 1970)

Byrds, The   'Eight Miles High', *Fifth Dimension* (Columbia: 1966)

Byrds, The   'Why?', *Younger Than Yesterday* (Columbia: 1967)

Catherine Wheel   'She's My Friend', *Ferment* (Polygram: 1992)

Chandra, Sheila   'Mecca', *Roots and Wings* (Caroline: 1995)

Colour of Memory, The   'Always With Me', *The Old Man and the Sea* (Lismor Records: 1994)

Colour of Memory, The   'Changed Days', *The Old Man and the Sea* (Lismor Records: 1994)

Colour of Memory, The   'An Emotional Fish', *The Old Man and the Sea* (Lismor Records: 1994)

Colour of Memory, The   'The Grace', *The Old Man and the Sea* (Lismor Records: 1994)

Colour of Memory, The   'Rigmarole', *The Old Man and the Sea* (Lismor Records: 1994)

Cornershop   'Brimful of Asha', *When I Was Born for the 7th Time* (Luaka Bop/Warner Brothers: 1997)

Cornershop   'It's Good to Be Back on the Road Again', *When I Was Born for the 7th Time* (Luaka Bop/Warner Brothers: 1997)

Cosmic Rough Riders   'The Gun Isn't Loaded', *Enjoy the Melodic Sunshine* (Poptones: 2000)

Country Joe and the Fish   'Eastern Jam', *I Feel Like I'm Fixin' to Die* (Vanguard Records: 1967)

Fadela, Chaba   'N'Sel Fik' ('You Are Mine'), *You Are Mine* (Mango: 1989)

goldenhour, the   'beyond the beyond', *Beyond the Beyond* (Raft Records in association with Contact High Records: 2003)

goldenhour, the   'tonight becomes tomorrow', *Beyond the Beyond* (Raft Records in association with Contact High Records: 2003)

goldenhour, the   'west sky picture show', *Beyond the Beyond* (Raft Records in association with Contact High Records: (2003)

Graham, Davy   'Maajun' ('A Taste of Tangier'), *Folk, Blues and Beyond* (Decca: 1965)

Jan, Gauhar   'Bhairavi' (The Gramophone Co. of India Ltd: 1902)

Joi   'Asian Vibes', *One and One Is One* (Astralwerks: 1999)

Joi   'Fingers', *One and One Is One* (Astralwerks: 1999)

Joi   'Joi Bani!', *One and One Is One* (Astralwerks: 1999)

Junoon   'Saeein' ('The Mystic'), *Inquilaab* (EMI Music International: 1995)

Junoon   'Talaash' ('Quest') *Talaash* (EMI Music International: 1997)

Kader, Cheb   'M'Hainek Ya Qalbi' ('I Eased My Heart'), *Cheb Kader* (Blue Silver: 1988)

Kaleidoscope   'Taxim', *A Beacon from Mars* (Epic: 1997)

Khan, Nusrat Fateh Ali   'Mustt, Mustt' ('Ecstasy, Ecstasy'), *Mustt, Mustt* (Real World Records: 1991)

Khan, Nusrat Fateh Ali   'Mustt, Mustt' (Massive Attack remix), *Mustt, Mustt* (Real World Records: 1991)

Kinks, The   'See My Friends', *Kinda Kinks* (Reprise: 1965)

Krishnamurthy, Kavita and Sonu Nigam   'Satrangi Re' (The Seven Colours), from the soundtrack to Dil Se (1998)

Krishnamurthy, Kavita and Sonu Nigam   'Satrangi Re' (The Seven Colours) (reprise), from the soundtrack to *Dil Se* (1998)

Kula Shaker   'Great Hosannah', *Peasants, Pigs and Astronauts* (Sony: 1999)

Kula Shaker   'Mystical Machine Gun', *Peasants, Pigs and Astronauts* (Sony: 1999)

Kula Shaker   'S.O.S.', *Peasants, Pigs and Astronauts* (Sony: 1999)

Kumar, Kishore   'Om Shanti Om', from the soundtrack to *Karz* (1980)

Kumar, Kishore   'Ye Kya Hua Kaise Hua?' ('What Happened, How Did It Happen?'), from the soundtrack to *Amar Prem* (1972)

Madonna   'Shanti/Ashtangi', *Ray of Light* (Warner Brothers: 1998)

Mahmood, Talat   'Chal Diya Caravan' ('The Caravan Is Leaving'), from the soundtrack to *Laila Majnu* (1953)

Mangeshkar, Lata   'Chalte Chalte' ('While I Was Walking'), from the soundtrack to *Pakeeza* (1971)

Mangeshkar, Lata   'Mohe Bhool Gaye Saavariya' ('My Lover Has Left Me'), from the soundtrack to *Baju Bawra* (1948)

Mangeshkar, Lata   'Tere Mere Beech Mein Kaisa Hai Ye Bandhan Anjaana?' ('What Is This Strange Bond Between You and Me?'), from the soundtrack to *Ek Duje Ke Liye* (1981)

Morente, Enrique and Lagartija Nick   'Omega', *Omega* (El Europeo Musico: 1996)

Mukesh   'Bhooli Hui Yaadon' ('Forgotten Memories'), from the soundtrack to *Sanjog* (1961)

Mukesh   'Chal Ri Sajni Ab Kya Soche?' ('Come, Beloved, You Have To Go, What Are You Thinking Now?'), from the sound track to *Bombay ka Babu* (1960)

Mukesh   'Chal Ri Sajni Ab Kya Soche?' ('Come, Beloved, You Have To Go, What Are You Thinking Now?') (reprise), from the soundtrack to *Bombay ka Babu* (1960)

Mukesh   'O Jane Wale Ho Sake To LauT ke Anna' (You, Who Are Leaving, If You Can, Please Return), from the soundtrack to *O Jane Wale* (1948)

Mukesh and Lata Mangeshkar   'Kabhi Kabhi Mere Dil Mein' (Now and Then, It Occurs to Me'), from the soundtrack to *Kabhi Kabhi* (1976)

Negresses Vertes, Les   'Ce Pays' ('This Country'), *Trabendo* (EMI/Virgin: 1999)

Page, Jimmy and Robert Plant   'Kashmir', *No Quarter* (Atlantic: 1994)

Primal Scream   'Crystal Crescent', 12 inch single (Creation: 1986)

Primal Scream   'Spirea-X', B-side of 'Crystal Crescent' (Creation: 1986)

Rafi, Mohammad   'Chho Lene Do Nazuk Hunton Ko' ('Let Me Touch Your Lips'), from the soundtrack to *Kaajal* (1965)

Rafi, Mohammad   'Khilona' ('Toy'), from the soundtrack of *Khilona* (1970)

Raman, Susheela   'Ganapati', *Salt Rain* (Narada: 2001)

Raman, Susheela   'Maya', *Salt Rain* (Narada: 2001)

Red Crayola   'Parable of Arable Land', *Parable of Arable Land* (International Artist: 1967)

Saigal, K L   'Diwana Huu Diwana' ('Mad, I Am Mad'), from the soundtrack to *Jindagi* (1940)

Santana   'Migra', *Supernatural* (Arista: 1999)

Sawhney, Nitin   'Market Daze', *Migration* (Outcaste Records: 1995)

Sawhney, Nitin   'Migration', *Migration* (Outcaste Records: 1995)

Shamen   'Happy Days', *Drop* (Communion: 1987)

Shamen   'Ω Amigo', 12 inch single (One Little Indian: 1989)

Singh, Talvin   'Sutrix', *OK* (Polygram Records: 1998)

Richard Strange and the Engine-Room   'Damascus', *Going Gone* (Side: 1986)

Stranglers, The   'Golden Brown', *La Folie* (EMI: 1981)

Stravinsky, Igor   'The Rite of Spring: Scenes of Pagan Russia' (1913), from *Stravinsky* Philharmonia Orchestra conducted by Eliahu Inbal (Teldec Classics International: 1998)

13th Floor Elevators, The   'Roller Coaster', *Psychedelic Sounds of The 13th Floor Elevators* (Sunspot: 1966)

13th Floor Elevators, The   'Slip Inside This House', *Easter Everywhere* (Sunspot: 1967)

13th Floor Elevators, The   'You're Gonna Miss Me', *Psychedelic Sounds of The 13th Floor Elevators* (Sunspot: 1966)

Wind Machines, The   'The View From Below', *Reverberation* (Ghalib Music Unlimited: 2004)

Yardbirds   'Happenings Ten Years Time Ago', *Roger the Engineer* (EMI/Columbia: 1966)